OUTLANDER CHRONICLES

BOOK ONE

PHOENIX

C.H. COBB

DOORWAY PRESS

Published by Doorway Press,
Greenville, OH, USA
www.doorwaypress.com

Available from Amazon for the Kindle
Available from Barnes and Noble for the Nook

Print version is available on Amazon and may be ordered
with
ISBN: 0984887504
ISBN-13: 978-0-9848875-0-7

Library of Congress Control Number: 2011944619

First Edition, 2011
Second Edition, 2012

Cover design by Dani Snell, www.refractedlightreviews.com.
Cover photo © mikenorton / www.fotosearch.com Stock
Photography, used by permission.
Cover design uses some elements by James Myers,
www.1987clothing.com, used by permission.

ACKNOWLEDGMENTS

There's nothing that quite resembles a widow so much as the wife of a wannabe writer who also holds down a full-time ministry. My wife has been my greatest cheerleader through my first project, then this one, and is encouraging me to begin the next one. Thanks, babe, you're the love of my life!

Thanks also to my oldest daughter, Dani Snell. Dani designed the cover, performing the digital wizardry on the original stock photo. She also carefully guided me through the Indie publishing process.

I owe a debt of gratitude to my son, Joshua. Josh taught me about character development, and then wrote a comprehensive critique of the first version. Nearly all of his recommendations found their way into the final version.

My youngest daughter, Laurielle, read the detailed timeline behind the story, and thinks I need to write a prequel. Her excitement helped me to commit to writing this tale.

My brother Lou (great encouragement), my sister Elizabeth (virtually professional editing assistance), and my sister Georgia (one of my "beta-readers") all deserve thanks for their part in this project.

Soli Deo Gloria!

CHAPTER 1

The rusting sign twisted back and forth in the cold February wind, its post corroded paper-thin. A good storm would finish it off. Faded letters announced *SPEED LIMIT 45*, but it was a message no longer necessary. Hadn't been, not for eighty years.

Beyond the sign, just cresting the hill, ten men trudged north on the crumbling road. The bluish spider tattoo covering the left side of their faces identified them as *Anarchs*, and specifically as members of the clan inhabiting the rusting ruins once known as Exton, Pennsylvania. Predators without a conscience, they were equipped with assault weapons and a hatred of social order. Their target was a dying community of *Townies*, just up the way, which had been struck with some illness or other. Their intent was to help the poor pilgrims to their natural end, perhaps just a bit ahead of schedule.

Hidden in a dense thicket of laurel, a tall, bearded man crept forward on the frozen ground. He surveilled the approaching group with dark, intelligent eyes, missing nothing. Arabic in features, he was clothed in an eclectic collection consisting of stained deerskin leggings, military-grade boots, and a heavy but worn coat retrieved from the ruins of some forgotten mercantile. His movements and the way he handled his weapon betrayed careful training and long experience.

His one-man ambush had been prepared for the men who now approached from the south. He knew that the moral calculus of what the ten were about to do mattered not at all to them. Unfortunately for the Anarchs, it did matter to the tall Arab. They had planned murder and plunder, but Hakim Abdul al Malik had laid his own plans, and the collision was but seconds away.

"Why couldn't you guys just *leave the kid alone?*" he muttered to himself. "He's suffered *enough* without your help." Hakim grimaced. He hated killing. *Isa, forgive me!*

He could hear their feet crunching on the old highway. The familiar adrenaline rush kicked in, controlled by the terrible calm that always came over him as he prepared for battle. He selected full-automatic on his M14, and forced himself to regard the Anarchs as targets, not men. He shifted slightly on the cold, hard ground, pulling the butt plate tightly into his shoulder. His measured breath created momentary puffs of fog.

A little closer . . . a little closer . . . and, fire!

The staccato bark of his rifle shattered the morning stillness as the spray of bullets etched a lethal pattern across the group. Three men dropped, screaming, the foliage behind them spattered bloody red. The remainder scattered off the road into cover.

Shoot and move, he reminded himself as he slid backwards then moved laterally to a new firing position.

The tall Arab rammed a fresh magazine into his gun, then peered through the heavy undergrowth. The far side of the road erupted in the flame and sound of automatic weapons fire, as the Anarchs raked the spot where he had just been.

Stupid amateurs!

Picking a target, he rapped out a three-shot burst, killing a fourth Anarch. Hakim wormed his way to a new position. Another brief burst, another kill. Again he relocated.

"Hal, how many of them are there?" a voice wailed.

"Hal's dead. I'd guess there are three or four of them," someone responded.

"I thought Hal said that there was just the kid left, and that this would be an easy raid!" the first voice protested.

"Yeah, well, Hal was wrong. Any more questions, moron?"

Cloaked in thick brush and silence, Hakim waited for the Anarchs to make another mistake. He peered through the undergrowth, looking for a target. Five minutes lengthened to ten, and he began to get cold.

"I'm pulling out!" a voice declared, thick with disgust. Several others muttered agreement.

Hakim listened to the diminishing sounds of the withdrawal, and then gathered his pack and walking stick, and disappeared into the wilderness.

****

About a mile away, a young man was digging a grave. An inch shy of a solidly-built six feet, he had a wide mouth accustomed to easy smiles, sandy-colored hair, and brown eyes. He was wearing a worn pair of blue jeans, a ratty denim shirt covered by an equally ratty coat, and old leather work boots that showed signs of too much use. His normally friendly face was contorted with grief at the moment; he was preparing a grave for his mother.

The rattling percussion of the distant firefight startled him and he threw down his shovel, grabbed his rifle, and jumped into the fresh hole. He waited a bit after the sounds of the gunfire ceased, then climbed out of the hole and wearily resumed his digging.

As he lowered the sheet-wrapped body into the grave, he began to weep. "Gonna miss you, Mom. I love you. I wish I could say that to you just one more time. Sorry dad can't be here, Mom, but he's just too sick to leave his bed."

A week later, Jacen Chester threw the last shovelful of dirt on his father's grave, and then leaned on the shovel, surveying the end of his sad task. Seventeen fresh mounds encircled the top of this low, green Pennsylvania knoll. Those graves represented all he had loved and lived for, family and friends. Laid low by some sickness, one by one they had died, and one by one he had buried them on this accursed hill. In the end, only he himself was spared.

Staring at the mounds, he figured he was all cried-out. Tears had been replaced by a bleak, throbbing anger at the injustice, the sheer unfairness, of it all. If there was a god, he hated him and was sure that he was hated by him in return. He and all his loved ones were in the grip of Fate, and the dice had been rolled and they had all lost. All except him.

Well, he'd lost too, the twenty-three year old figured, because he was still alive, and now very much alone. He leaned over and picked up his rifle.

"I'm very sorry."

Startled, Jacen whirled around and brought up his rifle, jacking a shell into the chamber in one smooth movement. In the edge of the trees stood a tall bearded man. The stranger appeared to be about forty, like Jacen's own dad had been. His face was tanned and wind-burnt, with high cheekbones and an aquiline nose. It was a rough face, but the deep, black eyes were filled with pity and sincerity. The man wore a large pack and held an ornately carved walking stick. He also wore a shoulder-holster with a pistol, and had an assault rifle slung over his back.

The man's simple compassion penetrated Jacen's guard, and he did not trust his voice to respond. Jacen held the rifle steady, but said nothing.

"I'd be mighty thankful, son, if you did not pull that trigger."

Surprised, Jacen relaxed slightly. He'd not been aware that his finger was curled around the trigger. It was only then that he understood just how numb he'd become. He didn't even know what day it was. The last week had been a nightmare of death and mourning.

Angry that his grief had again risen to the surface, Jacen demanded, "Who are you? What do you want?"

"I've been watching you for eight days now. I've seen you caring for these people, and digging the graves."

"I haven't seen you!"

"Didn't want to be seen," the stranger responded. "I've been keeping the Anarchs off your back."

"Heard some shots late last week. That you?"

"That was me. They were planning to raid your settlement; I spoiled their plans. Figured you had enough to worry about."

Jacen lowered his rifle and fought a losing battle with his emotions. His shoulders began to shake, he leaned against the tree, then sank to the ground, weeping uncontrollably. He was furious at himself for losing it, but was unable to control his grief any longer. The kindness of this total stranger undermined his defenses, and he was undone.

The man retreated into the trees twenty yards, pulled off his pack, and began to build a fire. Soon he had coffee boiling and venison roasting. He clattered about with such noise that Jacen realized the man had not moved on, but was extending an invitation.

Jacen struggled for a few moments with the whirling vortex of emotions that his grief and anger had generated. He needed to be alone and he needed someone to talk to and all at the same time. It was overwhelming. Finally he followed the sounds and approached the stranger's campfire.

"Who are you?" Jacen stepped close to the fire, and sat down on the ground.

"I am Hakim," the man said, and then tossed Jacen two cups. "Pour the coffee, would you?"

"You look like an Arab. You belong to the People of the Prophet?"

"It depends," Hakim responded.

"On what?"

"It depends," Hakim repeated. "Of which prophet do you speak?"

Jacen's anger flashed. "Give me a straight answer!" he demanded. "Are you a Muslim?" His parents had taught him that the Great Disaster had been triggered by religion, particularly Islam and Christianity.

"I was; I once was a Muslim. I am no longer. I am of the people of the prophet Isa, not Muhammad."

"I've never heard of Isa!"

"That's because you don't speak Arabic," Hakim chuckled.

"Who is Isa?" Jacen demanded bitterly.

Hakim's face darkened with anger. He looked at the young man and asked hotly, "Look, do you want to interrogate me, or do you want to enjoy _my_ coffee and _my_ venison with me?"

What's the matter with me? I am so angry I could kill right now, thought Jacen. He looked down, and put his head in his hands. "I'm sorry; I'm not myself. I'm just having trouble with my emotions. I've lost everyone, I'm furious, and I don't even know who I'm mad at."

"You gotta knife on you?" Hakim asked.

"Yeah, why?"

"Because I'm really hungry. Cut off half of that venison for yourself, and then pass the rest to me."

They ate in silence. Jacen had not realized he was famished. For two days he hadn't paused to eat, and it was all he could do to avoid wolfing the meat down.

"What's your name, son?" Hakim asked as he sipped his coffee.

Jacen stared thoughtfully at the man sitting across the fire. _Why should I trust this guy? I don't even know who he really is. On the other hand, he'd have no point in scamming me. All he's got to do to take everything I own is kill me. If he was going to kill me, he'd have done it while I was burying dad. Get a grip, Jacen! Why shouldn't I trust him? Why does it even matter anymore, anyway?_ Jacen made a silent decision, and took a leap of faith. It was a leap that he would later realize changed the course of his life.

"Jacen. Jacen Chester. These were my folks, my community. Some sort of sickness wiped us out. I buried my mom a week ago; I buried my dad today. Folks I love have been dying for the last three weeks. Seems like all I've been doing is diggin–" His voice left him as his throat constricted with emotion. Tears began to roll down his cheeks again. Hakim sat nodding, saying nothing.

After a moment, Hakim asked, "Why'd you burn down your cabins this morning?"

"Didn't know if maybe the whole place was somehow contaminated. Didn't want anyone else to catch the sickness if they should happen along here. So I burned the whole settlement down. My house was the last to go. Everything I'm keeping is in that pack over there."

"What are you going to do, Jacen?"

"Gonna go west. Get away from the east, all these ruins, and all the Anarchs."

"And all the memories?"

Jacen nodded. "My dad said the folks in the middle of the country were relocated to the coasts when the dying started, some eighty years ago. I figure there's no one left there now. So that's where I'm headed."

"Okay, so you're headed west. What then?"

Jacen's face brightened as he said, "That's the good part; that's where my dream is. I'm going to build a town that will replant a whole new civilization."

A flicker of a smile ghosted across Hakim's face. "A new civilization? Right. Have you always dreamed such small dreams?" Hakim asked dryly.

Jacen stood and began to pace as he elaborated on his vision of the future. He was obviously excited. "Look at us! I don't mean just you and me—all of us. Here we are, surrounded by the remains of a once-great civilization, and all *we* can do is scavenge in the ruins for rotting clothes and the few leftovers of a former time!"

"And so you intend to, what? Stop scavenging?"

"Yes! Well, no! Not at first, anyway; eventually. But that's not really the big idea. I want to build a town, Hakim, that somehow gets *beyond* mere survival. There's *got* to be more to life than just avoiding death. I want to start a community committed to creating, producing, and learning, instead of just . . . scavenging in the ruins." Jacen scowled and sat down. He'd never shared his vision with anyone. Somehow this stranger had loosened his tongue, and he wasn't sure if it had been wise to share everything.

Hakim sat, sipping his coffee, pondering the young man's words. "How will you populate your town?"

"As I travel west, when I run across good folks, I'll invite them to join me."

"Hmm. You married, Jacen?" Hakim queried.

"No, why?"

"If you want a growing population, everyone needs to do their part, including you," the older man chuckled as he refilled his cup.

The fact that he was still unmarried was a sore spot for Jacen, and he retaliated, "Well, look at you, Hakim! Are YOU married?"

"Nope, can't say that I am. But I'm not bragging about starting a new civilization, either."

"You're old enough to be my father!" Jacen needled. "How come you aren't married, Hakim? What have you got to show for your forty some-odd years, huh?"

"That's personal, kid, and it's none of your business!" Hakim snapped, suddenly irritated.

For a few moments the two men drank their coffee without speaking, staring into the slowly dying fire. Dusk fell, and the west glowed with a pastel pink. Clouds trailing on the lower rim of the sky were momentarily gilded, and then the sun sank below the horizon and the clouds resumed a foreboding gray.

"Why don't you get some sleep, son," Hakim suggested gruffly, still irritated. "I'll take the first watch." He doused the fire with the remnants of the coffee pot.

"Watch?? Do you really think it's necessary? I thought you eliminated the Anarchs last week!" asked Jacen, surprised.

"Yes, I got some of them, but not all of them. At least five got away. And you can bet that they know what's happened out here. They might wait until tomorrow morning to ransack the remains of your community, but they may decide to come tonight. If they do, we'd better see them first unless you fancy getting your throat cut while you sleep. So keep that gun right by your bedroll, and keep it loaded! I'll wake you up a little after midnight and you can keep the morning watch."

****

Two weeks earlier, Hakim had been walking up from the south on deserted byways. He had no destination in mind. He was wandering alone, as he had for years. He was a man of insatiable curiosity, which meant he read everything he could get his hands on, and always had to see what was around the next bend.

Nearly out of ammo for his M14, he had been scavenging in the ruins of Philadelphia. He was searching in the remains of an old hardware store when he heard someone approaching. He found a hiding place just before three men, each toting a shotgun, sauntered into the store.

"The Townies at Ludwig's Corner have been hit by a bug. I was scouting their settlement the other night, and counted six new graves on the hill above it," said the first.

"This is a good time to roll 'em! Let's go get their stuff," urged the second man, as he foraged through piles of rotting merchandise.

"No, pinhead," scolded the third man, "d'ya want to catch what they've got? I say wait for them all to die, then we'll move in."

"Huh-uh," disagreed the first, who seemed to be dominant. He was pawing through a near-empty rack of rusted tools. "We're not going to wait for 'em to die. Can't wait that long. We've got to have food, and they have it. We'll kill any Townies left alive, and then we'll take their stuff."

"What about their sickness, Hal? We might catch it from them!" whined the third fellow.

"Naah. We're immune! We've been hanging out in the ruins for years without catching a bug. We *must* be immune. Besides, we've got to have food before we starve. We'll hit 'em soon," directed Hal.

At that moment, Hal turned and Hakim had a clear view of his face. It was covered by the tattoo of a spider, the body of the spider occupying the front of the left cheek. *Oh, great,* Hakim thought to himself, *Anarchs. And I've only got seven rounds left. I'd never survive a shoot-out, not when they have shotguns.*

As the men rummaged through the store for anything useful, Hakim observed the same tattoo on each man, in the same location. Tattoos were the identifying marks of the Anarchs; the facial tattoo indicated their specific clan. Townies rarely wore tattoos, and never on the face, considering it a barbaric custom.

Luckily for Hakim the three left several minutes later, unaware that their plans had been overheard. After finding ammunition in the ruins of an old police station, Hakim next located the Townies' settlement. It was then, during his covert surveillance, that he had noted the young man serving as the lone caregiver of the dying group. Some intangible quality of the young man had impressed him, and Hakim had made a decision. Whatever the dying fortunes of the little community, it was not going to be interfered with by the Anarchs. Not if he could prevent it.

****

"Jacen! Jacen! Wake up! It's your turn for watch." Hakim waited until the young man began to dress, then asked, "Have you ever stood watch before?"

"Sure, many times," Jacen replied, digging the sleep out of his eyes.

"How were you trained?" Hakim asked doubtfully, eyeing the sleepy young man in the cold moonlight.

"Trained? What's to train? You just walk circles around the settlement," Jacen yawned. "At least, that's how we did it."

"Actually, it's a little more involved than that, if you do it right. Listen! When you are standing watch, the lives of those who are sleeping are in your hands. It's serious business. Understand?"

"Yes."

"Good. In the old days, in the military, people who fell asleep on watch were sometimes executed. It's that serious, so stay awake. I don't care to have my throat slit by the Anarchs while I'm sleeping."

"Got it. I'll stay awake."

"Good. Every thirty or forty minutes, patrol the perimeter of our camp, but never take the same route twice. Don't establish a pattern, unless you want to get jumped while you are patrolling. Understand?"

"Sure. Got it. Don't set up a pattern. Anything else?"

"Yeah. Always carry your rifle, and if you use it, shoot to kill. No mercy, do you understand? If they come at us, they are coming to kill us; that's just the way the Anarchs operate. If you don't kill them first, they will certainly kill you. This is serious business, boy; if you're gonna survive, you need to defend yourself without a second thought. You follow?"

Jacen was now fully awake, and nodded soberly in the moonlight. He pulled on his boots and his coat and then jacked a shell into the chamber of his rifle. He noticed that when Hakim spread out his bedroll it was not near the dying embers of the fire but well away in the shadows. A shiver ran up his spine, and as he circled the camp he remembered all the nasty things he'd ever heard about Anarchs. He had no trouble staying awake.

CHAPTER 2

It was a cold, clear night, and the sky was brilliant with stars. Puffs of a gentle breeze scattered the frost and brought sound and motion to the treetops. Jacen was tired, but he welcomed watch duty and the silence of the night. It was the first time in weeks in which he was not serving, or burying, someone.

He forced himself to think of his parents, see their faces, and remember their voices. He recalled images of his neighbors, all of whom were now dead, buried, and lying cold in their graves. Jacen did not want to avoid the pain of bereavement; he wanted to sear it into his memory. He wanted the anger of the loss to energize him so that he might deny Fate the last victim of his community. He would go west and build a new community, a community with many families, the rule of law, and the protection of civilization. And no Anarchs!

With a start he realized that he'd been buried in his thoughts for a long time. A look at the stars told him it had been over two hours since his last patrol around the camp. After listening intently for several minutes, Jacen stood, walked out about one hundred yards, and began to patrol the perimeter of his camp.

****

It was a little after 5:00 AM when he heard them approaching on the trail. What had once been Route 100 running from Exton to Pottstown was now little more than an overgrown path between the two ruins. Eighty years without maintenance had had its effect. Small trees and weeds were growing from the cracks in the crumbling asphalt.

The soft, crunching sound of feet tramping in the old roadway and the murmur of hushed voices was transmitted through the cold night air with amazing clarity. Jacen silently drifted back into camp, and moved toward the shadow where Hakim had spread his bedroll. It was empty!

Jacen struggled to control the rising fear in his chest. *Hakim must have heard the intruders and gotten up. What do I do now?* Something touched his shoulder and he stifled a gasp of surprise. It was Hakim.

Using hand signals, the older man directed Jacen to take a position on the ground behind some thick, fallen logs, and he made it clear that Jacen was not to shoot until Hakim did. Then Hakim disappeared into the shadows again.

The young man got into position amongst the logs. He noted with approval that it was a good site with lots of cover. Selecting the burst mode of his M4, he hunkered down and waited.

The M4 was carried almost universally; there was a large number of them available, as it had remained the personal weapon of choice for the military into the twenty-first century. The arms had been stored in crates packed in grease before the Great Disaster, so they had not corroded with age. While ammunition had been plentiful for scavengers the first fifty years or so, it was getting harder to find. There was no manufacturing to replenish the supply.

Jacen listened as the Anarchs drew close. One stumbled and fell, with much cursing and hissing and shushing from his companions. The group stopped as their companion clambered to his feet. Jacen peered through his barricade and counted five men in the moonlight. He could overhear their conversation.

"I can't believe someone burned down the cabins. We could have used them."

"Somebody must have survived the sickness, and torched 'em."

"Well, where's the survivor?"

"How should I know, idiot? I don't care anyway. If he's not there it just saves us a bullet. Or five, rather," the speaker snickered, looking around the group.

Jacen trained his rifle on the one on the left. He figured that Hakim would probably aim at the dominant speaker, who was standing on the right. As the small group continued to talk and argue, Jacen maintained his aim, waiting for Hakim to open up.

It was clear from their talk that they intended to kill him. A shiver ran up Jacen's back; if not for Hakim's insistence that they keep watch, they would have been murdered.

The group of Anarchs was beginning to head away, when one held up his hand and whispered, "Wait!" His companions turned and stared at him.

"I smell a camp fire."

"No you don't," one disagreed. "You smell the burnt cabins."

"Nope. Wind's coming from the wrong direction for us to smell the cabins here. It's a camp fire, and it's nearby."

Jacen was grateful that the fire had burnt itself out several hours ago. Though the man could smell it, at least he could not see the remaining embers. The Anarchs fell silent and began to creep in Jacen's direction. He knew that they could not see him but he felt the chill of fear nonetheless. Closer and closer they came, and still Hakim did not open fire. Jacen was about to fire when the loud rattling bark of an assault weapon came from his right. The muzzle flashes from Hakim's M14 illuminated the scene with an eerie, deadly strobe effect.

Jacen settled on his own target, and squeezed the trigger. His M4 stuttered a short burst. Answering fire from three weapons forced him to dive down behind the logs. The Anarchs' weapons were shredding his cover, but Jacen was too frightened to move. He heard an M14 open up again, and fire a long burst. Jacen was puzzled, because the shooting came from much further to his right and front than where Hakim had last been.

This time there was no answering fire. An agonized cry rose from out in front of his position. It wound down into a drawn-out moan, punctuated by the unknown man's tortured breathing. Jacen heard movement, then a pistol shot. The moan ceased.

The night became still once more, the wind exercising in the treetops, the stars twinkling but perhaps a bit dimmer than before. Jacen stirred, looked over his log barricade, and began to get up.

"Stay down! Stay put!" a commanding voice hissed from far to his right. Jacen dropped back to the ground behind his barricade, wondering.

****

When he next opened his eyes the sun was coming up. He heard a fire crackling and smelled coffee. Jacen was cold and stiff. *I must have fallen asleep*, he thought. He peered out of the network of fallen logs where he was lying, and saw Hakim tending the fire and fixing breakfast. He stood, picked up his rifle, and approached the fire.

Hakim looked up. He held a cup of coffee out to Jacen, and said, "Morning. I figured I'd just let you sleep. I know you needed it."

"Thanks. I really did," Jacen admitted as he gratefully accepted the steaming cup.

"First things first, son. While you're drinking your coffee, clean and reload your weapon. Always tend your weapon first, so it's always ready." The Arab turned back to the fire. He was frying a couple of chunks of venison with some thin sliced potatoes and wild onions.

After a silent breakfast, Hakim said, "We got some graves to dig. Five of 'em. Why don't you clean up breakfast, and I'll start digging."

"Where are they?"

"Right where they fell."

Jacen got up and turned to walk over to the site of the battle. Hakim called after him, "It's not pretty, Jacen."

It was awful. The Anarchs were sprawled in various positions, anger and shock written on their immobile faces. Dried blood was everywhere. One, who had taken several rounds in the stomach, had a pistol in his hand, the muzzle still in his mouth. Jacen thought back to the moan, and the shot of the previous night. He felt sick. He bent over and threw up, retching until it was just dry heaves.

He straightened, furious, balled his fists and shook them at the beautiful early morning sky, screaming at the top of his lungs, "Aaaaaaagggggggghhhhhhh!" He shouted again, then turned and faced his companion, who was looking at him with a shocked expression. Jacen raged, "I hate this! I hate this! Death is everywhere! I don't ever want to kill anyone else in my life! Aaaaaaagh!"

The young man turned his face up to the sky, shook his fist at the puff-ball clouds and shouted, "Why are you doing this? Why don't you stop it?"

Jacen turned away from the macabre scene, and stood trembling, eyes squeezed shut, shaking his head. He heard Hakim come up and felt the older man's hand squeeze his shoulder. Jacen muttered, "I don't *ever* want to kill anyone again! Never! Life is _precious_. This is wrong, Hakim. We were wrong."

"Come with me, Jacen." Hakim turned and walked toward the hill with the graves of Jacen's community. Jacen followed, tears once again running down his cheeks.

The Arab selected a place on the hill, set his rifle down and took off his coat, and then began to dig. Neither man spoke for fifteen minutes or so, then Hakim stopped and leaned on his shovel.

"Jacen, you are right; you're spot on, son. Life *is* precious. And in the world in which we live, there are fewer and fewer people, fewer and fewer lives. The loss of even one is tragic. Each person is irreplaceable, each one completely unique. Understand?"

"Yes." Jacen wiped his coat sleeve across his eyes.

"Did you seek this fight, Jacen?"

The young man shook his head, no.

"Did your community ever go into the ruins, looking for Anarchs to kill? Ever?"

No again.

"Did you hear them talking last night, just before I opened fire? Yes? What did they say?"

"They said they were coming to kill me," the twenty-three year old admitted.

"That's right, Jacen. Why? Have you ever in your life killed someone who was not trying to kill you?"

"No, of course not!" he snapped.

"No, and I wouldn't think it of you. Have the Anarchs ever killed needlessly?" the Arab pressed.

"Yes, sir. We've had lots of trouble with them."

"Uh-huh. Okay, I want you to think about something. Maybe when we defend ourselves and our communities against the predations of the Anarchs and others who kill wantonly, we _are_ fighting for the preciousness of life."

"But I hate killing!" Jacen insisted.

"So do I. But if you were to be killed, what about the fate of those around you who depend on _you_ for their protection?"

"There is no one anymore," Jacen said.

"No, but there was. And if I'm any judge of character, there will be again. You need to be ready to defend those whom you lead, and those who look to you for protection. If you hesitate in a firefight, it will be more than just you who dies. Never forget that."

Hakim climbed out of the grave, tossed Jacen the shovel, and said, "Keep digging. I'll bring the bodies over."

After Hakim dragged the bodies to the grave he pulled out a knife and slit the right sleeve on the clothing of each one, and gathered the material back. Spreading out their bare right arms, he called Jacen over.

"Take a good look, son. What do you see on their right arms?"

"Tattoos of tiny spiders."

"Right. Count 'em, but don't count the red ones, and tell me how many there are, total."

Jacen counted both. "Between all five bodies, there are twenty-seven spider tattoos, and eight more red ones."

Hakim nodded his head, and replied, "An Anarch records his kills on his right arm, in tattoos. They use a tiny version of their clan tattoo. It's known as their 'tally'. The red ones are for other Anarchs that they have killed. The blue ones are for Townies. These five men have killed twenty-seven Townies between them, plus eight Anarchs. Last night we put a stop to their tallies. Don't forget it, Jacen."

****

That evening as they sat sipping their coffee, Jacen reflected on what he knew of his companion. It was precious little. Hakim had simply appeared on the scene when Jacen needed someone. The Arab was not much for talking, especially about his own past. But Jacen was quickly learning that when Hakim did speak, he said something of value. Jacen was beginning to listen to the older man, and was recognizing that Hakim was a resource of knowledge, generally, but specially with respect to specific survival skills and fighting tactics.

"You did well last night. Or this morning, actually."

Jacen looked across the fire. Hakim was studying him. "You didn't do so bad yourself," Jacen replied dryly.

"Hmm. Jacen, whenever you make camp, whether you are going to stay or move on after a day or two, always size up the terrain from a defensive standpoint. Always. You never know when you'll need it. I knew you'd be safe in those logs because I'd picked the spot out earlier, in the daylight. So get in the habit of looking for good defensive positions, and figure ways to get between them safely under fire. Look for lines of retreat. Examine the fields of fire. Make this a habit. Understand?"

"But what if there are no Anarchs in the area? What if there is no danger?" protested the young man.

"There's always danger, son. And you have no idea who might be around, looking you over, deciding whether or not you make an easy target. Did you know I was around?

"I haven't survived this long, especially considering the places I have been, without learning caution as second nature. You're in the greatest danger when you are completely ignorant of it. Consequently, you should expect trouble, always. So learn to get an eye for terrain. Whenever you come to a campsite, think: 'How would I attack this camp?' And then figure out what to do to defend it."

Jacen nodded slowly, absorbing the information.

"What happened last night, Jacen, after you opened fire? Were you able to get off more than one burst?"

"No. Just one burst. After that they were pouring it at me. I couldn't lift my head without getting it shot off."

"Right. Learn to *shoot and move*. Shoot, then change positions immediately. Otherwise you'll get pinned down. When you are out-numbered or out-gunned, never fight from a fixed position unless it's unapproachable by your enemy. Stay on the move. Make 'em guess where you are, how many men you have."

"Where did you learn all this stuff?"

"Maybe someday I'll tell you. In the meantime, I might hang around long enough to see you get your town started, if it's okay with you. I like your thinking, son. It *is* time to try to put this old world back together, and I 'spose everyone has been waiting around for someone else to do it. Might as well be us. Do you mind if I stick around?"

Jacen considered the dark-eyed man sitting across the fire. Hakim was a mystery. But as he thought about it, he realized that asking *anyone* to join in his plan was a gamble, for he would know nothing of those he came across as he traveled west other than what intuition and first impressions could tell him. It was time to roll the dice, the young man decided. "I could use your help, Hakim. I hope you will stay."

The Arab nodded, and said, "Then I figure I'd better start your education right away, if we're going to rely on each other. One of these days I might need *you* to rescue *me*. So I'm gonna make sure that you learn enough to be capable of it."

Hakim set his empty cup on a rock, looked at Jacen, and said, "I've got first watch. I'll wake you about 1:00 AM."

CHAPTER 3

"What are you writing? And where on earth did you find a notebook?" Hakim had awoken to a crackling fire and the aroma of coffee. Jacen was sitting on a log, writing in a notebook with the stub of a pencil. The eastern sky was brightening, but the sun had not yet appeared over the rim of the horizon. Frost lay on the grass like a wooly white blanket. After banging the pine needles out of his cup, Hakim poured himself some coffee and sat down opposite the young man.

Jacen dug into his pack, pulled out a small, unused, spiral-bound notebook, and tossed it to the surprised Arab. "Here. Have one. Dad and I found a pallet of supplies last year in the back of a truck. The truck was still weather-proof when we found it, and there was a whole case of notebooks wrapped in plastic. The pages are a little yellow, but otherwise it's fine."

"What are you writing? A book?" Hakim teased.

"No, I'm keeping a journal. Started the habit last year after we found the paper. It's like I woke up one day and got fed up with everything being so temporary. Our community was just surviving. Not building. No one had any hope for the future. So I began to write about our experiences as a show of faith."

"A show of faith in what?" asked Hakim.

"The future, Hakim, the future!" Jacen answered passionately. "Someday kids will read what great-grandpa Jacen wrote. Someday people will be more consumed with *living* than with *trying to stay alive*. I have faith that the world won't always be marked by death, and I want to be part of making that transition happen."

Hakim smiled at the young man. Jacen grinned back, happy for the companionship.

****

Three days later Jacen was ready to leave. He had visited all of his old haunts, burning the images into his brain. He had spent time at his parents' graves, weeping, remembering, thinking. He knew he would never return.

That night at the campfire, he announced, "It's time to go. I'm headed west tomorrow. I need to do this. Do you still intend to go with me?"

Hakim nodded, "I'd like to. Got nothing else to do. Been wandering for years; I've seen much, and learned more, but I reckon it's time to put all that experience to good use. We don't really know each other all that well, but if either had malicious designs, I think it would have shown up by now. If the partnership doesn't work, I'll just bail out. Neither of us will be the worse for having tried."

"Sounds good to me, Hakim. I'm glad you're coming. Other than my basic goals, I really don't know what I'm doing. I know I'll need help."

"Okay then, let's start right now with the basics: destination. Where do you want to plant this community? When we leave tomorrow, where exactly are we going?"

"I want to go west, into the interior."

"The interior of this continent covers a lot of territory; can you narrow it down just a bit?"

Jacen chuckled, "A reasonable request." He paused, thinking, then admitted, "I don't know; I guess I'll recognize it when we get there. I want to locate near a large ruins with plenty of natural resources; somewhere with good water where we can farm, and plenty of timber. If we start somewhere near the center, I figure we stand an even chance of finding a spot with no Anarchs, and where no scavenging has occurred."

"I thought you weren't going to scavenge."

"No, I don't want to *rely* on scavenging. We'll need to at first, but if we're really going to start over, we'll have to learn how to do more than basic farming. We'll need to learn how to build, study, and create. I don't want to be forever dependent on the labors of an earlier people."

Hakim walked over to his large pack and dug around for a moment. He pulled out a slim book the size and shape of a large magazine. "One of my most prized possessions," he explained as he sat next to Jacen on the log. "It's a 2036 Rand-McNally road atlas of the country, with plasticized pages, so it hasn't decayed. I found it way down south in a ruin last year where no one was living. It's a little old, but I don't expect anyone has changed the roads," he said dryly.

The Arab turned to Jacen and asked, "How much do you know about the geography of North America?"

"Very little," admitted Jacen.

"Hmm. Okay, look," Hakim instructed as he opened the atlas to a page displaying the entire continental United States. "This is where we are," he started, pointing. "The great ruin about thirty miles to the east of us was once called Philadelphia. We are in what used to be the state of Pennsylvania. This whole land was once called the United States of America."

"Yeah, Dad taught us these things, but I've never seen a whole map," Jacen said. He was fascinated by the atlas.

"Surely you could have found maps around here," Hakim said, shocked. "I located the library in the Exton ruins, right down the road. The roof was leaking badly, but otherwise it was still standing. I'm sure it would have had maps."

"That's just it, Hakim! Our community had *no* curiosity about the larger world!" The young man's frustration began to pour out. "We knew of the Great Disaster, and that the government had plans for recovery. We were waiting for the government to step in and save us. For eighty years, that's been the story of our town. Other than basic reading, writing, and arithmetic, little else has been taught. We've been farming and scavenging, just barely existing. We've learned nothing and we've done nothing! We've wasted so much time! It makes me so angry!"

Hakim put the atlas down. "Jacen, it's not just your community; it's everywhere. I have been as far south as Florida, and as far west as the southern Mississippi river. I've seen several dozen little communities, just like yours. And the outlook you describe is everywhere the same. Everyone is expecting someone *else* to do something."

"But why, Hakim?"

"That's a story for another day, but I can tell you this; according to what I have read, the culture of the country for forty or fifty years prior to the plague was one of dependency. The citizens had come to expect the government to solve problems and care for them. Unfortunately, we are living that heritage. *Now listen to me,* Jacen!" the Arab said with such vehemence and frustration that Jacen wondered if Hakim had tried unsuccessfully to convince others before him. "There *is no more government, anywhere,* so far as I can tell. I've been through Washington, D.C., and other than a large concentration of Anarchs, it's nothing but an empty, decrepit ruin. People are waiting for help that will never come, and have been for two generations. It's a total myth!"

"I know! I believe you! Ever since I realized the truth, I've been dreaming of this project. If anything is to be done, we have to do it ourselves! So we're back to the original question: where will we plant this town? Tell me what you were going to tell me before we both got frustrated."

A wry smile traced itself across Hakim's weather-beaten face. "Sorry, Jacen. I've been trying to tell folks wherever I meet 'em that there is no government savior out there, and when I finally meet someone who believes me, all I can do is get frustrated about the ones who didn't. Okay, back to the map.

"The North American continent was made up of three nations. Up here was Canada; down here was Mexico; the U.S. was in the middle. These three had their own governments, customs and traditions. The U.S. had a strong central government, called the federal government, that bound the states together. Each state also had its own government, as did cities and towns.

"But when the plague happened, which we call the Great Disaster, so many people died so suddenly that government at all levels simply ceased to exist. The remaining authorities decided it was easier to care for people if they were concentrated in just a few spots. One of the last efforts of the federal government was the relocation of the remaining population to the east coast, around Washington and Virginia Beach, as your dad taught you.

"That was about eighty years ago. It appears that publishing stopped in 2038; I haven't been able to locate any published records more recent than that. What has happened since I know only through the stories I've heard. But it is safe to say that there are no organized nations or governments anymore, because there is no population sufficient to sustain them. The Great Disaster was world-wide. There isn't any way to find out what is going on in the lands that used to be Canada, Mexico, or even the central U. S., short of walking there and exploring it first-hand.

"Let's look at the lay of the land across the broad sweep of the country," said Hakim, motioning again to the map. "The basic idea is this: you've got three major mountain ranges spanning the continent from north to south. These are the mountains in the east, the Appalachians. Then there are the Rockies, right here," said Hakim, his finger tracing the range from Canada to Mexico, "and here in the west are the Sierra Nevadas and the Cascades together.

"Splitting the country right in half is the Mississippi River, also running north to south, right here. I've actually seen it way down in the south: it's huge—over a mile wide—and impossible to cross that far south without a boat; the bridges are all gone. It floods every spring, inundating the land for miles around it.

"Now," continued Hakim, "where are you thinking of starting your town? Do you have any general ideas?"

Jacen had no clue, other than knowing that he wanted the starting place to be far from the East. The two men talked over their plans late into the night. By the time Jacen stood first watch, it had been settled: their destination was the ruins of Denver, Colorado.

****

Two weeks after the the gun battle at Ludwig's Corner, Jacen and Hakim were crossing the Appalachian mountains on their journey west. Each carried a heavy pack, weapons, and ammunition. Hakim was teaching Jacen daily about backcountry travel, the plants and animals, the proper use of his weapon, survival skills, and many other practical subjects. He had a skillful way of using daily events to provide examples and sometimes even the main lesson. The younger man was a quick study, but it was a credit to the Arab's teaching craft that Jacen was usually unaware until after the fact that he was being taught some point or principle; Hakim wasn't preachy.

The grief of loss hung upon Jacen, but the twenty-three year old was taking it in stride. He did not linger in self-pity. Jacen was driven by the future, by the desire to build and create.

They were walking on what had once been known as the Pennsylvania Turnpike, Interstate 76. Like all other roads of the time, its top surface had eroded to little more than crumbly gravel, although its deeper roadbed had kept most of the trees at bay. Here and there a sapling was growing out of a pothole, of which the road had not a few. Occasionally the two men would come across the rusting hulk of a vehicle whose owner had not been fortunate enough to die in his own bed. They wasted no time scavenging the derelicts as they did not care to add to the weight in their packs.

Springtime was coming to the Pennsylvania mountains and the laurels were blooming. If eighty years with minimal human presence had been tough on the roads, it had been heaven for the wilderness environment. The streams ran clear and clean; the air was pristine; the forests were tall. Wildlife and game were plentiful. Even natural herds of elk had found their way into the western reaches of the state.

****

Jacen walked cautiously into the old tunnel. Rocks fallen from the ceiling were strewn all over the deteriorating road surface. Thirty feet or so past the entrance, the damp walls became icy, with stalactites of ice hanging from the ceiling.

"I don't know, Hakim; it looks pretty dangerous to me. I think we ought to go out and around."

"Nonsense. We'll be okay, Jacen. If it has lasted this long, it will last another thirty minutes or so while we walk through it," the Arab replied with more confidence than he felt. They walked a little further into the increasing gloom and then found the way forward blocked by fallen rock.

"Well, apparently it *hasn't* lasted this long," Jacen observed, his voice echoing.

Hakim observed the rock pile for a moment, and then tossed over his shoulder as he turned back toward the entrance, "Rub it in, kid, rub it in. Okay, I guess we'll do it your way. We'll find a trail over the mountain."

****

The obstacle was the collapsed Blue Mountain tunnel. Hakim walked back out of the tunnel, and located a game trail that plunged into the laurel in a generally upward direction. The path climbed steadily, and within an hour they had topped a low saddle about a mile north of the tunnel. As they began to descend, Hakim emerged from a dense thicket of laurel and came upon the carcass of a small deer. It was a fresh kill.

"Look out, Jacen! Get your rifle!" Hakim's voice was tense. His hand went directly to his shoulder holster, and he pulled out an old but expertly maintained Colt pistol. It was an antique M1911A1 model, but there was nothing antiquated about the stopping power of the eight .45 slugs it carried. Hakim adopted a shooter's stance, and surveyed the underbrush as he slowly backed up.

"What's up? What's wrong?" asked Jacen, coming up behind him but still immersed in the laurel thicket.

"Is your rifle at the ready?"

Hakim heard the weapon being unslung and a round being chambered before the response came from over his shoulder, "It is now. What am I looking for?"

"A cougar, I'd guess, and he is probably circling right now, if I'm not mistaken. Turn around and cover our back trail. Don't look the same direction I am, for crying out loud!

"Advance slowly back up the trail, but don't leave a gap between us. I want to back out of this little clearing. There's a fresh carcass not thirty feet in front of me. Must have interrupted the cat's lunch. If we are paying attention, he'll probably leave us alone. Otherwise, one of us is liable to be dessert."

"One of us?" Jacen asked.

"Yeah, 'cause if he comes after you, I'm running off like a crazy man."

"Thanks, O Brave Warrior."

"Don't mention it."

A chill ran up Jacen's spine when he spotted the big cat perfectly blended into the foliage. It scared him to realize that the mountain lion had been there undetected, staring at him for several moments. It was crouched in the underbrush, black-tipped tail barely twitching, cold yellow eyes locked on him.

"I see him. He's about sixty feet off, and he's crouched."

Hakim turned around slowly and spotted the cat. It was a big male, probably eight feet from nose to tail.

"Okay, cover him, but don't shoot unless he charges. Don't want to risk wounding him, lest we have a very unhappy cat on our hands. I'll make some noise and try to scare him off." Hakim fired three rounds up into the air and the big cat darted away. For a moment they could hear it crashing off in the brush.

"Hakim, you look a little spooked. You okay?" the young man asked as he reset his safety and reslung the rifle on his shoulder.

"I'm fine," the Arab said, dismissing Jacen's question.

"No, you're not. Look at you, white as a sheet, and your hands are shaking."

"Well, yeah, I probably overreacted," he muttered as he popped the magazine out of the pistol, inserted a fresh one, and then refilled the original before returning it to a side-pocket on the holster.

Hakim looked at Jacen's concerned face, and relented, "It's been about eighteen years. My sister and her little boy had gone hunting for mushrooms. They were overdue, and I went to find them. A cougar had gotten them. I followed that killer's tracks later. He had stalked them all the way and they never knew it. It was too late when I found them; they were dead. My brother-in-law felt responsible, had let them go out." Hakim scrubbed his face with his hands, and then added, "He killed himself that night. Couldn't handle it." The Arab pursed his lips, and exhaled noisily.

"Ever since, when I run into sign of a mountain lion, it all comes back." He returned his pistol to its holster and picked up his pack. "Never did find that cat. Never did even the score." Wheeling around, he plunged back onto the trail and continued down the mountain to the road.

31

CHAPTER 4

The game trail crossed a rock slide which brought them out of the trees, and a vista opened before them. There was a second, higher ridge due west, less than a mile away. From their vantage point in the middle of the slide area, they could see that the Blue Mountain Tunnel was actually two tunnels: the road emerged from the tunnel right below them, and then immediately disappeared again into a tunnel that bored through the ridge to their west. Hakim correctly surmised that the second tunnel was also blocked and figured they'd have to cross that mountain, too.

Jacen eyed the dark, lowering clouds and the rising wind. The temperature had been falling since midday yesterday. "Hakim, we're about to get clobbered by the weather," Jacen warned.

"Yeah, I've been keeping an eye on it since this morning. Think it's going to be snow?"

"It's a little late for it, but yes, I do. Maybe we ought to ride it out in this little valley. It's pretty sheltered here between these mountains."

"Bad idea, Jacen. If it does snow, it will be deepest in this fold between the ridges. It's a perfect place for drifts. We could get stuck here for a week or so, waiting for it to melt. Let's cross over and get down to the road again."

It took another two hours for the men to regain the road. Sprinkles of cold rain mixed with sleet were falling intermittently, and the light had begun to fade. Dropping their packs inside the tunnel entrance on the west side, they spent the next hour collecting firewood. A sharp ridge just north of the roadway blocked the cold, wet, northerly gusts, and the two managed to set up a fairly comfortable camp just inside the mouth of the tunnel.

****

Freezing rain during the night had turned into a wet, heavy snow by daybreak. *No travel today,* thought Jacen as he lay in his bedroll watching the wind whip eddies of snow around and around at the mouth of the tunnel. The water that had been oozing from various cracks in the ceiling the previous night was now frozen solid. A soft snore from nearby told him that Hakim was still asleep. Because of the intensity of the storm, Hakim had not thought it necessary to set a watch. It was the first night in weeks in which either had gotten enough sleep.

Jacen was reluctant to move from his bedroll, but he wanted some hot coffee so he got up and dressed, and rekindled the fire. He inched as close to it as he dared, and sat absorbing the warmth. When the coffee was ready, he poured himself a cup and allowed his thoughts to wander.

The world was a strange place, and he did not understand it, he decided. Not at all. For one thing, though he enjoyed living and was committed to the idea that life was precious, he was utterly unable to account for why he felt this way, nor even why he should. For beyond those two facts, the enjoyment of life and the preciousness of life, existence itself seemed rather pointless. The wind blew round and round, the sun went up, the sun went down, and then it came up again. And again. And again. Rain fell, and ran to the rivers, and the rivers ran to the sea. And more rain fell, and more, and more. Winter turned to spring, spring to summer, summer to fall, and fall to winter again. And again. And again. *Big deal! Why? What's the point? Maybe there is no point. But then, why do I want to build something enduring? Why bother? If there is no point to it, why not just relax and enjoy life? And if life is unenjoyable and hurts too much, why not just end it? Why not? Well, that's obvious. I don't end it because life is precious, and if life is precious, then mine must also be. Somehow I <u>know</u> this. But <u>how</u> do I know this? <u>Do</u> I really know this?*

No, not gonna go there. Whenever I go down this blind canyon, I get depressed. C'mon, Jace, pull yourself together. No answers anyway.

Jacen took a sip of coffee. *Mmm. That's good. Real good.* He savored the taste as the hot beverage warmed his throat and stomach. He enjoyed watching the steam of his breath dissipate as he slowly exhaled in the cold tunnel.

The other really strange thing Jacen could not understand about the world was why he was sitting in a cold, damp tunnel this morning when it was quite obvious that people used to live in the most beautiful, wonderful houses filled with a variety of machines and strange but wonderful devices. There were cars and trucks in the ruins, on the roads, and parked at every house. They had obviously been designed to travel these roads, but Jacen had never in his entire life seen even one moving. They were immobile, derelict hulks of glass and metal.

Everything was collapsed, decayed, rusted, rotted, and unusable. And wires! Wires everywhere. Up high, spanning hills. On poles. Even underground. *What were all these wires for? 'Electricity,' yes, according to dad. But what on earth was electricity? What was it for? And all the cities, towns, and villages: now just ruins. Why? What happened? How did such an advanced civilization come upon such hard times? And why have we not bounced back? Why can't <u>we</u> use their technology ourselves?*

His father had told him of the Great Disaster. A disease came on people and they began to die very rapidly. He knew that it was connected with a war, and that it had something to do with Muslims, but his knowledge was vague, fragmentary, and without context. His dad had not known a great deal himself. The one man in the community who had known of these things was killed by the Anarchs when Jacen was but five. There had been no one to take his place, and the town at Ludwig's Corner had been left with incomplete and fading memories of the past. It was a world filled with questions, but equally filled with a dearth of answers. *Hmm. Can you fill something with absence? With emptiness? It seems a contradiction. But this world is filled with it. FILLED with it! And so am I!*

Oh, bother! STOP IT, JACEN! Enough with this philosophical doubletalk! Let it go, Jacen! There are no answers!

But he was completely unsatisfied. And he intuitively realized that if his mind could formulate the questions, somewhere there was a mind that could formulate the answers. Someday he had to get some answers. Maybe Hakim knew something.

CHAPTER 5

The storm blew for two days before it deteriorated into individual snow squalls punctuated by blue patches of sky. It left behind about eighteen inches of heavy wet snow. On the third day the sky cleared and the temperature rose in the face of a soft, southerly breeze. The icy coating that had developed on the ceiling of the tunnel began to drip, and then commenced peeling off in sheets, occasionally bringing rock with it. Jacen and Hakim moved their gear to the mouth of the tunnel, as Hakim was fearing that additional cave-ins could occur as the mountainside became lubricated with excess groundwater. Reflecting brilliantly off of the snow, the sunshine made their eyes ache from the glare.

Rivulets of water from the melting snow, running across the crumbling road surface, soon became small rivers of water. Within hours, there was not a square inch of ground that was not either snow-covered or wet with running or standing water. Finally the men donned their packs and waded through the wet snow up the hillside to the north of the road, until they found enough flat ground at the top to pitch camp in the snow. It was not perfect, but it did not have the running water they experienced down on the road. After two more soggy days, they resumed their westward walk.

****

A week later, they arrived at the ruin of Bedford, Pennsylvania. The two left the old highway to scavenge clothing, shoes, and other equipment. It was sometimes possible to find items that, because of their packaging or storage, had withstood the ravages of time. A metal building with a pitched roof, standing behind a small department store, had proven to be such a place. It was a small warehouse of sorts, remarkably intact, and had remained quite weather-proof. Inside were several shrink-wrapped pallets of shoes and clothing. Both men were able to locate a good pair of boots, several pairs of pants, and other essentials. In another crate, Jacen discovered a compact pair of binoculars, which he added to his heavy pack.

"This building has some great stuff in it. I wish we had a way of carrying more of it with us," Jacen said.

"What? Are you into hoarding now?"

"No, Hakim, of course not. It's just that we'll wear this stuff out fairly quickly, and we have no guarantee we'll find more."

"If we don't find what we need, son, we'll make do. I thought you wanted to get away from this scavenging sort of life, anyway."

"Well, yeah, I do. I want to learn how to be a producer, not just a user. But it's going to take time to make the transition. And in the meantime, I'd like to have clothes to wear."

"I know, Jacen. I was just pulling your chain. Unfortunately, everything we take with us, we carry on our backs; there's no way we can carry extra."

Leaving the building, Hakim made sure to carefully latch the door, to preserve what was left for the next needy traveler. The two started out of town on a small road that appeared to be going in the direction of I-76. As the path rounded a curve, both men stopped suddenly. In the field across the road, grazing in the new spring growth, was a herd of about thirty horses. The men were downwind of the animals, and had not been noticed. They slowly crouched to the ground.

"Oh, bless Allah! What a find! This is great," whispered the Arab. "I have never in my life seen so many horses!"

"You're telling me," agreed Jacen as he quietly removed his pack. "But hey, I thought you weren't a Muslim! What are you doing talking about 'Allah?'"

"I'm *not* a Muslim. Not anymore. Maybe someday I'll explain."

"You say that a lot, you know?" rejoined Jacen, unslinging his rifle from his shoulder. Neither had taken their eyes off of the horses. Seeking better cover they crawled behind a nearby patch of forsythia, whose branches were just beginning to blossom.

"What? 'Bless Allah?' What are you talking about? That's the first I've said it since we met!" Hakim objected. Both men were still whispering.

"No, no, not that! That bit about, 'maybe I'll tell you sometime'. Whenever I ask you a personal question, that's how you always answer. You're always evasive." Still watching the herd, Jacen chambered a round as quietly as he could.

"Hmm," Hakim grunted. "Well, *maybe* someday I *will* tell you," the Arab muttered stubbornly.

Jacen shook his head, rolling his eyes. "Fine. Keep your secrets." He raised his weapon and took aim on the nearest horse, a large bay mare.

"*What* are you doing?" hissed Hakim with irritated surprise.

"Harvesting a little meat," Jacen whispered back, not taking his eyes off of the mare.

"Are you crazy?" Hakim demanded, shoving the barrel of the rifle down.

"What do you mean? They're good eating, Hakim. We need meat."

"You're kidding me, right?"

Jacen looked at him blankly, and shook his head, no.

"Jacen, we *need* these animals, but not for meat. These creatures are priceless for riding, hauling, plowing, and half-a-dozen other uses. They're worth a whole lot more *living* than they are as food! And I've never in my life seen them in a herd this size. All over the East Coast they've been hunted to extinction by people who are appallingly ignorant of the value of a good horse. Don't you dare shoot them!"

The two watched the horses graze for several more minutes. Finally a big lineback dun stallion spotted them. He snorted with a sharp whinny, and the whole herd galloped across the field and disappeared into the forest on the far side.

"So," said Jacen, standing up and retrieving his pack, "if we aren't going to eat them, what are we going to do with them?"

"We'll capture them and break them to the saddle. Then we can ride 'em and use them to carry our stuff. If we can find a wagon, or somehow rig one up, these horses can haul a whole lot of gear. Jacen, this is exactly what you need to get your town started! You'll need horses as your basic work animal."

"Have you worked with horses before?" Jacen asked dubiously.

"Nope. Never. But I've read a good book on them. In fact, I carry it in my pack because I've been hoping to run into a horse in my travels," replied the older man.

Jacen studied Hakim, thinking that he was being teased again. But Hakim's expression told the young man his friend was quite serious. Suddenly, the humorous image of Hakim perched on a horse while consulting a book formed in his mind, and Jacen began to chuckle. "You've read a book?" he chortled incredulously, "You're serious? *A book?*" The more he thought about it the funnier it seemed. Soon he was roaring with laughter, and he collapsed weakly on the ground, howling with mirth. "You've, hahahaha, you've read a *book*–hahahahaha–and you think you can train hor-hahahaha-horses!" The pent-up emotional energy of the last month now poured forth in gusts of laughter that Jacen found himself powerless to stop.

The Arab looked indignantly at the young man, who was rolling on the ground with glee, tears coming out of his eyes. Hakim insisted stiffly, "Of course. I have learned a great deal from books."

"Hahahaha, uh-haha, uh-ha, oh my," exhaled Jacen as he slowly regained his composure. "Oh, my!" he repeated, wiping his eyes on his shirt sleeve. "Oh, I *needed* that," Jacen muttered, half to himself. He looked up at his friend and exclaimed, "Hakim, that's really rich! You are something!" Jacen slowly clambered to his feet, still smiling and chuckling. "Do you think that you can teach, hahahahahaha, tea-hahahahaha," the young man's laughter resumed in gales, and he fell weakly back to the ground, "teach me, too, hahahahaha!"

The older man looked at Jacen in irritation, turned on his heel, and retrieved his pack. "We are staying here tonight," he snapped, as he began to set up camp.

CHAPTER 6

After setting up camp the two men sat by the fire, and discussed what the horses could mean to their plans. Hakim was excited; Jacen was skeptical.

"Jacen, this is a marvelous stroke of fortune! Let's capitalize on it! We should not leave this valley until we can take that whole herd with us."

"I guess I don't see it the way you do, Hakim. Why is this such an important find? I think it's wiser that we keep moving. According to your map, we've nearly two thousand miles to travel. It's going to take four or five months, at least. We can't stay here chasing after horses. Nuts, neither of us knows what to do even if we did catch one!"

"That's not true, Jacen. I know exactly what to do with them. Let me give you a few examples. Did your community have a plow of any sort?" Hakim asked.

"Sure. We had something that a man had patched together. One guy would stand on it, and four would try to pull it. It was hard work. I hated plowing. But it did turn the soil over, and once it got going, it was faster than using a shovel."

"Hmm. Well, a horse can be trained to pull a plow. One man, one horse, and one plow can cultivate more ground in a single day than eight men. And we can ride horses: our travel time to the Rockies would be cut down substantially. All those clothes you wanted to carry earlier today? We can pack them on horses, with all kinds of supplies. We might even be able to rig up a wagon of sorts. If we come across any cattle, and we probably will, we can drive them ahead of us if we have horses."

Jacen listened with growing interest, and then asked with a wicked chuckle, "Did you *read books* on all this stuff, Hakim?"

The Arab smiled. "No, Jacen, I did not 'read books on all this stuff'. But I have read one book on horses, and I think we can do it. It'll take a lot of work. We'll probably wind up spending a month, maybe even two, right here. But it will be worth it in the long run. Until we can figure out how to restore the technology of our grandfathers, horses could advance us well beyond where we are right now. This town of yours will be in a better position to accomplish your goals if it has the advantage of horse-power.

"Look, son, it was *you* who said you wanted to build and advance, not merely exist. Why not start right now? Why not re-discover how to domesticate and use horses?"

As Hakim poured himself another cup of coffee, Jacen pondered the matter and decided Hakim's logic was unassailable. *Why not begin the great advance back to civilization right now?* Jacen nodded slowly. "Why not?" he agreed. "Let's do it!"

"Good! Now, there are several challenges we need to overcome. Obviously, we have to find and capture the herd. We'll need a corral of sorts. We'll need to round up all the tack, or 'horse-hardware,' we can find, like saddles, bridles, and so forth, from the surrounding area. I'm guessing that since there's a herd here, there were probably one or more outfits in the area that had horses. We can scavenge for equipment. We'll also need to set up a more comfortable temporary camp for ourselves. We've got two weeks of hard work ahead of us before we even go after the horses."

****

It was an oddity of the times, and a major distinguishing factor between the Townies and the Anarchs: Townies hated to live within the ruins or in old existing structures. There was a palpable sense of human filth and death hanging about the old deserted buildings; on the other hand, the new cabins they built themselves, even those with dirt floors and leaky roofs, seemed cleaner, more habitable, and more inviting. In a pinch, a Townie would take shelter from the weather in an old structure, but given a choice between living in an ancient-but-still-weather-proof shelter, or building their own rough cabin, Townies would build the cabin every time.

For Anarchs it was quite different. They scavenged everything, including living spaces. There was no thought given to prior occupants, no discomfort with evidence of human filth, and no desire to create something new. They were content to 'live off the land' in every respect. If their dwelling required maintenance, they would move on to a different place rather than do maintenance or fix-up tasks.

If a Townie and an Anarch were each asked to build something new, the Townie would respond with *"what?"* and the Anarch would respond with *"why?"*. While there were exceptions in both groups, the scarcity of these established the norm.

****

For the next twenty days Jacen and Hakim worked without a break. Both men were already accustomed to hard, physical work, and so they made rapid progress. Scavenging the existing buildings, plus what had evidently been a lumber yard, they were able to construct a shed-like structure in which they could sleep and shelter their gear from the weather, although when the weather was good both men preferred sleeping under the stars.

They located the remains of a farming supply store in the ruin of Bedford, and salvaged what they needed to build a large pen, including two post-hole diggers and fencing material. Locating a steep embankment, where the old interstate highway had been elevated, they constructed a corral using the embankment as one of the sides. Soon they had a six-foot high fence enclosing the other three sides, encompassing an area of about 1600 square yards. A gurgling brook wound through one corner.

They erected another hundred yards of fence on either side of the corral's main gate, laid out like a funnel. If they could get the horses into the mouth of the funnel they stood a chance of being able to drive them into the corral. On the opposite side from the main gate, they added another gate and a smaller fenced-in area to be used for training the horses.

*** * * * * * * * ***

"What do you 'spose the date is, Hakim?" Jacen was sitting against a tree, eating some roasted venison still hot from the flames of the fire. It was late afternoon, tending toward evening and the two exhausted men had called it a day.

"I *know* what the date is, Jacen. I don't have to guess."

Jacen looked up, partly to see if Hakim was pulling his leg. The Arab stared back at him, completely serious. "How could you possibly *know* what the date is?" Jacen asked.

"Easy. I take sun sightings at dawn or dusk with a good compass, and maintain a journal to keep track of it. I *know*, plus or minus one day, the date. Why don't you take a guess at it?"

"Umm . . . I would guess that it is probably, oh, May, maybe the twenty-eighth."

"It's May the fifteenth, 2120."

"Really? Can you teach me how to do that?"

"Sure. This valley's not good for it, because we can't see the sun at either sunrise or sunset. So I just keep track of it on paper at times like this, so to speak. But when we are where we can see, I'll show you how to do it."

The men ate in silence as they finished their meal, and then sat enjoying the fading light. The bright green of spring growth had not yet darkened into the mature green of summer, and so the valley still looked fresh and new. The haunting sound of a lone whippoorwill came floating across the meadow, and a thin band of translucent cloud gradually started to glow orange in the distant western sky. The moon above them began to shine more prominently as the dusk deepened.

"Hakim, what happened?" Jacen asked softly as he watched the cloud turn from orange to bright red.

"Huh?" asked the Arab, stirred from his own thoughts.

"What happened to the world? How did we get to this point? What really happened?"

"Well, Jace'," he responded, shifting to make himself more comfortable, "it's a long story."

"It's not like I have anywhere to go, Hakim," the twenty-three year old chided. "If there is anything we have a lot of, right now, it's time. So, what happened?"

"The real answer has to do with something that happened long, long before, but you aren't ready for that story yet, so for now I will tell you the tale of the Great Disaster.

"About one hundred twenty years ago, the planet was filled with people, over six billion of 'em. The world—"

Jacen interrupted, incredulous. "SIX BILLION PEOPLE? You're joking!"

"No, I'm quite serious. As I was saying, the world was divided into nations, such as the United States, Britain, France, Russia, Saudi Arabia, Egypt, and many, many others. Each nation maintained its own government, laws, military, and its own interests in the wider world. Nations who shared common interests frequently forged alliances together, such as the European Union and the League of Arab States. The country of my great-grandparents, Jordan, belonged to the Arab League."

"Was this land a member of one of these alliances?"

"The U.S. was a member of many different alliances, but in some respects, America was its own alliance."

"What do you mean?"

"The nation was, at that time, more powerful than any other nation in the world, and by far. She spent more on her military than all the other nations of the world put together, and yet the country was so wealthy it was but a small part of her total budget. Her weaponry was more advanced, her soldiers better trained and better paid than any other country's armed services."

"What did America do with all that power?"

"She protected her own interests, as well as those of other countries to whom she was friendly. Some accused her of aggression and imperialism. She was occasionally guilty of the former, never of the latter. America was mostly a benevolent force for stability in the world. But she was defeated by the Arab peoples, and died as a country."

"Your people?" asked Jacen.

After a long silence, the Arab replied softly, "Yes. My people."

The stars above were beginning to appear through the deepening purple of the dusky sky. A damp chill spread as the temperature dropped, and dew began to form on the grass. The light breeze that had been drifting up the valley all day reversed, as the cooling air began sinking, seeking the low dells, valleys, and meadows. Hakim shivered, and after adding a log to the fire, poured himself some steaming coffee.

"My people," he said again, "my people unleashed the terror that destroyed the world. It even destroyed the Arabs themselves. But there is blame enough, in this tale, to be shared by all. The West committed suicide, and the East merely feasted upon the carcass. Your people," he said, looking sadly at Jacen, "destroyed themselves. They exalted the autonomous self, like the Europeans before them, and lost the soul of their civilization. They dehumanized themselves, and found themselves not worth saving."

The fire popped, as some moist pocket in the wood burst with steam, scattering sparks about. In the distance, coyotes began a mournful serenade of the moon. The Arab sat, uncharacteristically staring into the fire, sadness and weariness written in all the wrinkles of his leathery brown face. Jacen watched him silently, waiting for him to continue.

Hakim finally stirred himself and said softly, still staring into the flames, "It is enough for tonight. We will continue this later. You have the first watch, Jacen. Wake me at one."

CHAPTER 7

Three days later their shed was filling up with saddles and tack. Hakim had decided that they should recover as much serviceable gear as they found in the outlying ruins. The rotted and the ruined they left behind, although Jacen did recover several good saddle trees for future use by removing the old leather. He realized that the skills required to make saddle trees would not be soon available, and figured he'd better preserve what he could.

They had recovered seven good Western saddles, three English saddles, several dozen assorted bridles, headstalls and hackamores, and several boxes full of various bits, belts, straps, piggin' strings, stirrups, and other parts. A dozen saddle blankets, four decent sets of saddle bags, and eight fairly well-preserved ropes completed the haul.

"What in the world are we going to do with all this junk, Hakim? A month ago you were telling me I could not bring extra clothes! Now we have piles of stuff that you want to take, most of which I could not identify if my life depended upon it," Jacen groused.

"Patience, son. Soon you'll understand what all this stuff does, and you'll be glad we got it," Hakim replied, outwardly confident. What he did not say is that he hoped he would understand it all, too.

****

It was time to capture the horses. They had seen the herd around every couple of days. They had even begun to notice that when the wind direction was right they could smell the horses before they saw them. It appeared that the big animals had become more accustomed to their presence, and less skittish. The stallion, a big brown dun, continued to maintain his distance even while asserting aggressive control over the herd.

Hakim and Jacen did not have any apples or carrots to attract the horses. In fact they had no feed of any sort, and would have to rely on the grass growing in their corral, supplemented by what hay they could cut, to keep the animals fed once they were corralled. The one thing they did have to sweet-talk the horses was sugar. They had located a shrink-wrapped pallet of dry groceries that was undamaged. In it were several cases of boxed sugar cubes.

"We need to nab that stallion, Jacen. The whole herd follows him. If we don't grab him in the first batch, he'll take all the horses we missed and clear out of the country."

"How are we going to catch *any* of them, Hakim? I've no idea what I am doing."

"I've got it figured out, son. It will take around two weeks, and a lot of sugar. But we'll have a big batch of horses penned in that corral before you know it."

"How?"

"Tomorrow we will make a small wooden table and set it out beyond the mouth of that funnel we built with the fencing. Every day we'll put several dozen sugar cubes on it. As long as we give 'em plenty of space, the horses will come after it. Once they've begun to expect the sugar, we'll start moving the table further and further into the funnel. As long as we keep baiting it with sugar, they'll keep coming to it. We might even be able to bait them right into the corral."

"So, what's special about the table?" asked Jacen.

"Nothing special. It simply gives them a visual object to associate with the sugar cubes, and gives us a place to set them. After a few days, when they see it they'll come to it expecting sugar."

Jacen just rolled his eyes and shook his head.

"Oh, you of little faith," chided Hakim.

"Huh-uh," Jacen said, shaking his head, "*no* faith!"

"You just watch. You'll see," retorted Hakim.

The next day, they cobbled together a table from scraps of lumber, and placed it at the very far edge of the clearing, at the edge of the forest. Hakim dumped half a box of sugar cubes on it, and then spent the rest of the day chasing the squirrels and the deer away from it, much to Jacen's delight. The horses never did show up.

*** * * * * * * * * ***

That night after they had cleaned up dinner, Jacen asked the older man, "What did you mean several nights ago, Hakim, when you said that the people of the United States dehumanized themselves? You said, 'they dehumanized themselves, and then found themselves not worth saving.' What does that mean?"

Hakim picked up his rifle and moved to a spot across the fire from Jacen. He began to break it down and clean it. Jacen followed suit with his own weapon. He had known the Arab long enough to recognize when Hakim was getting settled to begin talking.

After several moments of silent activity, Hakim began, "Man is the only creature on the planet who has advanced rational capabilities, as well as capacities that go beyond mere rationality. For instance, only mankind can identify and appreciate beauty. Only humans can deal in genuine abstracts. Animals can not. Only mankind can deal in ethics and morality; animals don't have an 'ought' or a 'should,' but men do. Men can make decisions in a way that animals can not. When those mares are in heat, the stallion will mate with them. It's that simple. He does not 'decide to' or 'decide not to.' He simply does. But men and women can decide whether or not to mate. They may decide based upon a huge variety of factors, only a few of which have to do with the biological urge itself.

"If an animal is hungry, he will eat. If a man is hungry, he might nonetheless decide not to eat, or to wait on his spouse, or even to fast for religious purposes. While an animal might exercise something that looks like compassion toward his young, there are very few, if any, examples in the animal kingdom of one adult male exercising sacrificial compassion for another adult male. But human beings will do such a thing."

"You mean, like, when you helped me out?" Jacen asked.

"Actually, I was thinking about you caring for the other members of your community, including your father, when they were dying. Animals don't exercise that kind of gratuitous compassion. Only humans can, understand?"

"Yes, I can see that. But what does that have to do with my question? How did the people of this country 'dehumanize themselves?'"

"They, like Europe before them, mistakenly equated *liberty* with *license*. They began to give in to their lusts and passions, and defended their choices by talking about personal rights, moral freedoms, and so on. Instead of becoming more free, however, they became slaves to their lusts. They no longer exercised the moral—the uniquely human—component of their decision-making. They copulated like cats and dogs, gave themselves to alcohol and drugs, ate without regard to their bodily need, and generally pursued pleasure without restraint. They spent way beyond their financial resources, and according to the materials I read, denied themselves no pleasure.

"Before long, their pursuit of absolute autonomous freedom began to impact one another. If angered, they lashed out. If needy, they took, violently if necessary. Alternatively, if they did not feel like contributing to society, they simply stopped working and leeched off of those who did. If they desired power, when they got it, they oppressed others."

"Sounds a lot like the Anarchs," the younger man mused.

"That's right, Jacen. The Anarchs represent the complete, untrammeled pursuit of personal autonomy. Originally the anarchists were not violent, according to their philosophy. They simply wanted to be left alone. How that philosophy eventually produced the modern Anarch is another story for another time." Hakim fell silent as he reassembled his M14.

Jacen waited, then prodded the silent Arab. "You still have not answered my question."

Hakim nodded, and resumed, "Humanity in the twenty-first century stopped using the unique gifts that distinguished them as *humans* and separated them from animals. They stopped factoring morality into their decisions. The whole notion of denying or delaying gratification in favor of some greater good ceased to exist. Just like the brute animals of nature, they followed their lusts and passions, rather than their hearts and minds. In this way, Jacen, they 'dehumanized' themselves."

"Okay, I think I can understand that. But how was it that, in your words, 'they found themselves not worth saving'?" Jacen queried.

Hakim raised his eyebrows and thought for a moment before responding. "Well, that's a little more difficult to understand. I had to read a great deal of their literature before I could see it myself. Let me see if I can explain it to you.

"Late twentieth-century America had come to view nearly *everything* through the lens of the self. They had largely stopped thinking in terms of the good of others, and had begun to measure everything by the self. Their academicians saw this trend, were disturbed by it, and began to critique the new 'freedoms' of society. Some of their critique was well-warranted and well-aimed. But it lacked any compelling moral authority."

"Why?" asked Jacen.

"Because these same academics, as well as most Americans, had long before rejected God. When you throw out God, you necessarily throw out any sort of transcendent, universal values. At the very moment that these academics, clerics, artists, and lawyers were needed to measure their culture and sound the warning that it was coming up short, they found that they no longer had any yardstick by which the culture *could* be measured. There was no longer any universally acknowledged set of criteria by which the excesses of society could be evaluated.

"The late twentieth, early twenty-first century saw the final flowering of privatized belief. For most, the self had now become the only recognized authority. Traditional authority was disdained. Centuries, millennia even, of accumulated wisdom fell before the arrogance of the omniscient, omnipotent modern self.

"Twenty-first century America became a virtual anarchy of opinions with no genuine arbiter who could parse their relative value. This was soon followed by a cynical loss of confidence in the idea of *knowledge itself*. Once it was accepted that there was no larger authoritative narrative against which to judge truth claims and morality, then the very possibility of *knowledge*, of truly knowing, became suspect."

Hakim finished reassembling his rifle. Wiping his hands on a rag, he filled both of their coffee cups and handed Jacen's to him. Sitting back down, he sipped his coffee and continued.

"Understand, Jacen, that now you have two simultaneous crises. The culture has forsaken its ability to govern its desires, and is consequently ruled by its passions rather than its wisdom and self-discipline. Secondly, it has jettisoned confidence in knowledge and any sort of belief in universally valid truth.

"What happens next, Jacen, is that the West begins to view knowledge and truth claims through the paradigm of power, aggression, and oppression. If I claim to 'know' something, then I am exerting power over and oppressing others who disagree. 'Knowledge', then, ceases to be an accurate grasp of things as they really are. Knowledge no longer serves the pursuit of truth, now it serves the pursuit of an agenda; it is reduced to propaganda.

"There are many ways that this loss of confidence in knowledge affects a culture, but for the West its impact on how one writes and understands history was ruinous. History-writing became unhitched from knowledge related to facts and actual events, and was instead joined to political and moral agendas. Typically, history was reduced to a narrative of oppression. This is important, because what a culture thinks of itself depends largely on what it thinks of its past.

"The result of all this is that the history of Western civilization became the history of monsters and criminals, imperialists, robber barons, sadistic right-wing dictators, and the like. Oppressed people were granted nobility by these nouveau historiographers merely by virtue of *being* the oppressed. As a result, within a generation Western civilization became the scourge of the civilized world."

"But *didn't* the West commit great atrocities?" Jacen asked. "That's what my dad taught us."

"Certainly! As did _every other_ civilization, I might add. I am not arguing for the essential goodness of the West, Jacen. What I am saying is that it was due *no special opprobrium*. If anything became its undoing, it was actually the *success* of Western culture. The West advanced far more rapidly after the Middle Ages than its counterparts did. Consequently, it wielded far greater power and was able to subject every other culture with which it came in contact. But recognizing and admitting the failures of the West is a far cry from demonizing it and promoting other cultures to noble status simply because they did not advance as fast the West did.

"Now we come to our point. Jacen, if you believed that your civilization was the cause of virtually all evil and oppression in the world, would you work hard to save your civilization from collapse or a grave mortal threat?"

"No, of course not. If I truly believed it was evil, I would make no move to save it. I might even destroy it myself," Jacen said, understanding beginning to glimmer in his eyes.

"That, then, is what I meant. 'They dehumanized themselves, and found themselves not worth saving.' Western culture destroyed itself, and their academics, by and large, administered the poison. Their *critique* of the culture became a *condemnation* of the culture through a radicalized and selective reinterpretation of the facts. They made the classic mistake of historiography: they judged the past by the present. The irony is, despite their denial that universal narratives exist, by which morals and knowledge and cultures can be judged, they turned their own favorite narrative into a universally applicable one, applied it to the past, and found the past wanting. They were fatally inconsistent."

"So your claim, Hakim, is that Western culture committed a sort of cultural suicide?"

"That's exactly what I am saying, Jacen. One of the West's own historians, a British scholar by the name of Toynbee, put forward the idea that 'civilizations die from suicide, not by murder.' I think that is exactly what happened to the West. Now, mind you, there is a lot more to the story, such as the war that pushed them over the edge, but the condition that really destroyed the West was not outside pressure but internal decay.

"At just the time it was most needed, America no longer had the moral authority to correct its own excesses. It had demonized its Western heritage, which contained the foundations of its shared sense of morality. In the arts, law, politics, and the academy, the dominant view was that America needed to be destroyed, or at least greatly weakened. Nations eventually tend to act out the dominant beliefs of their cultural gatekeepers. And so it happened.

"It is ironic that by the time of its destruction, between abortion, infanticide, and euthanasia, the West had turned *actual* death into a functional tool to serve the whims of the people. The normal guardians of culture, such as educators, lawyers, and artists, had become the most vocal proponents of free and liberalized death. They fought to keep convicted criminals and murderers alive, but dispatched their own babies and their own elderly without a second thought. The distance of some one hundred years provides us with the big picture that they themselves missed at the time. In every respect, the West literally killed itself."

Jacen fell silent as he considered what Hakim had said. He thought for a while, and then asked, "What was the point, the real point of failure, of the culture? At what point was the damage done?"

"When the West decided that God was dead, or God was irrelevant, they lost the ability to promote universal values, the ability to properly critique, and the ability to correct. That was the point of no return. From then on it was just a matter of time."

"But Hakim, I don't believe in God either. But I do believe in morals, and right and wrong!" Jacen said defensively.

"I can see that. You truly do. For example, your insistence that life is precious is a moral value," Hakim acknowledged.

"It sure is! I think your analysis is wrong! Dead wrong!" Jacen was becoming angry. He felt as though Hakim was attacking him, and he did not care for it.

"But Jacen, why is life precious?"

"Because it just is!"

"That's an assertion, but it's not a reason. So I repeat the question: 'Why is life precious?' Sez' who?"

Jacen looked at him, mouth open. He did not know how to answer. "It's obvious, old man!" he finally retorted.

"Is it obvious to everyone?" Hakim asked mildly, pressing the point.

"Of course it is!" Jacen shouted. He was furious at Hakim, and felt as though he had been personally assaulted.

"Is it obvious to the Anarchs?" Hakim asked softly, staring into the fire.

Jacen glared at him, boiling with rage. He stood up and hurled his cup across the fire. As he clinched and unclenched his fists, he realized that he had no answer for the Arab. He wheeled and stalked off into the darkness.

CHAPTER 8

"Hakim, hush!" Jacen hissed.

The Arab looked up from their fire pit, where he had been snapping sticks, preparing to build up the fire. He grabbed his rifle and crawled over to Jacen.

"Looks like the horses found your sugar cubes," whispered the younger man.

"Hmm. Took 'em long enough," muttered Hakim.

The two watched for several moments. Once the sugar was gone, the horses began to graze in the lush grass around the table. The stallion was standing back, at the far end of the clearing, testing the scents on the breeze and keeping a watchful eye over his harem.

After watching for awhile, Hakim said, "Let's get back to the fire and fix breakfast."

"Aren't you afraid they'll hear the noise?"

"Nope. Want 'em to hear. I want them to get used to the fact that we're here. Want 'em to discover that there's nothing to fear. But I don't want them to *see* us today, just to hear us."

A week later, the horses were coming to the table nearly every morning looking for sugar. Once they had come four days in a row, Hakim moved the table thirty feet further into the funnel-like entrance to the corral. After another week the two men began to allow themselves to be seen at a distance. They made no attempt to approach the big animals, but pretended to ignore them.

✳✳✳✳✳✳✳✳✳

If prospects were improving with respect to the horses, they were deteriorating steadily between the two men. Jacen was inwardly furious that he'd been unable to defend his moral viewpoint. He had convinced himself that the Arab had judged and condemned him as immoral, but he knew, deep in his heart, that all Hakim had done was expose the weakness of his beliefs. His anger simmering just below the surface, Jacen became very critical of everything the other man did, not realizing that his focus on the other's perceived shortcomings allowed him to avoid facing his own.

For his part, Hakim was losing patience with his young friend. Jacen no longer seemed to want to learn, and discussions were getting dangerously out of control. Jacen had begun to intimate that Hakim was trigger-happy, and the older man deeply resented the insinuation. There were times when Hakim was ready to abandon his young friend; the only thing that kept him at Jacen's campfire was the hope that they would eventually work through their disagreements.

✳✳✳✳✳✳✳✳✳

It had been a hot, muggy, Pennsylvania day. All afternoon long, the two men had seen, or heard, thunderheads building up around them, and they longed for a rainstorm to cut the stifling heat. But despite the roiling clouds and rumbles of thunder, their little valley had missed

59

out on the rain. The two found some relief swimming in the creek below their campsite.

With nightfall, the heat energy drained away and the clouds dissipated. Starlight pierced the muggy air, and a downslope breeze brought some relief. The fire had burned down to coals, and Jacen sat against the bole of a tree, watching the fireflies. Hakim was standing in the shadows, looking across the meadow, which was drenched in pale moonlight. Tendrils of fog were forming in the low places. The disharmonious wails of a pack of coyotes floated on the evening air. The evening was otherwise quiet, if not just a bit eerie.

"Jacen, we need to talk."

The young man jumped. Somehow he had not noticed when Hakim moved back to the campsite. The tall man moved like a cat, something Jacen had yet to learn how to do.

"About what?"

"About the fact that we aren't getting along. About the fact that we're harboring grudges against one another. About the fact that we can't go on much longer like this. I'm not going to, anyway."

Jacen sighed, perhaps a bit too loudly. The young man's arrogance hit Hakim in the wrong spot, and the Arab muttered, "Forget it," and stalked back out into the meadow.

Jacen knew he had gone too far, and jumped up and followed him.

"Hakim, I am sorry. That was uncalled for. Look, I'm ready to talk. What's on your mind?"

"Well, for starters, why did you just react to me the way you did? What have I done to you? Why have you shut me out?"

Jacen stood silently in the darkness, chewing on his lip, wondering how to say what was in his heart. Maybe it was best just to take the plunge, and pick up the pieces later.

"Hakim, I feel like your analysis of how America failed was aimed right at me. You know I'm an atheist. It does not matter how you dance around this issue, you are calling me an immoral person. According to you, people like me destroyed the country. I find that deeply insulting."

"No, Jacen, I'm *not* calling you immoral. I believe you to be a good, solid man; the kind with whom I would enjoy the challenge of trying to rebuild this country. What I *did* say about you is that you have no foundation for your morality. You can't defend it. You can't go to someone and say, 'what you are doing is wrong, and here's why.'"

"I can, too!"

"No, you can't. You couldn't even tell me why one of the highest moral values, the value of human life, is and should be a moral value. You're planning on starting a town, and more than that, replanting a culture. Not everyone will share your moral values. You'd better be able to defend what is right and wrong, and be prepared to enforce it, when necessary."

"Well, not everyone reads as much as you do! I've never read about philosophy, how should I know how to answer that question?"

"It is not a question of reading or study, Jacen, it is a question of beliefs, and whether our beliefs provide us with good answers for the difficult issues of life."

"Okay, Hakim, let me throw the question back at you: why is life precious? How would you defend your beliefs about it?"

"Life is precious, Jacen, because all human beings are created in the image of God, and God has commanded us not to murder. God alone has the right to take life. An assault on life is basically an assault on God. Life is precious because God says it's precious, Jacen."

"But I don't believe in God, so why should I accept your moral reasoning? Why should anyone?"

"Point granted. My reasoning is not going to be compelling if one does not believe in God. However, at least I do have a logically consistent source of authority outside of myself—God's will expressed through His Word—that I can cite, and that will keep *me* on track, if I choose to obey it. The problem for atheists is that they have no reason whatsoever for believing in any moral standards, at all. A world without God is a world in which one is quite justified in doing exactly as he desires to do, regardless of the consequences to others."

"There you go again—you're calling me immoral because I am an atheist!" Jacen said hotly.

"No, I am *not* calling you immoral, nor do I *think* you're immoral! How many times must I say that?" Hakim said with vehemence. "What I *am* saying is that you don't have a *good reason* for being the moral person that you are! Your atheistic beliefs are inconsistent with your morality. Atheism gives you no genuine means for constructing morality! None!"

"If that's the case, then how did I arrive at my morals to begin with?" Jacen challenged.

"Just like the West was, Jacen, you're running on the fumes of a prior Judeo-Christian culture. Your forebears were surrounded by it, and even though they may not have believed in God, they nonetheless imbibed the culture of which they were a part. The bottom line is that you have unconsciously borrowed your morality from the Bible. In any case, you were created to instinctively know the truth of God's authority on basic morality. Rejecting that ingrained truth, as the Anarchs have, requires conscious effort."

Jacen shook his head, and turned his back on Hakim. He was furious. Over his shoulder he flung a bitter parting shot, "This conversation is over. I find it odd that for someone who claims to believe in God and the value of life, you find it so simple to kill, and you are so . . . accomplished at it!"

* * * * * * * * *

A week later, the two men were stalking a small herd of deer as the animals moved up into the laurel to bed down for the midday. The supply of meat was running low, and they needed the skins for clothing. After Hakim had made a deerskin vest and gloves back in late May, both had concluded that properly tanned deerskin made finer clothing than was available in the dwindling supply of old scavenged stuff.

Jacen was stepping over a small brook, when he stopped suddenly. In the dried mud of the creek bank was a bootprint, just as clear as day. He stared at it. For a moment the significance of the track refused to register in his brain. They had not seen another human since leaving Ludwigs Corner. Jacen had believed they were alone in this valley.

He silently motioned Hakim over, and pointed down. The two avoided speaking while hunting, if possible. The Arab was teaching the young man to communicate everything through hand signs. "You'll never know when we'll need it," the older man had said, back in the early spring. "One of these days we'll probably have to fight again. If we can communicate without talking, we'll have a leg up."

Surprise registered on Hakim's face as he saw the print in the mud. He motioned that they should track the human.

"What about the deer?" Jacen asked, breaking the silence. The sound of his voice spooked the deer, and they bounded away.

Hakim allowed the sounds of the deer crashing though the brush fade away before he answered. "Forget them. They can't shoot at us."

"What makes you think this person wants to shoot at us? Why are you constantly dividing the world between 'us' and 'them'?" Jacen asked with disgust.

"Son, we're not going to get into this right now. I have no idea what this person's intentions are, and neither do you! I'm just exercising due caution."

"No, you're exercising paranoia," Jacen muttered. "Lead the way, I'm following you," he sighed with resignation.

Hakim ignored his young friend, and concentrated on the track. The mud had dried completely, so it was probably several days old. It was a little bigger, and quite a bit deeper than Hakim's own track.

"Must be a pretty big guy. His feet are bigger than mine."

Jacen made no response, but stood waiting. Hakim began to follow the man's trail. Within thirty minutes they had tracked the unknown man to a deserted campsite, where they identified three additional sets of prints. The ground was well-trampled. Hakim guessed that the group had been at the site for about three days.

"I think they must have pulled out this morning. Looks like they left this way," he said, staring at the ground and pointing toward the north. "Judging from the campsite, I don't think we're dealing with Anarchs here. They tend to leave trash and junk lying around. These guys stacked their wood, for instance. See?" He pointed to a neat pile of firewood at the base of a tree. "I've never seen an Anarch stack firewood. Other than that, I've no idea who we are dealing with. But for safety's sake, Jacen, I think we should conclude that they're unfriendly. I can think of no other reason why they would not have announced themselves at our campsite. We're right off the road—they couldn't have missed us. They must not have wanted to be seen."

"Well, *I'm* not shooting on sight, if that's what you are saying," Jacen interjected.

"*Of course* I am not saying that! We don't ever shoot first unless we know their intentions," rejoined Hakim, irritated.

"Don't get mad at *me!* You *did* shoot first at the Anarchs back at Ludwigs Corner," Jacen accused.

"Yes, I certainly did! Do you remember why? Do you remember what they were planning?" Hakim prodded, his voice raised.

Jacen nodded, "They were going to kill me."

"Umm hmm. And how did you know that?"

"We could hear them talking."

"Right. You know, Jacen, you really make me angry with your snide little implication that I'm some sort of homicidal maniac. If you don't care for my company or the way I do things, maybe I'd better leave. But get this straight, son: I don't plan on dying to prove some stupid point to you. And

I don't plan on getting killed because you want to prove some stupid point to me. If we are going to stick together, I need to know I can count on you in a firefight. I'd rather be knowing that I have to watch my own back, than to be counting on you, when you can't decide whether or not to pull the trigger. Understand, Jacen?"

"I don't like killing, Hakim."

"Are you implying that somehow I *do* like killing?"

"No. But you sure are ready to kill."

"That's why I'm still alive, boy. And frankly, the fact that I'm ready to kill when I have to is why *you're* alive, and not in some six-foot hole on that hill at Ludwig's Corner."

Jacen said nothing. The argument of a week ago was still unfinished business, and the two were finding it harder and harder to communicate. Both had been avoiding the topic, but the potential danger brought on by the unknown visitors to their valley forced the simmering disagreement to the surface.

Disgusted, Hakim muttered, "We'd better get back to camp."

The walk back was a study in contrasts. Hakim was vigilant and careful. Jacen's face was rigid with anger, and he made an effort to appear as though he was not being watchful, as though no danger existed. Hakim saw the young man's act, but said nothing.

Dinner was a silent affair. When it was time to turn in, Hakim picked up his weapon, and started out to the perimeter to keep first watch. He said over his shoulder, "It's your turn for midnight watch, Jacen. I'll wake you."

Jacen stood up and called after him, "I'm not keeping watch, and you don't have to either. There're no Anarchs about. There's no point to it. I'm not going to do it."

Hakim stopped and slowly turned around. "You're not going to keep watch?"

"No, I'm not. I'm done with all that. Listen, Hakim, I appreciate everything you've done for me, and everything you've taught me, I really do. But I'm not paranoid. I have no idea what you have been through in your life that causes you to keep one eye over your shoulder, because you never talk about yourself. But you know what? It's okay. No one is going to kill you out here. You're quite safe. As for me, I'm done playing army, and I'm done with midnight watches. It's beyond silly—it's becoming offensive."

"Jacen, do you think the only danger in the world is from Anarchs? Do you think Anarchs are the only people in this world who are warped?"

"_Enough_ of your lessons, Hakim! I am _done_ absorbing your view of the world. I've had quite enough."

The Arab shut his mouth and swallowed. He nodded to himself. Jacen recognized that with the peculiar nod of the head, Hakim had just made some silent decision. "Okay," he responded shortly, "suit yourself. I'm still keeping watch. I'll keep both watches." He turned and disappeared into the dark.

"YOU DON'T NEED TO!" Jacen shouted after him.

Jacen stood for a moment, staring after his friend, knowing that some sort of rupture had just occurred. Although his pulse was still racing with his anger, he was not sure that whatever Hakim had just decided was a good thing. Jacen climbed into his bedroll with a deep sense of foreboding. Sleep fled from him. Finally in the early morning hours he drifted off to a troubled sleep, filled with angry dreams.

****

Jacen opened his eyes. The sky was already light, but the sun had not climbed above the ridge to his east. The birds were singing, and in the distance he heard the soft coo of a mourning dove. The hollow rat-tat-tat of a woodpecker drilling his way after an insect hung in the air. As his awakened senses continued to register sights, sounds, and smells, he heard clothing rustling in the direction of the campfire, and smelled fresh coffee. He sat up and stretched. Hakim was sitting on a log by the fire reassembling his rifle.

"You're going to wear that thing out cleaning it like you do," he said to the Arab. He intended his comment to be playful.

"Hmm. It will be ready for use when I need it. That's all I care about," Hakim said, rather sharply.

Jacen noticed Hakim's backpack neatly packed, leaning against a maple. His heart sank, and he stood up and pulled on his pants, then his boots. "What's going on?" he asked.

"I'm pulling out."

"Leaving? Why?"

"No point in talking about it, son. If the world is as you say it is, you don't need me. If the world is as I say it is, you're going to get me killed. Either way, sticking around is a waste of time. Beyond that, I'm tired of you intimating that I'm some sort of heartless killer."

"That sword cuts both ways, old man. The other night you were telling me that I had no morality," Jacen responded angrily, "well, I'm tired of that!"

Hakim did not reply. He rinsed his cup out and tucked it into his pack. "Jacen," he said, "I've left you pretty much all the supplies. On my way out, I'll stop by that little warehouse and scare up another can of coffee to take with me.

"Good luck to you, son. I mean that; I wish you no ill. Maybe someday I'll come see your town in the foothills of the western mountains. I pray that Isa will keep you safe."

He stuck out his hand, and Jacen walked over and shook it. The young man was at a loss for words. He knew that he'd made a tremendous mistake, but his pride would not allow him to admit it. The best he could do was croak, "Thanks, Hakim."

Hakim nodded, turned, picked up his pack and got it settled on his shoulders, and then took up his walking stick. With one more nod to the young man, he strode out of the camp, heading south. Jacen didn't see the several tears that rolled down the Arab's face.

Jacen stood until he no longer heard Hakim's footsteps in the underbrush, and then slowly sank onto the log. For the first time since Ludwigs Corner he felt very much alone.

"What have I done?" he murmured disconsolately to himself. "What have I done?"

CHAPTER 9

Jacen stared morosely into the campfire. He missed Hakim's company. He could not stir up the motivation to do anything. In fact, he didn't know what *to* do, or even what he *should* do. While Jacen's vision of starting a town had provided the overall goal and purpose, it was the Arab's practicality and experience that had, up to this point, answered the question of *'what do we do next?'* in the pursuit of the larger vision. Now Jacen had no idea what to do.

Night had fallen, and it was time to turn in. Tonight no one would be patrolling the perimeter of the camp. For all his bold words, Jacen felt naked, exposed, vulnerable. He banked the fire, picked up his bedroll and rifle, and walked into the darkness. He was hearing, unbidden, one of Hakim's many lessons in his head: *whenever you are traveling alone, never sleep by your fire. If anyone attacks you, your fire is the first place they will look to find you. Bed down back in the brush a hundred yards or so. Spread a few small sticks on all the approaches to your position. If anyone tries to sneak up on you, they might step on a stick, and it will wake you up.* Jacen shook his head. What had then seemed like so much paranoid excess, now made perfect sense. *I'm such an idiot!*

****

Twenty miles to the south, Hakim had made a cold camp. For reasons he could not explain, he did not feel comfortable building a fire. He knew that his position was visible from old Interstate 76. In case there were any wayfarers on that old path, he did not want to advertise his presence.

He chewed on a tough piece of jerked venison as he lay back, looking at the stars. His anger at Jacen had subsided, and he began to examine himself in the light of Jacen's accusations. *Maybe the kid is right. Maybe I am getting paranoid. Oh, Lord Isa, maybe my finger does stray too quickly to the trigger. Maybe I need to trust You more, and me less.*

He thought about the last four or five firefights he had been in, and for the hundredth time, analyzed his actions and reactions. Because Hakim was so close-mouthed about himself and his past, Jacen was completely unaware of the fact that Hakim agonized over the knowledge that he had killed. It was indeed in self-defense; but it was killing nonetheless. He came to the same conclusion after each bout of soul-searching: his actions had been necessary. But the sting and lingering sense of guilt of taking a life stayed with him, nonetheless.

Early morning found Hakim reading from his sacred book, the *Holy Injil.* He had not been particularly faithful to his reading for several months, but the morning dawned clear and bright and Hakim had no grand plan for the day. It was a perfect time to read about *Isa al Masih.* After a steady diet of English, it was refreshing to read the Arabic language of his childhood, even though he had not read the *Injil* while a youth. A quiet hour of reading passed before he was willing to admit that it was his own wounded pride, not his wisdom, that had responded to Jacen's arrogance. He had allowed his pride to spoil a great friendship, one of the few true friendships he had known since leaving his father's clan in Florida as a young man, many years before. Hakim snapped the book shut, and thought, *I'm such an idiot!*

****

Jacen leaned against the fence and watched the horses as they grazed. Some of the graceful creatures were even wandering into the open corral. He realized that there was no way he could do anything with the powerful animals. Not by himself. He smiled sadly, and thought, *After all, I didn't read the book on horses.* Walking around the fence line until he reached the gate, he wired it open. He didn't want the horses to get trapped accidentally within the fence.

As he tramped back to his campsite his dark mood broke and he realized that he still had his dream, and that he was no worse off than before he had met Hakim. In fact, the friendship itself, and Hakim personally, had taught him a great deal. He was now much better prepared than he had been before. The thought so encouraged him that Jacen decided to resume his westward trek in the morning. He would keep alive his dream of starting a town. *Somehow.*

The rest of the day was spent picking through his supplies, deciding what to take and what to leave behind. Though he felt he would not need his assault rifle as much as he had in Ludwigs Corner, nonetheless, it would come with him and along with it all the ammo he could carry. He sorted through his other belongings, clothing, and food, until his pack was filled but not unmanageable.

That night he prepared a big meal from the supplies he could not take, and a big pot of strong coffee. The stars were beginning to twinkle in the deepening dark of the evening sky when a voice from out of the brush startled him.

"Helloooo the camp! Can we come in?"

He sprang up and ran for his rifle, which had been leaning against a tree on the other side of the campfire. He didn't know what to do.

"Hey! Can we come in?" the voice repeated, a bit testily.

"Come on in," Jacen called out.

After a few seconds of crashing sounds in the brush, three armed men walked into the camp. One, in the middle, was a tall, well-built man with shoulder-length black hair and a long beard, appearing to be in his late forties. Jacen guessed he must have been four inches over six feet, and probably two-hundred fifty pounds or so. From the looks of it, none of those pounds were fat, either.

To the big fellow's left was a man about Jacen's age, height, and weight. There was a cruel curl to his lip, and an unpleasant look on his face. The third man was a larger, heavier, and slightly older version of the younger man. All three were dressed in dirty buckskins and carried M4's which could have been twins of his own. Jacen surmised, accurately, that he was looking at a father and his two sons.

The four men stood staring at one another. Finally the big man asked, "Where's your partner? Weren't there two of you?"

Jacen felt a chill run up his spine. The only way they could know that would be if they had been watching him for several days. He remembered then that Hakim had discerned from the tracks that there were four men. Maybe these, and one more? *Two can play this game, mister.*

"Where's *your* partner? There are four of you, aren't there?"

A flicker of surprise showed in the big man's face, but he quickly recovered and grinned at Jacen. "*Touché.* One of our men returned to the settlement."

"My partner pulled out yesterday morning. He's heading south, I'm heading west." Jacen offered.

"Mind if we join you at your fire?"

"Go ahead. There's coffee in the pot, and plenty of food left over. Help yourselves."

The men took seats around the fire. Jacen felt a little uncertain, but was glad for company. The big man was named John, and the two younger men, Tim and Gary, were his sons. Jacen felt vaguely that John wore the expression of a cat about to eat the canary. But the men seemed friendly enough. They swapped stories well into the night, though Jacen said nothing about his plans. Finally it was time to turn in.

"Tim," John instructed, "you take the first watch, then wake your brother up for the second."

Good grief, thought Jacen, *why? There's four of us now. There's no one else for miles. Is everyone out here paranoid except me?*

"Yes, sir, pa. Isn't it time yet? I wanna watch," Tim asked, a cruel grin breaking out on his face.

"I reckon."

Jacen looked mystified. "Time for what?"

"Why, time to turn in, son, of course!" John turned about on the log, and fished around in his pack behind him for a moment, and came up with two pairs of handcuffs and an evil grin to match his son's. Jangling the cuffs and smiling, he got up and came around the fire and stood in front of Jacen. "Why don't you put these on, so we can turn in?" He jangled the cuffs in Jacen's face, about six inches from the young man's nose.

"What are you talking about? I'm not putting those on!"

Without saying a word, the man drew back, and backhanded Jacen, hard, knocking him into the bushes. Jacen was stunned, and tasted blood in his mouth, and felt it running down his cheek.

"Would you like to try that again, son?" John said gently.

"Who are you? What have I done? Why are you doing this to me?" Jacen spluttered angrily as he staggered to his feet, barely comprehending what had just happened.

Again, without answering a word, John drew his big hand back and slapped Jacen hard. Blood showered from his nose as he pitched headlong back into the bush out of which he had just climbed.

"Get up."

John stood patiently watching as Jacen wobbled to his feet, bleeding from the nose and the mouth, head buzzing.

The big man spoke slowly, "Let's try this again: put these on. One set goes on your ankles; one set on your wrists. Make 'em tight, 'cause I will check 'em myself and if they are not tight, I'm going to knock your butt back into that bush. Savvy?"

Shaking with pain, rage, and confusion, Jacen nodded and reached out to take the cuffs. John dropped them in the dirt, then reached over and picked up Jacen's M4.

"You won't be needing this anymore. Now, put the cuffs on, then grab something and stop that bleeding from your nose. You're no good to me if you lose too much blood. Then turn in. Don't even think about wandering off in the night. Tracking you down would be too easy, and when we found you, we'd just kill you anyway. So, stop the bleeding, go to bed. I don't want to hear a word out of you till morning."

****

The morning dawned clear and beautiful, but Jacen did not enjoy it. His head throbbed, and he could feel a crust of dry blood under his nose and on his cheek. He lay in his bedroll, afraid to move. He heard the others stirring, and after a moment Gary crouched over him, and unlocked his wrists. He left the cuffs on his ankles.

"Get up and fix breakfast. Do what you are told, and you won't be beaten. Back-talk my dad and, well, you have had a taste of what life will be like for you."

"What's this all about? Why are you doing this to me? Can't you at least tell me something?" Jacen whispered in desperation.

"I guess there's no harm in saying," Gary lowered his voice, looking cautiously at his father. "You'll find out anyway, sooner or later. We're slavers. We're part of a community west of here, and we need slaves to work our fields. Dad, Tim, and I go out and find them. You'll probably be put to work in the fields when we get back. It's that simple."

"But that, that's WRONG!" Jacen hissed. "It's not fair. You can't do this!"

"Sez' who?" Gary sneered as he stood. Louder, he said, "Get the fire built and the coffee going. Hurry up, you fool!"

That morning the fourth man, Kincaid, was present at the campfire. Shanks had lied about him returning to the settlement. Kincaid had remained hidden, gun at the ready, prepared to jump Jacen's partner if he showed up. By now it was obvious that Jacen had been telling the truth, so Kincaid joined them for breakfast.

****

"They were trying to capture those horses," John said to Tim, as he inspected the fencing, and watched the small herd disappearing into the woods on the far side of the field.

"For food?"

"No, bonehead, if they had wanted them for food they would have just shot them. Looks to me like they planned on breaking them for the saddle. I've never seen it myself, but I understand it was once pretty common."

"What are we going to do next, dad?"

"This afternoon you and Gary will start back to the settlement with the slave. We need to get that kid in the fields while there is still some summer left. He's a pretty good catch. He's in good shape physically, and he looks pretty intelligent."

"What about you and Kincaid?"

"We'll spend the night here, then we're going to track down this partner of Jacen's. When I was spying on them, he looked as if he would make a pretty good worker, too."

****

Under the watchful snout of Gary's M4, Jacen strapped on his backpack. It had been crammed with as many supplies from the little warehouse as possible, and probably weighed close to one hundred pounds. He'd never carried so much weight before.

Then Tim handcuffed Jacen's wrists, and removed the handcuffs from his ankles. "Get used to it, slave. When it's time to work, you're shackled about your ankles. When it is time to move, you're shackled about your wrists. When it's time for bed, you're shackled both places. If you give us trouble, or if we simply don't like the look on your face, we'll tighten 'em enough to rub you raw. If you cooperate and work hard to please us, we'll leave 'em loose and comfortable. It's your choice."

Jacen nodded grimly, and said nothing. But inside he was seething. *I let down my guard one time, just once, and look what happens! I can't believe it! How am I ever going to get out of this mess?*

After getting final instructions from John, Tim mockingly bowed low before Jacen, and swept his hand toward the old interstate. Jacen lowered his head and acknowledged sarcastically, "My liege," and began climbing the embankment to the old roadbed surface. He took one last look down at the field where he and Hakim had worked so hard to build the fence. At the far end of the meadow, the big stallion was watching him. It whinnied once, then wheeled and galloped into the woods. Jacen turned, and began to trudge wearily toward the west.

****

"Hellooo, the camp!"

John shot a surprised look at Kincaid, who picked up his weapon and silently disappeared into the darkness. Then the slaver shouted into the night, "Come on in, but keep your hands where I can see them."

"I'm coming in," shouted Hakim. He walked up to the edge of the firelight, empty hands spread wide. "Hello, stranger," Hakim said in a friendly voice. "Pardon my surprise, but I was expecting someone else. Last time I was here, several nights ago, my partner was camped here."

"Young fellow, early twenties, tall, buckskin jacket?" John queried.

"That's him."

"Passed him yesterday on the turnpike. I was headed east, he was headed west. He asked me to keep an eye out for his partner—I guess that's you—and to tell you which direction he went."

"Much obliged, stranger. The name's Hakim." Hakim unslung his rifle, and propped it against a tree, and wearily wrestled out of his backpack.

"John Shanks. Coffee's hot. Help yourself."

Hakim poured himself a cup and settled on to a log. He was beat; he had walked a long distance today.

They talked in a friendly way for a few minutes, and then, convinced that Hakim was clueless, John called into the darkness, "Come on in, Kincaid. The man's not dangerous." He turned to Hakim apologetically, "Sorry friend. You just never know who you can trust nowadays. No offense."

Hakim chuckled, "Know what you mean. None taken."

The three men talked through a supper of venison and tubers about hunting game, the right way to skin a deer, whether or not they were getting enough rain, and so on, as though they had been friends all their lives.

Finally John yawned and stretched, and said, "Well, I 'spose it's time to turn in."

Kincaid laughed unpleasantly, looked squarely at Hakim, and replied, "Yep, I think you're right. It's time." As John turned about on the log and began rummaging in his pack behind him, Kincaid continued, "You know, John. This is sure a lot easier than having to track him down."

Pulling two sets of handcuffs from his pack, Shanks got up and replied, "You got that right." He walked around the fire and held the cuffs in Hakim's face and ordered in a not-unfriendly tone, "Put 'em on, my friend."

Hakim stood slowly. He sized the man up and figured that John was two inches taller and about forty pounds heavier. He replied softly, "No, thank you."

Like lightening, John drew his hand back and swung to backhand Hakim across the face. But the Arab had been expecting something and was ready. He ducked the blow, and jabbed a quick shot to Shanks' nose with his left. Knuckles extended, he threw a right cross, putting his hips and shoulders into the blow, and punched Shanks in the larynx. It was a strike designed to kill. The big man collapsed, blood showering from his nose. He lay in the dirt, eyes wide, pawing at his throat and making gurgling noises. Complete shock was stamped on his cruel features.

For an instant, Kincaid was frozen into stunned inactivity. It had never happened this way! Always in the past, after a little knocking around, the victim had meekly complied. Shaking off his surprise, he snatched up his M4 from behind him. As he rotated about and raised the muzzle, he found himself looking into the barrel of Hakim's .45 caliber Colt. The ugly black hole on the end of the pistol blossomed twice with flame, and Kincaid felt as if he'd been kicked in the chest by a mule. Confused, he became aware that he was lying on the ground. *What happened to me?* He tried to raise his rifle again, but his hands were empty. *What is going on?* Looking down, he saw his life-blood pumping out of his chest, and he understood.

Hakim shook his head sadly and rammed a fresh magazine into his pistol. *It has happened again. But I don't know how to avoid it. We have no common values, these men and I. There is nothing to appeal to. They simply take what they want. What could I have done differently?*

Shanks was wheezing on the ground, struggling to breathe, but slowly drowning in his own blood. Hakim bent down and grabbed his shoulders. "Where did you take the boy? Where did you take Jacen?"

No sounds came from the slaver's mouth, but he framed the words "Pittsburgh, airfield." And then John Shanks' days came to an end, and Hakim was alone again.

****

The next morning, after he had buried the bodies, Hakim lightened his pack as much as possible, removing everything not absolutely necessary. He knew that Jacen and he would return to this camp to work with the horses. At least, he hoped they would.

Grabbing his walking stick, he climbed the embankment to the interstate, and began striding rapidly west.

CHAPTER 10

On the fourth day of walking Jacen and his captors were at the eastern outskirts of the sprawling ruin that had once been Pittsburgh, Pennsylvania. They had left behind old Interstate 70 and Jacen did not know what route they were now walking.

"Are we going through the ruins?" Jacen queried. He had discovered that Gary, if not pushed, could be civil, even friendly, and didn't mind answering questions. But Tim, Gary's younger brother, was pure cruelty.

"Uh-huh," Gary replied as they trudged along, "our community is on the far side of the ruins, and this is the quickest way. We farm the open space that used to be the airport. It's just good, flat land now, well-drained and level."

"Aren't there Anarchs in the ruins?"

"Nah. They died out 'bout three years ago. Dad killed the last two in a gun fight. No one lives in the ruins now. About twenty years ago, when I was just a kid, a thunderstorm sparked a massive fire and most of what was left of Pittsburgh just burnt to the ground. It devastated the Anarchs, killed most of their women and children. Their numbers began to dwindle after that. So we turned tables and raided them four years back. Got nearly all of 'em. Then dad polished the last two off."

"You raided them? Your people went after them?" Jacen asked with disbelief.

"Sure," Gary replied in a matter-of-fact fashion.

"Did something in particular provoke that raid?"

"Nah. Nothing in particular. We were just tired of 'em. They caused trouble whenever we came close to the ruins. So we stamped 'em out—same way we'd kill a rattler, or a rabid skunk."

"Is it that easy to kill another? Don't you figure that human life, any person's life, has at least some value to it?" Jacen was beginning to see that maybe his values weren't quite as universal as he had thought.

"Not the life of an Anarch," Gary replied.

"Nor that of a slave," Tim chuckled. He'd been listening to the other two men. Gary looked at his brother with an odd expression that Jacen couldn't quite fathom, but he sensed disapproval.

The men trudged on in silence for another mile. Then Jacen spoke up again.

"How big is your community?"

"'Pends on whether or not you count the slaves, slave," Tim answered. "We've got fifteen families, and a total of twenty-seven men. Four of us are slavers for the community. Nine more watch the slaves in the fields, and the others handle other tasks in the community. We all pull a watch shift at night."

They walked in silence for another moment, and Jacen adjusted the heavy pack on his back. He was getting used to the weight.

"Well, aren't you going to ask?" Tim snickered.

"Ask what?" Jacen replied, knowing full well what Tim was hinting at.

"How many people like you we have, bonehead. How many slaves?" Tim responded. He seemed to enjoy saying the word 'slaves', drawing it out so that he pronounced it 'suh-LAVEs'.

"Okay, I'll bite. How many suh-LAVES do you huh-AVE, muh-AS-tor?" Jacen asked, mimicking Tim.

Gary smirked at Jacen's comeback, but Tim was enraged. He walked over to Jacen and brutally clubbed him in the head with the butt of his rifle. Jacen was knocked off his feet and hit the ground hard, hearing a loud sound of roaring in his head, and seeing brilliant flashes of light explode in his vision even with his eyes shut. He blacked out.

Slowly Jacen regained consciousness. The roaring sound gradually subsided, and as his hearing returned he became dimly aware that Tim and Gary were shouting at each other.

"YOU MORON! You could have killed him with that blow! What do you think you're doing?" Gary shouted at his younger brother.

"He was mocking me! He got what he deserved! Besides, he's just dirt. He's just a slave," Tim retorted furiously.

"Listen to me, blockhead, and listen good. We-need-these-slaves. Understand? We need them! We *don't* need *you* caving in their heads. That's the third time I've seen you do that, and you killed the first two. We don't go scouring all over the country for days, looking for slaves, just so you can bash their brains out!"

"What? Are you getting soft? Are you getting squeamish? You never have liked this slaving idea to begin with. I'm telling dad that you're going soft on these slaves," Tim taunted.

"You do that, Tim, you just do that. You tell dad I'm going soft. And then you and I will explain why we have been sent back with slave captures *three* times, but only arrived home with *one* living slave. You know dad was furious with us the last two times it happened. And you know he really doesn't believe the little lies you tell him to try to cover up your stupidity. So let's do tell dad that I'm going soft on the slaves and that you're *killing* them!" Gary's voice dripped with sarcasm. There was no response from Tim.

Jacen was face down on the dirt, pinned beneath the heavy pack, so he could not see the two men. He managed to mumble, "Hold on. I'm not dead yet, although I might feel better if I was." He felt someone loosening the pack straps from his shoulders and lifting the heavy pack off of him. A booted foot wedged itself under his shoulder, and he was roughly rolled over. Jacen felt warm blood trickling down his face. His head throbbed, and he could not open his eyes to the glare of the sun.

"Can you stand?" asked Gary coldly, still angry.

"I don't think so. Not yet, anyway. Give me a minute."

"Listen, slave, if you don't want to get battered, keep a civil tongue in your head. You keep prodding my brother, and he *will* kill you. Savvy?"

Jacen kept his eyes shut, but nodded and affirmed, "Got it. I got it. This time I really do."

After a few minutes, Tim dumped part of a canteen of water on Jacen's face, and commanded, "Get up. Now."

Jacen wobbled to his feet, head spinning, and stumbled to the ground again, falling on his face once more.

Gary rolled him over again, then squatted down. "Listen, buddy," he said, "the next ten or twenty minutes are a pretty crucial time in your life, okay? We're not going to free you, because we don't want you bringing any friends back who may not appreciate the sweet labor arrangement we have, what with all our slaves and everything. So we can't turn you loose, no matter what. And secondly, we aren't going to wait forever for you to feel better, because we've got places to go and people to see. Are you following me?"

"Yeah, I follow."

"What all this means, then, is that if you aren't on your feet in ten minutes or so, with that big pack on your back, we'll kill you right here. I'll do it myself. So if I were you, I'd find me a way to stand up, and to stay on my feet.

Otherwise, you're not going to grow any older than you are today."

****

As the sun settled into a crimson western sky the next evening, the three men reached the slavers' settlement. There were a good fifty acres of ground planted in crops of all kinds. The ancient landing strips had nothing growing on them, but anywhere there was not crumbling pavement, there were crops. The hangars and buildings of the airport were in poor condition, although there were parts that were usable. Most of the families, however, had built comfortable log cabins similar to what Jacen's family had lived in, back in Ludwig's Corner. The eighteen male slaves were kept under constant guard in crowded conditions in a small outbuilding that had survived the ravages of time.

As the men walked the last half-mile to the slave building, Jacen looked in wonder at the neatly tilled fields.

"What do you do with all this food?" he asked, making sure he kept his tone of voice respectful, and even injecting a little awe, for effect. He was learning what was required to get through a day without abuse.

"Well, a lot of it is canned for our use in the winter," Gary responded, "and we also trade a lot of it with another slave community about five days northwest of us. We give them vegetables, both fresh and canned, and they give us dried fish, finished lumber, and coal. We meet them several times a year to trade. You'll be making the trip yourself with us in September. You'll be hitched to one of the carts with the rest of the slaves."

"How do you manage to can stuff?"

"We have tons of glass jars that were discovered undamaged in the ruins, complete with lids. One of our men went through the stock to take inventory and figured that we won't run out of new lids for another fifty years. And the jars will last forever, if we take good care of them."

So you are building a town, a town on the backs of slaves, Jacen thought sadly. He began to appreciate that he was not the only person with a dream of rebuilding society, and he decided that he didn't care for this particular vision of the future. Jacen hoped that his own dream wasn't coming to an end in chains.

This was not at all the way he planned the new society to be. The civilization he hoped to spawn was one built upon freedom, a commitment to the dignity of all men, mutual respect, mutual responsibility, and equal justice.

Tim and Gary Shanks' world was based upon injustice, and was a living nightmare for the slaves. It was wrong, all wrong. As soon as Jacen had admitted that fact to himself, he heard Hakim's quiet voice speaking in his thoughts, confronting in that gentle, persistent way: *How do you know it's wrong, Jacen? Wrong according to whom? Wrong according to you? What's your source of authority? You, yourself? In this little society, you are the minority. Your captors think they are right, and they out-vote you right now. Is that how your morals are built, Jacen? Are they based upon what society, or the majority, thinks is right? You know these people are wrong, though, don't you? But you have no court of higher appeal, do you? You have no higher authority by which their error can be revealed. And you have no hope of ultimate justice.*

****

That night Jacen was bedded down in the slave shelter. They had arrived after dinner, so he received nothing to eat. The guard had warned him not to talk to the others, or he would be beaten. So Jacen painfully lowered himself onto what apparently passed for a bedroll. As he lay there, head still throbbing, he realized he had not even been given a chance to wash the blood off or to clean his head wound. *I hope it doesn't get infected,* he thought as he drifted into a tormented sleep full of exhausting dreams.

****

"I *said*, NO TALKING, slave!"

Crack!

The whip cut a red welt across his back, causing Jacen to gasp. He could not see the damage, but he could feel the fiery sting as his salty sweat dribbled across the wound.

Crack!

The face of the slave to whom he had been trying to talk contorted into a mask of agony as the whip made its mark on his sunburned back. Then he shot Jacen an angry look. When the guard had walked on, the man tossed a pebble at Jacen to get his attention, then subtly shook his head and half raised a finger to his lips, motioning for silence. He indicated, wordlessly, for Jacen to pace him in his hoeing as the two moved down parallel furrows in the cornfield, cultivating the ground.

Ten minutes later the guard was at the other end of the field.

"Hey, you!" the man called to Jacen quietly. "No, no! Don't look at me, look at your work! Don't let your lips move. We have to choose very carefully the times and places that we talk, otherwise they'll see or hear us and, well, you just got a taste of what will happen."

"You're telling me. I'd like to kill that bozo with the whip."

"Get in line, stranger. The rest of us out here would, too. It's all I dream about. What's your name?"

"Jacen Chester."

"Gus Blackwell. Welcome to hell, Jacen. Shhh! He's turning back our way."

The guard walked past the two, and continued to the near end of the field. Jacen stole a look at Gus as he worked his hoe, but Gus shook his head. Jacen guessed that his new friend was about five feet, ten inches tall, and would probably weigh about one hundred seventy pounds. He was wiry, but his bare arms and chest looked powerful. Black hair hung, matted, over his sunburnt, sloped shoulders. When

Gus turned the other way, Jacen could see that his bare back was engraved with multiple scars from the lash. Jacen flushed with anger, but held his tongue. *Somehow, someday, there will be a settling of accounts with this wicked community*, Jacen thought, *and I hope I get to see it.*

"Okay, it's clear again for a minute," Gus said under his breath, several minutes later.

"Has anyone ever escaped from this wretched place, Gus?"

"Sure, since I arrived here in the spring, three years ago, seven good men have 'escaped' into a hole about six feet deep and six feet long and three feet wide," the man replied cynically as he bent over and pulled a large rock out of the ground, dropping it into a basket brought along for the purpose.

"Buried 'em myself, Jacen," he continued. "No, no one ever gets away from these people. Not alive, anyway. There are too many of them and they have those stinkin' handcuffs, which they attach to any body part that moves, twenty-four hours a day. You're going to die here, my young friend. There's no one to rescue us. Not in this god-forsaken world."

They fell silent again as the guard turned their way, and made another pass to their end of the field, then back to the far end again.

"Careful. Keep an eye on him. He's trying to catch us talking again. Better cool it for the rest of the day."

****

By the end of the third day, Jacen knew what the pattern of the rest of his life was liable to look like. The slaves were wakened at dawn. The handcuffs were removed from their wrists, though the shackles on their ankles were not. Nine men with assault rifles herded them to several long, makeshift tables. Women, also wearing shackles, served them breakfast out of a big common pot. The food, at least, was not too bad, and Jacen guessed that the women sought to do the best they could with what was made available to them. Breakfast was one of the few times the slaves were permitted to communicate with one another, so there was a lot of noisy talk. Thirty minutes later they were divided into three groups and escorted into the fields by their guards, where they worked in silence for what Jacen guessed was about five hours before breaking for lunch.

Lunch consisted of a heavy black bread, and water. The bread was good and the water was clean. Apparently their masters realized that slaves work better if they are not starving, thirsty, or sick. By this time of the day it was hot, and the guards were getting surly, and were looking for opportunities to take their discomfort out on the slaves. Lunch was a time where you kept quiet, kept your head down, and tried not to be noticed. Any infraction was met with the whip or the fists of the guard. Their keepers had no mercy, and treated the slaves as chattel.

Another six hours of heavy field work, and then the worst of the day was over. The guards would walk them to a nearby creek and allow them to clean up, and then it was back to the slave shelter for supper and bed.

It was a dull, dehumanizing, and brutal existence. The routine was so unvarying that by the end of fourth day, Jacen could predict the furrow that he would be started in next morning. Apparently some decision had been made to pair him with Gus, because they continued to work together each day. Four days stretched to six, in unbroken monotony.

****

Under the cover of darkness, Hakim crept to a position in a small clump of bushes on the far side of the settlement from the slave shelter. To the casual observer it would seem that no one could hide in such meager foliage. Hakim's skills, however, were such that he was all but invisible. A crescent moon bathed the scene in a faded, ghostly white light. Night sounds filled his ears. An owl hooted into the darkness. Mosquitoes buzzed about his ears and face, but he dare not move to swat them. It was a sticky, humid, evening.

This was his fourth night of surveillance, and he had already learned most of what he needed to know. The most important was that he had discerned the patterns of the guards. The second most important finding was that the slavers had no dogs. No animal was going to give his presence away. *Four dogs would have been worth twenty men on guard. Somebody here made a big mistake when they set this operation up,* he thought to himself.

Farthest out, there was a picket layer of six guards, scattered about the outer perimeter. They were trying to protect not just the settlement, but the crops as well. Hakim shook his head. *Amateurs,* he thought, *they're spread too thin trying to cover too much territory. They're too far apart for mutual support, almost too far apart to even hear what happens to each other. Taking them out, or getting past them, neither will be a problem.*

In the settlement itself, two guards patrolled among the buildings at night. The village was sufficiently compact that their coverage was adequate. Penetrating the village proper was going to be a little more difficult than getting through the pickets.

All the guards worked in four-hour shifts and made their rounds in an unvarying, predictable pattern. In four nights he had been able to observe all the different shifts, had learned to distinguish the men by the way they moved and walked, and had mentally cataloged the patrol habits of each. It was obvious to the Arab that they had never been trained. Hakim guessed that the main reason the settlement had survived thus far was that they'd never faced a determined and skilled enemy.

Well, they did now; and as far as Hakim was concerned, he badly outnumbered them!

CHAPTER 11

The day was hot and muggy, and there was no breeze, nor was there any sign of cloud nor thunderstorm. The guards were late in moving the slaves to the fields for the morning work. The whole settlement was concerned that John Shanks and Kincaid Davis had not yet reappeared. An argument had arisen concerning whether or not to send a search party after the two, but the idea was ultimately rejected.

Jacen was about halfway down his first furrow of the morning when his hoe clanked on a rock, just the tip of which was on the surface. He stood for a moment, wiped the sweat off of his face with his forearm, and then dug around the rock with his hoe and pulled on it. It came up easily. Too easily. He dropped the rock in his basket, turned back, and noticed a piece of folded paper lying in the hole left by the rock. *Huh? That's odd. It must have been under the rock.*

The guard was moving close. There wasn't enough time to do anything else, so Jacen picked up his hoe and smoothed the dirt over the hole, hiding the paper in the process. He resumed hoeing until the guard had walked to the other end of the field, and then he dug up the paper. It was a note!

In a neatly printed script, the note read: *ARE YOU ABSOLUTELY SURE THAT WE DON'T NEED TO KEEP WATCH?* For the first time in two weeks, Jacen laughed out loud. The guard turned his head and Jacen covered his error by getting into a fit of coughing. The guard scowled at him, but turned away.

Gus gave Jacen a curious look, and asked under his breath, "What was that all about?" He kept a nervous watch on the guard.

"The cavalry just arrived, Gus. The good guys are here," Jacen responded, smiling as he resumed working. He was careful not to look at his friend.

"What on earth are you talking about? That knock on the head must have damaged something between the ears!"

"Gus, how would you like to learn to ride a horse?" Jacen's heart was filling with hope again. There was no doubt in his mind that Hakim was more than a match for the slavers.

"You *are* nuts, aren't you?"

"Nope, not at all. Just be ready to leave this nightmare when I wake you up tonight, or maybe tomorrow night."

"Right. Uh-huh. What about the guards, dreamer?" Gus retorted.

"There won't *be* any guards, Gus. Not close enough to matter, anyway. Trust me."

****

By the seventh night of surveillance Hakim had formulated his plan of attack, and was ready to move. It was a good night for it. The moon would not rise until well after midnight.

After observing through binoculars the cruelty with which the slavers treated their prisoners, Hakim had concluded that he was justified in using deadly force to free them. He felt an old rage rising within him. When he cut loose his dogs, he knew it would be difficult to get them back in the pen. But it had to be done.

Hakim's base camp was in a thickly wooded glen about one mile east of the slaver's settlement. From this position he was able to have a campfire without the danger of detection, as long as the breeze was blowing the right way. But tonight, he didn't light the fire. He took cold, charred ends of last night's logs from the firepit and smeared the soot and ashes over every exposed patch of skin. He rubbed the blackest soot onto his buckskins, to create a mottled pattern of camouflage. Then the Arab checked his weapons and ammunition, belted a combat knife onto his lower leg, picked up his walking staff, and then stopped to pray.

"O Lord Isa, I detest what I'm about to do tonight, but I don't know what else I can do. Grant protection to those whom I'm trying to rescue. Be especially near to Jacen and keep him safe. May the evil deeds of those who enslave and who engage in bitter cruelty come down upon their own heads. Limit, I pray, the bloodshed. Deliver me, and deliver Jacen, and deliver all those whom I seek to liberate on this dark night. Your will be done. Amen."

****

When the midnight shift change occurred on the southeast edge of the outlying fields, Hakim was not more than thirty feet away from the guard on duty, watching in hidden silence.

"Hellooooo, Sam," the approaching replacement called. "It's me, Arthur."

"Hey, Art. 'Bout time you showed up. I'm beat. I want to get to bed," complained Sam.

"Anything going on?" Arthur asked, lighting a cigarette. The settlement had been able to grow a small crop of tobacco last year, although they were too far north to ever get a good harvest.

"Yeah, I've had one of those summertime colds the last day or two, and I'm re–"

"NO, idiot," interjected Arthur roughly, "I'm talking about your shift, not you! Is there anything I need to know about? Anything going on out here tonight?"

Sam stood burning with anger for a moment before he trusted himself to answer. "No, Arthur. There's never anything that goes on out here. Not since we wiped out the Anarchs. You know that as well as I do." Sam sneezed twice in quick succession, and then muttered, "I'm going to bed," and walked briskly back to the settlement proper.

Arthur stood smoking his cigarette, looking at the stars for a few moments, then stamped his smoke out in the dirt and began his patrol. Hakim let him pass unhindered, knowing that the habit was to make contact with the next perimeter guard in the first thirty minutes of a shift change. When both men had disappeared, Hakim counted to one hundred, and then ghosted along the same path that Sam had taken toward the settlement.

****

Hakim knew the patrol route of the interior guards. Every night in which the interior guards had been the focus of his surveillance, it had never varied: the same pattern, at predictable intervals. It would be the guards' undoing.

The Arab crept up to the outer edge of the patrol route around the settlement's outlying buildings, and then melded into the darkness of a full cedar tree. He waited until he heard the boots of the guard crunch on the gravel, approaching from his right and then fading away to his left. He listened intently for another thirty seconds, but the night was silent. Crouching low, he moved stealthily another hundred feet or so, and then stepped into the shadows of the open tool shed. He knew that the guard would be coming around its corner in about ten minutes, if he adhered to the pattern.

The musty smell of rich earth, and the sharp scent of compost wafted through the shed. Over the fields, the plaintive cry of a loon floated. Little scurrying sounds betrayed the presence of field mice running up a wall somewhere close. Other than night sounds, the air was still. Hakim waited, waited for the peaceful night to turn violent.

The crunching sound of boots materialized from somewhere behind the shed. The Arab set himself in the black shadows, heavy walking stick in hand. The guard came around the corner, suspecting nothing. Hakim knew himself to be virtually invisible in the shadows of the shed. It was so dark that the guard himself, out in the open, was nothing more than a faint silhouette. Waiting until the man was even with him, Hakim swung his stick hard, impacting the slaver at the base of his neck, breaking it. The unfortunate man collapsed without a sound. He was dead within seconds. Hakim searched his pockets, and found what he was after. During his daytime surveillance, it had appeared that just about every free member of the settlement must carry keys to the handcuffs. The dead guard had a key in his pocket, as the Arab had hoped.

Hakim figured that he had about three and a half hours to complete the job before the next shift of guards came on duty. By that time, he and those he freed had to be at least two miles away for his plan to work. He began creeping toward the second interior guard's patrol route. The second assassination would be similar to the first; both interior guards had to be taken out before he could proceed.

****

One thing the tall Arab had not been able to determine was where in the slave quarters Jacen slept. Once the second guard was dead Hakim trotted to the open slave shelter. Standing in the opening, looking into the darkened area filled with sleeping, snoring men, he wondered what to do. No idea came to him. He was on the verge of simply waking the nearest man, when he heard handcuffs rattle and then sharply stop. They rattled again, and sharply stopped again. It happened a third time. After a moment of silence, the sequence started again. Knowing his silhouette would be dimly visible to anyone within the shelter, Hakim raised his arm. The rattling stopped. He entered the structure, walking between the sleeping forms, and headed in the direction from where he had heard the rattle.

"Hakim!" whispered a voice that he didn't recognize.

He squatted down next to a bedroll on which a dim form lay. "Who are you?" he whispered to the nearly invisible figure in front of him.

"The name is Gus. I'm a friend of Jacen. It's my turn for watch duty. He said you'd appreciate that. We've been watching for you the last two nights."

"Hold out your hands."

Gus pressed the chain between his hands on Hakim's knee. Hakim followed the links to Gus's wrist in the darkness with his fingers. He fumbled with the key, and cuffs opened with a snap. In another few seconds he had removed the ankle cuffs.

"Thank you, oh, thank you," Gus breathed quietly, rubbing his ankles with his hands.

"Where's Jacen?" Hakim whispered. Close by, the steady snoring stopped and a dark form snorted once, then rolled over. Both men froze until the sound of steady breathing resumed.

"He is right at my head, lying the other way."

Hakim moved over to the sleeping figure, and touched him lightly on the shoulder.

"Jacen! Jacen! Wake up," he whispered.

Jacen stirred, and then mumbled, "What is it, Gus?"

"Hey, Jace'. Are you ready to leave this place, or did you want to stick around a couple more weeks?" Hakim asked.

The sound of the Arab's voice roused him to instant alertness. "Hakim! It's you! Man, am I glad to see you!" Jacen said with a husky voice. He got a lump in his throat, and was glad he didn't have to say anything more at the moment. A few tears squeezed out of the corners of his eyes, but he shook them off. *There will be time for a proper reunion later*, he thought.

Hakim quickly removed Jacen's cuffs, and then motioned for the two to follow him out of the shelter. The three crept out, and then went behind it so they could talk without waking anyone.

"Okay, both of you, shut up and listen. There's no time for greetings," Hakim said in a low voice. Both men nodded, and so Hakim continued, "We have less than three hours now for the next shift change. By then we must be at least two miles away. Understand?"

They nodded again.

"I need you to do exactly what I tell you, without argument or debate. Got it?"

Again, Jacen and Gus nodded their assent. Hakim breathed a sigh of relief. He'd been unsure what sort of attitude to expect from Jacen.

"If we are successful, we'll be able to free the entire slave population, but it's going to take two separate steps. If we try to free everyone right now, we'll make too much noise and wake the whole camp up. We'd be facing over twenty armed men with only a few weapons of our own. We'd be dead in minutes."

"What do we do?" asked Jacen. "I'm ready to do whatever you ask, without argument. I think I've learned my lesson."

"What lesson? What's that all about?" asked Gus.

"Maybe I'll tell you some time," answered both Jacen and Hakim, in unintentional unison. The two grinned at each other, and Gus just shook his head.

"Never mind. We'll explain everything later," Hakim promised. "Gus, can you identify ten tough and healthy men in this group? They *have* to be in good shape. It would be helpful if they knew how to handle weapons, too."

"Yeah, no problem."

"Wake *only* them and *keep them silent*! Get their cuffs off, have them get dressed, and then gather back here until we are ready. *No talking!* If you can't keep them quiet, this thing is going to fall apart real fast, okay? Here's the key. For mercy's sake, don't lose it. We'd never find it again in this gloom. Hang on to it when you're done. And bring all the cuffs with you, too. They might come in handy.

"Jacen," Hakim continued, "do you know where the tool shed is, and the outhouses?"

"Yes."

"There's a dead guard on the floor of the tool shed, and another behind the outhouses. Get their weapons and search the bodies. Take everything that might be of value, especially ammo. Bring it all back here."

"Got it. Where are you going?"

"I've got one perimeter guard I need to take care of. I'll be back soon. Be ready to pull out when I get back."

****

"Do the slavers have any good trackers?" Hakim asked the group of now wide-awake men standing around him.

"Yeah, they have two," a barrel-chested man responded, "John Shanks and Bob Beaufort. 'Tween those two, Beaufort is the best. Nothin' gets away from Beaufort."

"Three," another voice piped up, "don't forget Jackson."

"Nah, Jackson just thinks he's good. He couldn't track a lame man across a wet mud-flat. We really only have to worry about Shanks and Beaufort," the big man said confidently.

"Shanks is dead, so that leaves just Beaufort, then," said Hakim.

"How do you know Shanks dead? He hasn't gotten back to the settlement yet. He could still be alive," someone challenged in the darkness.

"Shanks tried to put some of these cuffs on me. We had a little disagreement about it. I won. That's how I know he's dead. And his buddy, too. I think his name was Kincaid," Hakim responded.

"Say, mister, you're right handy. Name's Philip Gonzales," said the barrel-chested man under his breath, holding out a meaty hand. It felt to Hakim like he was shaking hands with a man built of stone.

"Pleased to meet you, Gonzales, but introductions will have to wait. Listen up, everybody; we've got three assault rifles that I took off of the guards. I also have mine, and Jacen, I brought yours. So we have five weapons. Gus, you and Phil each take one. Who else here has had plenty of experience with weapons?"

Four more hands went up. Hakim selected a short, wiry man, named Randy, who looked as if he had staying power.

"Okay, I need two of you other men to swap boots with Jacen and me. We need to play a little mind game with Mister Beaufort."

Ten minutes later, Hakim, Jacen, Gus, and ten other men walked down the road that headed southwest out of the slaver settlement. Just before they left the slave shelter, Hakim had gotten the small group together.

"We need to make plenty of tracks for Beaufort to follow. I want the trail to be obvious. But go in *single* file, and you men we swapped boots with need to be at the end of the line. Remember: we're not out of the woods yet. We've got to get off the settlement without waking anyone. So, *no noise*! Got it?"

All the men nodded.

"Okay, let's move out."

CHAPTER 12

When the early morning shift change occurred three guards were missing, although no single individual was aware of the fact. At first no one raised the alarm. The replacement guards figured that the man they were relieving had perhaps gone to the outhouses, or was at the other extent of their patrol area and would turn up before long. It wasn't until the two interior guards made contact with each other in the first thirty minutes, according to pattern, that they learned that neither had encountered the man they were to relieve.

"It's probably nothing, Gary, but we'd better check into it. Who were you supposed to relieve?" asked Jim Trebane. Trebane was a trimly built forty-year old, just shy of six feet. He and his son Buck were the settlement's carpenters.

"Marshall Williams. How 'bout you, Jim?"

"Dave Smedley. Marshall's cabin is closer. Let's check on him, make sure he got home."

The two walked over to the Williams' cabin. Gary Shanks spoke in a low voice into the open window, "Marshall! Marshall! Are you in there?"

A slight stirring could be heard. A moment later Sandra Williams spoke softly through the window, "Who is it? What do you want?"

"Sandy, it's Gary. I'm looking for Marshall. Has he come in from watch duty yet?"

"No. Why? Aren't you supposed to relieve him tonight?"

"Yes, but I haven't seen him. Don't worry. I'm sure he's around, Sandy. Probably just having a smoke before he comes in. Go back to sleep."

The two men walked out of earshot, and then Gary said to Jim, "We'd better check the Smedleys, Jim. But I really doubt it's anything serious."

A check at Dave Smedley's place revealed that he, too, had not come home.

"I hate to wake anyone else, Gary, but we probably should. One guy missing is nothing to worry about, but both men? Something's up. We've got to get back to our own patrols, especially if something nasty's going on. Who's not pulling any duty tonight?"

"Beaufort doesn't come back on watch duty for two more days. He'll be home."

The two woke up Bob Beaufort, and after asking him to check on all the perimeter guards, Jim Trebane and Gary Shanks resumed their own patrol routes.

****

The eastern sky was brighter when Beaufort completed his check of the perimeter guards. Bob Beaufort was the Pittsburgh settlement's chief tracker. He was an excellent woodsman and hunter, and an expert marksman with any weapon. Beaufort was forty-eight, sandy hair, dark brown eyes, and tough as dry leather. Because of his skills, he was one of the settlement's main hunters, and whenever slaves escaped, Beaufort tracked them down and brought them back. He hadn't lost one yet.

The tracker had discovered that the guard in the southwestern sector was missing. His relief had not seen him. Beaufort knew from the duty roster that Ed Sims was assigned to that sector.

Bob Beaufort walked back to the settlement proper, and began to look for Jim and Gary to tell them what he had discovered. He passed the outhouses, turning his head about, looking for the two interior guards. That was when he noticed a dark form on the ground behind the privies.

Uh-oh, he thought to himself. He walked over, and his fears were confirmed. Stooping down, he reached to feel for a pulse, and then drew his hand back when he saw the victim's neck. There was no longer any need to check for a pulse: the corpse's neck was very obviously broken. Beaufort whistled softly to himself, and shook his head; the aggressor had known exactly what he was doing, how and where to strike to achieve an instant, silent kill. A quick search of the victim's pockets found them to be empty. At that moment, both of the interior guards appeared, each walking their patrol route. He got their attention and waved them over.

"Take a look at this," he said, motioning to the lifeless figure on the ground. The grey light of dawn revealed that the unfortunate victim was Dave Smedley.

"He was clubbed in the back of the neck," Beaufort pointed out. "There's not another mark on him. Whoever did this knew exactly what they were doing. And he wasn't killed here. Whoever did it dragged him back here so he wouldn't be found right away."

"His rifle is missing," Jim observed.

"Uh-huh, and so's his handcuff key. Checked his pockets —he's been cleaned out."

"You reckon one of the slaves did this, Bob?"

"Nope. Look at those boot prints in the dust. None of our people have boots like that. And I don't think any of the slaves, nor us, for that matter, know how to kill with this sort of efficiency. Whoever whacked poor ol' Dave knew exactly what he was doing. And he had to get past our guards to do it."

"Did you follow the trail to see where he was murdered?" Gary asked.

"Not yet. Just now found him. I'll do that next. And Gary," Beaufort said, "we're missing one perimeter guard. The southwest sector."

"Ed? Wasn't he on duty this morning?"

Beaufort nodded. "Supposed to be. But I couldn't find him anywhere."

Gary looked at the body, shook his head and said, "We'd better get everyone up and armed. Something nasty's going on, and we need to be ready for it."

"No, not yet," Beaufort said, scratching the stubble on his chin, "give me twenty minutes to work out the trail first, otherwise it will get lost under the footprints of our own people. You two stay on your patrol, but be ready for anything. I'll find you when I've finished looking around." He looked at the body, considering, and said, "Let's just leave poor Dave right where he lies until we've got things figured out. I've got a feeling this is going to be a bad day."

****

Hakim led the twelve others southwest for a mile, until they picked up old Route 30. They turned and followed the old trail west, making sure to leave plenty of trail sign. The four with the weapons brought up the rear. Hakim picked up the pace, and led them for about four more miles. When they reached the spot where Raccoon Creek flowed under the road, he called a halt and gathered the group. It was getting brighter, and light fog was rising off the dew-drenched ground.

"Okay, listen up. The slavers will be getting their pursuit set up about now, since it is light enough to follow our trail. I killed three of their men this morning, and they'll be furious, bent on revenge. Probably some of them will take out their anger on the remaining slaves, though I doubt they'll kill any, since they need 'em now more than ever, now that they've lost you men.

"As far as I'm concerned, you're free to go wherever you will. I don't hold any authority over you at all. But the weapons stay with Jacen and me: we'll need 'em to complete my plan. I can't tell you to stay, but I am asking you to stay until we have freed the remainder of the slaves. It's your choice, but it'll be much harder to do without your help. But know this: if you stay with me, I'm calling all the shots until everyone is free and safe. If you can't handle that, then don't stick around."

A big, rough-looking man set his jaw stubbornly, and challenged Hakim, "Why should we follow you, stranger? Especially if you intend to lead us back to that snake-pit! We don't know you from Adam!"

Hakim looked at the man, his black eyes steady and dangerous, and responded, "Because I've been trained for this. I know what I'm doing. You don't."

Jacen's head snapped around and he stared at Hakim, exclaiming, "*What?* You've been *trained* for this? What on earth do you mean?"

Hakim answered without taking his steady gaze off of his challenger, "Maybe someday I'll explain, Jacen."

Jacen smiled and shook his head. He should've known what Hakim would say. Jacen turned and faced the burly man. "Listen to me, Joe. Hakim and I have been together for several months. There's a great deal about him that *I* don't know. But I *do* know this: he knows how to fight. If I was in a scrap there's no one I'd rather have beside me. I know that I've been with you guys only for a week or so, but I'm asking you to trust him, and to help him. I'm asking you to help *us*."

Hakim looked at the men standing around him. He could only imagine what they were thinking. Finally free after being enslaved, some for years, and now he's asking them to risk it all and go back.

A whippoorwill called plaintively in the distance, the gentle sound wafting through the early morning mist. No one said anything until Phil spoke up, "Way I figure it, if not for you we'd still be in chains. You got past all their guards, and let us go right out from under their noses. Let's see here, 'tween Kinkaid and Shanks, and the three guards this morning, you've already done for five of their men. I reckon you know what you're about, all right. You've helped me, I 'spose I can help you. 'Sides, I don't much want to see those other slaves stuck in that awful place."

Gus nodded, "Count me in, too. I'm with you, Hakim."

"Me too. I'm in for the duration," affirmed Randy, cradling his M4. He was bored, and just wanted to get on with it.

Several of the other men nodded and murmured their assent. The remaining four gathered into a little knot, weighing the situation and debating amongst themselves, but soon they turned back to the others.

The big man named Joe spoke up, "You can count on us, Hakim. We'll follow your lead," he said, looking around, "all of us, 'til this thing plays out. What do you want us to do?"

Hakim nodded, and then motioned them all to gather around. "Look at it this way, men: we've given the nest a couple of good whacks with a stick, and now the hornets are swarming out to get us. We have a lead on them, but we can't get lazy or careless. If we pull off what I have planned, by mid-day tomorrow we'll all be armed and every slave on that settlement will have been freed.

"If we're not successful, there's a good chance that most of us, maybe all of us, will be dead.

"Here's the plan. We've got to get as many of their armed men as possible out of the camp, and we've got to keep them out overnight. That's the only way we can free the rest of the slaves. So we're about to split into two groups. The first group will circle back to the settlement without leaving any tracks. We'll re-infiltrate the camp tonight. The second group will lead the pursuers on a wild-goose chase through the hills. The second group will take a separate, longer, trail today that will loop back toward the settlement, arriving at a rendezvous point tomorrow morning.

"If all goes well, the posse won't realize that four of us have bailed out. Beaufort is going to be tracking those boots that Jacen and I were wearing, which now two of you are wearing. Beaufort will chase you, while we double-back to the camp."

"Now, wait just wait a minute!" said one of the men doubtfully. "You're using us as *bait?*"

"That's right," Hakim answered coolly, "that's exactly what I'm doing."

"Well, that ain't right! What about us? You'll be leaving us unarmed. We won't have any way to fight! Those men will murder us!" The man's face was flushed with anger.

"What's your name, friend?"

"Elijah Moore."

Hakim sighed, and then answered, "Okay, Elijah, let me explain. I knew I couldn't free all of you last night, especially not the women. Just one scream, and it would've all been over. There were at least twenty armed men in that camp. They would've had all the advantages, not to speak of all the weapons. We'd have lost the fight very quickly.

"So I had to find a way to empty the settlement of as many of the slavers as possible, and then sneak back in and finish the job in much more favorable circumstances. Last night we poked them in the eye, hard, and this morning they will chase us because they want to poke us back. I need them to chase you and your group, Elijah, so that four of us can re-infiltrate the camp tonight and set everyone else free."

"That still don't help us," Elijah scowled. "What are we 'sposed to do when they catch us? Throw rocks at 'em?"

"It's okay, Elijah," Joe broke in, unexpectedly. "This fellow has a good plan. I see what he's doing, and it's the best way. We'll be several hours ahead of the pursuit the whole time. As long as we don't dilly-dally they'll never catch us. We'll get back to the settlement before they do, and we'll be armed by the time they catch up. Then it's gonna be pay-back time!" Turning to Hakim, Joe asked, "Let me lead the second group. This is gonna be good!"

"Joe's a good man," Gus agreed, "we all look up to him."

"Okay, Joe. You're leading group two. I'll lead group one, and the overall operation. Are we all in agreement?" Hakim asked, looking around.

Elijah looked at Joe, who nodded his head, and then affirmed reluctantly, "I don't know you, stranger, but if Joe's in it, then I'll throw my hat in the ring, too."

Everyone else nodded. Hakim said, "Okay, I've got Gus, Phil, and Jacen. That gives me three men, and we're all armed. Joe, you take all the others. You've got Randy, and he's armed, so you've got one man with a rifle, just in case. And here," Hakim said, holding his Colt pistol out to Joe, "take this. But by all means, bring it back to me safely. That gun and I've been through a lot together. I'd hate to lose it.

"My group is going to drop over the side of the road into Raccoon Creek. We won't leave any tracks in it: I checked it yesterday, and it has a good limestone and gravel bottom. We'll walk the creek north and east for a mile or two, and then come out and double back to the settlement on another trail. Hopefully their tracker won't pick up on the fact that we've left the group.

"Joe, your group will continue on Route 30 another half mile or so. A trail will come in from the west. It's old County Road 3042."

"I know it," Joe affirmed, "we did some logging up there last fall."

"Take it west, and stay on it. Make sure you are leaving plenty of sign for Beaufort to follow. Just don't make it *too* obvious.

"Head for the ruin of Frankfort Springs. When you get there, go south to Burgettestown. From there, take the most direct trails back to the settlement. Meet us early tomorrow morning west of the old Route 60 bridge over Raredon Run. It's a total of about 35 miles you men will be walking. Once the posse sees that you are heading back east, the game is up. They'll forget about tracking you and they'll make a beeline for the camp. If you want to stay ahead of them, you'll need to walk all night long. We'll be watching for you. But if you see *any* of their people instead of us, it means we've failed. In that case, you'd better scatter and clear the country on your own.

"Hopefully, when we link up tomorrow morning, we'll have weapons for everyone. Then we'll prepare an unpleasant greeting for the returning posse, who should be several hours behind you.

"Any questions?" Hakim looked around at the group. Just hours ago, all the others had been slaves, without any hope. Now he'd given them a taste of freedom, and he was asking them to walk right back into the mouth of the lion. *Isa, please keep these men safe!*

"Nope! Got it. And it's a good plan. You can count on us," Joe affirmed. Everyone nodded.

"Okay, let's get moving, then. Remember, go *single file*. It makes it harder for their tracker to know how many men he is following. And put the men with our boots at the end of the line. I want Beaufort to think he is following the guy who killed his guards."

With that, Hakim, Jacen, Gus, and Phil dropped carefully into the creek below, and began to wade downstream.

****

Dawn found the slaver settlement filled with a miserable combination of anger, recriminations, a thirst for revenge, and comfortless grief. It was only by the dint of heated words ending in a showdown with weapons drawn, that Jim Trebane, Gary Shanks, and Trebane's son Buck, had prevented the rest of the camp from taking outraged revenge on the remaining slaves. Fractures were slowly appearing in what had appeared to be a united community.

There was also a growing sense of doom among some. Some with guilty consciences felt that the just payment for their cruel subjugation of other human beings was now coming due. The more thoughtful among them had long known that their slave operation was a grave injustice, even if they were unable to verbalize why. A few had even spoken against it, such as the entire Trebane family, Gary Shanks, and one or two others. But a combination of perverse justifications, peer pressure, and the seemingly inevitable economic realities had always managed to blunt the voice of conscience. And it had not helped that Jim Trebane's wife was John Shanks' sister. Though Melissa Trebane was intensely uncomfortable regarding the notion of slavery, she loathed opposing her brother. And Jim Trebane had hitherto not been a man of sufficient moral courage to either leave the community outright, or fight for an end to the slaving. But that was beginning to change.

The three bodies of the men killed during the raid were buried, and then in the early morning the members of the settlement began to debate what they should do. The camp was divided into two factions. One group wanted to send all the men out to recapture the escaped slaves. The other group thought it foolish to leave the settlement with its women and children unguarded, especially since the remaining slave population would exceed that of the free adults.

In John Shanks' absence, Bob Beaufort was the de facto leader of the settlement. After watching the meeting descend into a shouting match, Beaufort stood up, fired his assault rifle into the air, and shouted out, "QUIET! BE QUIET, ALL OF YOU!"

Shocked silence fell on the group.

"Every second we spend arguing we are wasting precious time! So here's what we're going to do. We'll leave four men to guard the camp. We'll arm the women. We'll form a posse with the remaining men. And the slaves will remain locked up in their shelters until the posse returns, except for the women who are needed to cook. Now let's get on with it!"

While his orders were being carried out, Beaufort discussed with Gary and Tim Shanks who should remain as guards.

"I'll leave Sam Oxford, Art Miller, and Jim and Buck Trebane. The rest of you will come with me."

"Not a good idea, Mr. Beaufort," responded Tim Shanks.

"Why not, Tim?"

"You know how those Trebanes are. They're slave-lovers. We're liable to return and find that they've let the remaining slaves loose while we've been chasing the escapees. You'd be better to keep them with you, and keep an eye on 'em."

Beaufort nodded slowly. "You're pretty sharp, Tim. I hadn't thought of that, but you're right. Hmm. Maybe I'll take the two Trebanes, and then leave you and Willy Jackson here instead. Willy's been nursing a turned ankle anyway, he'd just slow us down."

"Yes, sir. I'd love to go, but if you think I ought to stay, I will." The truth of the matter was that Tim had been hoping to stay. He'd been wanting to rape one of the female slaves, but there had always been too many others around. This might be his chance. So he thought.

Thirty minutes later, the posse left the settlement. Bob Beaufort and two others were walking point, following the trail. The other fifteen men followed twenty or thirty yards behind. Revenge was on the minds of most. If they caught up with the slaves, it would not go well for their former captives.

CHAPTER 13

It was a day for revenge, bloodshed, and sorrow. Two angry and opposing forces of men, one armed to the teeth and the other wishing to be so, were in the field and hunting for one another. And there would be very little quarter given when they collided.

The one thing Hakim feared most of all was that once he had freed and armed the slaves they would execute a swift and bloody revenge upon the entire slaver community. He knew that it was likely that there would be little he could do to control it. He was caught in a dilemma, and had come down on the side of freeing the slaves, come what may. In his calculation, it was better that slavery be stamped out, than that it become the new norm for the new world.

****

It was a beautiful day from the aspect of weather: suitably hot and muggy for August in western Pennsylvania. One hundred years prior, it would have been a day filled with the gleeful shouts of children splashing in the community pool while parents sat in the shade of an umbrella with a cool drink and a good book. It would have been a day in which the sharp *crack* of a bat making contact with a baseball, chased by the excited roar of the crowd, would have resounded in a thousand different ballparks across the land.

But that was the old world, and this was the new one. There were no longer any crowds and there were no longer any pools and there were no longer any ballparks, and there might never be again. Both worlds, the old and the new, were fallen worlds, to be sure. But up until June 7th in the year 2036 the fallenness of the old world had been for millennia subdued, more or less successfully, behind a social contract of societal and governmental civility. The corruption of fallenness was still there, of course. But because of truly good things happening in the world, such as the success of science, governments growing responsive to their citizenry, the vitality of the Judeo-Christian ethic, global growth in economic prosperity, and a handful of other factors, those who should have known better began to deny that fallenness, or more precisely—evil—even existed.

Theologians, philosophers, and scholars, wooed by the certain and definable results of empiricism, bifurcated the concept of truth. To the material world was ascribed a knowable, firm, objective quality of truth. It was claimed, however, that the unseen world, the spiritual world, had no such truth, no such firm reality. Spiritual truth was deemed to be relative to the background, the experience, even the whim of the individual. As such, the genuine reality of the existence of spiritual beings and of life beyond this material world was denied in objective fact if not in religious notion. From there it was but a short leap to deny the reality of evil.

The unintended consequence of this division of truth into a 'real' lower story of the physical world, and the 'relative' upper story of the religious or spiritual world, was the loss of a genuine grounding of ethics and morality. No longer was, for instance, the taking of life in situations other than self-defense considered wrong simply because God said it was. Rather, it was wrong *only* if the majority of a society deemed it to be so. Pandora's box was open, and mankind eventually discovered that they could not control the consequences.

Once it became apparent in the late 20th century that science would be unable to answer ultimate questions, even faith in the objective existence of 'lower-story' of truth began to fade. Beginning with the academic world but quickly spreading to popular culture, the whole notion of truth itself was discredited. Science became politicized, eventually becoming a means of propagandizing particular ideologies.

Lost in the philosophical free-for-all that developed was the intuitive understanding that mankind, indeed the world itself, was corrupt and bent toward evil. Ancient prophets had warned of fallenness in their ecstatic utterances: "all our righteous deeds are like a filthy garment . . . and our iniquities, like the wind, take us away." But in a world of scientific progress, and industry, and economies, and law, and functioning courts, legislatures, and government, it became too easy to dismiss the prophets. Their voices were atavistic, unsophisticated, unreal, and unwelcome. Instead, it was human *goodness* and human potential that was considered real, and indeed, limitless. The world congratulated itself in a hundred different ways for rising above the primordial ooze, and for putting away tribalism and racism and nationalism and greed and several dozen other ills, whose presence, rather than being understood as harbingers of evil were viewed as something far lesser. But certainly not evil.

There had been other warnings, of course. Auschwitz and Darfur and Kosovo and the Khmer Rouge and the Crusades and the Inquisition and the Stalinist purges and the Crucifixion, to name a few. But these were dismissed as anomalies, or reclassified as the just actions of oppressed peoples. Anything but evil. There could be no true evil. And if there ever was, it had no home in the hearts of men. Certainly not evil.

At least, not until June 7th, 2036. On that date, four conventional devices containing a hemorrhagic strain of the small-pox virus of a specially engineered virulence, were detonated in the atmosphere above four American cities: Los Angeles, Chicago, Dallas-Fort Worth, and New York. It was an attack by the Islamic Forces of the European Union, with whom the United States, Russia, and China were currently at war. The EU had never intended that the virus break through the tight quarantine of the North American continent. But intentions and outcomes are often two different things in the world of war. Within a few months the entire globe was under the onslaught of the deadly virus, for which no antidote had been developed.

Eighty-four years later the global population had bottomed out at just over eight million souls, whose 'luck' in the genetic roulette-wheel of life (as some considered it) provided natural immunity to small-pox. Eight million scattered across the surface of the planet was an insufficient critical mass to support infrastructure, electricity generation, refining, manufacturing, industry, government, or even rudimentary civilization on virtually any level.

Among the casualties of that dreadful day was the sophisticated intellectual casuistry that passed for intelligence and wisdom in the the old world. The justifications of a narcissistic and irresponsible society no longer held sway in a world in which one very well might die before one's next meal. There was very little room for error.

Among the Townies in the new world, no one questioned the benefit of the birth of a child: every infant was considered precious. No one made excuses for irresponsibility or laziness anymore: the margin of survival was simply too thin. If you didn't work, you didn't eat, and no one argued the point. And it wasn't because philosophy had suddenly improved upon men's minds. It was simply because the calculation of starvation versus survival was easy to compute: once the aged, ill and truly infirm had been cared for, there was nothing left for freeloaders.

And few doubted the reality of evil any longer. Most doubted the existence of good.

****

It was a story Hakim knew very well, because it had been passed down with great care in his family. Hakim's own great-grandfather had been part of a secret Islamic Jihad Special Forces unit. They had been inserted as a sleeper cell into American society some years before Islam's successful, and primarily peaceful, takeover of the European Union in 2028.

But in a Sunni-Shia clash in Gaza five years earlier, the headquarters of Islamic Jihad had been destroyed and most of the HQ personnel killed. The building burned to the ground, with the result that all records of the sleeper cells in the U.S were lost. As a consequence, all those cells were orphaned.

Not realizing that his controllers in Gaza no longer existed, Hakim's great-grandfather remained faithful to jihad, waiting for a signal that never came. When the small-pox virus swept across the States, his family was among those who found that they were immune. In the maelstrom of global death that followed, all nations of the earth ceased to exist as political entities.

Years passed. Though the cause had long before died out, jihad remained a part of the belief of Hakim's forebears. As the advance of age caused Hakim's great grandfather to lose the edge on his combat skills and special-forces training, he passed his training along to his sons, and taught them to teach their own sons after them. Hand-to-hand combat, martial arts, infiltration and surveillance techniques, explosives, small-unit actions, survival skills, and jihad was part of the lifeblood of the ancestry of Hakim Abdul al Malik.

It was a life that Hakim ultimately rejected, resulting in a separation from his family, but not before he had mastered the skills of his father. Wandering without a destination in mind, Hakim had traveled over the entire eastern seaboard, and as far west as the southern Mississippi. He found that pockets of human life were rare, and generally of two varieties. The Townies were comprised of those who had bound themselves together in small, tightly knit communities, and who had managed to survive by scavenging and the hard work of primitive agriculture. Those few communities composed of more than thirty or so couples actually experienced slow population growth. But smaller communities struggled to merely maintain status quo, and a single disaster of weather, fire, or sickness could easily wipe them out.

The second kind of community was the Anarchs. The forerunners of the Anarchs were anarchists, primarily peaceful people who found fault in any sort of centralized social authority. The anarchists who survived the plague formed small communities based solely upon scavenging. When the wealth and resources left over from the pre-2036 world began to run out, they turned to stealing from the Townies. The Townies within their small communities soon organized to protect themselves and their crops. At this point it dawned upon the Anarchs that their one opportunity to forge a world without government was staring them in the face. All that was necessary was eliminating the Townies before they and their organized communities could gain a foothold. Thus the Anarchs morphed into a violent, predatory society.

There was no communication between communities (other than the occasional wanderer who brought news), and so the transformation of the Anarchs was not a coordinated event. It happened only as local food supplies were exhausted. And yet, because of the governing ideology of the anarchists, it happened repeatedly across the land.

There were, of course, exceptions. There were Anarchs who rejected violence, and there were Townies who preyed upon others, as did the Pittsburgh slaver community. There was something of a continuum existing between the two opposite ideologies. But the fact of exceptions is made

significant only by the existence of the norm, and the norm
did exist.

Thus had Hakim found the new world in his travels. It
was an aggregate of two radically different cultures, with two
radically different visions of the future.

****

"Jacen, bring up the rear and watch our backtrail, just in
case Beaufort doesn't take the bait. For the next thirty
minutes or so, it doesn't make much difference how much
racket we make, so let's move fast." With that, Hakim started
striding downstream in the shallows, sloshing as he went.
Gus and Phil followed at fifty-foot intervals, with Jacen
coming last. Over the months since Ludwig's Corner, Hakim
had taught Jacen much about survival and fighting and was
confident he would take his role as rear-guard seriously.

The brook looped considerably, following the contours
of the land as it meandered towards its eventual destination
at the Ohio River. The men stayed in the water for about a
mile and a half, until, in a sharp bend, Raccoon Creek turned
back to the west. There Hakim held up, waiting for the
others.

"We're going to leave the creek here," he said in a low
voice. "Follow me, and stay on the rocks. We don't want to
leave them with a trail to follow." A tilted limestone shelf ran
from the center of the creek out onto the eastern shore, and
continued for several hundred feet before it was overtaken
by the soil around it and disappeared into the side of the hill.
Hakim stepped onto the shelf and walked it right up to
where it met the hillside. A faintly visible game trail traversed
the side of the low ridge, headed gently uphill. Hakim gained
the trail and then followed it over ridge to the east.

Branches of massive white oaks extended above their
heads. Shagbark hickory trees and red maples stretched
higher with grey squirrels chattering angrily at the men from
the safety of the highest branches. Under the thick forest

canopy there was relatively little undergrowth and the men made good time.

Jacen continued an attentive study of their back-trail as they walked, but also was able to enjoy the early morning beauty which surrounded him. A blue jay flitted off to the side, disturbed by their passage. Jacen could hear several tiny warblers in the tree tops, too shy to be seen. Once, as the trail plunged through a thicket, he could hear the sound of deer bounding off, unseen, to his left.

When they reached the top of the ridge, Hakim left the game trail and turned northeast, hiking down into a steep gully. As they continued to descend, the hillside to the left fell away, and the men saw Raccoon Creek wandering lazily below them. They came upon the washed-out remains of an old bridge, with an old roadbed heading off to the east. Hakim called a halt, and the three gathered around him.

"According to an old sign I ran across, when I was checking out this route several days ago, this is the East Hookstown Grade road. We'll take it to the east. If we stayed on it, it would allow us to approach the settlement from the cornfields on the north side. But we'll take it to another, smaller trail which will put us on Raredon Run. We should be able to follow the creek bed to a drainage ditch that will put us just behind the slave shelters, with good cover nearly all the way."

"That's a good plan. I know that ditch; it does go right behind the slave shelters," agreed Gus.

"Yeah, but there's a lotta' snakes in that there creek, Hakim," Phil drawled.

"You afraid of snakes, Phil?"

"No! . . . Well, yeah, I guess so," the big man admitted.

"Me, too. But we'll be moving slowly enough that they'll clear out well before we come upon them, so don't worry. And we're too far north for water moccasins, anyway. I'm more worried about snakes of the two legged variety. We need to penetrate the camp undetected, and that creek is our best bet."

Phil nodded, and said, "Guess we'd best get started then."

****

"Joe, are you sure this is a good idea?" The speaker was Elijah Moore. He was having second thoughts about the wisdom of the whole plan. The group had just turned west onto Route 3042 and were leaving the creek bottom, beginning the climb to the ridge.

"Elijah, are you still worried about being bait for the trap?" Joe asked his nervous friend.

"Yeah! What if something goes wrong?"

"I agree," chimed in Fred Sutherland, a heavyset man with broad shoulders and powerful arms, "I sure hope they're not playing us for the fool!"

"Gus would never stand for that," Mike Eggleston retorted. The wiry man scowled as the others walked up and gathered round. "I'm surprised you'd even think that, Fred! Listen to me: first of all, if not for that Arab guy we'd still be in chains, all of us. Second, you know that Beaufort and Shanks would send out a posse after us anyway. So we're not in any more trouble than we would have been had we stuck together."

"That's right, 'Lijah, Fred," Joe agreed. "Plus, we're several hours ahead of them, and that's a pretty lazy bunch. All we've got to do is follow Hakim's plan, and by tomorrow morning we'll be well set to turn tables on those slavers and wipe them out."

"You trust him, Joe?" asked Elijah, doubtfully.

"He freed me, didn't he? He gave every last one of us an opportunity to bail on him once we'd gotten out of the camp, didn't he? I do trust him, and you ought to trust him, too."

"C'mon, guys. We don't have time to stand around and talk about it. We need to keep moving," insisted Eggleston. "Okay, Elijah?"

Elijah sighed, and said, "Okay. I'm in. I'm just a little nervous about it, but I am in."

****

The trail was easy to follow. All signs back at the camp indicated that one individual had somehow gotten past the outer perimeter guards on the southeast side, and then slain the inner guards, as well as the perimeter guard on the southwest. Twelve slaves had been released.

What wasn't clear to Beaufort, and he gnawed on this as they hiked, was why only twelve had been released. Perhaps the unknown person had been interrupted unexpectedly? Or maybe he simply felt like he was pressing his luck? In any case it had not yet entered the tracker's mind that the one who delivered twelve slaves was intending to come back and make a clean sweep.

Beaufort held up his hand, and his men stopped well behind him. He was walking out in front so that the tracks wouldn't be obscured by his own men. The tracker examined the signs. His quarry had stopped here for a break of some sort: the escaping slaves must have stood around for a few moments as something was being discussed.

A few moments of study enabled him to identify thirteen sets of tracks. Up until now the group had been traveling single file, and he had only known there were thirteen because of the number of slaves that had been released.

Bob Beaufort walked over to the side of the road, and observed where several had climbed down to the bank of Raccoon Creek, apparently to get water. Satisfied, he called back to his waiting men, "Okay guys, grab some water here and let's keep moving."

****

Thirty minutes later, Beaufort was no longer satisfied. For the last ten minutes or so he'd been plagued with the nagging suspicion that something about the tracks was different. But he was unable to pick out what it was that was bothering him until now.

The escaping slaves had stopped again for some sort of conference, shortly after turning off of old Route 30. They'd come out of their single file configuration, and had gathered around several others, evidently discussing something. Now there were only nine sets of tracks. Somewhere, between here and the last stop, four men had left the trail. But where? And where were they going?

He'd not seen any evidence of four sets of tracks peeling off. And he knew that the tracks of his own posse now made it useless to go back and look.

"What's going on, Bob?" called Maxwell Baker. "Why have we stopped?"

"Take a break, men. I've got a problem to work out," the tracker ordered.

Max walked up to him. Max Baker was a natural leader, but he was also a good follower. In the weeks since Shanks had turned up missing, like cream Max had bubbled to the top, and had helped to provide leadership to the community.

"What's up, Beauf?"

"We've only got nine men here, Max. We had thirteen at the bridge over Raccoon Creek. Somewhere along the way four men turned off, and I don't know where or why, and it bothers me."

"You think they may be up to something?"

"No, not necessarily. Maybe they've just started breaking up, now that they've gotten away. But still. . . ," Beaufort did not finish his sentence.

"What?"

"I don't know. I don't like it."

"Any idea where they might have split up?"

"That's just it. I don't know."

"Okay. Put yourself in their shoes. If you know you're being followed by a bunch of angry armed men who have a good tracker, where would you bail out?"

"In the creek. I'd hop into the creek and hope that the posse follows the other guys," said Beaufort, nodding to himself. "And I'll bet that's exactly what they did."

"Probably. So what do we do now? Split up?" Max asked.

"No. We've no trail to follow other than this one. And I'm really the only man here that can read trail sign, anyway. We'll have to stick with this group we're following here. But I *am* worried. According to the tracks, the man who got past our security and killed our guards last night is still with this group. These are his prints right here," Bob said, indicating a particular set of boot prints on the dusty ground. "But any man canny enough to do what he did last night is also smart enough to trade shoes with someone else. What if he and three others bailed out and are doubling back to the camp?"

Max raised his eyebrows. "Maybe we ought to send someone back, and warn everybody."

"That's what I am thinking, too. Just in case."

The two men walked back to where the others were resting.

"Neil, Matt, and Allen! I want you to head back to the camp. Somewhere along the way, four of the group we're following split off, and I didn't pick up on that fact until right here. I want you men to go back to the camp, and get them ready for a possible attack later today or, more likely, tonight. While it's still daylight, find some good positions you can use to defend the central area of the camp, especially around the slave shelters and the armory in Shanks' cabin. Don't waste any men guarding the crops. Make sure everybody is armed. Whenever we come back, we'll do it in the daylight. So if anyone comes on you at night, you know it's not us. Shoot first and ask questions later. Understand?"

"You bet. We'll take care of it. Luck to you guys," Allen Wyse affirmed.

"Luck, Allen."

****

"Can I walk with you for a few moments, Hakim?" The questioner was Jacen. The four men had arrived at the spot Hakim referred to as the rendezvous point, where they were to meet the other group early the next morning. Hakim was setting out to do some reconnaissance and had left Gus and Phil snoozing, hidden in a thicket.

"Sure, Jacen. What's up?"

"Listen, uh, I really don't know how to say this, but, uh, I was really, really wrong back there at our old camp. I'm so sorry. I never should have accused you of being some sort of bloodthirsty, paranoid person. Over and over again since we split up, you've been proven so right. And I've been shown to be completely wrong. I'm sorry."

The big Arab stopped, turned around, and faced the young man. He placed a firm hand on Jacen's shoulder. "Jacen, I forgive you. Completely. And I think you saw something in me that I must constantly guard against. I am as capable of perpetrating evil as I am at fighting it. It resides in me as pride, and yes, sometimes self-righteousness. You sensed that in me, and for good or ill you threw it in my face. Lord Isa has used it to humble me. And that's a good thing.

"I must also ask you to forgive me. Isa says that '*love endures all things*'. I knew that, but I chose to ignore it, and to disobey Isa. I bailed out on you, and left you without protection. It's not the way friends are supposed to behave. I failed you and as a consequence I placed your life at risk. Thankfully, Isa is taking my wrong action and pouring his grace upon it."

"Oh, Hakim, don't worry about i–"

"No, no, Jacen. Someday I will explain this to you, but for now just trust me. I'm asking you to forgive me."

"Really, Hakim, it's nothing. It's water under the bridge."

"Jacen!"

"Okay! I forgive you!" the young man exclaimed with a grin.

Hakim grinned back, and hugged him with a big bear hug. "Now it is done. We need never mention it again. Go get some rest with Gus and Phil." The big Arab wheeled around, and continued up the hill.

Jacen turned to go, and noted with no small wonder that he felt much lighter and happier than he had in at least a week. He shook his head. *Some day I'll have to ask what that was all about, and why it has made me so happy.*

CHAPTER 14

Allen Wyse circled the settlement and came in from the south, where he, Matt, and Neil would be seen from a distance. He didn't care to get shot by mistake by the nervous community. They were nearly up to the cabins when Tim Shanks walked out to meet them.

"What happened, Mr. Wyse? Why are you three coming back?" Shanks asked.

"Beaufort is concerned that there may be another attack on the settlement. We came back to warn you, and to add to the defense if there is."

"Really? What makes him think they'll come back?"

"Four of the slaves separated from the group not five miles from here. Bob wasn't able to see where they jumped off, but he knows they did. It was somewhere between where Raccoon Creek goes under old 30, and where the high trail to Franklin Springs takes off. He's uncertain of their intentions, and doesn't want to take a chance."

"Well, I'm glad you're back, but we shouldn't have any trouble with just four slaves," Shanks said carelessly.

"Bob doesn't share your confidence, Tim. After all, just one man took out three of our guards, freed twelve slaves, and got clean away without any of us being aware of it. I'd say the character who did this, whoever he is, is more than a little trouble. Sounds pretty salty to me," Allen Wyse said. He was starting to get tired of Tim Shanks' cocky ways.

Shanks face reddened with anger, but he knew better than to fly off the handle with Wyse. "Yeah, well, we weren't expecting them last night, Mr. Wyse. Tonight we will be."

"Uh-huh, let's hope we do better. Now, let's get to work planning the defense."

They had seven men available for defense. Wyse guessed that one of the targets would be the armory in the elder Shank's cabin, so they decided to position Tim in the cabin with his mother, John Shanks' wife, Gladys. She was one tough old lady and would be armed with a semi-automatic shotgun while Tim would have his M4 assault rifle.

The remaining six men were divided into three groups of two. The slavers figured that the axis of attack would be from the west, and so one group was tasked to defend the western approach to the camp. Will Jackson and Sam Oxford constructed a thick log barricade just outside the Trebanes' wood shop, located on the western edge of the settlement. They could cover any approach from the west or the south. However, their view of the Shanks' cabin was blocked by Maxwell Baker's home, and they were unable to see the slave quarters from their position. They were also exposed if the attack came from the east.

The slave quarters would likely be the other main objective of the attackers. Two groups were designated to cover that part of the settlement. Art Miller and Matthew Hamm threw up a strong barricade, with two angles, allowing them to cover every direction in relative safety. But Miller's cabin, while protecting their back, also blocked their view of the entire southwest quadrant. Of all the teams, they had the best fire lanes and could see both the Shanks' cabin and the slave shelters.

Allen Wyse and Neil Coker hid in the canning shelter due north of Miller's cabin. They didn't put up any barricades that might give away their position; their role was to ambush the attackers. Since the canning shelter was open on three sides and they were basically mobile, they could deal with an assault coming from any direction but the southwest. Their field of fire in the direction of the slave quarters was unhindered.

All the women in the camp were armed with semi-automatic shotguns. By the time dusk had fallen, their plans and preparations were complete. The defense of the Pittsburgh slaver settlement was about to begin.

****

Unknown to those in the settlement, they were being watched. Hakim left his three companions well hidden in a thicket about three thousand feet to the west of where the old Route 60 trail crossed Raredon Run. All afternoon he lay in hiding, studying the settlement through his binoculars from several different vantage points, and counting the armed men. At first there were but four, but after a bit he observed three more return to the camp from the south. Hakim felt sure that they must have come from Bob Beaufort's posse. At first the Arab was uncertain why the men had returned; but the hurried preparations for the defense of the settlement that commenced within an hour of their return made it clear. Apparently Beaufort had noticed that four sets of tracks were missing, and sent the three back to warn the camp and add to its defense.

As he watched the men throw up log barricades, it became obvious from the fields of fire they were establishing that they expected to be attacked from the west. Hakim noted the groups of two that had been designated, and further observed how they stayed close to particular defensive works. As darkness fell, he withdrew from his observation point and returned to the others.

****

For the group with Joe Nolen, the day had become a hot, humid, nightmare of plodding on, putting one foot down in front of the other, knowing that no matter how much you needed to, you just couldn't stop. The price of failure was just too high. They were traveling on empty stomachs, digging into physical reserves they didn't know they had.

The day wore on with a hazy sky, but no clouds to block the sun. They passed plenty of creeks on their trek, so getting water was not a problem. But without food their strength was beginning to ebb, and their pace was slowing. Only by driving his men relentlessly did Joe's group walk into the outskirts of the Burgettestown ruin just after 3:00 PM. They had covered twenty miles since leaving the settlement before dawn. He called a halt, and they took a thirty minute break before resuming their march.

If Joe Nolen's men thought they had it rough, the posse was in worse shape. Though they had the advantage of food, they were weighted down with weapons, ammunition, and supplies. The slaves were accustomed to hard labor and the heat; the slavers were not. It was not until 7:00 PM that Beaufort's party dragged into Burgettestown.

****

"Okay, men, take a break. Jim, you and Buck see about getting coffee started, and pass around some venison jerky," Beaufort instructed. The Trebanes both nodded, and set to building a fire and boiling some coffee. Bob shrugged out of his heavy pack, and stretched. His feet ached, his back ached, and he was ready to call it a day. But he knew he couldn't.

Some of the men sat in knots, talking quietly, while others stretched out on the ground and tried to nap. They knew that Beaufort would have them up again soon, using the remaining light of the day.

"Surely we must be gaining on them," Max said hopefully, standing next to the tracker.

"Well, they haven't stopped to fix any food," Beaufort observed, "which means they don't have any. They're traveling much lighter than we are, so they have probably widened the gap between us. But sooner or later they'll have to stop to scavenge and eat, or they'll just run out of steam. We'll run 'em to ground tomorrow, I'm sure of it."

"When are we stopping for the day?" Max asked.

"Not until it's so dark I can't see their trail. We've got to use all the daylight on both ends of the day, if we want to catch them quickly. They'll not be as disciplined as we are. Every minute that we're walking when they aren't, we close the gap between us."

The two men were ambling forward, following the footprints in the dust, glad to be free of their backpacks. When they came to an intersection of the old roadways, the footprints unexpectedly turned northeast. Beaufort stopped, disconcerted, and stared up the other trail.

"Hmm. I wonder why they went this way?" mused Max, who turned and followed the footprints on their new course. He walked for twenty feet, stopped, and stooped over. "This is odd. Come take a look at this, Bob. What do you suppose it means?"

Beaufort walked over, examined the ground, and turned pale. "NO!" he shouted, and then commenced to unleash a tirade of angry curses.

Scrawled in the dust was one word: "SURPRISE!"

Max looked at him with a blank expression, "What? What's wrong? What does it mean?"

With an effort, Bob brought his temper under control, and turned to his friend. "What it means, Max, is that *I bought their ploy, hook, line, and sinker!* Their whole job was to lead us away from the camp, and like *idiots* we followed them. Now we're worn out, and we're at least fifteen miles from the settlement. They'll attack the camp tonight, and we're too far away to protect our homes and families!"

"But they're only three hours or so ahead of us, and they must be exhausted and weakened. Even if they do get all the way back tonight, there's no way they'll have the strength to attack."

"No, no, no! You don't get it, Max! These nine that we're following are just bait. It's the four who left the trail this morning that will be attacking the camp, probably as soon as it gets dark."

"But there are only four of them! We've got seven good men protecting the camp tonight," Max protested, worry written across his face. His wife and three daughters were back in the settlement.

"Yes. Let's hope they are enough. Otherwise, if they defeat our people they can get to the armory in John's cabin and arm the remaining slaves, as well as any of this group ahead of us that makes it back. We could be facing over twenty guns when we return, and there are only fifteen of us."

"You don't really think that's likely, do you?"

"If the man who planned the neat little trick that got us way out here when we're needed way over there is running the attack tonight, all bets are off. He's quite the general."

****

The four men blackened their faces and all other areas of exposed skin with ash. They double-checked their pockets and equipment to insure that nothing would rattle or click. Even the slightest sound could give them away.

"Gus, what are we likely to be up against?" asked Hakim. "What sort of weapons do they have? I've seen M4s; do they have anything else?"

Gus nodded and replied, "The M4 is their primary rifle. They've a few outfitted with scopes, too, by the way. But they also have a lot of semi-automatic shotguns. All the women in the compound have been trained to use the scatter-guns. And, since their men are out of town, you can bet they'll be armed with 'em."

"Where's the armory?" Hakim queried.

"It's the big back room of Shanks' house. I know that because last spring a small detail of slaves, including me, was sent to the cabin to repair a leak in the roof. It was right over the armory, so I saw the whole thing. There's a heavy oak door on iron hinges, with a padlock. Both of the Shanks wear a key on a chain around their neck. It's rumored that Bob Beaufort and his wife also have keys for it."

Hakim nodded, and then asked, "Where's Shanks' cabin?"

"The commons area of the camp has a little circular path around it, with another path running north-south through the center of it. The Shanks' cabin is the second structure to the west, where the north-south path intersects the commons circle on the north side."

"Yeah, I remember seeing that during my surveillance," Hakim affirmed. "Are there enough weapons in it for all of us?"

"Oh, yeah. You could probably outfit seventy-five or eighty men from that room, easy. Probably more than that. The Shanks have scavenged all the ruins within fifty miles and copped all the guns and ammo they could find."

Hakim nodded again, and picked up his gear. "Good. Okay, guys, let's move out. No noise!"

****

Just north of the settlement the trickle of Raredon Run had completely dried up, as it usually did in the late summer. The four men crept along in the dry, sandy creek bed in silence. Suddenly a stiff breeze from the west sprang up, and with it the temperature dropped about ten degrees. Hakim looked up to the black sky. No stars. And the wind had the smell of rain on it, with a mutter of distant thunder. *This could work to our advantage*, thought the Arab.

Twenty minutes later they had circled around the north side of the settlement proper, and had advanced up the drainage ditch. From their present position, the slave shelters

130

were about 600 feet due west of them. The stench of the nearby outhouses occasionally wafted by on the stiff breeze. The little group crouched in the ditch around Hakim as he explained his next step.

"I'm going to go up by myself to do a little recon. I want to see if they have any sort of patrol keeping watch, although I doubt it, since the whole camp seems to be on the alert. Stay here and stay quiet. And don't shoot me when I come back!"

When Hakim had disappeared, Jacen whispered to the other two, "I am pulling back down the ditch about thirty feet. I've got your back. Stay put."

Spits and spurts of rain began to fall, and heat lightning occasionally illuminated the churning clouds overhead, but not with sufficient intensity to expose the landscape below. The distant rumbles of thunder were growing closer. The gusting wind drowned out the night sounds, and would make their approach simpler.

Hakim was gone for about an hour, although to Gus and Phil it seemed forever. When Hakim crept back, he identified himself with a loud whisper when he was close enough to be heard. As he rejoined Gus and Phil, he noted with silent approval that Jacen was not there, and only appeared once Hakim had begun to explain what he had found. The boy was learning.

"No patrols that I could detect. Based on what I saw earlier today, there will be a pair of men hidden somewhere in the buildings three hundred feet west of the women's slave shelter. There are two more behind a log barricade three hundred feet west of the men's shelter, and two more a couple hundred feet farther west of them. I don't know where the seventh man is; he's the wild card. In practically every cabin is a light, which probably means the whole community is alert and prepared. If things go south it's going to get ugly very quickly. So if shooting starts, hug the ground. Most of these people are amateurs and will probably have their weapons on full automatic. The muzzle tends to pull up a bit during an automatic burst, so stay low. And put your own weapons on semi, or on threes; we don't have a lot of ammo.

"Okay, here's how it's going down. We'll do the men first. Gus, you're with me, Phil, you're with Jacen. Gus, pick a good level-headed man, wake him up, give him instructions and hand him the keys. Then you come join up with me again.

"Here's what you tell them: *no talking, no noise, stay low*. Tell them to go straight down to the drainage ditch, and *stay there*. They should go down one at a time."

"Tell your man to free all the men first, then crawl to the women's shelter and release them. Same instructions. *Everybody waits at the drainage ditch for us*. Got it?"

"Got it."

"Okay. Jacen, Gus and I will be to the south of the shelters. You and Phil will take up a position between them. God forbid that shooting starts, but if it does, our job is two-fold: first, draw all fire away from the shelters, so our people can get away safely. Second, neutralize the defenders."

"What's that mean?" Phil asked, confused.

"It's just a fancy way of saying that you need to kill anyone who's shooting at you. Now listen, if shooting does start our plan is likely to unravel quickly. Don't take any foolish chances. If your partner is hit, try to get him back to the drainage ditch. If your partner is killed, by all means grab his rifle and ammo, and then go back down to the ditch. Remember, don't fire at anyone coming up or down this hill, because they're sure to be our own people."

"Why are you doing the men first, Hakim?" Jacen asked.

"Because we need more fighters. If we get enough men free, we could overcome the camp in broad daylight, and then free the women. But we've got to have some soldiers."

"Makes sense," agreed Jacen. "When do we do the armory?"

"Once the slaves are all free, we'll detail a few men to get the ladies safely back to the rendezvous point on Raredon

Run. The rest of us will circle the camp on the lower north slope of the hill, and come at Shanks' cabin from the northwest. If everything works right, they won't even know we're there until we hit the cabin.

"However, if we get into a fight here at the slave shelters, all bets are off. Besides, Jacen, haven't I taught you the first rule of combat?"

"Yep. You have."

"What's that?" asked Gus, "What's the first rule of combat?"

Jacen clapped him on the shoulder, and replied, "No plan of battle survives first contact with the enemy."

"What's that mean?" queried Phil.

"It means," said Jacen, picking up his gear, "that when we start up this hill, we simply have to adapt to whatever happens."

"Adapt and overcome," affirmed Hakim.

"Adapt and overcome," repeated Jacen, nodding.

****

In the old world, Hakim's remarks about the women might have been interpreted as sexist or misogynistic. But nothing was farther from the truth in 2120. The reality was quite simple. When pressed to the ragged edge of survival, some things had become abundantly clear to the inhabitants of the new world, male and female alike.

Men, on average, have greater brute strength, fifty-percent greater muscle mass, significantly larger cardiac capacity, and a much greater capacity for overt physical violence, violence which can be harnessed for aggression or protection. Women have a greater tolerance for pain, lower center of gravity, on average ten-percent greater body fat, and less bone mass. And women can bear children, a capacity which was neither a matter of averages nor stereotypes. No man possesses the ability to give birth to new humans.

No one disputed that a woman could pull a trigger as easily as a man. It was just that that particular observation was not relevant. What was more cogent was the fact that putting women, humankind's best hope of survival, needlessly in harm's way was not an intelligent idea. And as intelligence was not cornered by the male of the species, this opinion was not unique to men.

In a world in which the population was heading south of extinction, a woman's ability to reproduce and nurture children made them highly treasured, at least among the Townies. Women were no more offended by this than men were offended by the acknowledgment of their capacity for violence. It was simply the way things were. The battle of the sexes died out when society was thrust once more back into a world of tooth and claw, no longer isolated from nature by suburbs and cities and hospitals and environmental controls and power-assisted labor-saving devices. Radical egalitarianism vanished when civilization was no longer protected from itself by police forces and the rule of law. The truth of the differences between men and women could no longer be hidden. This was not a problem in the new world, however, as no one, male or female, was of a mind to hide it anyway. Everyone was too busy just trying to survive.

CHAPTER 15

The wind whipped drops of rain into their eyes as the four men crept stealthily up the hill. It was strong enough that the rushing sound in the treetops masked any hint of their approach. When they reached the back of the men's slave shelter, Jacen and Phil positioned themselves fifteen yards to the right in a weapons-ready prone stance. Hakim was by himself fifteen yards or so to the left in a similar posture.

****

Charlie Caine was tired, in pain, and discouraged. He had awoken that morning to discover that twelve fellow slaves had escaped during the night. Like the other remaining slaves, Charlie was angry that he'd been left behind. The slavers whipped a few of the men, including Charlie, when they interrogated them early in the morning in an attempt to discover what had happened. But no one knew anything. The missing slaves had evaporated silently from their chains like ghosts, for all Charlie knew. But no ghost had laid down those bright red stripes on his back! If he could just get his hands on that clown with the whip, he'd show him a thing or two!

As he lay on his stomach on the thin bedding, he listened to the wind in the trees and tried to fall asleep. It was a good night for sleeping, but tired as he was he just couldn't doze off. He detected a soft rustling at the south side of the shelter, but ignored it, figuring one of the remaining six men was stirring in their sleep. But then he heard a faint whisper at his side. He craned his head around, trying to see in the black darkness.

"Charlie, wake up!" the voice whispered. "Charlie!" it said again, with quiet urgency.

"What? Who's there?" he whispered back. In that instant heat lightning flickered just enough to reveal the silhouette of a man crouching next to his bedroll.

"It's me! It's Gus! We've come back to get you out of here, all of you."

"Why didn't you just take us all last night?" he grumbled as he sat up.

"Long story, tell you later. For now, just listen. You need to follow my instructions to the letter, if we are going to get everyone away safely, okay?"

"Okay, but some of us are pretty beat up. They whipped four of us this morning when they found you gone."

There was silence for a minute, and then the quiet response came, "I'm sorry, Charlie, I really am. We'll explain later; it had to be this way. But don't worry, buddy, tomorrow morning is payback time. Can you walk?"

"Yeah. We're just sore, that's all."

"Okay, listen to me. I need you to unshackle these men. Send them down one at a time, to the drainage ditch right below the privies, due east. Every minute or two, send a another man down. Make sure they go down there and stay put! Don't let them go anywhere! We need everybody to make this work, understand?"

"Yeah. Anything else?"

"No noise! No talking! Keep them quiet or the shooting will start! Just get them down to the ditch and make them wait for us. When you're done with the men, crawl over and free the women. Same instructions. Then go down and wait for us in the drainage ditch. Remember, keep 'em quiet!"

Gus removed the man's shackles, gave him the key with a stern admonition not to lose it, and then disappeared silently into the gloom on the south side of the shelter. He found Hakim and joined him. Together they waited.

At first things went very smoothly. The fourth man was preparing to leave when the thunderstorm finally arrived. A bolt of lightning hit a hill to the south and for an instant the entire scene was illuminated, bright as daylight. At that moment, Art Miller just happened to be looking in the direction of the slave shelters. Though he did not see the armed figures prone on the ground, he did see two men standing in the slave shelter and he could see that they were unshackled!

"HEY!" he bellowed, raising the alarm, "THEY'RE HERE! EAST SIDE! MEN'S SHELTER!" He unloaded a full thirty rounds in the general direction of the shelter. The entire settlement woke up. Within seconds, four shooters were hosing down the men's slave shelter with a lethal fusillade of bullets.

Isaac Kleppenhof had the great misfortune to be standing upright in the slave shelter when the lightning illuminated the scene. He was caught by only one bullet out of a torrent of fifty-seven shots fired in the first set of four bursts, but one was all it took. The 5.54mm slug hit him low down in the left side. Upon penetrating the flesh, the bullet tumbled, leaving a gaping exit wound the size of a man's fist. Isaac bled to death in less than two minutes. Charlie was standing right next to him. As soon as Art had shouted, he'd immediately dropped to the ground. His fast action saved his life.

Paul Yohanson was crawling downhill, halfway between the shelter and the outhouses, when the shooting broke out.

He panicked, and jumped up like a rabbit to race down the hill to safety. But a random slug tore through the thin back wall of the shelter and hit him in the head. He died instantly.

Jacen and Phil immediately engaged the pair hidden in the buildings across from the women's slave shelter, shooting in bursts of three. *Shoot and move*, Jacen muttered to himself, *shoot and move*. He unloaded a three-shot burst, and rolled about 10 feet to his right. Phil saw what he was doing, and did the same. The return fire surprised the slavers, and they dove for cover.

On the south side of the shelter, Gus and Hakim were pouring fire onto the position just opposite them. Hakim knew that the situation had changed, and he was going to need to take offensive action to regain the initiative. Otherwise his tiny force would be cut to ribbons.

"Gus, keep firing at the two directly in front of us. Make 'em keep their heads down. After each burst, roll a few feet to the right or left, to keep 'em guessing."

"What are you going to do?"

"I'm going to move up and take those guys out. That barricade is too good. We'll never nail them from here. Not when we can't even see what we're shooting at. See the window in the cabin that's lit up? Don't shoot at *anything* to the left of it, 'cause you might shoot me."

"Got it. Will do."

"Okay, give me some suppressing fire."

"Huh?"

"Just shoot enough to make them keep their heads down while I advance."

"Okay, I can do that. Here goes." Gus rapped off two quick three-shot bursts at the barricade, then rolled to his right.

Hakim quickly crawled left and forward, taking care to keep out of Gus's fire lane. Gus rapped off another quick burst, rolled quickly to his left, and squeezed off another. Meanwhile, the firing off to his right was intense.

****

Hakim rose to a crouch and ran left and forward, praying that there would be no lightning to reveal him while he was moving. After gaining sixty feet or so he dropped to the wet ground, not wanting to press his luck. Behind him, Gus squeezed off another burst. Hakim dashed another fifty feet, and dropped to the ground again. The night was pitch black. Other than muzzle flashes, lightning, and a few dimly lit windows, there was no light. He waited for a good flash of lightning. He had to get a better view of the barricade for his next move.

****

"Isaac! Isaac!" Charlie whispered. He was unaware that the man had been hit, but he was very aware of the interlacing streams of lethal lead, tattooing holes in the back wall of the shelter just three feet above his head.

"JJ! Ed! Stay down!"he called. "When I get your shackles off, stay on your belly and worm your way out to the back. Don't get off the ground till you are below the outhouses. Get straight down to the drainage ditch, and wait for me there!"

Ed Montgomery called back, over the noise of the firefight, "Think I'll try my luck right here, Charlie. Get these shackles off of me, but I ain't movin' an inch until no one's shootin' at me."

John Jacobs spoke up, "Charlie, do me first then, 'cause I'm outa' here. I think I can get down to the ditch safely. Want me to carry a message?"

Charlie crawled over and stumbled across Isaac Kleppenhof's body. "Oh, man," he said sadly, "Isaac's bought it. He's not going anywhere anymore."

He continued over to Jacobs and unlocked his wrists and ankles. "Tell 'em, JJ, to wait for me at the ditch. We're gonna release the women next, and Gus and his buddies have more plans for us. So tell everyone to stay put until I get there."

****

Joe Nolen was working hard to keep his band together and moving. All nine men were exhausted and weak with hunger. As the storm intensified, the blackness of the night finally made any further progress impossible. By the occasional flash of lightning they were able to move off of the trail into the woods. The men huddled together on the wet ground.

"Okay, everyone get some sleep. I'll take first watch. Randy, you're next, then Fred, then Mike. Each of you, when it's your turn for watch, just stay awake as long as you can, and when it's no use, wake the next guy. As soon as there's enough light, whether it's stars, moon, dawn, or whatever, wake us all up. We've got to get to the rendezvous on time and help Hakim and the others."

****

The posse was having an awful time. The men were exhausted, but fear for their families kept them stumbling along the trail. It was only with great effort that Beaufort kept them from discarding even their weapons, in their concern to get back to the settlement quickly.

It was so dark that tracking the slaves was out of the question. But that was irrelevant anyway, since the settlement was likely now the destination of both groups, Beaufort having guessed at the slaves' intentions. The tracker knew this area intimately, so he pressed on as long as possible, driving his men. It was impossible for him to know this in the darkness, but the slave group had turned off the main trail earlier, since they were headed for the rendezvous point on Raredon Run, west of the settlement.

The darkness, the storm, and a profound weariness finally overcame the men. Without an audible signal, they just stopped. They could go no further. Most just lay down where they stopped. Beaufort decided to give them several hours of rest, and then start them moving again. They were now about seven miles from the settlement.

****

This is not going well, thought Hakim. *If it comes down to a war of attrition, they win. They've got more ammo.*

North of Hakim, between the two shelters, Phil hugged the ground and decided he needed to make every shot count from this point. He had only two magazines left. He turned the selector on his M4 to semi-automatic mode. He'd noticed that Jacen, on his left, had done so several moments earlier.

Far to his left, a cabin door crashed open and a silhouetted figure holding a gun was briefly exposed. The deep boom of a shotgun rolled across the commons area, and the door closed again. He heard the pellets striking the wall of the men's slave shelter. *Someone is really out of his element,* Phil thought, *that target is way out of the lethal range of a shotgun.*

It suddenly registered in his mind that he'd been hearing that boom almost like clockwork for two minutes or so. Even as this thought pressed itself on his consciousness, the event repeated. The door swung open, a figure was dimly back-lit, *boom!*, the door shut.

That's your last time, sucker! Phil trained his sights on the general area of darkness, and waited. A few seconds later, the door opened. He aimed at the back-lit figure, squeezed the trigger, and noted with grim satisfaction that the individual tottered and fell to the ground, and the door remained open. What Phil did not know is that he had just killed Art Miller's wife, and that one event brought down the defense of the southern side of the camp.

****

Art Miller and Matthew Hamm had the feeling that they were about to be flanked. Where there had been two sets of muzzle-flashes right below them, now there was just one, and neither man felt as if he had scored a hit. Which could only mean that second man below them was on the move. They began a searching fire into the darkness toward the south, popping over the barricade to fire three-shot bursts and then huddling back down. Art called softly to his wife, Lauren, who was in the cabin, and recruited her help. While he and Matt concentrated on the ground to the east and south, Lauren began stepping out of the cabin to fire a round in the direction of the slave shelter. *"Just to keep them honest,"* Arthur had said.

Then he heard her cry behind him, and the shotgun clattered to the ground as she began to crumple.

"NO!" he shouted with anguish. Without thinking, both men jumped up to catch her. The light from the cabin door illuminated them, and that was enough. Three sets of muzzle-flashes blinked furiously in the night, and both men were killed instantly.

Seconds later, Hakim and Gus raced up, bending low, and gained the safety of the barricade. The sight that greeted them was tragic, but they had no time for sorrow. Perhaps sorrow would come with the morning light. They had not wanted this fight, but nor would they leave their friends in chains.

Not only had they gained the safety of the barricade, and eliminated three of the defenders, they'd also gained more weapons and enough ammunition to finish the job.

Hakim crawled over and picked up the shotgun, and took the bag of shells sitting just inside the cabin door. Then he shut the door, restoring the cover of darkness. After reloading the twelve-gauge semi-automatic shotgun, Hakim turned to Gus, and ordered, "Take these M4's and all this ammo down to the drainage ditch. Arm two of the men, and position them on the north side of the women's shelter. Resupply Jacen and Phil. Then come back here."

After Gus left, Hakim crawled to the barricade on the west side, and peered over, waiting for a flash of lightning. He knew that his ash-blackened face would not expose him. Because of his surveillance earlier in the day, he knew that two men had been stationed just west of his current position.

A sharp bolt of lightning lit up the scene, and a fresh squall of rain began to fall. In the flash, he saw two armed men crawling toward the barricade. They were at the edge of the scatter-gun's range, but he triggered four quick shots anyway. Cries of agony told him all that he needed to know.

"Are you ready to surrender?" he shouted over the log barricade.

"You gonna kill us?" Sam Oxford called back, obviously in pain.

"Not if you surrender I won't. I can't speak for all these people you've enslaved, but we didn't come up here for a massacre. You guys started all this, we didn't."

After a moment, Oxford called back, "We want to quit. Can we come in?"

"Hang on. Some of your own people are liable to shoot you by mistake, and I 'spose some of mine could, too. Stay put for a second."

Hakim triggered three quick shots with the shotgun straight into the air, and then shouted out, "HOLD YOUR FIRE! HOLD YOUR FIRE!"

The camp grew silent in the darkness as thunder rumbled ominously. He was careful not to expose himself. He could see no one, but figured that there was an anxious ear in every cabin, listening.

"TWO OF YOUR MEN ARE HURT, AND NEED HELP. THEY ARE OUT OF THE FIGHT. WILL YOU HOLD YOUR FIRE?"

He waited about three minutes, and then heard a cabin door open, somewhere to the northwest of his position. An answering voice called out, "WE'LL HOLD OUR FIRE FOR FIVE MINUTES. NO PROMISES AFTER THAT."

Hakim heard some discussion in the dark in front of him, and Oxford called out again, "Can we go to him? Or do we have to come to you?"

He crawled to the cabin door and opened it, being careful to stay below the barricade. The area was illuminated by the flickering lantern in the cabin. He crawled into the shadows where he couldn't be seen, and answered, "Bring your weapons here. If you're feeling lucky, use 'em. You leave 'em here and I'll let you go to your friends. Otherwise I'm going to let loose and fill every square inch of that space you're in with buckshot. So what'll it be?"

"We're coming in. Hold your fire!"

A moment later two bloodied men hobbled up to the barricade. They dropped their M4's over the edge, and stood for a moment, searching the shadows with their eyes. Hakim moved into the light, still below the level of the barricade.

Will Jackson had blood coming from several places, but did not appear to be mortally wounded. He examined Hakim, and observed, "I've not seen you before."

"That's because I've not been here before," Hakim rejoined, coolly.

"You the man who killed our guards last night?"

Hakim nodded impassively, waiting.

"Why are you doing all this?"

"I might ask you the same question."

"What do you mean?"

"Why are you holding all these people as slaves?"

Jackson looked stymied, and glanced at Oxford for support. His friend simply shrugged, and Jackson turned back to Hakim. "I don't know. Never really thought about it."

"Maybe you ought to start thinking about it," Hakim said dryly. "Who is this voice I'm shouting at, over there?" He gestured to the northwest with his M14.

"That would be Tim Shanks, John Shanks' son."

Hakim nodded. "SHANKS, THEY'RE COMING YOUR WAY. DON'T SHOOT. THEY'RE YOUR MEN."

Turning back to the two, Hakim ordered, "Go. And when you get over there, tell Shanks his dad is dead."

"Dead?" Oxford asked in surprise. "How did John die?"

"Tried to put some of those shackles on me, and I didn't appreciate it. Now go. If I see either of you with a gun in your hands again, I'll kill you."

****

The storm wound down, its fury exhausted. Occasional flashes to the east could be seen, sometimes the muted rumble of thunder sounded in the distance. The wind died down, and the night sounds emerged once more.

Jacen and Phil remained in position, resupplied with ammunition by Gus, and trading occasional shots with the two men who were still holding the north-center of the commons area. Hakim had found Jacen and instructed him to keep the two pinned down, if possible.

"Keep 'em busy, Jace'. Make them think we are still all over here. I don't want them looking back to the northwest," Hakim had instructed.

Charlie Caine and Ed Montgomery were detailed to see that the women slaves were escorted back to the rendezvous point on Raredon run.

Hakim, meanwhile, took Gus Blackwell, Bert Rawlings, John Sears, and John Jacobs north and west, skirting the north slope of the knoll in order to attack the Shanks' cabin and its armory from the northwest.

****

As they crept up the slope on the northwest corner of the settlement, the clouds broke up. Faint starlight, plus the sliver of the moon rising over the hills to the east, provided

145

just enough light to move through the forest without too much difficulty.

After several moments of moving stealthily up the hill, Hakim could faintly discern two structures about one hundred feet in front of him. He halted the group, and turned to Gus.

"What are those?" he whispered.

"Sam Oxford's cabin," Gus responded under his breath, pointing to the left-most structure. "Kincaid Davis's cabin," he whispered, pointing to the one to its right.

There were no lights on in the cabins. Hakim guessed that they were empty, but gave them a wide berth nonetheless.

Several minutes later, the five men were crouched a hundred feet behind the Shanks' cabin. To the south was another cabin. Dim light appeared at the windows. North, and closer, was also a cabin. It, too, was obviously occupied.

"Okay, listen up. Rawlings, you cover the cabin to the north. Jacobs, you cover the one to the south. Look, we don't want to kill anyone else unless we absolutely have to. If anyone comes out the door, or starts to poke a weapon out a window, just fire a burst and chase them back inside. Don't actually shoot them unless they look like they could become a danger to us. Understand?"

Rawlings and Jacobs both nodded.

"Gus, John, I'm going to take a similar approach with Shanks. I want you two at the windows on either side. Gus take the north, John, you take the south. Now listen, I don't want you to shoot anyone unless they start shooting. I'm going around the front of the cabin, and I'll try to call them out. If they refuse, John, I want you to empty that shotgun into their house through your window. Gus, you fire off your M4, the whole magazine, into your window. But don't hit anyone! And don't hit each other! Okay? And then reload quickly! Look through your window before we start, and pick a spot to aim at. I'd like to do this last piece without hurting anyone if we can avoid it. Got it?"

Both men nodded. Each crept into position, and Hakim waited until everyone was set. Then, remaining in the shadows, he went around the front of the house. Over his shoulder he could hear Jacen and Phil keeping the remaining two defenders in the center of the camp occupied.

There was a risk, of course, that an overheated villager could plunge through the front door of the cabin, firing. Or, if Jacen and Phil did not keep their men pinned, Hakim knew he could be shot in the back. But it was a risk he felt was justified, if he wished to avoid more bloodshed.

"SHANKS, CAN YOU HEAR ME?"

There was no answer. Hakim waited a few minutes, and repeated the challenge. Silence. Then the lights in the cabin went out and the door began to open very slowly and very quietly. In the moonlight Hakim saw the gleam of a gunbarrel. He switched to full auto and fired half his magazine into the air. The door snapped shut immediately. Hakim was glad the others had held their fire.

"SHANKS! I WANT EVERYONE IN THAT CABIN TO COME OUT WITH THEIR HANDS UP! DO THAT AND WE WILL NOT HURT YOU."

Silence.

"ARE YOU COMING OUT?"

A voice, filled with anger and scorn, came through the wall of the building, "NO, SLAVE, we are NOT coming out!"

"Gus, John, remember what I said? Go ahead."

The night erupted again with the punctuated deep roars of the shotgun, and the loud, staccato bark of the M4 as it ripped through a magazine full of ammo. It seemed the noise went on forever. Hakim noticed that the firing behind him had picked up also, and guessed that the two slavers still unaccounted for in the commons area were trying to move around in support of those in Shanks' cabin. Hakim hoped that Jacen would be able to pin them in place a little longer.

The inside of the cabin was briefly transformed into a maelstrom of splinters, smoke, and noise. The M4's slugs passed right through the log wall, shredding it. Half of the shotgun's pellets embedded themselves in the opposite wall, the other half ricocheted off due to the oblique angle, and flew around the cabin in a lethal spray of lead shards. Fortunately, everyone in the cabin had dropped to the floor when the firing began. Other than cuts, bruises, and some pretty wicked splinters, no one inside was seriously wounded.

Hakim waited until the sounds of his men reloading their weapons stopped. Then he asked again, "SHANKS, ARE YOU COMING OUT?"

The sound of a hot argument could be heard from within. Finally, a commanding female voice sounded forth, "We're coming out with our hands up. Don't shoot!" The cabin door swung open, and a burly woman stepped out with her hands up, followed by Tim Shanks, Sam Oxford, and Willy Jackson, their hands empty and over their heads.

"We meet again," Hakim said with dry humor to Oxford and Jackson, who merely nodded. The Arab breathed a sigh of relief. The hardest part of the rescue was complete. Only a few details remained.

CHAPTER 16

The overcast finally broke up. A sliver of moon emerged from the eastern horizon, and began its circuit across a star-studded black sky. Low clouds scudded past, but there were no further remnants of the storm that had made the night so inky black.

Maxwell Baker rose wearily to his feet, and awakened Bob Beaufort. "Bob, wake up! I think we have enough light to get moving again."

Beaufort scrubbed his face with his hands several times before responding. He stood up, damp, cold, and stiff. *I'm too old to be doing this anymore. Let the young bucks do it*, he thought. Outwardly he merely nodded, and said to Baker, "I agree. Let's wake 'em up."

Four hours of sleep had improved their energy levels somewhat, but it had done nothing for their tempers. Beaufort, Maxwell Baker, and Jim Trebane had their hands full preventing several angry fist-fights before the group finally got on the trail and began the final march back to the settlement.

****

It was full light, but still early morning when the weary men finally wound their way onto the slaver settlement proper. They had passed acres of corn and wheat, and were leaving the fields as they drew further into the settlement, when Beaufort noticed a man on the roadway about two hundred feet ahead of them.

"Max, I think my eyes are going bad. Who is that on the road coming out to greet us? I can't tell. Is that Allen?"

Baker's eyes were excellent. "No, it's not one of our people. I have no idea who it is."

They continued, eventually drawing up close to the stranger, who held up his hands, and motioned for the group to stop. The man was over six feet, with dark black eyes and fine aquiline features, an olive complexion, and a black beard.

"Who the devil are you?" Beaufort asked with evident irritation.

Hakim ignored the question, and spoke loudly enough for the whole group of fifteen men to hear, "I'm going to have to ask you men to put down your weapons and your packs."

"And just why in the blazes do you think we would want to do that, stranger?"

"Because you're liable to be killed if you don't," Hakim replied, adding as an afterthought, "stranger."

"You're a fool! You're not even armed! I could lift my finger and you'd be cut to shreds!"

"Yes, I suppose so. Or, on the other hand, *I* could lift *my* finger," and as he said this, he did. The two drainage ditches fifty feet off either side of the road erupted into gunfire as seventeen freed slaves fired into the air from concealed positions, just feet over the heads of the slavers.

The effect was electric. The surprise was complete, and the men on the road were startled out of their wits. Four of the slavers fainted outright, probably aided by their exhaustion from the forced march of the night before. Three or four cried out in terror and dropped to their knees. The rest nearly shot one another as they whirled about, trying to bring their weapons to bear on an unseen enemy that seemed to completely surround them. As it happened no one was injured, though a few soiled their pants. Then the shooting stopped, as quickly as it began. The morning air was silent once again.

"So what do you say? Shall I lift my finger again?" Hakim asked meekly.

Beaufort knew he had been beaten, totally defeated. His face glowed red with rage, but his anger did not keep him from thinking clearly. He carefully lowered his weapon to the ground, along with his pack, and instructed his men to do the same. When all the weapons were on the ground, and the men's hands were behind their heads, the former slaves emerged from the ditches and surrounded the defeated men, weapons at the ready.

"You're the man in the boots, aren't you?" Beaufort asked, knowing that Hakim would understand the question.

"I was," Hakim smiled, "I was the man in the boots, until I put them on Tiny, over there," motioning to Othello Samuelson, one of the freed slaves. At six feet four inches, Othello was an inch taller than Hakim, and about one hundred pounds heavier. The other men called him Tiny, which was a little easier to get your mouth around than 'Othello.'

"Where'd you jump off yesterday?" Beaufort asked.

"Raccoon Creek."

"Huh. Well, at least I figured that right. So what happens next?"

"First of all, there's not going to be any more shooting, at least not while I'm here. Not unless some of your people cause trouble. If you cooperate, none of you will be harmed. You're all going to need to put these on," and with that Hakim held up a set of shackles, "wrist and ankles, so you don't cause any problems while your former, um, *guests*, decide what they are going to do."

"It'll be a cold day in hell before I put those on, stranger! I'm no slave!" Beaufort growled.

"Very well," Hakim replied without rancor.

Raising his voice, he addressed the whole group. "Those of you who wish to be shot to death, please stand over here with . . . what's his name?" he asked, turning to Gus.

"Beaufort."

"Ah. Thank you." Raising his voice again, Hakim repeated himself, "Those of you who wish to be shot to death, please stand over here with Mr. Beaufort! Those of you who prefer to wear shackles for a couple of hours, stand over there by Tiny, and put them on one another. You have to the count of ten to make your choice. One . . . two . . . three . . . ."

For few seconds as Hakim continued to count, no one moved. Then Jacen rammed a fresh magazine into his rifle, and the other former slaves followed his lead, doing the same. That was all it took. Five minutes later, all the slavers, including Beaufort, were snugly shackled.

*** * * * * * * * ***

After all the discarded weapons were gathered up, Hakim herded the whole group of slavers into the settlement proper. Sitting on the grass in the commons area, also shackled, were the defenders who had survived the raid the night before. Not shackled, but standing around with red-rimmed eyes were wives and children. Everyone, slave and slaver alike, knew that a way of life was coming to an end, and perhaps an entire community.

At first, many of the former slaves wanted to kill their captors. They argued among themselves for an hour, emotions flaring and voices raised. Some had been held as captives for over three years, and their bitterness was implacable. One group argued that it was wrong to kill them in cold blood. The other group argued that it had also been wrong for their captors to hold them in slavery, and that they would simply do it all over again if they weren't killed. The slavers weren't permitted to speak.

Hakim had said nothing, waiting to see if the former slaves would solve it by themselves. He had been sitting off to the side with Jacen, Gus, and Phil, talking quietly. When it became apparent that nothing was being settled, he called out to get their attention. After everyone quieted down, he spoke.

"I'm going to settle this right now. If it wasn't for me, not a one of you would be free today, so I figure I've got a right to speak. As long as Jacen and I are here, no one is going to be killed or harmed in any way. If you want to come back later and settle scores, that's your business, but I'd advise against it. We can't afford to lose any more people on this sin-cursed earth. In any case, there will be no massacre here today.

"I encourage you all," he said, speaking to the former slaves, "to divide up the weapons and ammunition among yourselves, recover any of your personal possessions that might have been confiscated when you were brought here, get as much of the food stores as you can carry – you've certainly earned that with your labor – and go back to your own settlements."

"What right do you have to tell us what to do?" snarled Joe Nolen.

Gus jumped up, angry. "I'll tell you what right he has, Joe! We at least owe him a little gratitude, don't you think? Under his leadership we freed the entire slave population of this camp, with a loss of only two men. At the very least we can respect his request. If you, or anyone else wants to come back and shoot the place up, have at it. Just do it after the rest of us have left. I'm not about to be party to cold-blooded murder, even if most of these swine deserve it. Where does it stop, Joe? You gonna kill their women, and children, too? No sir! *They* may be murderous scum. But *I'm* not. And I don't think any of you are, either."

There was a rumble of agreement from most of the other former slaves. Nolen glowered at the group in anger. He walked up to Hakim, and returned the Colt pistol that the Arab had loaned him.

"Okay. Have it your way. I can wait. But I don't forgive, and I don't forget." He walked over to Beaufort, and spit on him. "Listen, Bobby-boy. You'd better make sure you post a watch every night. And there better be a double-guard outside your cabin. And your wife and kids better never go down to the river alone. 'Cause when I come back, I'll shoot you all down like the dogs you are! And you can bet on it . . . I _will_ be back."

Then he turned and looked at Tim Shanks, and said softly, "But for you, Tim, I've got something special planned. And you will beg me, _beg me_, to shoot you before I'm done with you. But you know what? I won't. No sir! You, son, are going to die real slowly. So keep looking over your shoulder, son, and don't sleep too soundly. I'll creep up on you, at night, when you don't expect it. And I'll show you just as much mercy as you showed us."

Joe Nolen turned on his heel, and looked at Hakim. "Hakim, I've got to admit it. From start to finish, that was a neat piece of work. I do thank you for setting us free. And you're welcome at my campfire anytime. If you ever need help, and I'm in the neighborhood, all you gotta do is ask."

He looked at his wife, who had been a slave with the women, "C'mon, Sue. Let's get what's ours, and go see if home is still where we left it. Are you coming, Murph?"

Mike Murphy and his wife, Josie, both among the freed slaves, were standing off to the side. "Yep," Murphy acknowledged, "we're ready. Waitin' on you. And when you come back here, Joe, to settle scores, I'll be right beside you."

The four dispersed into the settlement to recover what they could of their property. With their departure, the arguments ceased.

After they left, Gus looked at Hakim and Jacen with a sad expression. "When Mike and Joe were captured, that skunk," and he motioned to Tim Shanks, "killed their kids. In cold blood. He actually enjoyed it. I was really hoping to put a bullet between Shanks' eyes myself during the fight, when I could do it, natural-like, in the heat of battle." Tim Shanks' face was pale, and he was trembling with fear as Gus spoke. "But Tim, you're lucky I'm not like you. I'm not a cold-blooded murderer. Not like you. And besides, it sounds like you have an appointment with Mr. Nolen, and I don't want to interfere."

Gus addressed Bob Beaufort, "Bob, let me give you a piece of advice. That coyote, Tim, he's the one you want to put in chains. He'll be the death of you people yet. As God is my witness, if not for Hakim holding us back, not a one of you men would still be alive. And maybe none of you women, either."

He turned back to Tim, "If I ever, ever, see you more than two miles from this settlement, you are a dead man. No questions asked."

For several moments, no one spoke. The enormity of the cruelty with which they had treated the slaves, both by enslaving them to begin with, and then treating them with such brutality was beginning to come home to a number of the former slavers. The shame was as thick as fog. Some, of course, felt no accusations of conscience at all. But most, upon reflection, were distressed to see themselves as they really were, perhaps for the first time.

"Jacen, maybe you'll want to tell 'em our plans," Hakim said, interrupting the silence. But he whispered, "Say nothing about the horses."

Jacen stood up, and spoke to the group of freed slaves, "I don't know all of you. I've only been here for a little over a week. I'm from way out east. Some of you may have heard of the Philadelphia ruin. That's near where I used to live. This past winter a sickness wiped out our community, and all of my family. I'm the only survivor. As I grieved for my loved ones and friends, I made a decision that I was tired of simply existing, simply trying not to die. I determined to begin living with some purpose greater than myself, greater than my own survival.

"So I decided . . . I want to build a *new* civilization. I want to produce things instead of scavenging them, grow enough food to trade with others and to give to those who need it. I dream of a large community under the rule of law, a community that starts like-minded sister communities nearby with which it can trade and fellowship. A community not living under the fear of Anarchs, slave hunters, or any man. A community that is committed to justice, industry, hard work, art, beauty, and all the other things that make our lives special.

"I want to see men and women rediscover the old technologies, and put them to work once again. I want to have a settlement with craftsmen, tradesmen, builders, artists, doctors, scientists, teachers. A place where every person will have equal opportunity to work hard and pursue his dream. There will be no slaves, and no slave-holders. I want to build a community based on the notion that life is precious and must be protected.

"We've spent enough time as a people trying to survive, trying to eke out an existence from season to season. I am ready to stop being consumed with *not dying*. I want to be consumed, instead, with living, building, contributing."

As he spoke, weaving his dream, the entire gathering fell silent, former slave and former slaver alike. At some level he was speaking the same things that most of them were longing for: stability, opportunity, freedom, purpose. A world in which planning and preparing for the future was worthwhile, because the future was, at least to some degree, certain.

Jacen wrapped up his comments, saying, "Once we have completed our business back in Bedford, Hakim and I will head west, to the area once known as Colorado. It is far enough in the center of the continent that there are probably not any other people there. There certainly shouldn't be any Anarchs. We'll be far enough away from other people that we can build a community with our values, and there will be no one to interfere with us. There we will build a new civilization.

"Anyone who is committed to these same values is welcome to join us. It will be very difficult at first, because we will be constantly on the move until we arrive at a place that looks like a good location to start. And once we get there, we'll have to build an entire community from scratch. Neither Hakim nor I have any resources to make this work, besides our minds, our dreams, and a commitment to work hard. There are no guarantees. But we live amidst the ruins of a people that once, long ago, accomplished all these things. There's no reason why we can't do it again."

For several moments after Jacen had finished, the group stood by in small knots, talking. Then the weapons were divided up, and small groups began making preparations to leave. As the morning wore on, good-byes were said, and various ones departed for their former homes and communities, hoping against hope to find someone still there. Hakim and Jacen sat by, cradling their weapons in their laps, keeping the former slavers together, and protecting them from the still-burning ire of many of the former slaves.

In the early afternoon, Gus, Phil, Randy, and Elijah came and stood with Hakim and Jacen. The men, Jacen included, had been busy recovering the possessions that had been stolen when they were enslaved, and had completed that task.

"Jacen," Gus said, "we want to throw our hats in the ring, so to speak. Our entire settlement was destroyed when these jackals attacked us, back some three years ago. Elijah's wife, Julie, was killed in the attack. None of us want to go back there. Too many memories. We'd like to hitch up with you two. We've talked together with the girls, and we all like your plan. We'd rather die trying to make something new, something worthwhile, than survive just trying to hold on to what we've got."

A small group of women walked over as Gus was talking, and Gus began to introduce them. "This here's my wife, Katie. That there's Angela, we call her Angie. She's Randy's sister. Next to her is Ginny Moore, 'Lijah's daughter. And that's Misty Randall. Her momma and daddy died just after she was born."

Gus looked slyly at Jacen. He said innocently, "By golly, I don't say! Ginny looks to be 'bout the same age as you, Jacen!" Both young people blushed profusely, while the older ones smiled knowing smiles.

Gus continued, "And these two young ladies are the Linder twins, Lynn and Patricia. We call her Trisha. Then this is Mary Anders. She was widowed about ten years ago. She's uncommon wise. Of all of us here, I don't 'spect any one of us, nor all of us together, has as much sense as she does."

Hakim looked at Jacen and smiled. "I think what we have here is the beginning of your town, Jacen. Perhaps in the midst of all the heart-ache, *Isa al Masih* had his own purposes in our little detour here. They," he said, motioning to the slavers, "meant it for evil, but he meant it for good."

CHAPTER 17

The August sun bore down on the old interstate highway, producing heat waves that made the distant horizon an uncertain vision of shimmering ambiguity. Jacen and Gus each readjusted the cart harness, which had left red marks on their sweaty chests and shoulders. Phil and Hakim, and Randy and Elijah were similarly harnessed. The group had taken three of the largest two-wheeled carts, filled them with canned goods, and set out as a group from the Pittsburgh settlement. Four men and eight women had cast their lots with Jacen and Hakim, making a total of fourteen people. Jacen thought about that: nearly two weeks ago he had been walking in the opposite direction as a newly captured slave, his dreams dashed, and without hope. Now he was returning by the same path, with his dream of beginning a new civilization twelve people closer to reality. *How things change*, he mused.

"Everybody ready?" Jacen called out. With groans, the group got to their feet and picked up their loads, making minute adjustments on their packs and harnesses.

"You're worse than Beaufort was," grumbled Randy Bartwell.

"Pah! You're just lazy!" accused Gus.

"Now, now," Phil clucked. "You need to be respectful of your elders, Gus. Randy's gettin' old. He needs his rest. Ain't that right, Randy?"

"Old, my eye! You never saw the day you could keep up with me, Phil. I'll walk you into the ground any day of the week."

"Yeah, and you'll be complaining every step of the way!" added Gus, laughing.

Randy examined his harness carefully, made a slight adjustment, and then looked up, "I consider complaining to be the sacred right of the workin' man."

Elijah growled, "Yeah, and you exercise your rights constantly. Enough palaver! Let's get this show on the road! We stay here any longer, I'm gonna grow roots. Let's move."

The women watched the verbal sparring. Angie Bartwell, Randy's sister, explained, "Randy's not happy unless he's grumbling about something. It's when he stops complaining that you'd better watch out."

"Hey, sis! You're supposed to take my side, not tell my secrets!"

Angie rolled her eyes, and said, "C'mon, girls. If this sorry bunch is ever going to get anywhere, we're going to have to lead the way." With that the girls started down the trail, headed east.

Hakim looked across at Jacen, raised his eyebrows, and leaned into the harness.

****

On the third day, Jacen realized that he was recognizing ridges and landmarks. He was harnessed with Hakim on this particular day.

"Hakim, isn't that ridge just south of our camp?"

"Yep. I'd say we'll be there in another hour or two."

"Can't wait! I'm ready to get back to work with the horses!"

They walked for several more minutes in silence and then Jacen chuckled to himself a couple of times, and finally broke out in laughter. He looked at Hakim with a sly grin, still chuckling.

"What?" Hakim asked, wiping his sweaty brow, "What are you laughing at?"

"Just wondering. Do you remember all that stuff you read in your books?"

"What stuff?"

"All that stuff about how to tame and train horses."

Hakim shook his head, and rejoined gruffly, "You are not going to let that die, are you?"

"Not on your life! I think it's hilarious! I can't *wait* to watch Hakim, the great horse-trainer, do his thing. And all you've ever ridden, ha ha ha, is a *book*, ha ha ha! It's going to be a real show," Jacen chortled.

"Well, just remember one thing, funny boy."

"What's that?"

"If I am successful, next time we move out it will be a horse's *front* end wearing that harness you've got on, instead of the horse's *hind* end that's wearing it at present," Hakim said, laughing at his own joke.

"Very funny."

****

Late in the afternoon they arrived. The first thing they noticed was the horses. The beautiful animals were grazing in the meadow, some inside and some outside of the corral. As the party labored up with their carts, the stallion snorted and the herd raised their heads. The magnificent horse stamped his front hoof and whinnied, and the herd began to amble toward the forest. In a few minutes they had all disappeared into the woods.

"That's a lot of meat on the hoof, Hakim. I don't understand why we can't just shoot 'em," Phil said. His sweaty face was glowing red from the heat and exertion of

161

pulling the cart. He wiped his brow as he struggled out of his harness. The whole group had dismounted their packs, or shrugged off the cart harnesses, and were standing around looking with some dismay at the primitive state of Jacen's and Hakim's former camp.

"Tell you what, Phil: why don't we all get some water and get cleaned up? The stream is right down that little path right there. We'll get coffee on, and supper started, then I'll lay the whole thing out for you."

Several hours later, dusk had fallen and the hot August day had begun to cool. The fourteen sat around the fire, finishing up a stew of fresh venison and canned vegetables.

Jacen, acknowledged by all to be the leader of the group despite his young age, set his coffee down and began to speak. "Phil, this afternoon you asked about the horses, and why we can't shoot them for meat. Let's take some time this evening talking about the horses, our plans, and the new community we will build. And before we turn in tonight we need to set up our watch schedule, and I want to work on assignments for tomorrow."

They all nodded in agreement. Jacen looked at Hakim, and with a slight tilt of his head signaled the Arab to carry on the conversation. Hakim poured himself another cup of coffee, and began.

"Our goal is to build a new civilization: Jacen has established the dream. The fact that you're here means you've signed on to the dream even if we don't quite know how to accomplish it. The primary concept is pretty simple: in order to make advances in technology and culture we must first advance in efficiency. In many respects the slaver community had it right though they were going about it the wrong way. We want to advance the right way, without oppression or injustice." There were murmurs of agreement from several of the group.

He fell silent for a moment, thinking of the best way to explain their plans, then looked up at Phil and continued, "Phil, all your life long, what has been the major task that has occupied your time? What activity took the vast majority of your time before you were captured as a slave?"

"Why, that's easy," the barrel-chested man replied, "it's finding the next meal. Most everything I have done has revolved around establishing shelter and gathering food."

"Uh-huh. How about you, Randy?" Hakim inquired.

"Same."

"You, 'Lijah? What's taken up most of your time?" the Arab persisted.

"Finding food. Same as everyone else."

"Right. How about you, Katie?"

"I'm either finding food or cooking it. It's about all I get done," Katie Blackwell replied.

"Yeah, well, that's 'cause Gus eats enough for two people," snickered Phil. Gus glared at him.

"Okay. At present, our lives are dominated by the need to eat, right? There's not much time or energy left over for reading, learning, creative thinking, developing new skills, being artistic, and so on. In other words, there's no time to build or advance culture or civilization. All of our efforts are spent on survival.

"What we need is some change in our situation which allows us to produce more food than we need, and accomplish work more efficiently, right? Only then will we have time for other pursuits."

"I can see where you're going with this, Hakim," observed Mary Anders. "The horse is the change you are talking about. I've read a great deal about them in books."

At this statement, Hakim glanced at Jacen with an expression of triumph written on his face. Jacen grinned back at the older man, and shrugged his shoulders, shaking his head.

Mary continued, "A horse can be tamed and trained to pull a plow, or a loaded wagon. It can snake fallen timber out of a forest. We can learn to ride them, and travel much faster and much greater distances."

Hakim gazed at Mary with surprised admiration, as though he was seeing her for the first time. It was a look which didn't go unnoticed by the rest of the group, and it evoked some small smiles and a wink or two. Hakim, his attention focused on Mary, saw none of this. He continued, "Exactly, Mary! That's exactly right! You see, Phil, with a horse we can get far more work done than a man can do by himself. For example, suppose four men can plow half an acre of ground in two days. With a horse, one man can plow that half-acre in one day. That's an eight-fold increase in productivity."

Phil nodded, rubbing his stubbled chin with a large, rough hand. "I got it," he said. "If we get our chores done faster, there's more time left for doing other things."

"Right, and the horse is our ace in the hole for doing just that."

It had grown dark. The western sky had a hint of brilliant red, but it was rapidly fading. The group sat around the fire enjoying the sound of crackling wood, the night birds, and the coolness.

Phil broke the silence, "So, I reckon you must have a lot of experience with horses and such, Hakim. You done a lot of riding?"

Jacen snorted and struggled to suppress the laughter rising in his chest, but he was unsuccessful and sat chortling in the glooming light. All heads turned his way.

"What?" Phil asked, "What did I say? What are you laughing at, Jace?"

The young man's mirth overflowed. He weakly held up his hands, and between gales of laughter he pointed at Hakim and struggled to say, "Ha, ha, ha, ha! Ha, ask—aha, ha, ha, ha! Ask *him*, ha, ha, ha!"

In unison all heads turned back to the Arab, who was now sitting in a rather stiff, straight-backed posture. Even in the flickering firelight, the steely look on his face could be discerned.

"Well? What's going on? What's he finding so funny, Hakim?" Gus insisted. "Surely with all these plans you're spinning, you've got some experience working with horses? Right?"

The Arab hesitated, and then replied somewhat testily, "No, not exactly. But I *have* read some books about them, including how to tame and train them."

"*Books?*" Phil exclaimed incredulously. "You've read some *books?* Wha—"

Phil's rejoinder was cut off mid-sentence by an icy female voice, "And exactly *what* is wrong with reading and learning from books, Mr. Gonzales? I've learned a great deal from my reading. I suggest you try it some time!" Mary Anders retorted indignantly.

"Oh! No offense intended, ma'am!" Phil stuttered. "I surely did not mean to offend. It's just that, well . . . ," he finished lamely. He was embarrassed to say it, but the truth of the matter was that he was illiterate. The big man desired desperately to read, but was mortified to admit that he barely knew his 'letters', as he called them.

The group sat in silence for a moment, half of them wondering about the horses and the other half wondering if they had just seen a spark of human chemistry flare up around the fireside.

"Well!" exclaimed Elijah Moore, half to himself as he looked from Hakim to Mary Anders and back, "*that* was interesting . . . !"

CHAPTER 18

Over the next three weeks the community spent most of its time building cabins sufficient for the winter that they now realized would be spent in Bedford. Everyone pitched in to help and the work went quickly. Most of the structures were but one-room affairs, divided into sleeping spaces by hanging a blanket here or there. They also began the task of smoking and jerking meat in preparation for winter. Already the mornings were beginning to feel crisp, though the leaves had not begun to turn.

Hakim was spending most of his time in the corral, which had been enlarged and then subdivided into several different pens. They had continued to draw the horses with sugar cubes, and although the stallion stood defiantly off, the other horses slowly became accustomed to humans. Eventually they trapped ten horses in the largest pen. The Arab spent most of each day with the ten, talking to them and singing to them from just outside the fence. Within two weeks, the horses were accepting sugar cubes, and an occasional apple from a nearby wild orchard, from Hakim's hand through the fence.

****

"Good morning, Hadar! Are you going to let me pet you today?"

Hakim held out his hand and the big buckskin mare cautiously sniffed at it. Hakim slowly raised his hand to rub the mare's forehead. She began to swing her head away, and Hakim stopped, leaving his hand in mid-air. She snorted and twitched her ears, then moved her big head back toward him. Hakim waited, then continued to reach toward her. As he touched the white patch on her forehead, Hadar trembled but did not move away.

"There now, that's not so bad, is it?" he spoke as he rubbed her forehead and then scratched her cheek. If this was a first for Hadar, in that this was the first time she had ever been touched by a human, it was also Hakim's first contact with a horse. He had read several books on them, some of which had brief sections covering training a horse, but most of which dealt with the mechanics of bridling and saddling a horse, and *advanced* training techniques for horses that had already been broken to the saddle.

During the two weeks prior, as Hakim had acclimated the horses to his presence, he had singled out the big buckskin as the best prospect to work with first. She seemed to be less excitable than the other horses. He had named her Hadar, Arabic for 'civilization,' as she would be the first of the horses tamed and trained.

****

One of the new tasks made necessary by corralling the horses was cutting hay for feed. The men of the settlement had added that task to their others, and a supply of provender was slowly building up.

Jacen had worked with everyone to lay out work and watch schedules, tasks, and community responsibilities. Because the young man was fair-minded and teachable none

167

of the older members of the community found any reason to complain about his leadership. Jacen seemed to have an aptitude for leading and organizing, and as time went on his abilities grew.

Hakim continued to teach the young man various skills, as well as the rudiments of geography, history, mathematics, and philosophy. The others soon discovered that Hakim had a far wider breadth of knowledge than they had realized, and began sitting with Jacen as Hakim taught him in the evenings.

****

"Where'd he learn all that stuff he talks about in the evenings?" Phil asked, as he and Jacen struggled with the loaded cart. They had spent the day cutting hay in a large field south of Bedford, and were returning to the settlement.

"What? Who? Oh! You're asking about Hakim, right?" Jacen had been lost in his thoughts, and it had taken him a moment to realize that Phil was talking to him.

"Yeah. How's he know so much?"

Phil had been the first of the community to perceive that Hakim was tutoring Jacen. From that moment on, Phil had been at every lecture, listening with rapt attention.

Jacen looked at the big man harnessed next to him, and smiled. "He reads. That man reads everything he can get his hands on. You know, Phil, in many of the ruins some of the buildings have not sustained that much damage. Hakim has run across several libraries with books in usable condition. He told me once that he spent the entire summer in a ruin down south, I believe he called it Atlanta, simply because its library was fairly intact. He spent the whole summer just reading.

"You've seen his big backpack, leaning in the corner of our shelter? It's full of books. I'd say half the weight of what he carried when we came here to Bedford from Ludwigs Corner was books."

168

"You don't say! So he learnt all that from books?"

"Yep. Say! I've noticed you yourself have a real interest in history and such. You've not missed one of his lectures since joining us. I know he'd be glad to loan you any of his books."

Phil didn't respond. They trudged on in silence for a few minutes, straining against the harness, and then he confessed, "Can't read. Wouldn't do me no good to have a book in my hands."

Jacen looked at his companion and saw that his face was flushed with embarrassment and shame. He realized that Phil had just entrusted him with one of his most closely guarded secrets. He felt a sudden warmth of friendship toward the man.

"Would you like to be able to read?"

"More than anything. Just never learnt."

"Well, that settles it then. I'll teach you! Tell you what: why don't I rework the schedule? Hay cutting is the most hated chore in the community. You and I will take over all the hay cutting till winter stops us. Nobody else will mind. We'll get started a little early each day, so we can spend two hours in the middle of every day working on your reading. Nobody else needs to know. How 'bout it? Want to give it a shot?"

Phil looked at the younger man with an expression of grateful relief and nodded. "You're on, Jacen. Let's do it."

****

Each member of the Bedford community lived with ugly memories of their days in slavery. Several feared that one day the men of Pittsburgh would come with revenge on their minds and guns in their hands. Hakim, therefore, began teaching them the small unit tactics and advanced weapon skills that he knew so well. He discussed the mistakes of the guards at the slaver settlement: predictable patrol routes and schedules, and the assumption that there was no threat.

One day each week, as the late summer turned to fall, he taught them rudimentary hand-to-hand combat skills: how to fight with a knife, how to fight with a stick, and how to disarm an opponent. He reminded them repeatedly that that they were living in a world where there was no one else to help or protect them. Vigilance was the responsibility of the whole community.

They always went about their tasks armed, even the women. They had refined the night watch duty to the point that the schedule operated smoothly and everyone got enough sleep. As an additional precaution, two men combined the purpose of patrolling and hunting once each week, walking a wide arc in the country some twenty miles to the west. They were looking for game, but also for footprints or any other sign of human travelers. So far, they had found plenty of game, but no footprints.

****

"C'mon, girl. See what I have here? Nothing's going to hurt you. It's okay," Hakim purred soothingly. Gus and Randy had helped to separate the buckskin from the other horses in the larger corral, and had chased her into the smaller pen and shut the gate.

He showed Hadar the halter and coiled lead rope, and let her sniff them. After Hadar had satisfied her curiosity, Hakim began rubbing her down with them, then bringing them back to her face where she could see and sniff at them. This was repeated several times over the next several days, until the horse no longer shied from the halter. Finally Hakim was able to put the rope halter on the big mare, and begin leading her around the pen.

Hakim had practiced with the tack enough to know what to do with all the buckles and straps. He had a good idea of how to properly fit a saddle or a headstall. But he truly had no idea how to settle and train a wild horse. The books he had found all dealt with more advanced training, so the Arab was really relying on a little bit of information, and a lot of guesswork.

And he made a beginner's mistake. After a week in which he had established a good relationship of trust with the horse, he figured it was time to go to the saddle. The problem was not that he was too quick to reach for the saddle. Actually he had wasted several weeks in his own inefficient program of acclimating the horse to his presence. The problem was that he had not taught Hadar what she needed to know.

A horse is a social animal that observes a rigid pecking order in all its relationships. It tolerates, or sometimes bullies, any other horse (or creature) which is below its own position on the social ladder. It defers to any horse (or creature) which it acknowledges to be above its position. As of yet, the two-hundred pound Hakim had not demonstrated to the 1200 pound Hadar what their respective positions were on that all-important ladder. And Hakim was about to pay for the mistake.

****

Hadar stood trembling under the saddle. She was showing a great deal of white around her eyes, but Hakim was intent on making sure the saddle was fitting properly, and was not watching the horse's body language. At least he had done one thing right: he had recruited a little help rather than tackling the project today by himself. Jacen had a short grip on the reins and so was able to control the big horse's head.

Hakim flipped the cinch over the seat of the saddle, and looped the right-hand stirrup over the saddle horn. He picked the saddle up off the fence rail and carried it to Hadar's left shoulder, and gently swung it over her back. She snorted and side-stepped away from Hakim, until she came up against the fence and was able to go no farther. Her ears were flat back on her head.

He walked around and pushed the horse away from the fence, let down the cinch and stirrup, then returned to Hadar's left and ran the latigo through the cinch ring and finished it off. He'd already adjusted the stirrup length several days earlier when he'd thrown the saddle over a big log and sat on it.

Hadar snorted again and jerked her head against the reins, but Jacen held them firmly. Hakim collected the reins in his hand, though Jacen still held a firm grip just below the bit.

"Well, this is it," Hakim said nervously.

"Are you sure she's ready? She seems mighty skittish to me," Jacen observed.

"Well, son, this is new ground for all of us, including her," the Arab replied, without confidence.

"To the future, then."

"To the future," Hakim repeated. He put his boot in the stirrup and swung into the saddle. He wrapped his free hand around the saddle horn with a white-knuckle grip. Settling himself, he nodded to Jacen, "Let go, and then back out of the way. If I were you, I think I'd get out of the pen."

Jacen nodded and released the reins. He backed up ten feet, then turned and walked to the fence. Climbing through, he turned to watch.

Hadar stood trembling. Hakim forced himself to release his death grip on the saddle horn, and reached down to pet her neck. As he shifted position to do so, the heel of his boot accidentally touched her ribs.

It was like someone set off a bomb right under him. Hadar dropped her head low, almost yanking the reins out of Hakim's hand, then pitched forward and kicked up her hind legs. In a flash she swapped ends, then commenced crow-hopping and bucking around the pen. For four or five seconds, Hakim hung on to the saddle horn for dear life, one second almost flying off the back of the saddle, the next second crashing violently, face-first, into the bony back of Hadar's head as she bucked around the pen. Finally he was pitched over the horse's head and landed on the fence, the fence post itself catching him in the ribs with a sickening crunch. He dropped motionless inside the pen. Hadar continued to crow-hop around the enclosure until she finally stood exhausted and covered with sweat, trembling, in the center of the pen.

Hakim was unmoving, and lay in the dirt, face down, in a spreading pool of blood. Jacen was horrified. Vaulting over the fence, he shouted for help and ran to Hakim, finding him unconscious but alive. Hadar shied to the far side of the pen.

****

Oh, the pain! Excruciating, unending, throbbing pain! *Where am I? What happened?* His eyes seemed to be glued shut. His eyelids felt sticky, and would not open. Everything hurt. He felt a warm wet cloth bathing his face. It hurt like fire. He tried to raise his hand to touch his face, but nearly fainted from the pain that exploded with fresh vigor in his chest. He couldn't lift his arms: it hurt too much.

Breathing was so agonizing that he tried to hold his breath and just gulp some air every minute or two. He wondered again, *what happened? Have I been shot?*

"No, you've not been shot."

Hakim was surprised: he hadn't realized that he had spoken aloud.

"You got thrown off of a *fool* horse," the female voice continued in an almost angry and wholly unsympathetic way. She spit out "*fool* horse" like an expletive. "You're a fool!" she continued, "you could've gotten yourself killed!" With the last few words, the woman's emotions betrayed her crusty demeanor and her voice broke. Hakim finally placed the voice: it was Mary Anders.

As the fog cleared a few details began to come back to him. He remembered saddling Hadar, and stepping into the saddle. He remembered the horse dropping her head violently, but he remembered nothing else.

"How did I get here? Where am I?"

"You're in your cabin. Phil and Jacen carried you here, while Gus, Randy, and Elijah tried to get that *fool* saddle off that *fool* horse! You've broken ribs; don't know how many, but I expect darn near all of 'em. You've got a nasty gash over your right eye, which you received from the top rail of the fence. It's going to leave a lovely scar. I'll be surprised if the eye socket of your left eye isn't shattered. It's certainly swollen and badly discolored. Jacen said your head came down on the back of the horse's head when it was coming up, while she was bucking. And to top it all, Hadar stepped on your left leg. She didn't break that, but she left a good gash and an ugly bruise there. Other than that, you're fit as a fiddle."

****

For the next five days, Hakim was unable to move about much. The pain in his chest, which had been enough to cause him to faint when he sneezed, gradually began to lessen. Mary Anders was very concerned, but very busy trying to pretend that she wasn't. He enjoyed her attention, even if the extreme pain was troublesome.

The third day after the accident Jacen stopped in to talk. "What should we do now, Hakim? Should we release the horses, or butcher them for food?"

"Absolutely not! Why would we?" Hakim grimaced. The forcefulness of his response sent splinters of agony shooting through his torso.

"We can't continue with the horses! You're the only one who knows anything about them, and look what happened to you. The rest of us have no idea what to do with them. You could've died out there. We need you! We don't need those horses!" Jacen protested.

"Look, Jacen, there's never been a time in history in which an advance did not exact a human cost. Many of the early explorers simply vanished. The early days of flight were filled with deadly accidents. Madame Curie with her husband Pierre were among the first to study radioactivity, and it's thought that her death was brought on by radiation exposure."

"What's radioactivity? I've never heard of it," Jacen asked, puzzled.

"Oh, never mind! My point is this: we can't stop moving forward simply because I had an accident with the horses. They *are* our next step! They are *essential*! I'll just have to learn what I did wrong, and do better the next time," Hakim insisted.

"I don't know—"

"Jacen! We have no choice! What I explained to the group a month ago about the conditions necessary to advance wasn't some theoretical philosophy. It's reality. Unless we learn to harness and use more power than we as humans can provide, we'll never get anywhere. My accident won't be the last one with the horses. But we can't stop because we're afraid of accidents!"

****

Slowly Hakim regained his strength, and as his ribs healed the pain level became tolerable. One evening, at mealtime, Jacen sat next to him. "Found something for you. It's another book on horses."

Hakim looked at the young man, wondering if Jacen was teasing him. But there was no glint of mischief in his friend's eyes. "Where'd you find it?" Hakim asked.

"You know that old farm where we found three saddles last spring? I went back and searched the house. There was a glass book case in one room, wholly intact. This was in it." Jacen set a slim book before Hakim. It was entitled, *Lyons on Horses*, by John Lyons with Sinclair Browning.

Hakim picked it up. It was in good condition, though very old. He read the subtitle on the cover out loud, "John Lyons' proven conditioned-response training program." The Arab opened the book and flipped through it with a rising sense of excitement.

"Jacen, this is *exactly* what I have needed! This book isn't about horses generally, like my others. It's specifically about *training* horses, starting at the very beginning!"

****

It was now early October, and the nights were crisp. The leaves on the trees were in full color. Though there had been no frost yet, the mornings were getting snappy. The Bedford community was well into their preparations for winter, both for themselves and for the horses. Hunting parties were being sent out at least two days distance from the community, to preserve the closer game for winter hunting.

The horse herd had increased to twenty-three animals through Jacen's work of trapping horses with sugar in the big outer corral. Hakim and Jacen both knew, however, that they would have to release some of the herd during the winter if they were unable to provide enough feed.

It was a glorious afternoon, the one day of the week that the whole community rested from their chores. Jacen was sitting on the fence, watching the horses gallop around the inner perimeter of their fence. They had worn a track all the way around the big corral, just a few feet inside the barrier. The young man was growing to love the big, beautiful animals, and was thankful that Hakim had insisted they continue their plan of horse-taming and training, despite the accident. The beautiful creatures were impressive in strength, and seemed to the young man to be very intelligent, and insatiably curious.

Jacen jumped off the fence and walked over to the new training pen, the "round pen" as Hakim called it. There Hakim was combing the big buckskin mare, Hadar. She loved the attention. She no longer shied from humans and seemed to look forward to her daily meetings with Hakim, late experience with the saddle notwithstanding. Hakim's cracked ribs were healing, though they still caused him no small amount of pain in his movements.

"Hakim! Look at that!" Jacen called. The horses in the larger pen had stopped their romping, and had bunched together. They were all looking intently to the west, toward the old interstate, ears straight up.

The Arab took one look, and replied, "They hear something. The horses become aware of things much sooner than we do. Better go back and warn the others. Make sure everyone has a weapon on hand. I'll bet we're about to have visitors." He slipped the halter off of Hadar, patted her gently on the rump, and said, "That's enough for now, girl." She followed him to the fence and watched him slip stiffly between the rails.

****

"Gus, Phil, grab your weapons and get out of sight. Hakim thinks we are about to have visitors. Randy, head down to the creek and warn the women; stay close to them. 'Lijah, you come with me. Let's scout down the west trail just a ways, see what we can see."

Wordlessly, the men complied. Jacen rarely spoke with urgency, so the men did not resent it when he did, nor did they waste time with questions.

Jacen and Elijah Moore eased up the embankment of old I-76, and studied the western approach. Sure enough, about one mile down the trail was a small party making slow progress and struggling with several two-wheeled carts. He raised his binoculars.

"Well, I'll be! 'Lijah, looks like some of the Pittsburgh slavers are headed our way. I count, let's see, four men, and one woman. No, make that two women, and two young children. All four men are yoked to carts, which look to be pretty heavily loaded. All the adults are armed. I recognize the men, but I don't remember who they are. Here, take a look." Jacen passed the glasses to Elijah, as Hakim scrambled up the slope behind them.

Elijah studied the distant group for a moment, and said, "That's the Trebanes, Jace. It's Jim, his wife, and his son, Buck. The other man is one of the Shanks' boys, Gary, with his wife and kids. I can't make out the other guy, one of the women is in the way. Wait . . . okay, that's Sam Oxford. Huh! As I recall, Hakim, you loaded his britches with buckshot in August. Reckon he must be feeling better."

"And as I recall," Hakim responded grimly, "I told him that if I ever saw him again with a gun in his hands, I'd kill him. And here he comes with an M4 strapped to his back."

"You gonna shoot him on sight?"

Hakim had his own binoculars on the group. After a moment, he responded, "No, not unless he's asking for it. I'll give him an even chance to account for himself." The Arab swept his glasses from side to side, looking for others, and then faced his two friends. "Listen, this could be some sort of a trap, or diversion. Jace, why don't you and Elijah slip back down the embankment and go under the bridge, to the other side of the embankment. Don't let them see you. Go two hundred feet or so west and hide yourselves, let them pass, and then creep up the bank behind them so we can box 'em in. Keep a sharp eye, in case they have anyone traveling down in the brush. Let me do the talking. I'd rather they didn't even know you're behind them."

Jacen looked at his friend with concern. "Are you sure you're up to this, Hakim? If you have to pull the trigger on that weapon, it's going to be all you can do just to hang on to the gun, with those cracked ribs of yours. Elijah and I can handle this."

"No, I'll be fine. I'll put it on semi-automatic. If this is some sort of a trap, all three of us will be needed. If there's any shooting, make sure we don't hit each other in the crossfire. Try not to hit the women unless they're firing back. By all means, don't hurt the kids."

CHAPTER 19

When the small band of laboring travelers was less than one hundred feet away, Hakim stepped out from behind the foliage where he'd been hiding, and faced the group. He cradled his old M14, its worn grip fitting naturally into his hand. His dark eyes flashed with irritation, but he said nothing. With his dense black beard, the fresh scar over his eye, and his buckskin clothing he looked very intimidating.

The travelers stopped. The men carefully set the draft poles of the carts down, and slipped out of the harnesses. The two children crowded close to their mother, frightened by the fierce-looking stranger who seemed to have appeared out of thin air. None dared to move a hand toward their weapons. Sam Oxford stood motionless, as pale as a sheet, with his empty hands spread wide.

Out of the corner of his eye, Hakim saw Jacen and Elijah creep into prone positions some forty yards behind the group.

"Hakim?" queried one of the men, the oldest among the four.

"That's me. What do you want?"

"I'm Jim Trebane. This is my wife, Melissa, and my son, Buck. That's Gary Shanks, his wife Ellen, and their children, Peter and Elizabeth. And that's—"

"I know him," Hakim replied, interrupting Trebane. He looked at Sam Oxford, and asked, "You remember what I said last time I saw you, Oxford?"

Sam licked his lips nervously, kept his hands held wide, and managed to croak, "I surely do, Mr. Hakim."

"Hakim!" the Arab asserted, irritated.

"Huh?"

"Hakim is my first name. No 'mister.' Just Hakim. Why have you come here, when you know what I said?"

Oxford looked at Jim Trebane in a silent plea for help, but said nothing.

"We want to join your group," Trebane said. "We want to be a part of this new civilization you're building."

Hakim raised his black eyebrows with surprise. He hadn't expected this. He replied, "We don't allow slavers; we fight against slavers. There will be no slavers in the world that we build!"

"We understand, and we agree," Trebane responded quickly. "But will you allow *former* slavers? Will you allow people who have seen that they were wrong, and who now want to do right?"

Hakim blinked. *Well, I'll be!* he thought to himself. *I had not counted on this at all. I think Jacen needs to decide this one. Actually, I think the whole group needs to. Still, it could be a trap.*

Hakim didn't reply. Trebane took that as an opportunity, and with a brief nod to the others, kept his right hand outstretched and slowly, gingerly, took hold of the muzzle of the M4 that was slung over his shoulder with his left hand, removed it from his shoulder, laid it on the ground, and then stepped away from it. The others followed suit with their weapons.

"In your new world, can former enemies become friends, and former masters and slaves become equal co-workers?" Trebane asked bluntly.

****

"Absolutely *not*! These people killed my Julie! I think we oughta shoot 'em down right here and now!" raged Elijah, his voice breaking with a combination of grief and anger. Ginny Moore ran to her dad and wrapped her arms around him, tears streaming down her face.

"Elijah, I know what our community did to your wife, and I'm so sorry. It was horrible. But none of us here participated in that raid. In fact, we all spoke against it," the elder Trebane confessed.

The group had gathered around the fire pit. Each adult was carrying a rifle or shotgun in case the former slavers were meant to be a diversion preparatory to a surprise attack. Gus and Phil were scouting in the brush, keeping an eye out for trouble. Trebane and his people were unarmed and seated in a tight knot, looking very worried and anxious about their future. Some among them were silently questioning whether this had been such a good idea after all.

Trebane had repeated the words he had spoken to Hakim once the whole Bedford community had gathered. The response had been shock, disbelief, and not a small amount of anger. The brutality that the former slaves had received at the hands of the Pittsburgh community was not going to be soon forgotten, or forgiven.

Jacen watched the arguing and the bitter words for a few minutes, then walked over to Hakim and spoke quietly so that no one else would hear, "I don't think this is a diversion, Hakim. These people are risking their lives to come here. The whole scenario is so implausible that it's putting us *on guard* rather than causing us to be unwary."

"I agree," the Arab replied, "this is something these folks need to work out among themselves. If we try to insert too much leadership here, we are going to position ourselves as unwelcome interlopers. Let's go out and find Gus and Phil.

We'll take their place on watch and let them come and be part of the conversation."

Jacen walked into the middle of the group and waited for the debate to cease, then spoke up: "Hakim and I are agreed that this is something you folks must decide. We're going to replace Gus and Phil on watch, so they can be part of this. There's only one thing I ask of the Bedford group: no violence, please! We're not going to shoot anybody. The worst we will do is feed these people an evening meal and tomorrow morning's breakfast, and send them on their way. But we're not going to harm anyone as long as they behave themselves. Can we all agree on that one point?"

Sober faces nodded agreement all around the campfire, except for Elijah.

"Elijah, I need your word on this, too. I know that if you give me your word, I'll have nothing to worry about."

Elijah turned his back on the group, fists clenched. He stood motionless for a moment, shoulders shaking, then turned back, tears coursing down his sunburnt, leather-like face. He nodded and replied hoarsely, "You have my word. No violence."

Jacen nodded gravely, and said, "Good. Let me suggest one more thing. Today, just talk. Decide nothing until tomorrow. That'll give everyone a chance to think about it, and to sleep on it. Tonight Hakim and I will tell you what we think, but neither of us will vote. It's going to be your decision." With that, Hakim and Jacen walked across the meadow and plunged into the forest on the west side.

In a few moments, Gus and Phil walked out of the brush and joined the group. Katie Blackwell was talking at the moment. "I don't think we will give ourselves much of a chance at a new life, a new civilization, if we start with so much bitterness and anger."

"Not going to be much of beginning if we start with slavers, either," Ginny Moore, Elijah's twenty-one year old daughter, snapped back.

"But they have rejected that life, Ginny," objected Misty Randall. Misty and Ginny were best friends, practically inseparable.

"It's pretty convenient to reject it *after* we destroyed it. I'd be more convinced if they had rejected it when we were still wearing shackles," Elijah retorted.

"What do you say about that, Trebane?" Phil challenged roughly.

"I never was for slavery. All I can say is that I didn't have the courage to stand up for my convictions. I'm ashamed of that."

"Oh, yeah? Okay! And I guess we're just supposed to say, 'Welcome! Come right in! Join right up!' Right? You expect us to forget the murders, the abuse, the lash?" Randy replied angrily.

"Now wait just a minute, Randy! Be fair! In all my days there I never saw Jim Trebane or Buck or Melissa abuse a single one of us. Maybe they were part of that community, maybe they kept silent, but I never saw them mistreat anyone," Gus rejoined. "Did you?"

Randy began to reply, then stopped and shut his mouth, thinking. After a moment, he agreed, "Come to think of it, no. In fact, Trebane kept Tim Shanks from whipping me one day. Stepped right in between us. I guess I never even thought about it."

"I can speak for Melissa," said Katie. "She never even so much as said a harsh word to me. Last winter when I had the flu, she saw that I was well-cared for."

"Same here," Trisha Linder said. "She and Buck and Jim were always kind to me."

"As far as I'm concerned," Elijah said bitterly, "it's either me or them!"

"There's no need to say nothing like that, 'Lijah. You're part of us, you're part of our community. If we had to choose between you and them, there'd be no decision at all. You belong with us. We're not going to lose you and Ginny in order to gain anyone," Phil said softly. All around the fire murmured agreement.

The lump in his throat was too big to allow him to reply; Elijah just nodded his appreciation, turned from the group and walked a small distance away from everyone. He stood looking at the setting sun as he tried to control his emotions. After a few minutes, he returned, and sat down on a log.

The assembly sat or stood silent, not knowing what to do next. Lynn Linder finally spoke up, "I was there when Mr. Trebane spoke against the raid that killed Elijah's wife."

"What?"

"Art Miller was injured during the raid. Mrs. Shanks came and ordered me to help with the bandaging. I was there in the main building when Mr. Trebane and Buck started arguing with Mr. Beaufort and Mr. Shanks. Mr. Trebane was furious. Shanks finally told him that if he didn't shut up, he'd have Tim go shoot Mrs. Trebane down, right on the spot! Gary jumped up, looked at his dad and shouted at him that if Tim so much as reached for a weapon, Gary would kill him. I thought we were about to have a war right there. It was Tim that did it. It was Tim who killed Julie Moore. He said so during that argument. Acted like he was right proud of it, too. Gary and Sam, they sided with Mr. Trebane. I was there," Lynn affirmed.

Phil looked at Gary Shanks and demanded, "Why did *you* come here? Why did you leave your mother and your brother?"

Gary stared at Phil with a level gaze before looking down at his hands. After a moment he confessed, "I *hated* that life. I *hated* what it was doing to me, and to my wife, and to my kids. I guess I just didn't know how to break free. My mom, my brother . . . well, they're family. But after you guys shot up our camp, and I had to learn how to use the business end of a hoe again, well, I had a lot of time to think. And I realized – slavery is evil. And *I* was becoming evil. It had to stop.

"Ten days ago I told my mom that I was taking Ellen and my kids and leaving, for good. If you folks don't take us, we'll travel on and start somewhere by ourselves, I guess. I'm done with slavery. And if I ever see it again, I'm going to do the same thing you folks did. I'm going to put a stop to it, or die trying."

He looked up again at Phil with that level gaze, and said softly, "That's why I'm here, Philip. I'm hoping that maybe your community goes several steps beyond simply not having slaves. I'm hoping that you're willing to forgive, and to give us a chance to become a part of your group."

****

"I think we should accept them. So does Hakim," Jacen replied in answer to a query from Gus. It was growing late and the night air had become crisp. The discussion around the fire had lasted all evening, sometimes going far afield, but always coming back to the dilemma posed by the newcomers.

"But what if it's a trap?" Gus insisted.

"I might be wrong, but it doesn't have the feel of a trap. We could've just as easily killed these folks as invited them to share our supper. With what Elijah and Ginny and others have suffered from their hands, they must have realized the danger they were putting themselves in when they came. Furthermore, we've won decisively every firefight we've had with the Pittsburgh group. They couldn't have considered us an easy target. And I really don't think any of that group wants to tangle with Hakim again."

Gary Shanks spoke up, "If you fear that this is some sort of a trap, take our weapons away. Search through all of our belongings, and confiscate all the guns. We are five adults who are willing workers: post an armed guard to watch us. Let us prove ourselves, that all we wish to do is become a part of this new civilization that you're building."

"You'd accept terms like that?" Elijah asked.

"We discussed it before we ever left Pittsburgh, and we all agreed among ourselves. We understand the difficulty our request presents for you. But we are completely sincere: we want to be part of what you people are trying to accomplish."

"How long would this time of proving be?" asked Randy.

"That's your decision. We're prepared to accept what ever you decide on that matter," Jim Trebane replied.

For several moments no one spoke. A moisture pocket in one of the logs on the fire popped, sending a small cascade of sparks skyward. The full moon slowly began to peek over the ridge to the east. The plaintive cry of a distant coyote sounded. No one broke the stillness; everyone sat absorbed in their own thoughts.

Finally Jacen stirred himself and stood up. "Think on it," he said, addressing the whole group, "sleep on it. We'll delay tomorrow's work schedule until after lunch. After breakfast, we'll make our decision.

"We'll have a regular community watch schedule tonight. Randy and Phil, I believe you two are first up. In addition, Hakim and I will each do a stint guarding our visitors, for their safety and ours." He looked at Hakim and added, "I'll take first watch."

CHAPTER 20

The morning came with clear skies and unseasonably cold temperatures. It was a reminder that winter was approaching. Jacen lay in his bed for a moment, not wanting to get up just yet. It was still dark out, but there were sounds of activity around the communal campfire. Someone was building up the fire in preparation for making coffee.

When the weather turned bad, everyone did their own cooking in their own cabins. Otherwise, it was done at a large fire pit built for the purpose. Rough-hewn tables and benches were close by. It was a means of bonding as a community, sharing news and information, and discussing work assignments and community issues. Apart from all that, everyone simply enjoyed being together for a few moments prior to beginning the work of each day.

Jacen groaned. It had been a long night. Hakim and he had seen to the guarding of their visitors by themselves, in two long shifts. Jacen had been relieved at around two AM by his friend, and so the night had been shortened considerably. The normal community watch stint was a three-hour shift, every other day. Jacen had put in his time the night before, then last night had done the extra duty, and he knew that tonight he would have his turn on community watch once again.

He sat up, swinging his feet down to the rough floor, picking up a splinter in the process. "OUCH!" he grumbled. Luckily, items like tweezers, packaged in hermetically-sealed blister-packs that were all but impossible to open, were still readily available in the ruins of old drug stores. Jacen extracted the splinter by candlelight and then dressed. Hakim had not come in yet from his shift of the watch.

He stepped out of his cabin into the dim twilight of the predawn. Thirty yards away, Elijah Moore was busy getting coffee started. No one else was in sight. The fire created an inviting sphere of warmth and light in the early morning, and Jacen was drawn to it. The sky was clear overhead, stars fading into the purple, but a dense, cold fog hung low over the meadow. Though he could not see them, he heard the horses frolicking in the large corral.

"Mornin', Jace."

"Good morning, 'Lijah," he acknowledged with a smile. He loved the crusty older man. Elijah was stubborn, opinionated, and could carry a deep streak of resentment. But he was also reliable, steadfast, and loyal. And in rare moments he displayed a dry sense of humor that Jacen absolutely treasured. Elijah's daughter, Ginny, shared her dad's stubbornness, but was far more joyful than he. Jacen was slowly coming to treasure Ginny, too.

He located his and Elijah's cups, wiped out the ants and pine needles, and poured them each a steaming cup of coffee. They sat in silence, enjoying one another's company and the dawning of a new day.

They were each working on a second cup when Elijah broke the early morning stillness. "Don't know what to do about our visitors," he confessed. "I hate those slavers. I just hate 'em. I won't never forget that they murdered my wife in cold blood.

"But on the other hand, I also know that Gus is right. None of these that came yesterday joined in the cruelty of the rest of them, 'cept maybe Gary. I never knew him to go out of his way to be mean. But he *was* involved in capturing slaves."

"I know," Jacen replied. "He and Tim escorted me to the settlement when they captured me. Gary is, or at least *was*, a mixed bag. He kept Tim from killing me, but in his rage at Tim Gary threatened to kill me himself. I never had any dealings one way or the other with the Trebanes, or with Sam Oxford."

The two men lapsed into silence again. After several minutes, Elijah got up and added a few more logs to the blaze, getting coals ready for the morning cooking. "We need to find some chickens somewhere. I heard my pappy tell that they had found some good egg-layers when he was young. Anarchs stole the cluckers eventually, but he said those eggs were sure tasty while they lasted."

He sat down again, then confessed, "I am dead-set against allowing these slavers into our company. But I'd like to be convinced otherwise. I think it'd be healthy for us to grow. We need more people. And I got to admit, I love the Shanks' kids, Peter and Elizabeth. They're just pure sweetness, good-natured and respectful. I know that you're in favor of admitting these folks, Jacen. What can you tell me that might change my mind?"

For a moment Jacen said nothing; the question had caught him off-guard. Then a thought came to him, and he asked, "Elijah, did you ever hear how I came to be captured by old man Shanks?"

"Nope. Never did."

"Well, it was after Hakim and I had an argument, and neither of us was willing to forgive. Hakim's a religious man, worships somebody he calls *Isa*. I've never heard of Isa, but that's beside the point. Anyway, Hakim was trying to show me that I had no *reason* for my moral beliefs, since I don't believe in God. He was saying that, unless you believe in some sort of God, there's no way to justify moral convictions. I misunderstood him, thought he was telling me that I was *immoral.* I started firing back at him—with my mouth, I mean—and we got into a pretty good tiff. I started accusing Hakim of being ready to kill anyone who crossed him. You may have noticed that Hakim's a pretty good fighter?"

"Yeah, I'd say he's pretty fair," Elijah agreed, dryly, "he probably could have taken on all those slavers by himself."

"Yeah, he could've. They'd have started disappearing one by one over several days, and would've never caught him. He's taught me everything I know in the way of tactics. He's a formidable opponent.

"Anyway, I thought he was accusing me of being immoral, so I started accusing him of being bloodthirsty. I accused him of being trigger-happy, and killing when it wasn't necessary. Oh, I really hit him with some low blows —stuff I knew in my heart wasn't true! Then one night I refused to pull my watch stint; told him it wasn't necessary. Told him there was no danger, and that he was just paranoid."

"What happened?" Elijah asked.

"He pulled an all-nighter on watch. Next morning, when I got up, he was packing his gear to leave. Basically told me that he didn't appreciate my accusation that he enjoyed killing. He said that I would wind up *getting* him killed if we stuck together. Well, *I* told *him* that *I* didn't like being called immoral.

"Neither of us would get down off of our high-horses. We refused to forgive one another, or as Hakim puts it, we refused to 'grant grace' to one another. As I look back at it now, I realize that I was behaving like an idiot. I nearly destroyed the very best friendship I've ever had. He never did call me immoral, really. He simply pointed out that I have no anchor point for my moral beliefs, no *reason* to be moral. Since then, I've seen that he is exactly correct. I thought morality was universal, because I thought everyone was basically good. Hakim showed me I was wrong, and I was *furious.* In my pride, I was willing to destroy our friendship to get rid of this guy who had so easily exposed me.

"And in his pride, he was unwilling to overlook my insults against him. He simply pulled up stakes and left. Within twenty-four hours, I—who had said there was no danger—was in shackles.

"Now here's my point, 'Lijah. Both Hakim and I were in the wrong. We both nearly wrecked a friendship that we now treasure, because we refused to forgive one another. That stupid pride separated us. And it made it easy for the slavers to capture me. Nearly destroyed my life!

"Don't make the same mistake, Elijah. The Pittsburgh slavers have already destroyed one part of your life, when they took Julie from you. Don't let them destroy the rest of it by carrying bitterness against them for the rest of your life. Your bitterness will destroy *you*, not *them*. And these people were not involved in the death of your wife. You won't bring justice to Tim Shanks by taking vengeance on the Trebanes, or Gary, or Sam."

Elijah didn't respond. In his heart he knew that the sincere young man was right. He wondered how someone so young could have so much wisdom. He just didn't know if he was ready to accept it.

****

"We've talked, argued, discussed, and debated. Now it's time for a decision. First, we'll decide whether or not to accept these into our community. If the decision is negative, we'll return their weapons and allow them to go on their way without harm. If the decision is positive, then we'll move on to consider whether there will be some sort of probationary period." Jacen looked around the group, and decided to start with Elijah and Ginny.

"Elijah, you go first. You and Ginny have more riding on this than the rest of us. It's only right that your vote should have the most influence. What do you say?"

Elijah stood up and looked around at his assembled friends. He said, "What you and I talked about early this morning, Jacen, changed my mind. Until then, I was opposed. But what you said made more sense than anything else I've heard. I'm not going to allow the rest of my life to be ruined with bitterness. I have a lot of doubts about this, but I vote to include them, all of them."

He turned to Gary Shanks, and said, "It's liable to be many years, if ever, that I consider you a friend, or that I can look at you without being reminded of your brother and your dad. I may never like you. But I've decided that I can work alongside of you." Elijah returned to his seat.

"Ginny, how about you?" Jacen asked gently.

In a voice that was almost too soft to hear, the young woman replied while looking down at the ground, "I'm voting with my dad."

Ultimately the vote was unanimous to accept the newcomers, although each individual expressed great reservations. It was then decided that the former slavers would not be allowed to have their weapons or serve as part of the nightly community watch for the first six weeks, at which time the issue would be revisited.

****

The newcomers were not received with a complete cold shoulder, however. The whole community pitched in to help build their cabins, and the women and children were warmly welcomed immediately. It raised not a few eyebrows—and smiles—when Elijah Moore began taking great delight in carving wooden toys for the Shanks' children, which, needless to say, Peter and Elizabeth also found to be delightful. It was clear that he did not hold the children responsible for the actions of the parents.

Jacen and Hakim were happy to learn that Jim and Buck Trebane were both excellent carpenters, and blacksmiths as well, craftsmen who were capable of making barrels, buckets, wheels, furniture, and many other useful items. The Trebanes had made all of the Pittsburgh community's two-wheeled carts.

One of the two carts that the newcomers had brought was heavily loaded with the Trebanes' tools, including a large sawmill blade that Jim had scavenged, though he had not yet figured out how to power it. The other cart was loaded with the new group's personal belongings, and additional canned goods.

Sam Oxford was an illiterate but otherwise capable man of thirty-five. Of medium build and pleasant but taciturn disposition, he proved to be a hard worker with an uncommonly good grasp of farming. He'd never married, and was so quiet that the women tended to forget he was there. When Phil observed that Sam was open about his own inability to read, and equally open about his desire to learn, Phil publicly acknowledged that Jacen was teaching him to read. Soon Jacen had two students, and they no longer held the lessons in secret during hay-cutting breaks.

Gary Shanks was a study in contradictions. Though originally complicit in the Pittsburgh community's slavery operation, once he had become convinced of the fundamental wickedness of it, he had turned completely. Gary and Ellen were thoughtful and sensitive to the suffering of others—perhaps because of the sufferings they had caused—and showed themselves ready to serve the community in whatever way required.

****

"HIYAHH!" Hakim shouted, and waved his coiled rope at Hadar. The big mare began trotting around the inner perimeter of the round pen. Hakim continued to drive her by waving his hands and the rope. He made her trot for about two minutes, then he turned his back on her and walked to the center of the pen, making kissing sounds with his lips. She stopped trotting immediately and followed him into the center of the pen. He turned and stroked her nose affectionately for a moment, then backed up, waved his hands and drove her back to trotting, this time in the opposite direction. This went on for thirty minutes, until the horse's sleek coat was damp with sweat. Finally Hakim called the buckskin to himself, and patted her neck.

"Good girl, Hadar. You're learning, aren't you? We'll have that saddle on you again soon." He took an apple out of his pocket, and gave it to the horse. He then walked over to the pen gate, with Hadar following obediently behind him, and let the horse back into the big corral with the other animals.

Randy was outside the pen, leaning on the fence, and watching with bemused interest. He called out, "How are those ribs doing?"

Hakim walked over, and leaned on the fence. "Okay, I guess. It still hurts to wave my hands and this rope, but it's getting better. Thanks for asking, Randy."

"I don't see how this 'round pen work', as you call it, is accomplishing anything. Okay, I can see that you have Hadar trained to obey in terms of trotting around the pen and so on, but how is that helping you get a saddle on her back?"

Hakim smiled. "It doesn't look like much, does it?"

"Honestly? No, it doesn't."

"Hadar needs to learn that she is below the rank of a human, in terms of pecking order. She's learning that we call the shots and she obeys. I make her run when I want her to run. I make her stop when I want her to stop. Not when she wants to stop, but when I want her to stop.

"I'm taking longer with this than is probably necessary, but that's because, first, I've never done it before and I want to get it right. Second, I really don't want to get all busted up again, so I'm making sure she's really ready."

"Can you teach me to do it? Can I start on a second horse?"

"I can teach you the little that I know, and I can let you read the same book I'm reading. I'd be glad to. Are you really interested?"

"I am. I understood what you said several weeks ago about us needing to improve efficiencies, and I think you're right about that. I guess I've also got another, more basic, motive: I really, really don't want to haul a cart all the way to Colorado this next spring!"

Hakim laughed, and said, "Nor do I. I'd much rather ride than walk or pull. Tell you what: you pick a mare out of the larger corral, and we'll get started right now!"

CHAPTER 21

The next three weeks passed uneventfully. At mealtimes the separation between the former slavers and the former slaves was most obvious. Each group tended to sit by themselves, and while both groups were *civil* toward one another, there is a significant difference between civility and warmth. But Jacen sensed that the ice was thawing.

If the relationship between the two groups was slowly warming up, the weather was doing the opposite. It was definitely getting colder. All of the leaves had fallen, and frost had become routine. There had even been one day when everyone suspected that it would snow, though in the end it was but a very cold rain that had fallen.

Jacen compiled the coming week's community work assignments each Sunday evening. He made sure that the hotheads—Elijah, primarily—were not sent out unaccompanied on tasks with any of the former slavers. It was going to take some time before that was possible.

There were only a few weeks left in which hay could be profitably cut. He looked over his roster, and decided that it was Randy Bartwell's turn, with Gary Shanks assisting. He decided that on Tuesday they would try one more cutting on the meadow three miles to the the east. While they were there, they could also pick up the hay that had been drying since it had been cut the week previously.

****

"Ready?" Randy asked.

"Yep. Let's go." Gary Shanks responded. "Unfortunately, that hay's not going to cut itself."

"Nope."

The two men leaned into the harness and started the heavy cart rolling. Their scythes lay in the back of the cart, along with a file for sharpening the blades. Randy's M4 was slung over his shoulder; Gary was unarmed. It was part of the terms of the probation period, an arrangement that the former slavers chafed under but had accepted for the purpose of earning trust.

"How's the horse training going, Randy?"

"Great! I'll be putting a saddle on Doll this afternoon for the very first time! I'm really excited about it. I'm going to let her get used to it for a couple of days, and then maybe by the end of the week I can ride her for just a little. Can't wait!"

Randy was discovering a natural—if untaught—talent for working with the big, graceful animals. The slim, wiry man had picked a fine mahogany-colored bay mare and had been working with it for the last several weeks under the Arab's close tutelage. Somehow along the way the horse had acquired the name 'Doll', or 'Doll-baby'.

"Hakim seem to be healing up?"

"Uh-huh. He's not back to full strength yet, but he's getting close." Randy chuckled, and added, "He's got his nose bent out of joint because I'll be riding Doll before he gets back up on Hadar. But that's just because he has been so interested in training me that he's not put in a lot of time on his own horse the last couple weeks. The man is a natural-born coach."

198

"He really is. You know, Randy, my initial impression of Hakim was that he was little more than a civilized Anarch. I've never seen someone with such a capacity for violence. I think he could have treed the whole Pittsburgh settlement all by himself, if he had wanted to." Shanks paused for a moment, thinking, and then continued, "But watching him the last couple of weeks, he seems like he *hates* violence. The man has two different natures. What am I seeing, Randy?"

"Well, I'd say you're seeing him pretty much as we all do. Don't ever cross the man! Well, wait, that doesn't sound quite right. . . ," Randy hesitated, trying to put his thoughts in order. Then he continued, "Okay, it's not like he's got some kind of hair-trigger temper or something, Gary. He's actually very patient. I guess what I mean is, don't ever become his enemy. I think you folks at Pittsburgh found that out first-hand."

"Yeah, I'd say so," Gary agreed dryly, shifting his shoulders in the harness as they trudged along.

"On the other hand," Randy continued, still thinking on the matter, "he's not a man prone to violence unless he is defending something from attack. He's not one to search out trouble for trouble's sake. But if someone comes looking for trouble, they'll find that Hakim is a whole lot more than what they can handle."

****

The two men had been working steadily for several hours, and it was now mid-morning. They had first raked the dry hay that had been cut the week prior. The cart was now filled with the dry stuff, and both men were wielding scythes, cutting the remainder of the field. Randy had worked his way to the edge of the meadow, next to a dense thicket of evergreens and laurel. His M4 was cross slung on his back to keep it out of his way. Hakim had taught them all to never put their weapons down during work details away from the settlement.

199

Randy dropped his scythe, straightened up, and wiped his brow. It was one of those unusually warm late fall days, and the exertions of cutting hay had raised quite a sweat. As he stood resting for a moment, looking up into the sky, he realized that he was hearing something stirring in the thicket. He glanced around. Gary was working about sixty feet behind him, further into the field.

A stick snapped in the thicket. Randy's eyes narrowed, and he unslung his M4 and chambered a round. He moved stealthily into the thick, darkened, copse. Moving from the bright sunlit field into the dark shadows of the dense thicket left him briefly blinded as his eyes adjusted. He moved a few more steps.

Suddenly he heard a menacing, rumbling growl to his right. It took all his courage to remain still, but he managed to control himself. Slowly, ever so slowly, he pivoted his head to the right, and then froze. Peering at him out of the thick undergrowth was a massive black bear!

* * * * * * * * *

"I honestly don't think he even knows I'm alive," moaned Ginny Moore.

"Nonsense, girl! The boy is not blind! I've seen him look your way," assured Angela Bartwell, as the two worked on the settlement's laundry. Like most other tasks at present, each person served the whole community.

"Well, he's never tried to talk to me. He doesn't try to sit near me during meals. He's never put me in his work detail. Angie, I really don't think he notices me! Or if he does, he obviously doesn't think of me any differently than he thinks of, well, you, for that matter!"

Angie sighed. "Listen, honey, he notices you. Trust me. I've seen it. He's just scared to death. I think he's just scared of lovely young ladies. And I think he's scared of becoming attached to someone again, having lost his family so tragically."

Ginny thought on that as she rubbed the shirt across the old washboard. She had known enough of her own heartaches to understand Jacen's aloofness. Her own mother had died in her arms after being cut down in a hail of bullets when the Pittsburgh slavers had attacked their settlement. Unlike Jacen, however, she was not holding back on forming a new relationship; she greatly desired it. *Funny,* she thought to herself, *how differently we all react to tragedy. Jacen has shut down, but I'm the opposite.*

****

The bear snarled, and stood on its hind feet. Avoiding staring at the big animal, Randy slowly swung his weapon around, trying to bring it to bear on the threatening beast. Too late! Without warning the bear lunged at him, roaring ferociously! One swipe of a massive paw knocked Randy back into the field, the skin on his chest flayed and bleeding profusely. He lost his grip on his rifle and it went flying. The bear bounded out of the tangle of undergrowth, and then stopped, blinking uncertainly in the bright sun. It sniffed for a moment, located Randy, then rose up on its hind quarters again. Randy was struggling to his feet, staggering backwards, trying desperately to get away, yet afraid to turn his back on the enraged animal. He tripped over his scythe, and fell again. The bear stood before the bleeding man, fangs bared and snarling, and then charged the last few feet. It raked Randy's left leg with its claws, and Randy screamed, then fainted.

****

"Yeah! Good! I think you're getting the hang of it!" Jim Trebane said, encouraging Jacen. The two men were working with a whipsaw, hand-cutting planks from the long trunk of a felled tree. Trebane had built a rough frame that allowed him to stand on top of the log while Jacen stood below, with the other end of the saw. They were cutting boards to put a floor in the Shanks' cabin.

"Where'd you find this saw?" Jacen asked, brushing the coarse sawdust off of his hair and shoulders.

"The area to the west of Pittsburgh was once home to an Amish community," the carpenter replied. "Apparently they all died off long ago. On one of our forays we found the remains of an old, deserted community with several of their barns still standing. They were almost completely intact: those people really knew how to build! Anyway, one of the barns was filled with hand tools of all sorts. That's where I got most of my stuff, including this whipsaw."

Jacen knew about the Amish people. They were a folk who loved a simple lifestyle, and had eschewed all of the newer technologies. Consequently, they weren't significantly impacted by the loss of electricity generation, petroleum refining, and manufacturing that brought the rest of the world to a halt.

The Amish never visited the ruins to scavenge. Instead, they made or grew everything that they needed. Jacen had thought much about the skills possessed by the Amish, and hoped that on their way west next spring they would run across some Amish communities. He was hoping to find some skilled Amish who would join them.

West of Ludwigs Corner had been a good-sized Amish settlement. Years ago, Jacen's father used to trade with them. Then one day the Anarchs located the neat, well-maintained community, and massacred them all. The Amish folk had religious convictions against violence, even in self-defense. The Anarchs had no such convictions. It had been a one-sided battle, with an inevitable outcome.

"We're done with this one. Add it to the stack," Jim instructed. "I figure that ten more boards like this and we'll have all the wood we need for Gary's floor."

Jacen carried the heavy plank over to the stack of cut lumber, and set it down. He walked back under the cutting frame and looked up at Trebane's smiling face. He grinned in return and took hold of his end of the saw. "This'll put shoulders on a man, for sure," he moaned, as he pulled the saw down, beginning a new cut and unleashing a small avalanche of sawdust.

"That it will," Trebane laughed in agreement as he pulled the saw back up, "that it will."

****

Gary had not noticed when Randy disappeared into the brush. The first time he realized that something was happening was when he heard the bear roaring and snarling. He looked around in time to see Randy as he was knocked backwards out of the thicket. Racing over to assist the injured man, Gary shouted for help, forgetting momentarily that the two were alone. Looking around he spied Randy's M4 on the ground and snatched it up. The enraged bruin had clamped its jaws around Randy's calf but released him and stood on its hind legs again, preparing to charge this new challenger.

Gary jammed the mode selector to full auto, and raced toward the bear, shouting. His assault momentarily confused the animal, and the delay sealed the animal's doom. When Shanks was ten feet away, he held the trigger down and stitched a pattern across the bear's chest and up its neck, placing the last five or ten rounds into the stunned animal's mouth. The huge predator collapsed into a bloody heap.

"RANDY!" Gary shouted as he dropped the weapon on the ground. The older man was unconscious, and bleeding profusely from multiple wounds. Gary carefully removed what was left of the unconscious man's shirt, and then began working feverishly to stop the flow of blood. He ripped off his own shirt and rapidly began to tear it up, using the strips to bandage the contusions. *Gotta get him back to the settlement immediately!* he thought. *He's probably going to die anyway, but I've got to try to save him.* The pallor of Randy's normally leathery complexion worried Gary as he attempted to staunch the bleeding.

Randy's eyelids fluttered briefly, and then opened. He tried to move.

"Lie still!" Gary commanded fiercely.

"Wha, what, what ha, happened to me?" Randy murmured, disoriented.

"Hush! You've been mauled by a bear. Please, don't move."

Randy didn't respond, having fainted again.

****

The unmistakable staccato rattle of an assault rifle on full automatic stopped Elijah in his tracks. He and Phil were east of the settlement about half a mile, snaking downed logs into the encampment, later to be cut up as firewood against the approaching winter.

"Where'd that come from?" he asked the big man.

"Not sure, 'Lijah, but I think it was behind us, back farther east."

Elijah thought about it for a moment, then clapped his hands together sharply. "Randy is out that way, cutting hay," he exclaimed. He turned and looked at Phil, eyes flashing with anger and suspicion, and continued, "And he's with that Shanks boy. I bet Shanks tried to attack him!"

Momentarily infected by Elijah's suspicion, Phil cried, "C'mon, 'Lijah! Grab your rifle! Randy might need help!"

The two men began running down the trail, headed for the meadow.

****

Back in the round pen, Hakim heard the distant stutter of the M4 also. He slipped the halter off Hadar and opened the gate leading to the main corral. "We'll finish this later, girl," he said affectionately as he slapped her gently on the rump, and then slipped between the fence rails and ran into the camp with his weapon.

Locating Jacen, he asked, "Did you hear that gunfire?"

"I did. I was just about to come look for you."

"Organize a defense of the camp, just in case. I'm going to check it out."

"Hakim, unless I arm Jim, Sam, and Buck, it's just going to be me and the women. Gus, Phil, and Randy are all out on chores."

"Oh, for crying out loud!" Hakim said, slapping his leg in frustration.

"We'd better both stick around," Jacen advised. "I trust the new ones, but if there's trouble afoot, more likely than not it has something to do with them or their former community."

Hakim nodded. "Yeah. That makes sense. Okay, you get the Trebanes, Oxford, and the Shanks all into the Shanks' cabin. It will be easier to protect them, and to keep an eye on 'em. I'll arm all of our women with the shotguns, and put Mary and Angie outside of Shanks' cabin, to seal it off. You position the Linders out of sight, backing up Mary and Angie. We'll put the rest of the women in their own cabins, keeping watch."

Jacen nodded, then asked, "Where are we going to be?"

"Scramble up the embankment, Jace, and hide in those bushes. You should have a good field of fire over most of the camp. I'll do picket duty, out east about two hundred yards. If I hear any shooting back here, I'll come on the double.

"Let's get to it!"

****

Gary slung the M4 on his back then gathered the older man up in his arms, and started across the meadow at a stumbling run. He saw that the jostling caused by carrying the limp figure in his arms increased Randy's blood loss, though he could travel faster than with a cart. But it was more important to stop the blood loss, so he gently laid Randy in the cart on the hay, and struggled into the harness. Staggering briefly under the load, he began trotting back towards the settlement.

CHAPTER 22

Elijah Moore and Phil Gonzales raced down the trail toward the meadow where Gary and Randy had been assigned to cut hay.

"Whoa, Elijah, slow down!" wheezed the bigger man, after about eight minutes of running. Elijah stopped, also breathing hard. Phil leaned over, put his hands on his knees, and tried to catch his breath. "If I'm gonna be in any shape to be useful when we get there, we gotta slow down! Whew!"

He straightened up after a minute, and said, "Let's just do a fast walk, okay?" Elijah just nodded, too winded to talk. They resumed their progress, walking at a fast pace down the trail.

After a moment, Elijah snarled, "If that was Shanks we heard, he's a dead man. I just knew they were waitin' till we turned our backs on 'em. I'll bet Shanks has killed Randy!"

"Don't jump to conclusions, Elijah," Phil advised, "we don't know what happened just yet."

"True. Could be that Randy was holdin' off an attack by Shanks. Maybe it's Shanks that's dead."

"Oh for crying out loud, Elijah! Get a grip on yourself! I doubt there's been any trouble between Gary and Randy. It's probably something else entirely."

"You don't know that!" snapped Elijah.

"No, I don't! And that's my point! Neither of us have *any* idea what those shots were about. Don't invent trouble where there isn't any!"

"Hey, Phil! I didn't invent that slaver camp, did I! And Shanks and Trebane and Oxford were all part of it, weren't they!"

Phil didn't respond. He realized that it was useless to talk to the suspicious man. He'd have to wait until the facts came out. Stubborn as Elijah was, Phil knew his friend would accept the facts when they were made clear.

He didn't have long to wait. They rounded a curve in the trail and spotted one of the carts about three hundred yards distant. It was being pulled by only one man, who was struggling to move it along at a trot. The man saw them and began waving his arms and crying out. It was Gary Shanks! Randy was nowhere to be seen. And what's more, Shanks had an assault rifle slung over his shoulder: he was supposed to be unarmed!

"NO! NO! Where's Randy, you dirty . . . ?" Elijah shouted, not even finishing his sentence, so filled was he with outrage and accusation. He ran towards Shanks, chambering a round as he went.

For Phil, time suddenly slowed to a crawl. He knew with perfect clarity what was about to happen, as though seeing it in a vision. In that instant it registered in his mind that Shanks was crying out for *help*, not shouting threats. Phil tried to warn Elijah, but it was too late. Elijah raised the muzzle of the M4 and aimed at the figure in the distance. As Phil finally closed on the enraged man, punctuated spurts of flame began to jet out of the muzzle of the gun. The thought that the range might be too great for a hit passed through Gonzales' mind, but that brief hope faded as he saw Shanks crumple to the ground in the distance. Phil collided with the thin, older man from behind, and wrapped one burly arm around Elijah's chest, pinning his left arm; with his right hand he slapped the hot barrel down so hard that Elijah lost his grip on the weapon, which went spinning away into the underbrush. The two men skidded to a tangled heap on the old, gravel surface of the road.

"What are you DOING, you old fool?" roared Phil Gonzales, jumping to his feet and grabbing Elijah by the back of his shirt, jerking him upright.

"He's done away with Randy! He killed Randy!" choked Elijah, his rage matching Phil's anger.

Phil checked himself from escalating the situation, glared at the angry figure in front of him, and spat out, "*No*, he hasn't! He was calling for *help* when you shot him!"

"Help?" asked Elijah, confused.

"Yes, help!" growled Phil with disgust. He pushed the older man back to the ground roughly, turned, and trotted for the cart and the fallen figure in front of it.

****

All the inhabitants of the camp heard the distant gunshots echoing between the hills. The former slavers were gathered into the Shanks' cabin under guard, waiting until the situation was resolved. Melissa Trebane walked over and hugged Ellen Shanks, and said, "I'm sure it's okay, Ellen. They're probably just hunting. Or maybe it's target practice."

"No, no, that's not it," Ellen replied, "something has happened. I just know something terrible has happened. I feel it in my bones."

"I'm confident that Gary is okay, Ellen. He went out today with Randy, and Randy isn't holding any grudges, so far as I can tell," assured Jim Trebane.

Ellen pressed her lips together and shut her eyes, shaking her head. She felt in her heart that something awful had just transpired.

Peter and Elizabeth clung to her, sensing her fear.

"Mommy, is something wrong?"

****

Jacen heard the second set of shots, and cursed in frustration. He was stuck at the moment, unable to investigate. All they could do was wait.

The community had grown with the new addition of the Pittsburgh contingent. But since the newcomers weren't trusted yet, they couldn't help with tasks such as watch duty and defense. In fact, the former slavers required someone to watch *them*, someone who otherwise would be available for more productive duties. The situation left the whole camp short-handed. They couldn't send out a strong team to investigate the shots when they simultaneously had to care for the defense of the camp.

Jacen scanned the perimeter of the camp with his binoculars. Everything looked normal, and the horses, which he could see from his vantage point, showed no signs of being spooked. He had a growing sense that the camp itself was not facing a threat. But it would be foolhardy to yield to that intuition just yet. The shots could be a diversion to get them to leave the settlement unguarded. He smiled in spite of himself. It was more or less the same tactic Hakim had used to empty the slaver camp of its defense some two months ago. *That's not going to happen to us! Not on my watch!*

No, they would have to wait until some of the men returned from their work detail before they would be able to send anyone to investigate the shootings. Unfortunately, Gus was hunting somewhere far to the north, and probably would not return until tomorrow.

* * * * * * * * * *

Phil raced up to the cart. Gary Shanks lay on the ground, unconscious, bleeding from the thigh and the shoulder. It had not registered until just then, but he noticed that Shanks was not wearing a shirt. *That's odd. He was wearing a shirt this morning. Wonder what happened?* Phil thought to himself. He rolled Shanks over gently and inspected the gunshot wounds.

210

Ah, that's good. Two exit wounds. And they're both clean. Thank goodness our ammo is jacketed, otherwise I'd be able to put my fist into these exit wounds, and Gary would be already dead.

Phil pulled out his knife and slit Gary's jeans up to the thigh wound. He tore strips off, and bandaged Gary's leg first. Gonzales looked up and saw Elijah standing there, pale as a sheet, a look of shock on his face.

"You said, . . . you, . . . did you say . . . ?" Elijah stuttered.

"I *said* he was shouting for *help*. I couldn't make out anything else. Here, stop the bleeding on his shoulder while I take care of his leg. If we're lucky, we might save his life." Phil motioned with his chin to the pile of denim strips he had cut. Elijah got down on his knees and began to compress the wound. Phil noted with relief that the older man's color was returning to normal. For a moment he had feared that Elijah himself was going into shock.

"Where's Randy?" Elijah asked as he worked swiftly, bandaging the wound.

"No idea. Something must have happened. And look, there's no magazine in this weapon. It's not even loaded."

Elijah didn't respond. They finished bandaging Gary, who remained unconscious but was breathing steadily. Phil picked him up and carried him around to the back of the cart to place him in it for the trip back to the camp.

"OH, LORD, please, no, no, no! Oh, no!" Phil cried. The front and side walls of the cart had prevented them from seeing the body in the back of the cart. He gently placed Gary down in the straw next to Randy, and began to weep.

"What? What is it?" asked Elijah from the front. He had begun slipping into a harness and could not see what was in the high-walled cart. When Phil did not answer he slipped out of the harness and ran to the back of the cart. What he saw left him speechless.

There before him was Randy's lifeless body, with numerous blood-soaked bandages about his chest and legs. It was obvious that he had been mauled by an animal. Elijah dropped to the ground in a sitting position, and held his head in his hands. His shoulders shook in sobbing grief. Randy had been the best friend he'd ever had. It had been Randy who had gotten him through the death of Julie. Randy had always been there for him. And now he was gone.

After a moment, Phil stirred. "C'mon, old buddy," he urged, hoarsely. He gently stood Elijah to his feet. "We've still got to try to save Gary. If we get him back quickly, he'll probably be okay. But there's no time to lose."

Elijah nodded, and wiped his face on his sleeve. "Yeah," he choked, "nothing more we can do for Randy. Oh, why did this have to happen? How am I ever going to tell Angela? Poor Angie, this is gonna kill her. This is awful."

****

Hakim was positioned with a good field of fire, watching the road. When the second set of shots echoed off the hills, he clenched his teeth and shook his head angrily, but there was nothing he could do. They couldn't allow a diversion to pull them out of the camp.

Twenty minutes later, he spotted the two-wheeled cart. Whoever was pulling it was trotting, which was very unusual. He put his binoculars to his eyes, and looked again. It was Phil and Elijah. *Huh. That's odd. They didn't take a cart with them this morning. They were going to be snaking logs back to the camp.*

He remained in his hiding place, and carefully searched the woods around them with the glasses, just in case. But when the two started shouting for help, he grabbed his weapon and stood out on the road. As they saw him they redoubled their shouting.

"It was an animal attack, animal attack! We've got a wounded man!"

Hakim signaled that he had heard, and turned and raced back into camp. "ALL CLEAR! ALL CLEAR! WE'VE GOT A WOUNDED MAN COMING INTO CAMP!" he shouted.

The cabins emptied. Everyone was glad to stand down and get back into the open. Angie Bartwell and Mary Anders ran to Hakim and Jacen's cabin, which doubled as the infirmary, and put some water on to boil, cleared the table, and got bandages ready.

Their medical supplies were an eclectic mix of boiled linen bandages, and whatever manufactured supplies had withstood the ravages of time. Typically, eighty-year-old adhesives did not work. Some of the alcohol was still good. Occasionally sealed sterile pads could be found. Most of the medical and surgical tools were in good shape, having been packaged in sterile blister packs. Some antibiotics seemed to retain their efficacy. One of the biggest problems was that very few people really knew what they were doing, especially when it came to emergencies and trauma. Most adults understood infection at an elementary level. But conditions generally were not sterile enough to prevent its onset in the case of major injury.

The two exhausted men finally staggered into the camp with the cart. Everyone began to rush toward the cart, until Phil held his arms up, commanding, "NO! No. Stay away."

Phil turned and looked at Elijah. "We've got to hold it together now, old friend," he whispered. "It's probably best that I go to Ellen Shanks and tell her what happened. You go to Angie." He then turned back to the gathering crowd in front of him, and directed, "Hakim! Jacen! Please get Gary inside, quickly! He's been wounded. He's in the back of the cart."

As they came close, Phil whispered to them, "Listen, I hate to break it to you this way, but Randy's in the back of the cart, too. He's dead. Please, let us tell Angie and Ellen before you say anything to the others." Both men nodded.

Phil walked over to Ellen Shanks, and took her slender hands in his big rough hands. "Ellen," he said quietly, "Gary's got two bullet wounds. He was hit in the thigh, and just below the collar bone. No bones were broken, and no innards were damaged, far as I can tell. I believe he'll pull through, but he's lost some blood. He's unconscious, but I think that's just from shock."

She took the news stoically, though her face was pale. "How did it happen, Phil?"

"There was a mistake made. I'll explain later. Let's just get through this, first. We also have another big problem." His voice caught, and a tear edged out of his eye. "Randy Bartwell is dead," he whispered huskily. "It was an animal attack, probably a bear."

****

"Where's Randy, Elijah? He and Gary were working together. That's their cart. Where . . . ?" Angie's voice trailed off, cut short by the expression of agony on Elijah's leathery face.

"Angie?" Elijah said gently, chin quivering.

"Is he . . . ?" she quavered. One look at his face was all it took. She crumbled. Jim Trebane was standing next to her, and grabbed her as she went down, and helped her over to a bench. She began to sob, "Oh, Randy, Randy, Randy!"

Hakim and Mary were working on Gary, and saw what was going on through the open door. Hakim urged Mary quietly, "Go to her. I've got enough help in here. She needs you right now. Gary's going to be okay. Go to her."

Mary nodded, rinsed her hands, and went outside.

Ellen appeared in the doorway. Misty and Ginny were watching Peter and Elizabeth. Hakim looked up, and said, "Come in, Ellen. Gary's going to want to see your face, not mine, when he comes to."

"Is he going to make it?"

"Yes, I think so. He'll be as weak as a kitten for a couple of weeks, but as long as we can hold infection at bay he should do fine."

She walked over to the table. Gary's jeans had been cut off of him. Hakim was now probing the thigh wound for fragments of denim. Threads of clothing left in a wound was a surefire way to start an infection. Jacen was bathing and bandaging his shoulder. There was blood all over the table. She felt woozy, and sat down on a chair.

"Why is he unconscious?"

"I expect he is in shock. He's lost a lot of blood. In some ways it's better this way. I've got to make sure he doesn't have any clothing fragments inside the wounds, and probing the wound hurts like the devil. If he was awake he'd be crying out in pain, and we'd have to hold him down." Hakim paused, concentrating, working a pair of forceps. "Ah ha! Here it is!" He pulled a ragged, bloody patch of torn denim out of the wound. He sponged the wound, and then motioned to Jacen to bandage it.

Hakim washed his hands and pulled off the bloody apron he was wearing. "Come here, Ellen," he said gently, reaching down to help her up. Then he wrapped his arms around her in a big-brotherly hug. He felt her begin to tremble as she wept quietly.

"I am *so* sorry this happened. None of us quite understand what went on out there. When Gary wakes up, he'll be able to explain a great deal, I imagine. I'll do my very best to keep him from getting infected, and I will pray to Lord Isa that Gary will be healed."

She nodded her head, and then pushed away from him, tears still coursing down her cheeks. "I know you will, Hakim. I trust you. I know you'll do your best for my husband."

****

The news of Randy's death fell like an anvil upon the settlement. Randy had been a favorite of everyone, and Randy's sister, Angie, was disconsolate.

Angie, with Mary Anders comforting her, was in the cabin which the two women shared. Misty Randall and Ginny Moore were watching Peter and Elizabeth Shanks, in

215

the Shanks' cabin. Ellen Shanks was sitting with Gary: he had awoken briefly, and was now sleeping.

Everyone else gathered by the fire-pit. Jacen looked at Phil and Elijah, and asked, "What happened?"

Phil stood up, and began speaking, "I really don't know what happened to Randy. It looks like he was mauled by an animal, a bear by the looks of the claw marks. When Gary is able to talk, he can tell us the story, as I expect he saw the whole thing.

"Elijah and I were snaking logs out of that patch of dead-falls about a mile east of here. We heard automatic weapons fire, to our east, and we knew that Randy and Gary were cutting hay in that direction. So we decided that we had better go investigate."

"That was the first set of shots?" Jacen asked.

"Yes, those were the first ones. We were running down the trail and rounded a bend. There, several hundred yards ahead of us, was Gary, pulling the cart. There was no sign of Randy." Phil stopped, and looked at Elijah, who stood up, trembling, and rubbing his hands together.

"I, uh, . . . I, uh, . . . I, I . . ," Elijah stammered. He stopped, and scrubbed his face with his hands. "Well, uh, I . . . ." He shook his head, and looked back at Phil. "Phil," he asked hoarsely, "please tell them. Just tell them like it was. The whole thing." He sat back down and stared at the ground, shame written on his face.

Jacen looked from one man to the other, began to open his mouth, then thought the better of it, and just waited.

Phil glanced at Elijah, then turned back to Jacen. "Elijah," he began, "was worried that somehow Gary had attacked Randy, and that the shots we heard were a result of that attack."

"What?" Sam Oxford asked, astonished.

"Gary attacked Randy? What on earth for?" Jim Trebane jumped up, agitated. "Why would Gary do that?"

Jacen raised his hands. "Please, men, sit down. Let him finish."

Phil turned to Sam and Jim and replied, "Elijah has had a hard time accepting you all into our community. You know he's been worried that you were sent here as part of a plan to recapture us."

"But that's ridiculous, Phil!" Jim Trebane protested angrily. "We've all disavowed slavery, and our part in the Pittsburgh settlement! We want nothing more to do with those people!"

Phil held up his hands, "I know, I know! And for my part, I believe you. I'm glad you all have come. But you know Elijah's history as well as I do! You know that Tim Shanks *murdered* his wife! And each of you were aligned with the slavers while we were in chains. You can't simply erase that fact! Elijah's having a hard time making the transition from knowing you as slave-holders, to seeing you as neighbors."

"What happened next, Phil?" Jacen queried again.

"Well, we came around the bend in the trail and saw Gary Shanks pulling the cart by himself. We didn't see Randy. Strapped to Gary's back was an assault rifle. Elijah jumped to conclusions, and before I could stop him, he opened fire on Gary. I tackled Elijah and got the gun out of his hands, but it was too late. Gary had already caught two slugs."

Jacen looked at Elijah and asked, "Is this true? Is there any detail you would change about what Phil has said?"

"Everything he said is true. That's exactly how it happened. I shot Gary. I thought he had done away with Randy, and I lost my head," Elijah said quietly, staring at the ground.

"And that was the second set of shots?"

"Yes."

"Did Gary fire on you?"

"No."

"Was he making any moves that you interpreted as threatening?"

Elijah hesitated, and then answered, "Other than the fact that the weapon was slung over his shoulder, no, he did not."

"Did Phil fire any shots?"

"No. He was trying to stop me. All of the shots in the second set were mine."

Everyone sat stunned, disturbed by what they had heard. This was the first major incident they had faced as a community. Elijah's actions were reckless and clearly unwarranted. If Gary died, Elijah would be guilty of an unaggravated murder. Some sort of response from the community was demanded. But what? Vengeance? Forgiveness? Punishment? Overlook it as a simple mistake?

"Do Ellen or the kids know, yet?" Jacen finally asked.

"No," Phil replied, "I didn't tell her. Didn't know what to say."

Jacen was uncertain what to do next. As a community, they had no code of conduct. There was no single standard of right or wrong to which they all subscribed.

"Jacen, she's got to know the truth," Jim Trebane declared.

"Yes, she does," Jacen affirmed. "I just don't know how we as a group should respond to this. She'll want to know what we are going to do, and rightly so."

"What *are* we going to do, Jacen? Elijah could have killed him. He may still die," Katie Blackwell asked.

"I don't know, Katie. We need to think on this before we do anything. I want to be sure that whatever we do will be right."

He looked at Hakim, who responded mutely with raised eyebrows. The Arab had remained silent for the whole interchange. Jacen suddenly remembered the discussion he'd had with his friend the previous spring, when he'd asked Hakim what the point of failure had been in the old world. He recalled Hakim's response clearly: *When the West decided that God was dead, or God was irrelevant, they lost the ability to promote universal values, the ability to properly critique, and the ability to correct. That was the point of no return. From then on it was just a matter of time.*

Jacen felt sure that Hakim was wrong, that God was not the answer to this dilemma. He just didn't know what was.

****

They buried Randy that afternoon. Other than Angie herself, there were no loud displays of grief. Death was a constant companion in the new world. Most had learned to simply swallow their sorrows and go on with life. Survival was too much of a challenge to permit the luxury of extended mourning.

Late that afternoon, Hakim and Phil returned to the field where Randy and Gary had been cutting hay. A cloud of flies was buzzing over the bear's carcass. Hakim carefully examined the signs of the struggle and came to the conclusion that Gary had tried to save Randy's life, not only in his desperate attack on the bear, but in his efforts to stop the bleeding.

Jim and Melissa Trebane explained to Ellen the circumstances which led to Gary's wounds. She was understandably angry at Elijah, and demanded retribution against him. But in the end, Jacen decided that the event had been a regrettable mistake, and that no further action was necessary. The majority of the community sided with him. Throughout the entire debate, Hakim had remained silent, and no one had thought to ask his advice.

Both Gary and Ellen Shanks found the chosen "resolution" to be very unsatisfying, and both grew very bitter toward Elijah. But they were not the only ones who found the community's non-action to be inadequate. Oddly enough, so, too, did Elijah.

CHAPTER 23

Phil stacked another load of firewood outside of the Linder sisters' cabin. He knocked on the door, which was shut tightly against the chill. It was mid-November, and all signs pointed to a hard, cold winter.

"Who is it?" queried Lynn from inside the cabin.

"It's Phil. I just finished stacking another load of wood for you and Patty."

The door opened and Lynn stood in the doorway. She smiled and responded, "Thanks, Phil. You're a sweetheart."

Phil blushed and said nothing.

"How are you doing, Phil? I know that you and Randy were close," she asked gently.

"I'm okay. I miss him. Guess I always will. But it's 'Lijah I'm worried about. He's gotten really angry and defensive. He's not sleeping well. He's furious that Randy died and he's angry at himself for shooting Gary. I keep hoping he'll get back to his normal cranky old self. But right now, he's chock-full of rage."

"I'm so sorry. Give him time. I expect he'll work through it."

"I reckon so. Well, I best be gettin' along. Got to split more wood yet, get ready for the winter," Phil mumbled, jamming his hands in his pockets.

"Say, Phil, why don't you let me mend that rip on your shirt before it gets any bigger?" Lynn suggested, reluctant to end the encounter. Phil was wearing an old denim shirt he had scavenged some time ago, and the pocket had ripped and was hanging open like a little flag.

"Oh, it's nothin', ma'am. Just a little tear."

"Nonsense! You bring that shirt over tonight and I'll fix it right up for you," she insisted. "And while you're waiting, I'll fix you a piece of apple pie," she promised.

The labor involved in harvesting and grinding wheat made flour a semi-precious commodity, consequently pastries were usually reserved for special occasions. Phil found the generous offer irresistible. He grinned at her, in spite of his shyness. "Yes, ma'am. That sounds real fine. I'll just bring this shirt over after supper. Thanks, Lynn!"

Lynn watched him as he walked away, and thought to herself, *it's a good thing I can cook. I don't think he'd notice me otherwise.*

Phil was thinking, *Phil, old boy, you're dumb as a post. That woman ain't interested in you. She's just bein' kind and neighborly. Well, I am almighty pleased that she's my neighbor. She's one fine lookin' neighbor. Yes, indeedy.*

****

Gary Shanks' gunshot wound was healing rapidly. Two weeks had passed since the bear attack that had killed Randy Bartwell. The whole camp was on edge over the affair, and Elijah's near-killing of Gary.

But if Shanks was healing physically, he was deteriorating emotionally. Gary and Ellen were embittered by Elijah Moore's prejudice and recklessness, and they were deeply disappointed in Jacen's decision to overlook the shooting without any penalty or retributive justice. The whole affair seemed . . . unfinished.

Though no one had thrown the fact in their faces, Gary and Ellen also felt the guilt of their own past as slavers. That, too, seemed like unfinished business. They perceived a growing isolation and estrangement from the former slaves. It did not occur to them that the sense of separation was actually due to their own bitterness, and not a lack of welcome from the others. It began to appear as if their recent history as slavers would dog them forever.

The Shanks had taken to eating their meals privately in their cabin. Peter and Elizabeth were required to be with them. Gary's bitterness continued to mount, and was infecting Ellen. Though his children knew something was wrong, they didn't understand why they were withdrawing from their neighbors.

The unresolved issues from Randy Bartwell's death were threatening the fabric of the entire settlement. Fractures in relationships appeared, polarized around loyalty to Elijah or the Shanks. The situation demanded leadership, but Jacen didn't know how to respond. Hakim had his own opinions, but hadn't been asked and so kept them to himself.

Jacen knew that he was being confronted by the very moral ambiguity Hakim had warned him about, and yet the young man's pride kept him from seeking wisdom from his mentor. The Arab had already explained that morality and justice were anchored in God Himself, but Jacen didn't want to hear any more about Hakim's God.

****

One day, not long after, Hakim was digging post holes for an extension to the corral. Gary was watching, trying to be as helpful as he could without tearing his wound open again.

"You're not too talkative, Gary," Hakim noted. He had been observing Gary and Ellen for several days, and had perceived the tension and the anger rumbling just below the surface.

After an uncomfortable moment of silence, Gary mumbled, "Just got nothing to say, I suppose."

"Perhaps. But then, you haven't had much to say the last two weeks. Want to talk about it?"

The answer was quick and sharp: "No, I really don't!" After a moment, however, Gary relented and added, "Wouldn't do any good anyway."

"Oh, I don't know. Why don't you try me? Hand me that pole, will you?"

Shanks dragged one of the fence posts over to Hakim, who tilted it up and dropped it in the hole. Gary held his breath for a moment and then took the plunge, the words tumbling out of him with raw emotional energy. "Hakim, I don't feel like we'll *ever* be accepted here! Elijah shot me, for Pete's sake! He could have killed me! He was TRYING to kill me! And nobody did *anything*! That's just WRONG! And he virtually accused me of murdering Randy, when I had risked my own life going after that bear, trying to *save* Randy! I could have just turned tail and run! I get so mad at Elijah, I, . . . I almost want to shoot *him*! But then . . . ," he trailed off into silence, scowling.

"Then what?" the Arab asked. He paced off the distance to the next post-hole and began digging, while Gary tamped dirt around the one he had just finished.

The younger man did not answer immediately. He finally admitted, "Then I remember how guilty *I* am of having enslaved these people. And here I am asking Elijah just to forget *that*? Even though some of *my* family murdered *his* wife in that raid three years back? That was wrong, too, and justice was never done about Julie's murder. To this day, I feel awful about it."

It was Hakim's turn to be silent. He jammed the post-hole digger into the deepening hole, and heard a *clank*. He pulled the tool out, and knelt down to remove some rocks he'd uncovered. Gary stood watching morosely. Finally, the older man responded.

"Back in September, Gary, when your group arrived here to join us, you said that you hoped that we could *forgive* your involvement in slavery. Do you remember that?" Hakim queried. Gary nodded, and so Hakim continued, "What did you mean by that?"

"I don't understand what you're asking."

"What do you mean when you talk about *forgiveness*? What does it mean to *forgive* someone?"

"C'mon, Hakim, everyone knows what that means!" Gary replied with a scowl.

"Really? Maybe, then, you could explain it to me." Hakim fished another rock out of the post hole, and then resumed digging.

"You're serious?"

"Certainly! I want to know how you understand that notion."

Gary studied the Arab's leather-like face and his deep, black eyes, and saw there nothing but sincerity and compassion. "Well, . . . okay," he began, grudgingly, "when someone has done something bad to someone else, then that someone else can just pretend like it never happened. That's forgiveness," Gary asserted, dragging a new fence post over to Hakim.

"And that's it?"

"Sure. That's all there is to it," Shanks replied, looking at Hakim curiously.

"And what are the alternatives to forgiveness?" Hakim pressed.

"Revenge is one alternative, I guess. You could escalate the situation and try to pay your enemy back. You hit me, so I hit you back. Then you hit me back, a little harder. So I haul back and just wallop you. That's one alternative." He leaned over and knocked a dry burr off of his pants, then looked at Hakim again and continued, "But I believe that's a bad idea. Where does it stop? Or, I suppose, you could just get bitter and hate the perpetrator, but not take actual vengeance. That's another way of dealing with it. It's a better way than payback. But you still wind up carrying a knot of anger in your gut. I think it's best to just try and forgive the offender and let it go."

"So, how's the forgiveness going? Are you forgiving Elijah, Gary? Are you able to pretend it never happened?" Hakim asked pointedly.

Gary looked down, dejected. "I'm not, not at all. I've tried. But I'm finding it impossible, and my bitterness is eating me alive. Seems like I'm always angry. I can't sleep. I'm short with Ellen and the kids." He stopped for a moment, looking off into the distance, and then turned back toward the older man. "Hakim, it's killing my family and I don't know what to do."

Hakim dug in silence for a few minutes. He wanted to get this section of the corral done before the ground froze for winter. It would give the horses a little more room, and a little more forage.

"Gary, can I forgive something that Elijah has done to you? Is that legitimate? Would that grant Elijah forgiveness?"

"Not from me, it wouldn't. The one harmed must be the one to forgive, otherwise it's pretty cheap forgiveness. You weren't really hurt by Moore putting a bullet into my shoulder, nor by him accusing me of killing Randy!"

Gary handed the next post to Hakim, who slid it into the hole with a satisfying *thunk*. Neither men spoke again for a moment as Hakim stepped off the distance to the next hole, and Gary tamped the dirt around the post.

"That brings up another quest–"

"Hakim, where is all this going?" Gary asked impatiently, interrupting the other man. "What's your point? I feel like you're going somewhere with this, and I don't know where it is."

"Gary, it is going somewhere, and I do have a point. But first I want to learn what you believe. If you're tired of talking about it, I'll drop it," the Arab replied.

"Maybe we'd better drop it."

****

"No! Don't do that, Jacen! Never wrap the reins around your hand!"

"Why not, Hakim?"

"You weigh, what, maybe one-ninety, two hundred pounds? Hadar probably weighs over 1000 pounds. If she gets it in her mind to take off running, you don't want that thing wrapped around your hand, believe me. She could drag you like you were some sort of overgrown pine cone."

"Ah. Got it." He unwound the reins from his hand, and just clasped them tightly.

Hakim had saddled the big buckskin, and was about to climb aboard. It was his second attempt. The first time had resulted in a bunch of broken ribs and some nasty cuts and bruises, and Hakim was understandably nervous. *But this time*, he thought, *it will be different*. He'd spent weeks in the round pen establishing Hadar's trust, showing her who is boss, and teaching her to obey his every request.

The big horse looked completely at ease. She snorted softly, and shifted her weight. Hakim had hoped to step into the saddle with no one around other than Jacen, but word had gotten out and he had the entire camp for an audience.

"You be careful, Hakim!" Mary Anders called from outside the fence. "I just cleaned my cabin, and I want no mud nor blood on my floor. If you fall off like last time, you're going to have to fix your own self up!" She spoke with a rough edge but everyone knew she was worried to death. Mary had developed a soft spot for the hard-headed Arab, something she was desperately trying not to reveal.

"I did not *fall* off," retorted Hakim with irritation, turning to face the woman, "I was *thrown* off! There is a difference. You fall off of a *fence*; you get *thrown* off a horse!" Mary just rolled her eyes and shook her head.

Katie Blackwell laughed at the interchange. If no one else perceived the developing bond between the two older members of the community, Katie certainly did.

Phil called out laughing, "Either way, you got pretty busted up, Hakim. You sure you're ready for this?"

Hakim stiffened, his pride ruffled, and turned to face his new tormentor. "Would you people please just *shut up* and let me think about what I am doing? Better yet, *go away*!" he snapped, his black eyes flashing.

The onlookers found the bearded man's nervousness amusing. Hakim was deeply respected by every member of the community. He was an uncommon individual; he could be a cunning warrior one moment and gentle and meek the next. His knowledge of history and the world about them seemed encyclopedic. And he was normally unflappable, but not today. His gathered friends enjoyed seeing his uncertainty; it helped remind them that this mysterious, seemingly omni-competent man was, after all, just like them.

"Not on your life, Hakim! We don't get much entertainment 'round here, and right now, you're it," chuckled Gus, "I wouldn't miss this for the world!" The others nodded, smiling.

Hakim turned back toward Jacen, who was holding Hadar's reins firmly under the big mare's chin, and relented in his irritation. He shrugged his shoulders, the ghost of a grin playing about the sides of his mouth. "Well, Jace, I guess it's showtime, buddy. We certainly don't want to disappoint the audience. Hand me the reins, and get out of the way."

He patted Hadar's neck, and purred, "Okay, girl, let's see if you and I have learned anything in the last several weeks." Hadar's ears twitched, listening.

Continuing to talk softly to the big buckskin, Hakim took the reins, grasped the saddle horn, and in a fluid motion put his left foot in the stirrup, and swung his right over the horse's back, settling into the saddle. Hadar's ears laid back momentarily. She side-stepped a foot or two, uncomfortable with this new weight on her back. With a snort, the mare pulled her head down sharply, then reared back, her front hooves coming briefly off the ground. She crow-hopped twice and side-stepped once more, but her heart wasn't in the protest and Hakim knew it. After a final snort Hadar stood still, having made her point. Holding the saddle horn with one hand in a white-knuckled grip, Hakim reached forward and patted the horse's neck, speaking softly to her.

Hakim then dismounted, and spoke quietly to the horse, continuing to pet her. He remounted, and the mare fussed again briefly. Hakim repeated the sequence of mounting, dismounting, and reassuring Hadar until he was able to climb into the saddle without any protest from the horse.

After a few moments, once Hadar seemed to accept the idea of having Hakim sitting on her back, the Arab gently touched her ribs with his heels and clucked his tongue. She began walking around the pen calmly. An involuntary chuckle escaped his lips, and Hakim realized that he was grinning. The whole group began to chatter with excitement and call out congratulations. In that moment, the dream, which had been fading under the heartache of recent grief and sorrow, was renewed.

****

"Come here, Peter, I've got something for you," Elijah called, reaching for a leather bag at his feet. The camp was eating supper, and was flush with excitement from Hakim's first ride. The fire crackled brightly, throwing warmth and light about the circle.

Stars glittered overhead, and beyond the flickering light of the fire the night was cold. Despite the lowering temperatures, the settlement was reluctant to move indoors. No single building was large enough for them all, and each instinctively craved the company of the larger group. They had continued to take the meals outside together, and planned to do so until weather or illness drove them inside their individual cabins.

Ever since the Shanks had joined the community, Elijah had doted on their children, Peter and Elizabeth. They had become a source of unmixed joy to him. His suspicion and prejudice against their parents, Gary and Ellen, did not extend to the kids.

"No! Stay here!" Gary barked sharply as Peter got up. Peter looked at his father with a confused expression. Gary exclaimed, "Peter, I don't want you spending any time with Elijah! And that goes for you, too, Elizabeth. You just stay right here!"

The conversation around the fire came to a screeching halt as an uncomfortable silence descended upon the whole group. Though Gary's bitter attitude had been developing over the last several weeks, the vehemence of his feelings still came as a shock, especially since it was so publicly expressed. Peter sat down, and sadly looked across the fire at Elijah.

Elijah froze, his right hand in the act of pulling a beautifully carved toy horse out of the leather pouch. He blinked, caught off-guard by the open insult, then pushed the toy back into his bag. Something in him quietly died. The old man turned away and left the fire. Though none observed it, large tears were rolling down his leathery cheeks.

The chatter around the fire pit did not resume. Soon the silence became oppressive, and by ones or twos folks began to excuse themselves and return to their cabins. The evening was ruined, and Gary knew it. He felt embarrassed, but didn't know what to do. His bitterness was becoming unmanageable.

****

"We need to build up our stocks of meat, Jacen," Hakim observed as the two men sat alone at the campfire. Gus and

Elijah were on watch duty, and everyone else had turned in. Jacen and Hakim were enjoying some rare time together.

"I know. We've already had our first skiff of snow, and all signs point to a rough winter. If we don't lay in more meat soon, we might not get another chance before the really bad weather begins. What do you recommend?"

"Remember that elk herd we ran across a month ago, about twenty miles west? If I took Hadar with me to pack the meat out, I could probably bring back about half of what we still need."

"Is she ready for that?"

"I think so. I wouldn't try to ride her outside of the pen yet, but she'll do fine as a pack horse. I've trained her to carry burdens in the round pen, and haven't had any problems."

"You want to take anyone with you?"

Hakim nodded. "Elijah. He needs to get away before he just shrivels up and dies. He's carrying so much shame and anger that I'm afraid he's going to explode one of these days. Do him good to get away from everyone."

"Sounds like a good idea. But that brings up another problem: it cuts deeply into the defense of the camp."

"Uh-huh, well, there's an easy way to fix that problem. It's time we lifted the probation on our newcomers, Jacen. Even though things are still tense since Randy's death, it's clear that they simply want to join us. I say we let 'em in with full trust."

****

"I'd like to ask everyone to stick around after breakfast, before going to your work details. There's something we need to decide," Jacen announced to the group the next morning.

It was chilly and overcast, with lowering clouds, but little wind. Here and there a snowflake drifted lazily down from the gray sky. The group stubbornly continued to eat

230

outdoors, knowing that when they finally gave in and retreated to their own cabins for the winter, they wouldn't renew regular group meals until spring.

When breakfast was cleared away, they sat at the tables, wondering what was up. When the Shanks stood to return to their cabin, Jacen waved them back to their seats.

"It's time we made a decision about the Trebanes, Sam, and the Shanks. We've had them on probation for over six weeks. We either need to accept them into the community as fully trusted members, or let them know we'll be headed west without them, come spring. Hakim and I believe we should accept them, return their weapons to them, allow them to join in the watch details, and participate in every respect as full members. I think they have more than proved their good intentions, and their value to our community."

"It's about time," Gus called out. "They've earned our trust, as far as I'm concerned." Everyone else nodded agreement.

"Elijah, what do you say?"

The old man stood to his feet, and said, "I have no objections," and sat back down.

Jacen then conducted a secret ballot of all the original members. The vote was unanimous. He smiled broadly, and said, "Looks like we all agree. Gary, Sam, and Jim, you can pick up your weapons from my cabin. You and your families are full members of our community now. It's been a long time in coming, but welcome, and we're glad to have you all! I'll rework the watch schedule tonight, and add you men to it."

*** * * * * * * * ***

Two days later, Hakim and Elijah left for several days of elk hunting, with Hadar in tow. The rest of the community continued to prepare for the onset of winter, smoking and jerking meat, stocking up on firewood, improving the cabins,

and scavenging what few supplies remained around the ruins
of Bedford.

CHAPTER 24

"Hey, everybody! Look what I found today!" Sam Oxford called out as he walked up to the fire. He was waving a yellowed roll of old paper, the edges tattered and the corners dog-eared, but otherwise intact. The group gathered around with curiosity, and Sam unrolled the document on one of the rough tables they used for supper.

"What is it?" asked Patty Linder. Somehow, as the group gathered around Oxford, she managed to find a spot right next to Sam. Smiling, Mary Anders noticed that it was not the first time that Patricia had taken a seat next to the normally taciturn man, but she wisely kept her thoughts to herself.

"It's a blueprint," observed Jim Trebane, leaning over and inspecting the document closely.

"Right," smiled Sam, "a blueprint for a four-wheeled covered wagon! Exactly what we need for our trip west this spring!"

"Well done, Sam!" Jacen exclaimed. "Where did you find it?"

"There's a cluster of farms and buildings about eight miles north, and Phil and I were searching up there today, looking for anything useful," Sam replied.

"Yes, that's what's left of St. Clairsville."

"Well, there's an old wood shop, and a smithy, too. Looks like it might have been an Amish community long ago. There were a bunch of plans and drawings for various things, and a whole passel of tools, in pretty good condition, I might say."

"Is it worth sending a cart up there, Sam?"

"I think so, several carts, actually. Probably ought to send Buck and Jim with us, so they can get a look at the tools. There's lots of stuff we can use, including a good deal of iron stock. Jim will need that to make tires for the wagon wheels." Both Trebane and his son were accomplished carpenters, and adequate blacksmiths as well. The buzz of excited conversation continued as dinner was served.

****

"Hellooo, the camp! Hello!" The voice floated on the crisp evening air from the old I-76 embankment, startling everyone. Jacen silently signaled to Gus and Phil, and they picked up their rifles and melted into the darkness. The others located their weapons, and kept them handy. The women retreated quietly into the cabins, but Jacen knew they would be arming themselves with shotguns. He heard the squeak of the Shanks' door, and knew without looking behind him that Gary was ready.

"Hello the camp!" the voice repeated. "Can I come in?"

"Come on in, but keep your hands empty," Jacen shouted back.

"Sure thing. I'm comin' peaceful-like. You good folks have nothing to worry about, not from me, anyway." There was a distinct drawl to the unseen visitor's voice.

The stranger strode to the campfire, making no discernible noise as he walked, his movements graceful. His clean-shaven face was weather-beaten. He was of medium height, and powerfully built. The man wore a wide-brim leather hat, from under which a pair of sharp blue eyes carefully evaluated the scene, taking in at a glance the positions of all the men and their weaponry, and noting the cabins beyond. He carried a large backpack with apparent ease. An M14 was strapped to the pack, and the stranger had a Mossberg Persuader Tactical shotgun slung over his shoulder, butt up. Jacen knew from Hakim's training that a weapon carried in such a fashion could be put into use immediately, faster even than a holstered handgun.

"Welcome, stranger! There's coffee on," Jacen motioned to the fire, "help yourself."

"Well, that's mighty kind of you, son! Don't mind if I do."

The man unslung his shotgun and carefully leaned it on a tree. He removed his pack with a grunt, and placed it next to his shotgun, then fished a cup out of a pouch. As he bent over, Jacen caught sight of a shoulder-holstered gun inside his half-buttoned coat.

"That's quite a bit of artillery you're carrying, mister. Figuring on starting a war?" Jacen kept his voice friendly, but he also kept his M4 in his hands.

"Nope. Just don't like to be bothered. Folks usually leave me alone when they see all this hardware," the man replied cheerfully, heading for the coffee pot. He poured a cup then came over and sat at the table across from Jacen, sighing gratefully as he sank to the bench. Jacen observed that the man had distanced himself from his pack and shotgun, effectively telegraphing that he was not a threat. Jacen relaxed, then leaned his own rifle against the tree behind him and sat back down.

"Jacen Chester," he said, reaching his right hand across the table. The stranger smiled and shook his hand.

"Francis Tulley. My friends call me Frank."

Jim, Buck, and Sam introduced themselves, and sat back down warily.

"You traveling alone?" Jacen asked.

"I always travel alone. You can tell your boys hiding in the woods, there's three of 'em, that they can come in. And your women, there be nine of them, that they can relax. And you got two kids 'round here somewheres."

"Actually, there's only two in the woods," called out Gary Shanks as he stepped out of his cabin door, cradling his assault rifle in his arms. He walked over to the fire and sat on a log, but kept his weapon with him.

Jacen's eyes narrowed suspiciously. "You seem to know an awful lot about us, Mr. Tulley."

The man stared back at Jacen, a hard expression on his face, "I'm no trustin' pilgrim, son. You really think I'm gonna park all my hardware way over there against that tree without knowing what the situation is? I've been watching you folks since yesterday afternoon, and I decided that you all must be a decent sort of folk. I've gotten kind of lonely traipsing around in the woods all by myself, figured I'd enjoy a little company for a while before I keep movin'. If you're gonna be unfriendly, I'll leave right now."

Jacen smiled suddenly, and held up his hands, "No need to leave, Mr. Tulley. No offense, but we're not trusting folks either, and we've not been watching you. So, you're welcome in our camp, but my friends in the woods will stay hidden until we know that there aren't more of you out there somewhere. Otherwise, you're welcome to stay with us."

Frank grinned back, "Somebody taught you well, boy. Doesn't pay to be trustin' nowadays. No offense taken."

****

Frank Tulley proved to be an interesting guest. The whole group, except for Hakim and Elijah, who were still away hunting, gathered around the tables listening with fascination to Tulley's tales of travel. As Jacen listened, it struck him that Tulley reminded him of Hakim.

Gus and Phil prowled silently around the perimeter of the camp for several hours and assured themselves that the visitor was indeed alone. Once confident of that fact, they joined the others for the conversation around the campfire, which went on late into the night. This was the first visitor that had been received since the former slavers had walked into camp in early fall, and everyone was hungry for news of other places.

As Sam Oxford placed the third pot of coffee on the fire, Mary Anders brought out several freshly baked apple pies. "Oh, my, Frank!" cried Gus, "you're getting the special treatment tonight. Mary's pies are the best I've ever tasted."

Katie Blackwell looked at Mary slyly, and said, "Hakim's going to be heartbroken that he missed one of your pies. We'd better not tell him when he gets back."

Mary's face flushed briefly, and then she retorted, "Serves him right. He and 'Lijah went off gallivanting around the country and left us with all the chores. Besides, I'll bake him another when they get back."

Tulley had been debating with Jim Trebane about the best way to sharpen a knife when he heard Katie's comment. His head snapped around and he exclaimed, "Hakim? Hakim? Now that's an almighty uncommon name. You folks know someone with that name?"

"Sure. Hakim and Jacen are our leaders, so to speak," Katie responded.

"What's he look like?" Tulley asked. By now, everyone else had stopped their own conversations and were looking with curiosity at their visitor.

"Big, tall Arab," Jacen replied, "black eyes, heavy black beard. Probably about your age."

"Does he carry a walking stick, with funny looking letters carved into it?"

It was Jacen's turn to be surprised. "Yes, he does! How did you know?"

"Son of a gun! Can't believe it! Here I am, off in the north woods in the middle of nowhere, and who do I run into but Hakim," muttered Frank to himself.

"You know him then?"

"I should say I do! That old terrorist is my best friend! How in the world did you folks fall in with him?"

Jacen then told the story of the community, starting with the death of his own family and continuing up to the present time. For some in the group it was the first time they had heard the complete tale. Jacen left nothing out, including the trouble they'd had with the Pittsburgh slaver community. He hastened to add that the Shanks, the Trebanes, and Sam Oxford had renounced their former involvement and were now full members of their own settlement. However, Jacen did not relate Randy's death or the circumstances that surrounded it.

The group stayed up well into the night, talking and asking questions. During the evening, when Jacen had explained the vision of the new community, it was obvious that Frank Tulley was impressed. As the newcomer asked careful questions about their plans, Jacen began to wonder if they might have a potential new member.

When the group finally began to break up and head for their cabins, Jacen reminded the men of their assignments. "Gary, you and I have what's left of the first watch. Sam, you and Gus are pulling the midnight watch tonight. Phil, you and Buck are on from four until dawn. Don't get lax, people," he admonished.

"I'll be glad to help out," Tulley offered.

"There's no need tonight, but if you happen to stick around long enough, I'll work you into the rotation," Jacen grinned. "There's room in my cabin for your bedroll, Frank, unless you were really hoping to sleep under the stars tonight."

"I'll take a roof over my head whenever I can get it. It's getting a might nippy out here anyway," Tulley answered. He stood up and moved toward his pack muttering, "Can't believe I've found Hakim!"

****

For the next two days Francis Tulley joined in the community's chores with vigor and enthusiasm. He'd forgotten the pleasant camaraderie of community and was enjoying the interaction with others. He felt immediately at home and, in Jacen's estimation, fit right in with the collected personalities.

"So, what do you call yourselves?" asked Tulley as supper was dished up. The whole group, minus Hakim and Elijah, were gathered at the communal tables close to the large fire. Gary and Ellen had even broken their self-imposed isolation, so curious were they about the visitor.

"I beg your pardon?" Jacen asked, not understanding.

"Your new community. Your new civilization. What do you call it?"

Jacen looked stumped, and glanced around the group, "I, I guess we've never thought about it. It's never come up."

As they ate, they began to discuss ideas for a name. Nothing fit until Phil Gonzales offered hesitantly, "I think we ought to name our new town *Phoenix*. It comes from an old tale about a colorful bird who lives for 500 years and then burns up in smoke. Out of the ashes, the bird comes to life again. That's kind of what's happening here. Out of the ashes of the old world, we're building a new one."

Everyone looked at him in amazement. They knew that the man was just now learning how to read. He'd never before spoken about mythology, or shown any indication that he knew of ancient things.

"Phil, how in the world did *you* hear about this bird thing, the, the, . . . what'd you call it? The phoenix?" asked Gus with surprise.

Phil's face reddened with embarrassment, "Yeah, that's right, the phoenix. My momma used to tell us kids stories about old legends. The legend of the phoenix was my favorite. I guess it's kind of a dumb idea."

"No, no, it's a great name!" cried the Linder sisters, in unison.

"Really! I love that idea! Out of the ashes, new life. It fits perfectly!" exclaimed Jacen. The agreement was universal. After polling the group, Jacen declared, "Phoenix we are.

Out of the ashes of the past, we will build a new civilization, a new culture!"

CHAPTER 25

"You know what they call him, don't you, down where we come from?" Frank asked the group at large. The wandering topic of the fireside discussion had drifted toward the Arab.

"All we know him by is *Hakim*," Sam Oxford answered.

"Well, down south he's known as *The Outlander*," Frank said.

"The Outlander? Why? What's that mean?" Jacen asked.

"We call him that because of his travels. Down south he has been as far west as the great Mississippi River. The lands there and beyond are called the outlands. He's explored all the Blue Ridge mountains from Pennsylvania south. Hakim's a wandering man. I'm surprised he has stayed with you folks this long."

"Well," Katie Blackwell smiled, shooting a discreet glance at Mary Anders, "I think he's getting sweet on someone here." Mary blushed, but said nothing.

"Pshaw!" exclaimed Phil. "The man's a confirmed bachelor. Never been married and never will be, I'll bet."

"Oh, no, there you are wrong, Phil. He's not a bachelor. He's a widower," answered Frank, without thinking. The instant he said it, he regretted it.

"A widower?" several in the group exclaimed in unison, shocked.

"He's never said anything about it," Jacen asserted.

"No?" Tulley challenged. "C'mon, Jacen. Of everyone here besides me, you've been with Hakim the longest. Does he ever talk much about himself?"

"Rarely. He just says, 'Maybe—'"

"Maybe someday I'll tell you about it," Frank mimicked, imitating the Arab's deep voice.

"Yep. That's it. That's Hakim," Jacen agreed with a wry smile.

For a moment everyone was quiet, absorbing this new revelation about the mysterious friend they knew as Hakim. Then Mary broke the silence. "Tell us what happened," she pleaded, "he's our friend."

Those sitting close to Frank saw him pale slightly at Mary's request. He walked over to the fire and refilled his coffee cup, then cleared his throat.

"No," he answered firmly. "That's Hakim's business. If he wants you to know, he'll tell you about it."

"No, he won't. He never talks about himself. He's our dear friend, and yet we know almost nothing about him. I've learned more about Hakim in an hour, from you, then I have from him in two months. If not for him, half of us would be still holding slaves, and the other half would be slaves," Jim Trebane said.

"And I would still be alone, or more likely, dead. It was Hakim who taught me how to survive in this world. I'd be another tattoo on some Anarch's arm, if not for Hakim," Jacen confessed, gazing into the fire. He looked up, staring into the newcomer's face. "Frank, please tell us. Tell us about Hakim, and what happened to his wife. How can we truly know him, if we know so little about him?"

Tulley looked around the group of faces, and deliberated. *Sorry, old buddy,* he thought towards Hakim, *but it's not only your business.* He sat down heavily and stared into the fire, screwing up his courage. For years he had dreaded the day when he would have to tell this tale to those who had not heard it. *Guess that's today.*

"Well," he started, his voice slightly husky at first, "twenty years ago, Hakim had a sweet wife named Sarah, and two beautiful baby girls, twins. Ruth and Naomi. Oh, how I loved those little girls," the man said, his cup trembling a little in his hand. He took a deep breath, and continued.

"One day a young fella, friend of Hakim's, 'bout his same age, was felling trees, clearing a field. He'd cut about a third of the way through the trunk of a large pine when Sarah walked up. She wanted to pick berries in a patch some sixty feet way, and she was afraid that tree was gonna fall on the berries and ruin the patch. So she asks if she could pick all the berries before the tree was felled. He figures it's safe, still two-thirds of the trunk to get through, so he stops and says, 'Sure!' He walks off to get a drink, and she and her little girls head for that patch," Frank stopped for a moment, and rubbed his face with his hands. The group around him remained silent, absorbed in the tale.

"Well, about then a gust of wind comes up. We'd been getting winds on and off all day. There was a great *snap!* and that big ol' pine came down. Came down right on top of them. Killed 'em, all three. Crushed the life —" he was unable to finish. For a moment he said nothing. Gary Shanks looked across the table at him in the flickering firelight, saw Tulley's cheeks glistening, and realized the man was silently weeping.

"Turned out, y'see," Frank said hoarsely, controlling himself with effort, "turned out, the trunk was partially hollow. I didn't know," he said brokenly, "I did not know it was hollow; I didn't know. Oh, Lord, I didn't know," he rasped, putting his face in his hands.

"It was . . . you?" Mary Anders asked gently.

"It was me," admitted Tulley, wiping the tears from his face, "it was me."

The group sat in stunned silence, not knowing what to think. The tale itself was tragic beyond words. But Francis

Tulley had represented himself and Hakim as being the closest of friends. It simply did not add up, to their way of thinking.

A log in the fire popped, sending a small shower of sparks skyward. Overhead, stars glistened like diamonds in black velvet. A thin, crescent moon was slowly disappearing below the ridge to their west. None of the listeners around the fire stirred. No one knew how to break the silence, or what to say after such a terrible self-disclosure. The deaths had clearly been accidental, and yet Tulley obviously felt responsible, and they could well imagine that he must have been held responsible by his community.

"What happened? What did Hakim do?" asked Gary Shanks, finally.

Tulley did not answer at first, then replied, "Well, at first he was in shock. We, the whole community, buried them. Hakim just cried his eyes out. Then over the space of a week or so, he just got madder and madder. He went into a rampage, busted up everything in his cabin, shouting and screaming, and then he just burned it down. The whole thing. He was furious at God, furious at me, and furious at his wife for dying on him and leaving him alone. He was just consumed with anger. After he burned down his place, he just disappeared. I tried to track him, but I couldn't follow the trail. We were afraid he was going to kill himself.

"He was gone for two months. After he left I started thinking about suicide. I was miserable, felt like it was my fault. I was afraid to go to sleep, because I would see the crushed bodies of those little girls in my dreams. If I did get to sleep, I'd hear the *crack* of that tree trunk over and over again, and I'd awake from the nightmare, sweating and shaking. I became angry, and lashed out at everybody.

"Finally, one day I decided I'd had enough. Couldn't take it anymore. I'd lost my best friend and was responsible for the death of his family, who were so precious to me. I decided to kill myself. Took my gear and my rifle, and figured I'd walk several days west, so no one would ever find my body. I found a good spot, and sat down to think about it before I blew my brains out. Lo and behold, up walks Hakim. He'd come back to the settlement, found out that I had gone, and trailed me there. 'Don't do it, Frank,' he says. 'Please don't do it. I forgive you. I've already lost my family. I'm not going to lose my best friend, too. In the name of *Isa al Masih*, I forgive you.' Tulley paused for a moment, overcome with emotion. He struggled to regain control, and then went on.

"I never imagined I'd hear those words. Oh my, I'll tell you, it was like a crushing load was lifted from my shoulders. Suddenly I wanted to live again.

"Well, we just camped there for a week, talking, remembering, grieving and crying, and laughing too, and then we came home. He was hurting something awful for a good couple of years, and so was I. But we got through it. God brought us through it." Frank took a deep breath, and wiped his face again, then looked around the group.

"Hakim is the best friend I have ever had, and I love him like a brother. I can't wait to see him again. He's been wandering for the last fifteen years or so. I pulled up stakes about three years ago, myself. Got restless. Just started exploring. Can't believe I've run into him." With that, Tulley fell silent, and sipped his coffee.

Gary Shanks finally broke the silence with a question. He faltered as he spoke, as though he still trying to comprehend what he had just heard. "He forgave you? He just . . . forgave you?" he asked in a shaky voice.

"Yes, that's right."

"And you are best of friends now?"

"The very best."

Gary Shanks excused himself, and walked slowly back to his cabin.

****

Two days later, Hakim and Elijah returned from their hunt. They were leading Hadar, who was loaded down with a large elk carcass. The whole camp turned out to process the meat. Some of it would be canned, some jerked. Gary was present when Hakim spotted Frank Tulley, and watched the reunion intently to see if the men were indeed the best of friends.

"Hakim, you old terrorist! How in the world are you?"

"My word! Frank Tulley! It's great to see you, man! Where on earth did you come from? How did you find me?" Hakim gave his friend a bear hug, which was joyfully returned.

"Find you? Find you? You flatter yourself; I wasn't looking for you! I just happened to run into these good people, and when I learned that they had had the bad fortune to take up with you, well, I've spent the last couple of days giving them my sympathy!"

"Ha!" Hakim roared. "Sympathy? You've been free-loading off of these hard-working folks, that's what you've been doing! You never were much for work, you bum!"

The two mountain men spent the next few moments happily trading insults, and then sat down with coffee to catch up. As Gary watched and listened, he could not sense the slightest guilt on Frank's part, nor the first bit of blame or reticence on Hakim's. *So this is what forgiveness looks like*, he thought.

****

Over the next week Hakim continued to work with Hadar, riding her out of the round pen on longer and longer excursions. He was making many mistakes, but Hakim was a quick study, and rapidly learned from his errors. Little by little, he was also learning how to use the rope as a lariat.

He started teaching some of the others how to gentle the horses. Elijah, Sam Oxford, Jacen, and Linder twins had expressed a great desire to work with the powerful animals.

Frank Tulley was also drawn to the graceful creatures, and he began learning as well. Hakim helped each to pick their horse out of the bunch, and then taught them the basics of round-pen training, as far as he understood it. Soon, the round pen was busy all the time, almost from dawn until dusk. The horse herd became more and more accustomed to human contact, trotting up to the fence whenever anyone came to the corral.

To Elijah, Hakim gave Doll, the beautiful mahogany bay mare that Randy Bartwell had gentled. "I think you should finish up Doll, 'Lijah," he said, "I think Randy would have wanted you to. Besides, both you and I need to be able to ride soon. Before the snow sets in most of the game will have cleared out of this valley. We'll need to be able to range farther from camp if our hunting is to be successful."

Hakim had sensed the shame, guilt and hopelessness that Elijah was wrestling with, and knew that the man needed to be needed. After talking privately, Jacen and Hakim had decided to place the main hunting responsibilities on Elijah. The old man was an excellent shot, he was silent in the woods, and he seemed happiest when he was on the move. Hunting simply fit Elijah's needs at the moment, as well as those of the Phoenix community.

****

"So you're the *Outlander*, eh?" remarked Jacen, as the group lounged around the campfire. It was a bitter night, but no one wanted to turn in. Storytelling, reminiscing, and camaraderie had made this nighttime part of the community's life the favorite of each. Except for the Shanks. Gary Shanks and his family had resumed their isolation in their cabin. Shanks' wound had healed, but his heart had not. The bitterness had grown to the point that he no longer enjoyed the company of the others.

"Told you, did he?" Hakim said, casting a glare at his friend Tulley.

"Yep. We already knew you were a wanderer. We just didn't know you'd acquired such a reputation for it. The *Outlander* . . . hmm . . . it fits, Hakim," Jacen mused. "It fits you well."

"You talk too much, Francis," Hakim groused, good-naturedly. Frank just rolled his eyes.

"Tell us more about what happened to the old world, Hakim. How did this land go from the powerful, developed nation it was, to where we are now?" Mary Anders asked.

Hakim looked at his empty cup. "Any more coffee in that pot, Sam?" Oxford nodded, and filled the Arab's mug. "Thanks, Sam. Well . . . it was actually pretty simple. The countries of Western Europe simply stopped making babies. Or, I should say, the Europeans of Western Europe stopped. They were a culture that had lost its reason for being. They had no larger purposes, nothing larger than entertainment, comfort, and security. Parenting was a drain, a drag on their lifestyle. And so they stopped having kids."

Jacen shook his head and interrupted, "There you go again, Hakim! Mary asked for a simple history, and you're giving her a morality tale! Why do you always have to do that?"

"Patience, son! Hakim is not simply telling you *what* happened, he's telling you *why*. The 'why' is as important as the 'what.' Sometimes more so," Frank advised. Jacen shrugged and rolled his eyes. Hakim resumed his story.

"The Europeans stopped having babies, but the Muslim immigrants did not. In the space of two generations, the majority population of Europe was Muslim. In essence, they did peacefully what the Muslim invaders of centuries prior had been unable to accomplish with protracted wars: they took over Europe. The European Union, which was a confederation of nations such as Britain, France, Germany, Italy, and so on, became the *Islamic* European Union, the IEU.

"It happened in stages. Britain scrapped its system of laws in favor of Islamic Sharia law in 2022. By 2025,

Germany and France followed suit. The armed forces of those three nations discharged all non-Muslims in early 2028. If you wanted to be a member of the military of those three nations you had to be a confessing Muslim. By the end of that year, the combined forces of Britain, France and Germany forced all the other European Union states to adopt Sharia, and the EU officially became the IEU.

"There were many who did not go peacefully into the setting of the Western sun and the rising of the crescent moon and star. There was much bloodshed, and even organized persecutions of non-Muslims. But the tide had turned and it was too late to go back to the days of the old Judeo-Christian West."

"But I don't understand," Jim Trebane objected, "why would the West abandon its own heritage?"

"It saw no point in saving it," Hakim responded simply.

"But why not?" Buck asked.

"For years, Western academics had drilled into the heads of the students passing through their classes the failures of Western society. And not just the failures of the West, but the crimes of the West. The children of the West were taught that imperialism, racism, sexism, consumerism, and exploitation of the poor and the environment were the main characteristics of Western culture. After several generations had been raised with that sort of understanding, there was no cultural vitality left in the West. No one thought the West was worth saving."

Hakim fell silent, and sipped at his coffee. The others sat around the fire, thinking about what had been said. As they weighed the Arab's words, several found themselves remembering that they had been taught by their former communities that the Old World, particularly the Old Western World, was indeed corrupt.

Patty Linder was one of these. "But Hakim," she finally objected, "that's what *I* was taught about the Old World and their capitalist system of economy. I was taught that it *was* corrupt. And you're saying, or implying anyway, that it was *not?*"

"Patricia, what you were taught, and what generations of Westerners were taught, was true, after a fashion. But it was only a half-truth. The complete truth is that _all_ human governments, cultures, and systems of economy are corrupt, not just the West. Some systems are better than others, some worse. But all are ultimately corrupt, and they're corrupt because they are administered by humans, who are *themselves* corrupt.

"Let me give you an example of what I am saying. It was common in the West to fault the early settlers of this country for their treatment of the Indians, who were already here when European settlers arrived. The settlers lied, murdered, and cheated the native Americans out of their land, their crops, hunting grounds, and so on. Right?"

"Yes, that's what I heard," Patty affirmed, and several others nodded.

"And victim cultures, such as the Indians, have a certain implied nobility, correct? After all, they suffered at the hands of the European newcomers, right?"

"Well, yes! At least they weren't cheating the Europeans out of their land, or stealing it by warfare!" Patty said stubbornly.

"Right," Hakim agreed. "But did you ever wonder, or were you ever taught, how the native Americans *themselves* came by the land? Did you ever wonder *whom they displaced*, or how much killing, cheating, and warfare was involved? Or were you ever taught about the brutal wars between those many native American tribes, wars which were going on prior to contact with the white man?"

"What, Hakim? Are you saying two wrongs make a right?" Jacen retorted somewhat hotly.

"Not at all. I'm just pointing out that these ills of which the West is accused are, in fact, problems of _all_ cultures. They are not uniquely *Western* sins. They are, instead, *human* sins."

"That's true," Patty mused. "My mom—she's the one who taught me—never even raised that point about the Indians. I don't think it had ever occurred to her."

"Are you saying that all cultures are the same, Hakim? That they're all equally good or bad?" Jim Trebane asked carefully.

"No, I'm not saying that either. I do think there are distinct advantages that some cultures have over others. I'm just saying that the portrayal of the West as uniquely evil was either incredibly naïve, or perhaps ignorant, or perhaps connected with some other agenda on the part of the teacher. It certainly isn't an accurate portrayal, in any case."

"You're going down a rabbit trail, Hakim, get back to the main story," complained Frank Tulley. Jacen smiled to himself. *Guess I'm not the only one who's impatient.*

"Right! So, the European Union becomes the Islamic European Union in 2028. They begin a crash program of rebuilding the military, which during the days of the EU had shrunk to little more than a small police force. The build-up causes Russia to begin transferring troops to its western borders as a defensive move. By 2036 open war has broken out, with the Islamic nations on one side, and Russia, China, India, and the U.S. on the other.

"The U.S. military is pretty much a paper tiger by this point, but they still manage to invade and occupy the British Isles. This is supposed to be preparatory to an assault on Europe. However, the military of the IEU responds with tactical nuclear weapons, and manages to incinerate all U.S. forces in the British Isles. This effectively eliminates all offensive-capable U.S. forces. Some years earlier, the United States had signed a nuclear disarmament treaty. Unlike the other signatories, the U.S. actually did destroy its stockpiles of both tactical and strategic nuclear weapons. So, the country has no means with which to answer the IEU's first-use.

"Three days after the debacle in Britain, the IEU detonates four biological weapons over four major U.S.

cities. The bombs contain the small-pox virus. The IEU implements a comprehensive plan to put a strict quarantine on the North American continent, but it does not work out according to their preparations. The virus jumps the quarantine line, partly as a result of a Sunni-Shia flare up in the quarantine zone, and the smallpox virus spreads across the entire globe. Within a few years, the only survivors, world-wide, are those with a natural immunity to smallpox.

"This marked the end of the old world. There was no longer a sufficient population, anywhere, to support government, or manufacturing, petroleum refining, electrical generation, and so on. I located handwritten records in a government building the ruins of Washington D. C. The final entry was dated December 7, 2041. The writer indicated that he had barricaded himself in the building with a few remaining government employees, as they tried to hold off a mob storming the building."

"And we are the survivors?" asked Mary Anders.

"We are some of the survivors, Mary. In my travels I have come across small communities scattered throughout the south and east. I have no idea what the situation will be on the other side of the Mississippi River, for I've never been able to cross it. It's such a wide river that I think we'll need to go north in order to cross it."

An owl hooted in the distance, and Hakim yawned. He stood up and announced, "That's enough history for one night. I'm going to bed."

CHAPTER 26

"There's not much in that old lumber yard that's useable, Jacen," the elder Trebane affirmed. "Buck and I looked it over yesterday. It's been ruined by termites and rot. It's not much good for building anything, let alone wagons."

Jacen nodded, listening. Jacen, Hakim, and Jim Trebane were planning work details for the winter months. Phoenix had two goals to accomplish during the winter months. The first priority was to complete the gentling and training of the horses. All of the big animals needed to be broken to the saddle, the harness, and pack loads. The second priority was building wagons for the trek west.

Work with the horses was proceeding well, and all of the community members were learning how to ride and handle the horses. Most of the work of breaking the horses, however, was now accomplished by Hakim and the Linder twins. Elijah helped out when he could, but the constant demands for food and skins required that Elijah and Phil spend their time hunting and trapping. Everyone else was employed in some aspect of constructing the wagons.

"So what do you need us to do, Jim? You're the expert carpenter. Tell me how I should assign the rest of the people to this task."

Hakim noted with approval Jacen's growing ability to lead the Phoenix enterprise. He had learned to listen, delegate, employ the skills and expertise of others, and make difficult decisions swiftly. He worked well with people, and didn't abuse his authority. The young man was developing into a first-rate administrator.

"We have multiple problems, Jacen. Winter weather will complicate every aspect of building these wagons, from timbering the trees to working with the cut lumber itself. If I had some sort of indoor workshop, it would make things simpler. It's a pity that we haven't been able to focus on building the wagons until now. The second problem is that the wood is wet. If we build the wagons with undried lumber, we'll get severe warping, shrinking, and splitting problems once it begins to dry out. Unfortunately, by that time we'll be traveling. And third, I have no experience making wagons like this. A horse-drawn, four-wheeled wagon is quite a bit different from a two-wheeled cart."

"Which of these is our worst problem, Jim?" Jacen asked.

"Well, we can't do anything about the season, and I'll just have to learn on the job how to make a four-wheeler. The blueprints Sam found will help. So the only problem we can do anything about also happens to be the biggest. We've got to dry that wood, somehow. If we could build some sort of a crude dryer and let the lumber sit in it for three months or so, I could get it almost completely dry. But the amount of wood we would need to fuel the dryer would be huge, more than our capacity to provide. We couldn't do it," Jim affirmed.

"I think I can solve that problem," Hakim offered. "When 'Lijah and I were hunting this week, we ran across several huge piles of coal sitting near an old industrial site. If we could rig our existing two-wheelers to be horse-drawn, we could bring plenty of coal. We could use it to heat the cabins, and still have plenty left over to maintain the heat in a dryer."

"Coal would work well as a heat source," Trebane affirmed.

"What could we use as a dryer?" Jacen asked.

"What if we cleared out the small warehouse behind the Linder's cabin? The one that we scavenged last spring? It's nearly empty anyway, and it's structurally sound," Hakim suggested.

"That's a good idea," agreed the elder Trebane. "It's already divided into two sections. We could dry the wood in the larger area, and set up a workshop in the smaller one. It's not perfect, but we could make it work. It would need to be properly vented." He turned to Jacen, "You'd also need to create a new night shift to stoke the dryer, or maybe the existing watch duties could be expanded to include that."

"That works. Let's do it," Jacen said.

For the next week all the men except the two Trebanes worked together to clear the warehouse, set up a wood shop and blacksmith's forge, and make the alterations necessary to turn the larger half of the small warehouse into a wood-drying facility. The women worked with the Trebanes to fashion useable harnesses for four of the community's two-wheeled carts.

Within another week the Phoenix community had its own, growing stockpile of coal. Red spruce was being timbered, then plain-sawn with the whipsaw frame. It was then hand-planed, and stacked for drying on stickers in the warehouse. The spruce would be used for the wagon boxes, seats, and bows. A small amount of hickory was being prepared for the wheels, wagon tongues, and axles. A benefit of the vastly depopulated land was found in the unhindered, eighty-year growth of the forests. The result was not only the great size of the trees, but the resurgence of species formerly thought to have vanished.

****

The weather turned unseasonably warm and clear just before Christmas. Hakim and Gary Shanks were working together on the whipsaw, cutting planks from a huge red spruce log. Gary's bullet wounds had healed well and he was returning to a normal work schedule.

"Hakim, do you remember that discussion you tried to have with me, about forgiveness, some time back? We were putting up that length of fence."

"Yep. What about it?" Hakim queried as he pulled the saw on it's down-stroke, releasing a small shower of damp sawdust that added itself to the thick layer already coating the Arab's head, shoulders, and beard.

"I wasn't ready to talk about it then, but I am now," Gary ventured. Ever since hearing the tragic account of the death of Hakim's family, and witnessing the reality of Hakim's forgiveness toward Frank Tulley, Gary had been watching the two friends like a hawk. The more he saw Hakim and Frank interact, the more mystified he became. It was clear that not only was there no animosity between the two, but they really were the best of friends. Gary had decided that whatever Hakim knew about forgiveness, he wanted to know, too.

Gary paused and bent over to catch his breath, hands on his knees. "Whew! This ol' saw will make a man outta ya!"

"For sure! But you haven't regained all your strength yet, Gary. It'll get easier over the next few weeks."

"Hope you're right about that. I'm beat!" Shanks grunted. He wiped his brow, then looked down at Hakim standing below him, on the lower side of the whipsaw frame. "Go ahead," he encouraged, "what were you trying to tell me about forgiveness?"

"I've thought about that conversation, too, Gary. I can understand why you were so frustrated with me. Nobody likes to play 'twenty questions,' so I'll just get to the point. It's a whole lot easier to forgive someone else, if you've been forgiven a far greater offense yourself."

"Okay, you're going to have to explain that."

The Arab thought for a few minutes, then nodded to himself. "Well," he began, "let's say that I had one hundred fine horses, all broken to saddle and harness. And then you came along, saw them in the field, and all you saw was meat on the hoof. So you shot them all, and traded with the meat. I reckon I'd be pretty upset about that, and I'd come hunting for you."

"I 'spose you would! That's something anyone of us might have actually done, before we knew how useful horses are."

"Uh-huh. I had to stop Jacen from shooting the horses when we first found them last spring. Anyway, let's suppose that when I found you, you told me how sorry you were. You told me you didn't know the horses were mine. You didn't know they had been trained. And so I decide to forgive you instead of starting my own little vendetta against you. How are you going to feel?" the Arab asked, looking up at the other man.

"But how could you—"

"We're not ready for that part yet," Hakim said, cutting off Gary's objection. "Just think about it, imagine it, imagine that you killed all those horses and I forgave you. How would you feel?"

Gary stooped down and sat on the edge of the whipsaw frame, dangling his legs over the side. He closed his eyes and thought for a full minute before responding. "I'd feel free, I think. And very grateful."

"Good. I think you're exactly right," Hakim affirmed.

"But—"

Hakim stopped the younger man with an upraised hand, and then continued, "But that's not the end of the story. Let's say that several weeks later some kid steals, oh, a chicken, maybe, from you. Let's say he kills it and eats it. You go hunting for the thief, find him, and you're all ready to take it out of his hide. Just before you start to lay into him, you remember how you were forgiven for killing my horses, and you think about how grateful you are. What are you going to do? Imagine the scene."

"Don't have to imagine it. I know what I'd do: I'd give that kid a talking to, but I'd forgive him," replied Gary.

"Why?" Hakim asked, his black eyes penetrating. Gary suddenly felt as though those eyes knew everything about him. It was an uncomfortable feeling.

"Because I myself had been forgiven so much. I'd just killed all my neighbor's horses, and my neighbor forgave me. This kid just steals a scrawny chicken. Surely I can forgive him."

Hakim nodded, and smiled. "So if someone has been forgiven a really big offense, then perhaps it becomes easier for him to forgive someone else a lesser one?"

Gary stared at him for a moment, thinking. "Yes, I guess that's right. Never thought about it before."

"Hey! You two gonna work, or talk?" Jim Trebane's voice came ringing across the unusually warm December air from under the open shed where he was planing the rough-cut boards.

Hakim laughed and called back without thinking, "You're a real slave-driver, Jim!" The instant he said it, he regretted it.

But he needn't have worried. Trebane grinned at him across the open space and chuckled, "That I am, Hakim. That I am," and turned back to his work, whistling a tune.

In that moment the Arab knew that the community was finally beginning to draw together as one. He looked up at the man sitting above him and said, "We'd better finish these cuts or they won't be feeding us any lunch."

****

Some traditions were too deeply embedded for eighty years of suffering to erase. Most of the little communities in the North American continent retained several celebrations and holidays, and the customs and traditions long associated with them. Christmas was one of these. Where the calendar was uncertain, a day in early winter would be designated in advance as Christmas Day. The children in the community would begin a countdown once the date had been chosen, thus proving that some things never change.

In the case of Phoenix, Hakim had the date pegged with certainty, and Christmas morning dawned clear with a stiff, warm breeze out of the south. Each family had the morning breakfast to themselves in their cabins, but all the singles met together around the community campfire. By mid-day, everyone was outside participating in games and fun activities, including one that became a permanent tradition for Phoenix, weather permitting: the Christmas Day horse race. Hakim laid out a straight, quarter-mile course on the old Interstate. Six entered the race: Jacen, Ginny Moore, Elijah Moore, the Linder twins, and Sam Oxford. Ginny won, though Jacen was right behind her. Mary Anders claimed, with a twinkle in her eye, that Jacen would have come in last if he hadn't been chasing Ginny.

The special Christmas supper was finished and the dishes had been cleared away. The members of the community were sitting around the blazing fire, enjoying the glow of a satisfying day. The pall that had hung over the group since Randy's death seemed to be lifting. The progress with the horses and the wagons combined with a clear vision for the future gave the little community more hope than its individual members had ever before allowed themselves to entertain. While Elijah and the Shanks were still not speaking, the bitterness had gone somewhat underground.

"I hope the rest of the winter is this warm," Mary Anders said. "This is wonderful!"

"Humbug," the elder Trebane replied, "doesn't feel at all like Christmas, Mary. I want to see some snow!"

"You watch your mouth, Jim Trebane!" Melissa, his wife, admonished. "I'll take this warm weather any time I can get it!"

"Now, now, 'Lissy. With all this coal we've got, you'll be nice and toasty this winter. And if you get too cold, we can move into the wood dryer. It's really warm in there."

The fire crackled and sparked cheerfully. For a few moments the group was silent as they enjoyed the moment. All were present, as it was still early evening and the night watch duties had not commenced.

Gary Shanks broke the silence. "Hakim, I've heard that there's a religious background behind the traditional celebration of Christmas. Are you aware of it?"

Jacen groaned, and Ginny Moore, sitting next to him, swatted him sharply on the knee, prompting a surprised *'Ouch!'*

"I am. It's a great story," Hakim said, "and it's the main point of the Christian Bible."

"Tell us the story, Hakim," Ellen Shanks asked.

"Okay," the Arab replied. He settled himself more comfortably on his seat, and began, "The Christmas story begins when God created the world. God made us to fellowship with Him and glorify Him by serving Him. The first couple He created, Adam and Eve, chose instead to disobey. Their disobedience polluted the human race, separated them from God, and brought them under His righteous judgment. From that point forward, all humanity was in rebellion against God. Consequently, God pronounced the ultimate judgment on mankind: eternal banishment from His presence in a place of everlasting punishment."

Patty Linder frowned, "Hakim, this is depressing; it doesn't sound like anything I've ever heard associated with Christmas!" Murmurs of agreement came from several others seated around the fire.

"Patty, the true Christmas story is not about how God made good times better, but about how He mercifully rescued His people from an absolute disaster. God takes a situation that's really bad, really hopeless, and brings unspeakable joy into it," explained Hakim.

Frank Tulley spoke up, "Patty, haven't you ever wondered how our lives, which show so much potential for happiness, have so much heartache instead? Haven't you ever wondered why things break, why people get sick and die, why life is hard instead of easy? Of all people, we who have survived the Great Disaster should see this most clearly!"

"Sure, Frank, but isn't that just the nature of things?"

"It is now, yes," Tulley agreed, "but it's not how God designed the world to be. Disappointment, death, and decay became the 'nature of things,' as you say, only when Adam and Eve chose to rebel against God. The more you understand that, the more you appreciate the good news of Christmas."

"Would you like me to stop?" Hakim asked, looking at Patty. "I can tell the story later to anyone who still wants to hear."

Jacen was opening his mouth to ask Hakim to stop when Ginny slapped him on the leg again. He turned to look at her, and she mouthed the words, *don't you dare!* He raised an eyebrow and shrugged his shoulders, but remained quiet. A few snickers could be heard from those who observed the interaction.

"No, Hakim, go ahead," Patty answered dubiously, "but so far I like the myth of Santa Claus much better."

Hakim nodded, and then continued, "Well, because God is righteous and holy He punished His people's sinful rebellion. But He's also loving and merciful, so He promised to send a deliverer who would come and save them from their sins. Through a prophet named Isaiah, He told his people that a young woman, a virgin, would have a baby who would become their King and Redeemer."

"That's impossible!" exclaimed Patty, more forcefully than she intended.

"Mom, what's a virgin?" asked seven-year old Peter Shanks.

"Never mind, dearie. You don't need to know right now," answered Ellen Shanks.

"You've got to stop telling these racy stories, Hakim," Jacen teased, "you're going to pollute little mi—*Ooof!*" Ginny silenced him with an elbow to the ribs. "*Would you STOP that!*" Jacen hissed to her under his breath.

Ginny stuck her tongue out at him, turned to Hakim, and said with all sincerity, "I want to hear this. Please, Hakim, continue."

Hakim smiled at her, then turned back to Patty Linder, and explained, "Patty, in God's story of redemption there are *many* points of impossibility. But what's impossible for man is simple for God. Ultimately it's a story you accept by faith, or not at all.

"Anyway, God promised to send someone to save His people from their sins. Seven hundred years later, He did just that. A young woman, a virgin named Mary, was visited by an angel and told that she would give birth to God's chosen One, the promised Savior. He was to be named Jesus. At the time, Mary was engaged to a man named Joseph; the angel also visited him, and explained the situation."

"I'll bet that went over well," Jacen muttered, scooting out of Ginny's reach just in time.

Hakim ignored the comment. "Christmas, then, is the day on which the birth of baby Jesus is celebrated. If His birth was miraculous, His life was even more so. He was completely and perfectly obedient to God. He was kind and loving to everyone. And He began to display inexplicable miraculous powers: He turned water into wine, fed thousands with just a few pieces of bread, calmed a stormy sea with a simple command, healed the sick, and even raised some who had died back to life. He was compassionate and accepting towards those whom society had rejected and condemned. He taught them about God and showed them His love as no one ever had before."

"How did God's people respond?" Gary asked.

"At first crowds followed Him and hung on His every word. But the religious leaders became jealous of His large following and the fact that, though He had never been trained in their religion, He seemed to know their Scriptures better than they did. They also began to perceive that He was claiming to be God's own Son. In their eyes, this was blasphemy of the worst sort. When they challenged Him, He would say things like, 'if I don't do the works of my Father, don't believe me. But if I do the works of my Father, believe in Me because of the works that I do.'

"Many people have claimed to be God over the long years of human existence. But no one has ever done the things this man Jesus did. But His greatest work they hadn't yet seen."

"What was that?" asked Sam Oxford.

"I'm getting to that. During one of their great religious festivals, Jesus went up to their capital city, Jerusalem. As He entered the city He was welcomed by huge crowds of people who proclaimed Him as God's promised One."

"The religious leaders, long jealous of His knowledge, His special powers, and his popularity with the common people, had finally had enough. They began to spread rumors and lies about Jesus, falsely accusing Him of all sorts of crimes. They managed to get Him arrested, and the opinion of the crowd turned against Him. The same mob that was calling Him 'Savior' not five days earlier now began to demand his execution. The authorities held a trumped-up trial, and sentenced Him to die. They whipped Him until He was a bloody mess, then drove nails through His hands and feet, and hung Him on a cross until He died."

A stunned silence hung over the group. After a moment, Patty protested, "How can you call this 'good news,' Hakim? What a terrible ending! Why would anyone want to hear this?"

"Because it's *not* the end of the story, Patty," Hakim explained patiently. "It's just the *beginning* of a story full of hope and joy. You see, Patty, contrary to all expectation, three days later Jesus was raised back to life by His heavenly Father. He was seen by many people; the Bible says over five hundred saw the risen Jesus.”

“So He didn’t really die?” Gary asked.

“No, Gary, He really *did* die. But God did something impossible, something only God can do: He reversed death three days after Jesus was buried. God the Father proved that Jesus’ claim to be the Son of God was true.

“Jesus’ closest followers wrote the New Testament portion of the Christian Bible to explain what Jesus’ death and resurrection means. They explained that God loved us so much that He sent His Son to die for us, in our place. The judgment that should have been against us, was placed, instead, on Him. He died to pay the penalty for our sins. And once that penalty had been paid, because Jesus had no sins of His own, God raised Him from the dead. Now God offers eternal life and complete forgiveness of sins to all who will place their trust in Jesus’ death and resurrection.

“So you see, Patty, Christmas is a time of joy because it celebrates the birth of our Savior, who is the ultimate and complete solution to sin for all who will believe in Him. All of God’s wonderful promises to His people are fulfilled in Jesus, who was born as a little baby, to a virgin, on Christmas day.”

****

For several moments after Hakim finished, no one spoke. Each was immersed in his own thoughts. Then Frank Tulley added a few logs to the fire, and quiet conversations resumed around the circle. Jacen noticed that Gus and Katie Blackwell were whispering back and forth. He saw a small smile form on Katie’s face as she nodded to her husband. Gus jumped up and faced the group.

“Hey, everybody! Listen to this!” he proclaimed. A big ear-to-ear grin was etched on his face. “We’ve got an announcement! Katie's pregnant! We're going to have our first baby!"

The quiet about the fire was transformed into a general chaos of shouted congratulations and expressions of joy. The ladies gathered around Katie, plying her with questions and sharing in her happiness, and the men around Gus, slapping him on the back. Jacen watched the scene with deep pleasure. This would be the Phoenix community's first birth. *Signs of life,* he thought to himself.

"When? When?" shouted several in the group.

"I think it's going to be late May or early June," Katie replied, her face radiant.

The hubbub continued for several more minutes, and then Phil stood up, clapped his big hands to get everyone's attention, and said, "This calls for a celebration! Elijah, break out your fiddle, man! Let's hear a tune!"

Elijah retrieved an old violin from his cabin, and Francis Tulley produced a hand-carved recorder, and soon the two were playing a lively jig. A space was cleared out near the fire, and the group danced, sang, and celebrated late into an unusually warm Christmas night. For a time it seemed as if troubles and grudges were forgotten in the joy of a promised new life.

****

Good news seemed to beget more good news. On New Years day, Francis Tulley announced that he had decided to winter with the Phoenix community. "I'm not making any promises what I'll do come spring," he said, "but in the meantime, I'll pitch in and pull my weight."

In spite of the encouraging events, however, as the depths of winter set in the old conflict began to re-emerge, and the relationship between Elijah Moore and the Shanks family was as cold and bitter as the January winds.

****

"Good, Lady! Good! Okay, now whoa!" Lynn gently pulled the reins and the horse obediently stopped trotting, and stood in place. Lady blew gently, and stamped her front hoof.

It was a cold, clear January day. The wind was light, but filled with moisture and biting with chill. Lynn had graduated her third horse, Lady, from the round pen two weeks before and was exercising her on the old I-76 turnpike. Hakim was riding alongside, mounted on Hadar, as he monitored Lady's progress.

"You're doing a great job with her, Lynn," Hakim affirmed. Lady was a smallish four-year old chocolate dun, well-socialized to humans, and possessing a steady, cooperative disposition.

Suddenly Lady and Hadar both snorted nervously, and side-stepped. Hakim noticed that the ears of both animals were laid back flat, and Lady's eyes were rolled back in terror. Just as he called out a warning, Lady bolted, and raced down the old highway, followed an instant later by Hadar. Both riders were thrown to the ground. The ground was frozen rock-solid and there was no give to it. Lynn landed on her left arm, and it broke just above the wrist with a sickening snap. She screamed in pain.

Hakim rolled to break the force of the fall as he landed. His head smashed onto the hard ground, and he was momentarily dazed, but otherwise uninjured. He shook it off and scrambled to his feet. Lynn was sitting up, clutching her arm, and crying with the pain.

"Lynn! Don't move!" Hakim commanded as his hand reached slowly inside his heavy coat. He unsnapped the cover of his shoulder holster, and slowly drew his .45 caliber Colt pistol. Lynn sat still, whimpering and clutching her broken arm. She saw Hakim staring steadily into the brush behind her as he took a two-handed grip on his pistol and smoothly assumed a shooting stance.

"Not this time, you devil. I've got you now," he muttered softly.

The great cat crouched in the brush and studied her victims with a calm malevolence. Her tail twitched once. Like lightning striking, she sprang. But Hakim was ready, and his pistol barked twice in rapid succession. The mountain lion landed on Lynn, claws and fangs bared, knocking her flat. Lynn screamed again in pain and fear, but Hakim's bullets had both struck true, and the cat rolled off of the terrorized woman. Hakim fired twice more at point-blank range, directly into the animal's skull, and the ferocious animal kicked once, then lay lifeless on the cold ground.

Hakim fought back the flood of memories and emotions as he returned his weapon to its holster. In spite of the cold, beads of sweat rolled down his forehead and into his eyes, stinging, mixing with tears as he remembered discovering the remains of his sister and nephew so many years before. With an effort, he controlled his emotions, and wiped his eyes on his sleeve. "Not this time," he repeated, as he knelt to comfort the sobbing woman.

****

"Those were gunshots!" Mary Anders exclaimed, looking up. The sound had startled her. "Four of them!"

"Sounds like Elijah must have found some game already!" Sam Oxford commented cheerfully. Sam was carrying buckets of coal to each of the cabins, replenishing their supply. Elijah had departed two hours before in a search for more meat.

"No, Sam. Elijah was headed east; those shots came from the west! And besides, that sounded like a pistol, not a rifle."

Sam rubbed his stubbly chin. "You're right, Mary. Well," he sighed, "best get prepared. You spread the word to the women. Better have 'em set their shotguns close by, just in case. I'll get Gus and Phil, and we'll go take a look-see." He ran from the cabin calling for the two men. They had heard the shots also, and had already grabbed their weapons. A moment later the sound of galloping hooves drew their attention, and they watched as Lady and Hadar raced down the trail from the old interstate embankment with empty saddles and flapping stirrups. The two horses ran to the gate of the corral, and stood nervously, blowing and stamping.

"Uh-oh," Gus muttered, "that doesn't look so good. Wonder what happened to Hakim and Lynn?"

The three men ran to the corral, and quickly saddled fresh mounts. As they were about to ride out, Patty Linder ran up.

"What happened? Where's Lynn?" she called out, worried.

"Don't know, Patty. I'm sure she's okay," Sam lied. He was concerned that something had gone terribly wrong, but didn't figure it wise to worry Patty until they knew for sure. "You strip the saddles off of Hadar and Lady, and rub 'em down, will you? We'll go find Hakim and Lynn."

****

"Try to hold still, Lynn," Hakim instructed. He checked her carefully for injuries. In addition to the broken arm, she had deep bloody scratches on her shoulder from the big cat's claws. Between the cold and the shock, Lynn had begun to shiver uncontrollably.

The injury to her left arm appeared to be a complete, though clean, break. *Thank You, Isa, that it's not a compound fracture!* he breathed silently. "I'm going to need to set that bone, Lynn. I'm afraid it's going to hurt. Let's get you back to the settlement and into a warm cabin. I'll do it there. Thankfully, we're not a mile from the cabins. Can you walk?" She nodded, so Hakim gently helped her to her feet, and they began to walk back.

Within a few short moments Sam, Gus, and Phil rode up. Hakim and Gus helped the injured woman into the saddle with Sam, and Gus let Hakim have his horse. "I'll walk back," he said, "you go with her and set that arm."

CHAPTER 27

Two days after the incident with the mountain lion, winter set in with a vengeance. The day had begun clear and cold, temperature in the teens. Cloud cover slowly built, and the temperature crept up to the twenties. As the humidity increased, the rising winds penetrated clothing with sharp, biting cold. By late afternoon, flurries were coming and going with slowly increasing intensity.

The wood shop became the new community center once the cold had driven the Phoenix group inside. With the wood-dryer adjoining, the wood shop remained pleasantly warm.

"We're getting set for a major blow, Jacen. I'm worried about Elijah," Hakim said to Jacen as the others trooped into the wood shop and stamped their feet free of snow.

Jacen asked, "You really think it's going to be that bad?"

"Yeah, this is gonna be a big one. I've been watching the sky all day. And the horses were getting nervous this afternoon, clumping together. I think we're in for lots of snow, and when the snow stops, its going to get bitterly cold."

"He's right, you know." Francis Tulley had walked up and added himself to the private conversation. "I've been seeing the same things. Elijah's going to be in a world of hurt unless he can find some shelter."

"Well, he's supposed to be headed for that old house below Carson's Gap. He can weather the storm there," Jacen said.

"Yes, he can," Hakim agreed, "just as long as he doesn't get caught out in it and lose his bearings. Once the snow starts falling and you lose visibility, everything starts to look the same. You lose your landmarks, and it's really easy to get turned around. And he's alone. If anything happens, he's not going to have any help. Look what just happened to Lindy!"

Jacen nodded. "Okay, what do you suggest?"

"Send Frank and me out tomorrow morning with four of the horses. We can get to the cabin, since the old interstate goes right close to it. If Elijah's not there, we'll find him and bring him home. And Jacen, from now on, I suggest that everyone who leaves camp needs to do so in company with someone else. It's too dangerous in this weather to go off by yourself."

****

By the time supper was over and cleaned up, a blizzard was raging. The group broke up early, and returned to their own cabins. As he was about to leave, Gary Shanks found Hakim and put his hand on the older man's shoulder. "Hakim, I know it's an awful night, but I wonder if you would drop by our cabin before you turn in. We'd like to talk. We're prepared to bribe you with an offer of pie and coffee."

Hakim smiled. "Sounds good to me. I'll be over in a few minutes."

"Thanks. I appreciate it." He turned and gathered his family. "Come on, Peter! Come, Elizabeth! Time to get home while we can still find the way!" The children were excited by the prospects of a big snowfall, and eagerly buttoned up their coats for the short walk home.

271

Frank and Hakim spent several moments talking, making a few plans for their trip to Carson's Gap. Sam Oxford walked up, putting on his coat. "I'd like to go with you, Hakim. I'd like to help find Elijah. I'm worried about him."

"We'd enjoy your company, Sam. You'd be a big help."

"Count me in, too."

Hakim turned to see young Buck Trebane standing close by.

Frank suggested to Hakim, "That would give us two teams. We might be glad of it, before it's over. I can team up with Buck, and you with Sam."

Hakim nodded. "Yeah, that works. It will be safer that way, and we'll find Elijah that much faster. Okay, Sam, Buck! Glad to have you both along. Be ready to go at daybreak. Bring warm clothes, your weapons, and plenty of ammo. Frank, you work with Mary to get some provisions packed. We'll take three extra horses. If we find Elijah, and he's okay, we'll turn it into a hunting trip. Maybe we can bring home some meat."

****

Ten minutes later, Hakim was knocking on the Shanks' cabin door. The snow was falling thickly, and the wind howling. There was no outside light, making the darkness almost impenetrable. Then the cabin door swung open, and light and warmth spilled out onto the snowy scene.

Gary stood in the door. "Thanks for coming, Hakim. I've been telling Ellen what we've been talking about, and she's got some questions." Hakim stepped in, and Gary closed the door behind him, shutting out the stormy night.

"Glad to come, Gary. Hello, Ellen, Peter, Elizabeth," he acknowledged, nodding his head in a friendly greeting. He hung his coat on a rough peg by the door, and sat down on a chair near the fireplace, holding up his hands to its cheery warmth. Ellen sat down, opposite him. For a moment, she clasped and unclasped her hands, saying nothing.

"What's on your mind, Ellen?" he probed gently. "How can I help you?"

"Gary and I have talked about your conversations concerning forgiveness, and I must confess that I, too, am having a hard time with both bitterness and guilt. Gary and I want to be part of this community, but we feel that our own actions in the past, plus Elijah Moore's behavior toward Gary, are separating us from everybody. We don't know what to do." Ellen Shanks was somewhat reserved and proper, but not snooty. Ever since Gary had been shot, she had withdrawn even more.

"Ma'am, I've never lived in a community in which people didn't wind up stepping on each others' toes, somewhat, and I don't expect you have either. There'll come a day when Phoenix will be too large to care for everyone's relationships to everyone else, but that day has not yet arrived. As small as we are, it's pretty important that we be able to get along."

She nodded in affirmation, and then said, "Gary related to me the story, or the parable, whatever, that you shared with him: that story about him killing one hundred of your horses, and then someone else killing his chicken. It made sense to me—the lesson you drew out of it—that we forgive more easily when we ourselves have been forgiven something greater. But that still does not answer a question I have: what about justice? Shouldn't justice be done? Should not someone have to pay for those one hundred horses, or even that one chicken? How can we be a *just* society if we allow crimes to go unpunished, or if justice is not executed?"

It was a good question, Hakim admitted to himself. In his heart he prayed swiftly for an answer. He thought for a moment, and then said slowly, "Ellen, ma'am? That's a really good question. Somehow in a society you need both justice and forgiveness. We could not live in a society where there was only justice and no forgiveness, and we would not *want* to live in one in which there was only forgiveness but no justice." She nodded in agreement.

Hakim leaned forward, his elbows on his knees and his chin cupped in his hand. He looked down, as though studying the rough-hewn floor boards, and pondered how to answer. Suddenly he slapped his knee and looked up with a smile. "What if," he suggested, "just imagining now, what if some third party stepped in and made some acceptable payment for those horses? Or for that chicken? Wouldn't that be acceptable? That way there would be a recognition of the cost of the crime, but also the reality that the penalty had been paid. What if my forgiveness of Gary for shooting all my horses was based upon the fact that someone stepped up and covered all my losses? Then I would be free to forgive Gary, *and* justice would have been done. Would you agree?"

The low moan of the wind could be heard in the trees. Somewhere in the distance a cabin door creaked open, then shut again. Ellen stared into the fire, weighing Hakim's words. Finally she looked up, and said, "Yes, I think so. The crime would have been both paid for and forgiven. Justice is served in that, I think."

"Okay, so you're saying, at least in that circumstance, that a third party, a substitute, can agree to bear the cost of the crime, and that's acceptable?" Hakim clarified.

"Yes, I think so," she repeated.

"Alright, what if I, as the owner of those horses, knew full well the value I had lost from the destruction of my horses? Could I decide to bear the cost *myself*, in order to enable forgiveness? In essence, I would be taking the punishment on myself for Gary's crime against me. What if I did that knowingly and willingly? If some third party could bear the cost, surely I could decide to do that as well, could I not?"

Gary rubbed his chin, thinking, and nodding slowly. But Ellen shook her head, "I don't know. How is justice accomplished in that case?"

Gary jumped in before Hakim could answer, "It's the same, sweetie. What you are saying is that someone must bear the cost of the loss of the horses, in order for justice to be served. What Hakim is saying is that it is the privilege of the owner of the horses to decide whether or not he wants to bear that cost *himself*, so that forgiveness can move forward. Am I right, Hakim?"

"Yes, precisely. The point is, once you allow for the possibility of a substitute to pay the penalty, you have just opened the door for both justice and forgiveness to be executed. The offender is free from his guilt when the victim extends forgiveness, because he knows that the penalty of his crime has been paid by someone willingly bearing the cost. The victim of the crime is satisfied, because the debt has been paid in full, either by a third party, or by his own decision to shoulder the cost of the crime himself. When both parties are thus satisfied, they can be reconciled as friends and neighbors."

"But what about restitution? Shouldn't the offender try to cover the cost of what he has done?" Ellen objected.

"Of course—if it is possible. The offender should make up what he can to the one he has victimized. But many times it isn't possible. For instance, to make this abstract discussion personal, how can Elijah undo the fact that he shot Gary? He can't. He could help with the chores that Gary can't do because of the injury; I suppose that much is both possible and advisable. But unless you're suggesting that we line Elijah up and have Gary shoot him as payback —which would be *revenge* and not justice, by the way— there's no way to undo the fact that Elijah shot Gary. Exacting revenge won't repair the relationship between the two. But forgiveness will. However, if there's to be forgiveness, a third party must bear the penalty for Elijah's actions, or Gary must decide to absorb the cost himself."

"But I don't think I can do that! Every time I think about what Elijah did, I get furious! It was so UNFAIR! It was just plain WRONG!" Gary raised his voice as he poured out his bitterness. "He accused me of *killing* Randy, and I was doing everything I could to *save* him! Randy and I were *friends!* Elijah's accusation hurts far more than the gunshot wounds," Gary said, bitter tears trickling down his angry, red face.

Hakim said nothing. Gary wiped his eyes on his sleeve, and they sat in silence for a few minutes. Suddenly Ellen realized she had offered her guest nothing. She jumped up and exclaimed, "Hakim, I'm forgetting myself! What can I get you? I've got some coffee, and I made a pie this afternoon. Would you like something?"

Hakim grinned at her, "Well, ma'am, I've been admiring the smell of that baked pie ever since I came in. I'd love to have a piece."

As he poured three cups of coffee Gary confessed with a wry smile, "Sorry, Hakim. Didn't mean to be inhospitable. We are just so dominated by this thing. Between the fact that I was a slaver with the group that murdered Elijah's wife, and the fact that I've borne the brunt of Elijah's hatred and suspicions in Randy's death, not to mention getting shot by him, we've simply not been thinking clearly. In fact, we've not been thinking of anyone but ourselves. I reckon that's part of our problem."

Gary shoveled a few more pieces of coal on the low-burning fire. When they were all seated again, Ellen asked hesitantly, "Hakim, are you really a widower? Did you really have two little girls? Francis Tulley told us the story."

Hakim stared at the fire, and nodded slowly without saying anything.

"And yet Frank is your friend?" Gary asked. "How can that be?"

The Arab breathed deeply, then turned to look at Gary. His black eyes were penetrating in their intensity, and tinged with sadness. He replied, "Gary, I forgave him. God enabled me to forgive him. That doesn't mean that I didn't grieve over my wife and children. I cried my eyes out, and went through a whole mix of emotions: anger, depression, guilt. Sometimes I still grieve for them. Forgiving Tulley didn't put a stop to the grief, Gary, but it is what kept bitterness at bay. It's what made a renewal of friendship with him not only possible, but joyful. He's not just my friend; he's probably my best friend in all the world, he and Jacen."

"I don't see how that's possible. I could never do that."

"You could if God enabled you to do so. You could if you yourself had been forgiven."

"I don't understand. What are you suggesting?" Gary asked.

"Maybe there is a God, a Creator God, who made you, Elijah, and Randy. Maybe Elijah's crimes against you are primarily crimes against this God, for violating His law. Maybe your crimes against those you enslaved are primarily against this Creator God, for enslaving people who belong to Him. Perhaps the forgiveness Elijah needs must come from this God. Perhaps the forgiveness you need for your involvement in slavery must also come from this God. What if that is the *real* forgiveness, the *huge* forgiveness necessary before we are able to forgive others? Maybe that's the one-hundred horse, or ten-thousand horse forgiveness that we need, in order to forgive the scrawny chicken crimes we commit against one another."

"This sounds sort of like the story you told at Christmas."

"Same story, same God, same truth," Hakim admitted, nodding.

"That's funny. I thought you're a Muslim," Gary observed.

"Why does everyone always think that?" exclaimed Hakim, exasperated.

"Well, you are of Arab descent, are you not?"

"Yes, Jordanian, to be specific. I once was Muslim, but now I worship *Isa al Masih*."

"Never heard of him. Who's that?"

"It is simply Arabic for Jesus, the Messiah."

"Well, that explains your Christmas story, then. It's strange; I was always taught by my folks that it was Christians who destroyed our country," said Gary carefully.

"Christians over the centuries do have much to answer for, Gary," Hakim acknowledged. "We've fallen far, far short of what Jesus demands of us. We've spilled our share of blood. Much of the time it was done by people *claiming* to be Christians, but who had no genuine interest in Jesus Christ, people who tried to further their personal agendas by coming under His banner. As far as I am concerned, many of these were simply religious opportunists, not real believers in Christ.

"In any case, Gary, Christians did not destroy America. They were heavily involved in the founding, formation and development of this country. But by the time of the wars that did ultimately destroy America, Christian influence had evaporated from the political scene. It was Muslims, Gary, not Christians, who detonated the biological weapons that brought on a worldwide epidemic of small-pox."

Gary chewed on a forkful of pie, weighing what Hakim had said. The cabin was quiet for a moment. Peter and Elizabeth had fallen asleep on a blanket near the fire. Gary could hear their soft breathing. Ellen broke the silence.

"Tell us more about this God, Hakim," she asked.

"I'll give you the short story, then I'd better get back to my cabin. I think I've given you enough to think about for one night. Some of this you heard about at Christmas.

"It is not a complicated story. God created the world and all that is in it, including human beings. Mankind was made to serve and glorify God. In fact, God designed us to find our greatest happiness in worshiping and serving Him. But we humans fell into disobedience, and ultimately grew to hate Him."

"Woah, hold on one minute! I don't hate God," Gary objected.

"But you're not even sure that God exists; am I right Gary?"

"I'm not sure *your* God exists," Gary declared. After thinking a moment, he added, "Okay, I'll admit it: I'm not sure any God exists."

"Well, Gary, being uncertain that God is actually real is not a position I would interpret as loving and worshiping Him. If we refuse to acknowledge another human's existence, most of us would interpret that as hate, right?"

"Granted. But I can *see* another person; I can't see God."

"True. But according to what God wrote in His Word, He has made His existence obvious through the world that He has created. According to Him, you and I and this planet are all the evidence we need that He exists. So your determined refusal to believe, no matter how you may feel about it, is declared to be hostility against Him."

"I disagree with you, Hakim, but for the sake of the discussion, please go on," Gary replied.

"Having rejected the God who made us," Hakim continued, "it was but a small step for us to reject one another, because we are created in God's image. Mankind therefore began to sin against each other, sins of violence, hatred, lust, greed, envy, anger, rage, oppression, and so on. This present world is all the evidence we need of mankind's sins against one another. But the Bible makes it clear that all sins are first and foremost sins against the Creator and owner of all things, God Himself.

"The *Holy Injil*, known to you as the New Testament, tells us that God will one day punish our crimes against Him, eternally. God, who is perfect in justice and holiness, will exact perfect punishment against those who disobey Him, and that punishment will be entirely righteous and just. But God is not only perfect in justice, righteousness, and holiness, He is also perfect in love, grace, mercy, and, yes, forgiveness."

"But Hakim," objected Ellen, "how is that possible? How can God be perfect in love when He is also perfect in carrying out punishment? How can perfect mercy coexist with absolute justice?"

"It's a dilemma, Ellen, isn't it? For us it seems impossible. But the same God who declared that death is the perfectly just penalty for sin, also declared that a substitute can bear the penalty in the place of the actual offender. And so God sent His Son, Jesus Christ, to be the substitute who dies in the offender's place.

"That one fact has never ceased to amaze me. God preserves His absolute righteousness by exacting sin's full penalty for every transgression. And He preserves His perfect love and mercy by bearing that penalty Himself, as the sinner's substitute, in the person of His Son. Perfectly just, and perfectly merciful. Perfectly righteous, and perfectly forgiving. What an amazing and loving God!"

Hakim paused as he took a swallow of his coffee, and another bite of his pie. Both Gary and Ellen remained silent; he thought he could sense a glimmer of understanding.

"But what about Jesus' own sins, Hakim. No one can make it through this life without screwing up somewhere along the way," Gary said, after a moment.

"Jesus lived as an actual, historical person without sinning once. He always fulfilled His heavenly Father's will. Consequently He was not subject to the law of death, since He had never sinned. But He willingly offered to take the sinner's place, and receive God's righteous judgment against sinners in His own body. The story is a lot longer, but suffice it to say that the very people for whom He died executed Him upon a cross. The cross was the most cruel, inhumane method of capital punishment you can imagine. It was excruciatingly painful."

"But you said at Christmastime that He was raised from the dead," offered Ellen.

"Yes. Three days after He was laid in a tomb, God raised Him from the dead. The resurrection demonstrated at least two things. It showed that Jesus really was who He claimed to be, God's Son. And it showed that God accepted the payment Jesus had made for sin; there was no longer any need for Him to remain in death. The full penalty had been paid; God's justice was satisfied." Hakim looked at Ellen as he said this, and then continued, "God determined to fully and completely forgive all those who would make the death and resurrection of His Son their payment for their crimes against Him. And so He grants complete forgiveness, peace, and eternal life to all who will trust the payment of His Son, Jesus."

"So, to get back to you and Frank, you're saying, Hakim, that you were able to forgive Francis Tulley," Gary said, thinking through it as he spoke, "because you had received far greater forgiveness from God for all your sins against Him. And you're saying that full justice actually *was* done in Frank's case, because Jesus died for Frank, paying for his sin."

"That's exactly what I'm saying, Gary. After all I had done against this Creator God, Frank's carelessness against my family was small by comparison. How could I not forgive Tulley, when God had forgiven me so much? And, because Frank's carelessness had been fully paid for by Jesus, life for life, I was free to forgive Tulley."

Ellen looked at the tall, rough Arab sitting opposite them. Somewhere in the depths of her heart, she sensed a battle between her will and her understanding. What Hakim had been saying was adding up, but she was not ready to accept it. For reasons beyond her comprehension, tears were trickling down her cheeks.

"I think I understand what you're saying, Hakim," Gary said, "but I'm not sure if I believe the story about God and Jesus. There are many other religions out there, and they all claim truth."

"That they do, Gary, that they do," Hakim admitted sadly. He stood up and buttoned his coat. "Thank you, Ellen, the pie was wonderful. I hope you have more questions in the future. I love cookies, too, and if you're baking, I'll be glad to come over!" He winked at her, and turned to go.

"But wait, Hakim!" Gary stood up, agitated. "Aren't you going to try to convince us that this is all true, and that we need to believe it?"

Hakim had been reaching for the door, but he stopped and turned and looked at his friend. "No, Gary, I'm not," he responded gently. "I'll tell you the story as many times as you want to hear it. I'll do my best to answer your objections and questions. But I'll not try to convince you of the truth. The Bible indicates that, deep in your heart, you already know the truth and will either continue to fight against that knowledge, or you will embrace it. Believing in Christ is a step of faith, not the result of browbeating or cajoling. And if you're unable to see the reality of what I have said operating in my own life, I'll never be able to convince you with some sort of logical argument. Either way, you are my friend, and my neighbor, and I'm glad your family is part of Phoenix. You belong here, with us.

"Good night, Gary, Ellen." And with that he stepped out the door and closed it behind him. Gary and Ellen sank into their chairs and gazed into the fire, silently pondering, late into the evening.

CHAPTER 28

The old house was largely intact though there had been no human maintenance for over eighty years. It was just one of those odd coincidences of nature, Elijah Moore figured. In any case, he was glad that the place was here. In the late fall he had discovered it while tracking a herd of elk. A work party from the Phoenix encampment had come out and cleared the old stone chimney of nests and accumulated debris, done a few other minor repairs, and stacked a winter's supply of firewood on the first floor. It was to be a base camp for winter hunting trips.

After dressing, Elijah re-rolled his bedroll, and stowed it tightly in its proper place in his saddle bags. That was one of the first lessons of the backcountry he had learned as a boy. If you leave your bedroll lying about, you're liable to find that other critters and creepy-crawlys also enjoy its warmth.

Withdrawing a day-pack from his saddle bags, he filled it with a few supplies for the day's hunt. After banking the fire carefully, he drew his coat tightly around him, strapped the small pack on his back, picked up his gun, and started out. He knew of a low saddle between two steep-walled valleys, two miles to the north. On previous visits he'd seen a lot of deer and elk sign there. The animals used it as a natural pass between the two valleys. Elijah planned to sit in the laurel on the leeward side of the saddle, and ambush the deer as they passed between the valleys. The way he figured it, he'd have two or three kills by early afternoon. He'd walk back to the cabin, get his horse, and pack the carcasses back to the cabin by sunset.

As he stepped out into the early morning darkness, the stars twinkled brightly overhead. If he walked briskly, he'd be at his chosen spot before sunup. He checked the picket rope on his horse, Doll, making sure there was plenty of forage close by, and then set out for the small pass.

Elijah enjoyed being alone. Ever since the death of his dear Julie, he'd not had much use for company. Julie had loved people, and he had enjoyed her enjoyment of them. Their cabin had been a frequent spot for fellowship, games, and discussions in their little community in years long past.

Then came the slavers and their surprise assault on Elijah's community. Elijah and his neighbors had put up a good fight initially. Then, when several of the wives were killed, including Julie, the heart simply went out of the men. Elijah and the others surrendered, not wanting to endanger their children. And so had begun the long, bitter darkness of Elijah's soul. He had loved his wife with abandon, had doted upon her and their daughter, Ginny. When Julie died, it was as though Elijah's heart had been ripped right out of him. The only reason he went on living was because of his daughter.

Elijah later learned that Tim Shanks had coldly and methodically killed the women with a sniper rifle. Shanks had figured that the death of their wives would cripple the defenders with grief, and so it had. One day, Elijah vowed, he would find Tim Shanks and kill him, slowly, in the most painful way he could think of. He would get his revenge.

When Hakim had come along and freed the slaves, Elijah had listened to Jacen and Hakim's plans for the future. Something long dead within him stirred, ever so slightly. After watching the two men in action during the battle with the slavers, Elijah knew in his heart that Jacen and Hakim were men you could ride the river with, men you could count on. He joined his fortunes and future with Jacen and Hakim's dream to start a new society out of the ashes and death that characterized the old one.

But when the former slavers had come to join the Phoenix community in September, it had been all Elijah could do to tolerate their presence. He hated them. He just knew they were waiting until everyone let down their guard, and then the slavers would come upon them like a flood, and recapture them all. Elijah's bitterness and suspicions knew no bounds.

Then came the horrific death of Randy Bartwell. In his outrage, Elijah shot Gary Shanks, thinking that the former slaver had killed Randy. He was mistaken, however, and now Elijah felt the extra burden of guilt for very nearly killing a man in unbridled, irresponsible rage. In the secret places of his conscience he admitted that he was, in some ways, not that different from the slavers. His fresh guilt added to his bitterness, and consequently, to his desire for isolation. He did not want to leave the Phoenix group: his daughter was part of it, and Phil and Gus were his friends. But neither was he comfortable there once the former slavers had joined.

His assignment as the hunter for the group suited him perfectly. He was away for much of the time, not having to interact with the hated former members of the Pittsburgh slaver settlement. And yet, he was still a contributing part of the Phoenix community. It was an arrangement that was probably the best of all worlds, at least for one tormented with grief and guilt, as Elijah was.

*** * * * * * * * ***

"Come on. Come on. A little farther . . . a little . . . ," Elijah whispered under his breath. *BOOM!* The large-bore rifle leaped in his hands, but his shot was true. The big doe ran twenty steps, stumbled, and lay still, a crimson spot blossoming on her left shoulder. The other deer traveling with her scattered. He could hear them crashing away in the thick forest. Elijah emerged from his laurel-enclosed hiding place, and dragged the deer back to his spot on the leeward side of the saddle.

Cutting into her ankles, he poked a stout, green stick through the tendons of her rear hocks, and hoisted the dead animal into the tree with a rope he'd thrown over a thick limb. Elijah quickly field-dressed the deer. He left the carcass hanging in the tree to cool out, and then crept back to his hiding place.

By noon there were two deer hanging in the tree. Shivering, Elijah felt the bone-penetrating chill of the moisture-laden breeze which had been rising steadily and was now gusting with enough strength to bring down a rotten limb here and there. Thin wisps of clouds had begun overspreading a clear sky shortly after dawn, but the sky was now a solid and lowering overcast. *There's a nasty blow on the way*, he thought to himself. He waited in his hiding place for another hour, but no game was moving. The deer had probably bedded down for the day. But if nasty weather was developing, they would get nervous and start moving again in the mid-afternoon.

Elijah decided to walk back and get his horse, pack the two kills back to the cabin, and maybe he'd have time to try for one more in the late afternoon. He stood up and stretched noisily, no longer caring if the deer heard him. Picking up his small pack, he started back to the cabin.

A creek lay at the bottom of the valley. His trail crossed it, then continued up the other side, less than a mile from the old house. A rime of ice lay upon its edges, but the center still flowed freely. *Bet this is a good trout stream*, he thought to himself as he carefully picked his way across the brook, hopping from boulder to boulder. He was jumping to the final boulder just short of the far side, when the stone turned under his foot as he landed on it. Losing his balance, he fell heavily into the stream, striking his head on a rock.

For a moment he lay in the shallow, icy water, stunned and struggling to maintain consciousness. Had the water not been so cold, he would have succumbed to the concussion immediately. Dazed and only half-aware, he got to his hands and knees and crawled out of the stream. He had lost his gloves. His clothes, front and back, were soaked through. The cold was painfully intense. He staggered to his feet, his head bleeding and throbbing. He was shivering so violently he could barely control his movements. Looking around him, Elijah found that he was unable to make sense of what he was seeing, as the blow to his head had been so severe. He stumbled in circles, falling again into the shallow edge of the stream.

In the one part of Elijah's brain that was still functioning properly, he knew that he was in deep trouble. His clothes were wet, he was at least a half-mile from shelter, he couldn't see clearly, and he was in grave danger of freezing to death.

With great effort, he got back to his hands and knees, and began to crawl. It was the only way to avoid falling again. Slowly his vision stabilized, and he could recognize the trail. And yet his balance would not support him on two feet. He must remain on hands and knees. Painfully, slowly, he began the long crawl back to the cabin.

Elijah had no consciousness of the passing of time. He had no feeling in his hands. He looked at them stupidly as he crawled, wondering why they were leaving red blotches on the dirt and leaves as he moved along. Finally he began to feel warm and sleepy. He longed to simply stop crawling and lie in the dirt for a short nap. It was all he could do to keep his eyes open. At some point, he passed out.

Something woke him up again. Groggily, he raised his head from his comfortable bed. *No, wait, this isn't my bed. It's snow. What am I doing sleeping in the snow? Did I fall out of my bed?* He looked around, trying to find his bed. Nothing made sense. He was out in the forest, and it was about dusk, and there was a light coating of snow on the ground. All around him, snow was falling with increasing intensity, and he could hear the moan of the wind in the trees.

Some drive to survive got him up and to his feet, though he couldn't feel them. As before, he stumbled stiffly in a circle, but this time he managed to straighten it out. Perhaps instinct more than awareness put him back on the path to the old house. Fifteen minutes and three falls later, he stumbled through the door. He clumsily shut it behind him and fell against it. After a moment, he straightened up, wandered into a wall in the dark, and fell over. This time, he did not get up.

CHAPTER 29

The wind was blowing stiffly out of the northeast when Hakim awoke in the cabin he and Jacen shared. Snow was falling steadily, and had accumulated about nine inches through the night hours. In a few minutes the other men came in, and were stamping the snow off their boots and brushing off their coats. The Arab pulled the coffee pot off the fire and poured a hot cup for each. Though Jacen was not riding out with them, he was up and dressed, planning to feed the horses and get an early start on other chores.

"Other than where it has drifted, this wind has probably swept the trail to Carson's Gap clear. I don't expect we'll have much trouble traveling, as long as we're careful," Hakim said to Jacen.

"When should I look for you?" Jacen asked.

"Expect us back in no more than two days, unless the weather worsens. If Elijah is okay, we will hunt tomorrow, maybe even this afternoon. If something is wrong, we'll return as soon as possible."

"I've packed enough supplies for five days, Hakim, just in case," Frank Tulley said. "I've also packed some medical supplies—just in case."

Hakim nodded. "Good. Sam? Buck? You boys ready?" the Arab queried. Both nodded. "Well, then, let's get moving."

The four pulled on their coats, shouldered their rifles, hoisted their saddle bags, and stepped out into the storm. The dim gray light of dawn was only beginning to filter through the snow-covered trees. Snow swirled steadily, landing on their hats and shoulders. Other than the hiss of the wind in the trees and the soft, squeaky crunch of their boots as they trod through the snow, the world was utterly silent.

The horses were bunched up under a big three-sided shed that had been built in the large corral. The seven animals that were cut from the herd plainly did not relish the thought of going out into the weather. A few of them elected to make their displeasure known, and side-stepped and danced about as they were saddled. Hadar crow-hopped once, but Hakim was not impressed, and soon had her under control.

The men rode out, headed east toward Carson's Gap and the old house where Elijah would have made his base camp. They were riding directly into the teeth of the storm. The wind-driven snow soon made their faces red and raw. It was a nasty ride for both man and beast.

****

"Hello the house!" Hakim called, as the four rode wearily up to the old building on Carson's Gap. There was no response, and no smoke coming from the chimney. Sam Oxford handed the lead rope of the pack animals to Buck, and trotted his horse around the back of the building. There he found Doll, shivering, with her snow-and-ice-encrusted rope still securely fastened to its picket pin.

"Poor girl!" he cried as he dismounted. He pulled the picket pin and led both horses around to the front. "Hakim, Elijah would never leave Doll untended in this weather. He thinks more of that horse than he does of us. Something must be terribly wrong!"

Hakim dismounted and unslung his rifle, motioning for Tulley to do the same. They handed their reins to the younger Trebane. "We'll check the house first. If Elijah isn't here, we'll have a devil of a time finding him. The snow has covered all the tracks, and all we can do is pray that we locate him before he freezes to death.

"Buck, there's an old enclosed shed through those trees. Take the horses back there, strip the saddles off, and rub 'em down real good with some of that straw you're packing. Make sure you get Doll nice and dry, then cover her with several blankets. Give her some water and a bit of that dried corn, and she'll be a friend for life." Turning to the other two men, he instructed, "I don't think anyone is here, but let's not take any chances. Sam, go around and cover the back door. Frank and I will go in the front."

Hakim and Tulley took up positions on either side of the closed door, and each chambered a round in their assault weapons. Gingerly reaching out and testing the front door handle, Hakim found it unlocked and pushed open the door; it creaked inward on its rusty hinges. Snow, carried on an eddy of the wind, swirled into the darkened interior. There was no sound from the inside. The two friends looked at each other, and Tulley nodded. Suddenly Hakim made a rolling dive into the room, followed immediately by Tulley. They each came to a crouch, weapons ready, at either corner of the room.

As their eyes adjusted to the dim light inside the front room, they saw an unmoving figure on the floor. It was Elijah. There was dried blood on the side of his head, and all over his hands.

"Oh, no," Hakim murmured. He stood up and walked over to the prone figure, and felt the neck for a pulse. He was unable to find one, but the skin was still soft. He pulled his knife from its scabbard, and held the black metal blade gently in front of Elijah's mouth and nose for a moment, then examined it. Moisture had condensed on the cold blade! However weak his vital signs, Elijah was alive and breathing faintly, at least for the moment. Hakim looked up at his companion with urgency, and barked, "Get Sam in here, Frank, right now! Then get a fire started as quickly as you can! Maybe it's not too late to save him!"

Hakim noted that Elijah's clothes were frozen stiff, and realized that somehow, somewhere, the man must have fallen into water, injuring himself in the process. It was apparent from the shape of his hands, and the knees of his pants, that he had crawled back to the house. He located Elijah's saddle bags, and pulled out a dry set of clothes, which he set aside. As Frank built up the fire, Hakim spread out Elijah's bedroll, and laid the unconscious man on top of it. He then began to gently wrestle the frozen clothes off of the old man. He finally wound up cutting some of the clothing off of him.

"Sam, a hundred feet off the porch, toward that big old oak tree, I remember seeing a pile of big, round, river rocks a month ago when we came up here to clean out the chimney. It must have been an old property boundary," he said, as he worked on Elijah. "Bring about ten of those stones in here. You'll need to take a chunk of that firewood to whack them apart. I expect those stones have frozen together in this weather."

He called over his shoulder to Tulley, "Frank, heat up some water for me. And you might as well set coffee on, and start fixing some supper. And I'm going to need a warm, beefy broth for Elijah."

"Done, done, and I'm working on it."

Hakim smiled to himself. Frank Tulley was no pilgrim. Both men were experienced backwoodsmen and battle-hardened warriors. Hakim was glad they had found one another again, after all these years.

****

"Okay, Sam, here's your next job. You get those big stones cleaned up and dry, then set them by the fire. Let them get *warm* – not hot, mind you – just slightly warm to the touch, and then put them under 'Lijah's blanket, right next to his skin. I want a stone next to each side of his neck, one between his legs snug up against his groin, and then one between each of his arms and his chest, in his armpits. Have the other five rocks warming by the fire,. Every twenty minutes or so, swap them, so that he stays warm. Got it?"

"Got it."

"When you have the first set of stones in position, go get eight more. Clean 'em up and warm them and rotate them just like the others. Put one at each hand and each foot."

Hakim knew that Elijah's chances of survival were slim. The old man was in advanced hypothermia, and recovery was unlikely, especially in these conditions. He gently inspected the unconscious man's hands, feet, ears and nose for signs of frostbite. They appeared to be okay. Hakim shook his head. If Elijah survived, it would be in part due to the fact that the air temperature had risen in advance of the storm. The Arab bowed his head, and asked his God to preserve Elijah Moore's life.

****

That night the storm blew itself out after dropping a foot and a half of snow on the Phoenix community. The low pressure system that brought the precipitation ambled on slowly, skipping across Long Island Sound and trundling northeast up the Atlantic seaboard, its sights set for Nova Scotia. A blustery high pressure system pushed south from Canada in its wake, bringing strong north winds and sharply falling temperatures. The old house in Carson's Gap, however, stayed warm due to the blazing fire in its old, stone fireplace.

****

Elijah slipped into delirium. Too weak to move, he was able only to mutter. In his semi-conscious state, he began to babble incoherently. The hate and anger he had harbored bubbled to the surface in snarls and wild accusations. Hakim advised the others that they had best forget all they were hearing, as the poor man was not in his right mind.

But slowly, his body core temperature was rising. Sam kept the warm stones in place, and faithfully swapped them out every twenty minutes or so. Hakim had cleaned and bandaged Elijah's head wound, as well as his hands. Now it was just a matter of time.

Since they couldn't move Elijah, and only two were required to care for him, Hakim sent Frank and Buck out hunting. They went to the same laurel-covered pass where Elijah had hunted, and stumbled across his two kills. These they packed back to the cabin. By the end of the day, they had bagged three more deer and a brace of grouse.

****

Elijah moaned. Hakim set his rifle down, which he had been cleaning, and walked across the warm room. The older man's eyelids fluttered, and then opened.

"Welcome back to the land of the living, 'Lijah," Hakim said, "I thought we'd lost you for good last night."

Elijah worked his dry mouth for a moment, then managed to croak, "Where am I?"

"You're in the cabin on Carson's Gap. Yesterday we came looking for you during the snow storm. Found you passed out in here on the floor. Your clothes were frozen solid, you had a nasty wound on your head, and your hands were all torn up. I figure you must have taken a fall somewhere."

"Hands hurt. Head hurts," Elijah mumbled.

Hakim nodded. "I reckon so. I suspect that as you do inventory, you'll find that just about everything else is hurting, too. Think you can handle some soup?"

Elijah nodded.

"Can you handle a spoon?"

Elijah held up his bandaged hand. It was shaking badly. "Don't think so."

Hakim walked over to the fire and poured a cup of soup, as he said cheerfully, "Well, what are friends for, other than for patching you up when you go swimming in your clothes during an arctic storm? I think I can manage the spoon. Here, let me help you sit up."

Once Elijah got some food into his stomach, his condition began to improve. Later that afternoon, Hakim sent Frank and Buck back to the encampment, with the pack horses loaded with fresh venison. Sam and he would follow once Elijah was strong enough to sit in the saddle. However, the next morning the old man's condition turned again for the worse. He developed a fever, and a racking, rattly cough. Finally, Hakim sent Sam back to the community with instructions to come back with one of the carts which had been rigged to carry coal, and as many blankets as could be spared.

In this manner they were finally able to return a now-very-ill Elijah Moore to the Phoenix community.

****

"Put him in my cabin, Hakim," Mary Anders instructed as the coal cart rolled up with Elijah bundled up in the back of it. The old fellow was floating in and out of consciousness, and his fever had not gone down.

Hakim picked Elijah up and carried him into Mary's cabin. She took one look and exclaimed, "Oh, no! Hakim, look! His lips are blue."

Hakim examined Elijah's face closely and noticed the bluish hue of his cheeks and lips. "He must be cold," the Arab offered.

"No, you ninny! That's not from the cold, that's from pneumonia! He's going to suffocate unless we get some of that mucus out of his lungs! Angie," Mary said, "stoke up the fire, and get some water boiling! We need some steam. Hakim, put him in the bed there, and help me get his coat and shirt off of him! Then we need to roll him onto his stomach."

Together they removed Elijah's coat and shirt, and rolled him onto his stomach. Mary brought out several clean towels, and arranged one under Elijah's head.

"Now, you hit him on the back between and below the shoulder blades, like this," Mary demonstrated. "He's got mucus down in his lungs, coating them, and it's so bad that he's not getting enough air. That's why his lips and cheeks have that bluish tint. I'll bring a steaming kettle over. Between the steam, and you beating on his back, maybe we can loosen enough of it so that he can cough it up."

They worked with Elijah for several hours, and he was able to cough up a good deal of phlegm. Slowly his pallor returned to a normal color. They covered him up, and then let him sleep.

"We need to do this about every four hours or so, Hakim," Mary said quietly. They were sitting at the table drinking coffee. Elijah was sleeping peacefully. "If his lungs fill up with that stuff, he'll die. But if we can get him through the next several days, he'll probably recover." She studied the Arab and seemed to notice for the first time the weariness on his face. "Oh, Hakim, I'm so sorry! You've been up taking care of him for several days now. You look exhausted. Angie and I will get some help. Why don't you go back to your cabin and get some sleep?"

"Are you sure, Mary? I–"

"Oh, hush! Of course I'm sure! Here," she said, handing him his coat, "off with you now. If you don't get to bed soon, you're going to fall over!"

Not long after he left, there was a knock at Mary's door. She opened it, and found Gary and Ellen Shanks standing outside. "Gary! Ellen!" she said with surprise, having been caught off guard. Of all the people in the community, they were the last ones she had expected to inquire after Elijah.

"Hi, Mary," Gary began. "We understand that Elijah's been brought back, and that he's got pneumonia. We heard that you're taking care of him. Ellen and I know how much work that is, we've had some experience with pneumonia, and so Ellen and I, well, we, uh . . . we want to help out."

Mary was well aware of the trouble between Elijah and the Shanks, but as she looked at the couple and studied their faces they seemed, somehow, different. The hard bitterness had gone from their faces. The edgy lines of anger had disappeared.

"You? You're sure? You want to help Elijah?" she asked directly. Mary had never been accused of being subtle.

Gary flushed with embarrassment. "Yes, we do. We'd like to help him recover. We want him to get well. That probably sounds odd, I suppose, coming from us. But we've, well, we've changed. Can we help?"

****

Elijah awoke in a fit of coughing. He was hot, and cast off some of his covers. He was surprised to see Gary Shanks standing over him, a concerned expression on his face. *What's he doing here?* Elijah thought to himself. But he was too weak to give it much thought.

"Can I get you anything?" Gary asked.

"Water," Elijah croaked, "Water, please."

Gary brought him a cup of cool water, and helped him sit up enough to drink it. Elijah drained the cup and sank back into the bed. "Much obliged," he whispered as he drifted back to sleep.

****

Two days later, Elijah awoke to a cabin of activity. Mary was cooking. Angie was sewing patches in worn clothes. There was a wonderful aroma of coffee in the air. Mary saw him stir, and called out, "Morning, Elijah!"

"Good morning, Mrs. Anders," he responded, his voice stronger than it had been in days.

"Oh, stop that! If you call me Mrs. Anders one more time, I'm going to send you back to your own cabin, and you'll have to get your own self well," she carped, sharp-tongued as always.

"Yes, ma'am," Elijah responded meekly.

She wiped her hands on her apron, and walked over to his bed, looking down on him with a smile. "Your fever finally broke, for good, I think, late yesterday afternoon. You've been touch and go for a while, Elijah. There were several times in the last three or four days we all thought you were finished. I 'spect you're just too ornery to die. How do you feel, 'Lijah?"

"Weak as a kitten, but otherwise pretty good." He fell into a fit of coughing, but it was not the rattly cough it had been.

"I have three very special people who have been wanting to see you. They've been camped out on my doorstep for several days, hoping you'd get better. Do you feel up to having visitors?"

Elijah scowled, his characteristic caution overtaking him, "Well, I don't kn—"

"I'll take that as a 'yes'," Mary said, interrupting him. Elijah just raised his eyebrows, studying her face.

"You cantankerous old coot!" she admonished, "These visitors will do you good! Now, you'd better promise to behave!" Not waiting for a response, she turned and directed, "Go get 'em, Ang'. Tell 'em they can only stay for ten minutes." Angie pulled on her coat, smiled mysteriously at Elijah, and went outside.

Mystified, Elijah wondered what was going on. He studied the cabin door, waiting, and wondering who would walk through it. In spite of his curiosity, he fell asleep watching the door.

****

A cool hand caressed his forehead, and he heard a soft voice, "Hey, dad. Wake up! I've brought you some friends."

Elijah opened his eyes. Ginny, his daughter was bending over him. She kissed him on the forehead. "Hello, Genevieve," he said tenderly.

"Hi, daddy," she said, and then she hugged him tightly. "I thought I had lost you."

"No, baby. I'm still here. Reckon I've got a little mileage left in me yet, thanks to everyone who's been taking care of me." Then he noticed two little tousled heads at the foot of his bed, looking anxiously at him. He broke into a big smile, and cried, "Peter! Elizabeth! Hello! Now there's a sight for sore eyes!"

The children laughed, and before Ginny could stop them, they climbed up on the bed and sat cross-legged, after giving the old man a hug. The delight written across his face was quickly replaced by concern.

"Do your momma and daddy know where you are," he asked sternly, but not too sternly.

"Uh-huh!" Peter said happily. "They told us we could come over!"

"They did?" responded Elijah with confusion.

"Yeah!" replied Elizabeth. "They said we can come see you anytime now. Now that daddy and mommy forbade you, we can be friends again!"

"Forbade?" Elijah stuttered.

299

"No, silly," Peter said with a giggle, looking at Elizabeth, "*forgave* not *forbade*!"

"They forgave me?" Elijah said, still confused.

The children did not hear him, as they happily prattled on, talking a mile a minute. Ginny finally lifted them off the bed and sent them home. "Shoo," she said, smiling, "I want to talk to my dad."

*** * * * * * * * * ***

The next day, Elijah got out of bed for the first time in a week. He was weak, but was clearly recovering. A day later, he was able to move back into his own cabin. Ginny took over his remaining care. She watched him like a hawk for any sign of relapse, but Elijah continued to grow stronger.

Throughout Elijah's ordeal, the Phoenix community had continued its preparations toward the spring, and the long trek westward. As often as the weather permitted, timbering continued, as well as the work with the horses. The dryer held an increasing amount of lumber, with the coal-fired heat drawing the moisture from the fresh-cut wood.

Two days after Elijah returned to his own cabin, Hakim found Jacen waiting on him when he returned from a long day in the round pen.

"Brrrrh! It's cold out there! Guess what, Jacen! Patty Linder started our last mare in the round pen today. By spring they will all be gentled."

"That's great, Hakim! I'm pleased with all the progress we've made. But there is something that's bothering me."

"Oh? What's up?"

"I heard that Gary and Ellen Shanks have become Christians, Hakim. And I heard that you have been talking to them about it," Jacen said, accusingly.

"Yes, I have. So, what's the problem?"

"I don't want you proselytizing these people, Hakim!"

"What?" Hakim said, shocked.

300

"Keep your beliefs to yourself, Hakim. This isn't going to be a religious community!"

Hakim opened his mouth, ready to make a sharp rejoinder. But he thought better of it, and remained silent for a moment. When he had his temper under control, he queried, "Then what sort of a community do you envision it to be, Jacen?

"Phoenix will be a secular community. We're not going to have a bunch of religious fanatics running it, or setting standards of morality for everyone else," Jacen replied firmly.

"I see." Hakim thought for a moment, and then asked, "Since any system of law is ultimately a statement on morality, because laws generally establish what is or isn't acceptable behavior, then I assume you'll have secularists setting the morality for everyone else. Right?"

Jacen considered this, and then responded, "Yes, I expect that's about right."

"Hmm. Jacen, what's a secularist? Is it someone who believes that there is no god? In other words, is a secularist necessarily an atheist? And if so, does that mean people must be atheists to be part of your community?"

"No, Hakim," Jacen replied, "people can believe in a god and be part of Phoenix. It's just that they have to keep their beliefs in their god to themselves. They need to be more concerned about the community than they are about whatever god they have."

"So, a secularist is either an atheist, or someone who maybe believes in a god but believes the community is more important, right? And because of that belief, he doesn't find it necessary to talk about his god to others."

"Yeah. Yeah, that's right," Jacen said, feeling gratified that the conversation had not degenerated into another argument.

"Jacen, don't you see that the secularist, as you have defined him, is in fact a religionist who is constantly preaching and demanding his particular view of religion? Any statement about God _is_ a religious statement, Jacen, including the assertion that God does not exist. That's a _religious statement_. You have just defined a secularist in exclusively religious terms: he either denies the existence of God, or he affirms that God isn't really important, certainly less so than the community. In both cases you're building a doctrine of God, which means you're creating a theology for your particular religion.

"And don't you see that your particular religion is absolutely intolerant of any other?" continued Hakim. "You go so far as to exclude people like me from participation in your community. You want to muzzle my religious beliefs, and you want to do so in order to promote your own, your own secularist view of things. It is you, Jacen, not me, who's intolerantly preaching religion. _I_ am not saying that a secularist can't be part of our community, but _you_ are saying that a Christian can't be!"

"But Hakim, your brand of religion tells others that they're wrong. Who are you to judge that?"

"Yes, Jacen, my brand of religion does tell others they're wrong. What you fail to see is that so does yours. So do all religions. So do all beliefs."

"Not true, Hakim! My dad used to say that all religions are the same, and that they all worship the same god."

"Jacen, I in no way want to dishonor your father or his memory, but you need to understand something. People who say such things are themselves creating a god out of whole cloth. They are less interested in truth about God than they are in mollifying people who possess contradictory notions about God. In reality they are respecting no one's religion, and are asserting their own made-up god to the exclusion of others. Their insistence on an amorphous, elastic god who has no distinct moral characteristics is no less exclusionary than the belief of the fiercest proponent of Islam, who insists that there is no god but Allah and Muhammad is his prophet."

Jacen considered this for a moment. He'd never before allowed himself to think through the flip side of his argument, but now that he did, he had to grudgingly admit that Hakim had a point. In fact, as he analyzed his own feelings, Jacen began to see that he was pursuing his own idea of secularism with something of a religious fervor, intent on winning everyone to his own way of thinking. It wasn't that he was trying to win others to a particular view of God, but rather to the equally important notion that *whatever* your view of God was, at the end of the day God simply didn't matter all that much. Of far greater importance, Jacen thought, were people and communities. For a fleeting instant he entertained the thought that the community and its structures and people were god; but he immediately dismissed this thought, not as false, necessarily, but he dismissed it as an implication he didn't want the burden of thinking about. He just didn't want to go there.

"So what, Hakim, do you propose as a solution?"

"Just let people talk, Jacen. Don't allow anyone to force a belief on anyone else. But debate, proselytizing, conversation, and so on, just let it happen. If I don't like what my neighbor is saying, I'll just tell him to get out of my house. Let everyone else do the same."

"But what if I'm out in public, and I don't want to hear it?"

"Jacen, we're all exposed to things we don't care for every day. That's just life. The instant you try to protect people from being offended, we lose part of our freedom. If you don't like what I'm saying, walk away. If I don't like what you're saying, I can walk away. And if we can't walk away, we'll just have to realize that freedom means that sometimes those we disagree with get to speak their piece. That's just part of life."

Jacen didn't respond. He knew in his heart that Phoenix needed Hakim, and others like him, such as Francis Tulley. He also knew that if he tried to enforce secularism, both Hakim and Tulley would leave, and now the Shanks would leave. He wondered if there were others of the Phoenix group who wouldn't tolerate a muzzle on religious talk. He suspected there were.

"I guess I'll just have to think about it some more," he replied carefully.

"Good, Jacen. I think that's a good answer for now," said Hakim, nodding. "I'm not asking you to be quiet about your conviction that secularism is the way to go. I'm simply asking that you not prevent me from voicing my convictions when we differ."

CHAPTER 30

"Peter, Elizabeth, you two run along. Momma and I want to talk to Mr. Moore," instructed Gary Shanks. The two tousle-headed youngsters hugged Elijah, and then ran to the door. They struggled with their coats momentarily, and then turned to their parents.

"Can we go and watch Mr. Trebane?" asked Elizabeth. The warmth, the rich aroma of fresh-cut wood, and the piles of sawdust made the wood shop Peter and Elizabeth's favorite place in the Phoenix community.

"Yes, but don't bother him with a lot of silly talk! He's a very busy man."

The two bounded out the door, shutting it behind them. Gary turned back to Elijah. It had been about a week since the older man had begun to feel good enough to get out of bed. Slowly, his strength began to return to him. The entire community knew that it had been a close thing: Elijah had nearly died, first from the exposure and hypothermia, and then from the ensuing bout of pneumonia. Everyone stopped by at some point every day to check on him. It had greatly encouraged the old man, and the sense of isolation and estrangement from the community that he'd felt was swallowed up by the genuine concern shown for his health.

Elijah looked up warily from where he was seated. He didn't know how to respond to Gary and Ellen Shanks since his illness. Clearly they'd changed in their attitudes and opinions toward him. But he had no idea why.

"What can I do for you, Shanks?" he asked carefully.

"There's something Ellen and I would like to say to you. Have you got a moment?" Gary replied.

Elijah examined the man's face. There was no guile in it, nor malice, so far as he could see. He relaxed, realizing in the same instant that he had tensed up when Gary and Ellen had entered. He nodded and motioned to two seats across the table from him.

After sitting down, Gary glanced at Ellen, who nodded almost imperceptibly. He turned back to Elijah, drew a deep breath, and said, "Elijah, Ellen and I want you to know that we have forgiven you for shooting me, and for accusing me of hurting Randy. We want you to know that we will no longer think of those events, or talk about them to others, nor will we continue to view you through what happened that day. We desire to put it behind us, for good.

"And we also want to ask you to forgive our complicity in the actions of the Pittsburgh slaver colony. We realize that that whole affair was wrong, and we can not defend our involvement with them in any way. We were wrong to be part of that. Please forgive us. We love you, our children love you, and we sincerely desire your friendship."

Elijah was caught completely off-guard; he'd not been expecting this. For a long moment he stared at the couple opposite him. A confusing mix of emotions whirled in his heart: joy and relief, bitterness, and stubbornness. His instinctual caution wrestled with his great desire to be free of the exhausting burden of the hatred and bitterness that he felt toward the Shanks and all the former slavers.

Suddenly, in a flash of insight, he understood that the bitterness he felt was destroying *him*, while not affecting those against whom he harbored it, except perhaps in peripheral ways. *It was his own life he was destroying with his sour bitterness!* Pulling himself from the depths of his own thoughts, he realized Gary was speaking again.

"Perhaps, Elijah, you need some time to think about this. I know that the loss of your wife, Julie, to the murderous activities of those we were associated with, is a very bitter pill for you. I can't begin to express how ashamed Ellen and I are that we were ever a part of such an outfit. We are so sorry, so ashamed, at what was done to Julie. I expect that if our positions were reversed, I would feel the same way you do. Would you like us to come back another time?"

Tears began to well up in the corners of the old man's eyes. He nodded, not trusting himself to speak. Gary and Ellen stood, quietly put on their coats, and left the cabin, closing the door behind them. Elijah put his head in his hands and wept.

****

One morning, about two weeks later, Elijah came to a decision. After many late-night talks with Hakim and much internal wrestling, Elijah finally decided that he wasn't going to allow the past to destroy his future. He decided to release his bitterness, and to forgive Gary and Ellen their part in the community that had murdered his wife. From the instant that he made the decision, a great and heavy weight was lifted from his shoulders and an involuntary grin traced itself across his leathery face. He was still grinning when he found Gary Shanks down at the corral.

"Gary, been looking for you," the old man said.

Gary was in the process of throwing a saddle on the back of one of the mares so that he could take her out for a little exercise. "Well," he said, stooping down to grasp the latigo strap, "you found me." He straightened up, cinched the latigo, and then began to adjust the length of the stirrups. "How can I help you, Elijah?"

"You asked me, a couple of weeks ago, to forgive you for Julie's death. Well, I've got to admit that the last thing I've wanted to do was forgive you. I wanted to make you suffer, somehow, as I have suffered. But I've realized that the more I've hated you, the more unhappy I've become. Hakim's been trying to convince me of a bunch of religious stuff. I ain't buying what he's selling, but he has convinced me of this: I need to forgive you, or my bitterness will destroy me.

"So, Gary, I'm ready to bury the hatchet; I'm tired of my bitterness. I accept your forgiveness. And yes, I do forgive you." He held out his hand, a big smile written across his face. Gary smiled back, and shook his hand enthusiastically.

****

The reconciliation of Elijah Moore and Gary and Ellen Shanks produced a ray of warmth in the Phoenix community that even the short, cold days and the long, dark nights of winter were unable to extinguish. The members of the settlement drew closer, and learned to function as a well-oiled team. Divisions between individuals as "former slaves" and "former slavers" finally disappeared, and the difficulties of survival bonded the little group as one.

During the winter months, great efforts were made to create a common base of knowledge and skill across the entire group. Each learned the care and handling of horses, and gained experience riding. Hakim trained everyone in small-unit tactics and weaponry, as well as hand-to-hand combat techniques. Around the fire at night, they discussed what would be their priorities when they arrived at their intended destination, and how they would set up the governance of the Phoenix community. All agreed that Jacen should be the leader until the community reached fifty adults in size, at which point they would begin to elect leaders.

During the days, the wood shop and wood dryer became the focal points of activity. The dryer had done its job, and the wood was sufficiently dry that there were no fears of it warping, cracking, or splitting down the road. Jim Trebane was constantly at work, planing and smoothing the wood, or teaching others to do so. The stack of finished, dried lumber grew larger and larger.

As spring drew on, the activities of the settlement became oriented toward producing the first prototypical wagon. Not only would the wagon be used to evaluate the design and to work out the kinks in construction techniques, it would also be put to work to train the community members how to handle a horse-drawn wagon.

The final design was a sturdy, durable wagon composed of an eclectic collection of items, such as a few scavenged metal parts, including leaf springs from automobiles, with the primary portion being wooden pieces fabricated in the Trebanes' shop. After a week of road testing with and without loads, and a number of modifications, the wagon design was pronounced an unqualified success.

****

"What's the date, Hakim?" Jacen asked. The two friends were sharing a rare moment alone, drinking coffee at the fire, which had burned down to but a few smoldering embers glowing in the darkness. The night air was chill and damp with dew. Jacen could hear the horses nickering, and stamping their hooves down in the corral. Though he could not see them, he knew that eight loaded wagons were parked not far away in the darkness. Tomorrow morning Phoenix would say good-bye for good to the tiny ruin of Bedford, Pennsylvania, and begin the long trek to Colorado.

"It's April 22th, Jacen. We've been here for one year and twelve days."

"Seems like forever. Do you remember when we first found this place, Hakim? And that little warehouse back there?"

"I do. And do you remember what happened when we came out of the warehouse and were headed back up onto the trail?"

"No, I can't recall. What happened?"

"That's when we first saw the horses!" Hakim said dreamily, looking up at the stars.

"And I wanted to shoot them for food! What an idiot!" Jacen said, laughing at himself.

"Well, now we've got a good string of forty-five horses, plus that stud. We've got saddles, wagons, and most importantly, we have good friends, Jacen. This dream of yours is rapidly approaching reality."

Jacen nodded, also gazing at the stars. He thought over his adventures of the last year, and realized how prominent a part his friend had played. He looked affectionately at the Arab, and said, "Thanks to you, Hakim. It's becoming a reality because of you."

"No, boy. Not because of me. Because of *us*. And because of *them*," he affirmed, motioning to the cabins where the rest were sleeping. "This project is growing out of all of our lives. And I believe, by the grace of *Isa al Masih*, Phoenix will be successful."

"You know you don't need to do that anymore."

"Do what?"

"Call your God by his Arabic name. You can call him Jesus. I know who you're talking about. And I suppose I don't mind if you talk about him, now and again."

Hakim grinned, "In the beginning, I referred to Him that way because I didn't want to clue you in, too early, that I was a Christian. I was afraid you'd get all hung up on wrong-headed notions before we really got to know each other. But mostly I do it because Arabic is my native tongue, and I love the sound of His Name in my own language."

Jacen shook his head. "Whatever. You got your hardware close by?"

"Always. Why?"

"Because, by the looks of Orion the Hunter, it is time for us to relieve Gary and Elijah."

Hakim threw out the dregs from his mug, tapped the few grounds of coffee out of it, and then left the cup on the table. He picked up his M14, checked the magazine and the safety, and then looked at Jacen with a grin. "Let's go do the last watch, boy. Together."

Jacen nodded and grinned back, his M4 slung over his shoulder. They walked out into the darkness, together.

CHAPTER 31

"Shall we wake them?" Jacen asked, unable to contain his excitement.

"Hold your horses, Jace! It's still dark. This is liable to be their last good sleep for a while. Give it another thirty minutes."

Jacen nodded. He could not wait to get the group up and on the road. The two men were done with the last watch, and the eastern edges of the sky were turning gray, then gradually shading from deep orange through yellow with the onset of the sunrise.

Thirty minutes later Jacen was walking among the cabins, beating an empty pot with a spoon and shouting, "RISE AND SHINE! RISE AND SHINE! Time to get up, Phoenix! We want to hit the road early."

Groans emanated from the cabins. It had been a late night packing for most of them. Through the walls of the Shanks' cabin, Jacen could hear Peter and Elizabeth expressing their youthful excitement about the new adventure that was to begin today.

****

"Hold 'em still, for crying out loud!" Jacen snapped, irritated. The two horses were prancing about nervously, picking up the excitement from the larger group. "No, no, not like that! Like this!" He gathered the bridle right under the horse's chin, and held it still.

"Well, you don't have to speak to me that way!" Ginny Moore snapped back.

An angry retort formed in Jacen's mouth, but then he thought better of it. He let the wave of frustration pass, then replied, "You're right, Ginny. I shouldn't speak to you that way. I'm sorry, I was wrong."

She raised her pretty eyebrows at him, and turned to face the horses again, gripping the bridle tightly under the chin. But the stiff resentment was gone from her posture. "I've got her now," she said quietly over her shoulder, "you can finish harnessing her."

Ginny seemed to show up whenever Jacen was working on something that she was capable of helping with. Jacen had noticed her interest. In fact, Jacen had noticed a lot more than her interest. The beautiful girl was intoxicating, downright distracting.

Several wagons over, Gary Shanks was admonishing Peter. "Son, I want you to go use the outhouse."

"But Dad, I don't have to!" the seven-year-old whined.

"Just try, son. I know that as soon as we get rolling you're going to have to use the bathroom. So just do it now."

"But Daddy, I really don't have to go. Really!"

Gary closed his eyes, and breathed out with resignation, "Okay, but remember what I told you. We probably won't stop at all for the first two hours. If you have to go once we get started, you'll just have to do it in your pants."

Peter looked at him, eyes wide, "Oh! Gross! Well, maybe I can try to," he said, turning toward the outhouse.

Gary smiled to himself once the youngster was out of earshot, and muttered, "Works every time."

****

During the spring Jim and Buck Trebane had crafted eight heavy wagons, with the help of the others. The bed of the draft vehicles ran to ten feet long, by five feet wide with sidewalls three feet high. The wagon beds had been thoroughly caulked and sealed. Each was fitted with thin spruce hoops, called bows, over which was stretched good canvas sail material, obtained from the remains of an old sail factory on the east side of the Pittsburgh ruin. It was a location that the Shanks knew of from their days at the slaver settlement.

Axles had been crafted from sturdy hickory timber. At first the Trebanes had experimented with trying to use auto or truck rims for wheels. After wasting three weeks attempting to create a means of attaching them to the axles, Jim gave up and the two men began the difficult process of crafting the wheels from wood. They settled on an hickory design that was four feet in diameter for the rear wheels, with twelve stout spokes, and front wheels with a three-foot diameter.

With their crude forge, he fashioned iron tires, which he heated until they expanded, then hammered down around the wooden rim. As they cooled, they bound themselves tightly to the wheel, making a heavy, but very sturdy, unit. If they kept up good maintenance on the wagons and their running gear, Jim figured that they could make several thousand miles without too much wear and tear, especially considering that their trail was entirely composed of old crumbling interstate highways, which still retained a good level surface.

There was enough iron stock to fabricate four spares of both front and rear wheels. They were carried in the tool wagon. In addition to a lever brake, each wagon carried, slung under the bed, a heavy squared log attached to the coupling pole of the running gear with a heavy chain. On steep downhill grades the log could be dragged to help control the wagon's speed.

Each wagon was painted a deep forest green and trimmed in black. Onto the tailgates was stenciled in fancy script the word "Phoenix", painted in bright red. On the left side of each wagon, Ellen Shanks painted an image of a white dove in flight, the bird the group had chosen to represent the phoenix.

****

The lead wagon would be shared by Jacen and Hakim, followed by a wagon with Elijah and Ginny Moore, and Misty Randall, and a third wagon containing Mary Anders and Angie Bartwell. Gus and Katie Blackwell's wagon followed, with Gary and Ellen and their children coming behind them. Jim and Melissa Trebane shared the sixth wagon with Buck. It was heavily loaded with tools, as was the seventh, driven by the Linder sisters. Patty and Lynn's vehicle became known as the "Tool Wagon." The tools, plus the spare parts for all the other vehicles took up over half the wagon, but the sisters did not mind as they were traveling light themselves. Bringing up the rear was a densely packed wagon driven by Phil Gonzales, Sam Oxford, and Francis Tulley. Most of the blacksmith implements, as well as some spare iron stock, came in the final, eighth wagon. Each of the first five wagons were rigged to tow the community's two-wheeled carts. The carts themselves were filled with provender for the horses, plus water containers. Jacen figured that the carts could be traded for food as the group progressed west, if the opportunity presented itself.

****

Although each had been trained to handle the horses and hitch the wagons, the morning turned into bedlam. The animals knew instinctively that something big was up, and

315

several of the horses chose this morning to express their displeasure at being harnessed. The horses that weren't being hitched at the moment didn't help matters. With their reins looped around the bars of the corral, they shuffled and sidestepped nervously, whinnying to their neighbors being attached to the wagons up on the I-70 embankment.

Tempers flared and hot words were spoken, but with Jacen's patient leadership backed up by Hakim's quiet competence, the group began to sort itself out. Finally they were ready to move, and Jacen reminded them of the plans for the day.

"Okay, listen up," Jacen cried out as he sat astride Astor, a large black mare he had gentled. Everyone turned to face him. "All we want to do today is about five miles. Tomorrow we'll go for ten. Eventually we'll probably do twenty-five to thirty miles per day, if the roads are good. Remember, today we are _just_ working the kinks out. We know that things will break, mistakes will be made, problems will occur. So just relax, and let's take things in stride. I'm going to count today as a grand success if we make five miles and none of us gets killed in the doing of it."

"How are we going to know where to stop, Jacen?" Gus Blackwell called out.

"Whoever is riding point for the day will ride ahead and scout a good place to camp, then come back and guide you to it. Today, Frank Tulley and I have those duties. While we're gone, Hakim is in charge." Gus nodded in acknowledgment.

Buck Trebane was already sitting on the wagon box, ready to roll out. He asked, "We still going to change the teams at noon, even though we're only going five miles?"

"Uh-huh. We are, just so everyone gets the practice of doing it. Plus, it will keep the horses fresh. Any more questions? No? Okay, let's roll!" Jacen waved his hand at Hakim, in the first wagon, and pointed west.

With that, Hakim lightly bounced the traces on his horses' hindquarters, and they moved out. One by one the wagons followed, until it was Gary Shanks' turn. He bounced the traces and clucked his tongue. Nothing happened. He slapped the traces down a little harder. The horses refused to move, ears drawn back. "Hiyaah!" he shouted, slapping the traces down hard. With a lunge, the two horses took off. The quick start tumbled Gary backwards off the box and he sprawled out into the back of the covered wagon. Ellen kept her seat and very alertly grabbed the reins, keeping control of the horses, who were now briskly trotting and beginning to overhaul the wagon in front. "Whoa!" she cried, pulling back sharply. The horses tried to stop, but the momentum of the heavily loaded wagon drove them forward. Ellen grabbed for the brake lever and yanked it. Gary was just finding his feet in the wagon, and the sudden stopped tossed him suddenly forward, so that he wound up lying halfway in his wife's lap. As Jacen howled with laughter, Gary calmly looked up at his wife and said, "You're doing fine, hon'. You're doing fine."

He again took his seat and got his team moving out at a walk. The wagons behind managed to follow without incident. At long last, the Phoenix community was on the move!

CHAPTER 32

Maxwell Baker leaned into the harness. Next to him, his son, Maxwell junior, nicknamed Mack, was also pulling, and next to him Neil Coker was likewise harnessed. Standing on the plow which the three men were pulling through the moist earth was George Agee. It was hard work, but the field had been cultivated for five years running, and the ground was not as hard as it could have been.

The Pittsburgh settlement had begun falling apart after the departure of the slaves the previous August. When Sam Oxford, Jim Trebane, and Gary Shanks had quit the group in September, it was the final blow. Tim Shanks vanished with the two sons of Bob Beaufort, and built up a gang of wandering, murdering, rootless men. Most of the rest of the settlement migrated to the slaver community with whom they had traded, five days to the northwest. The Agees and their four sons, plus the Bakers and Neil Coker had remained behind. The land was productive; it was a good location, already developed. They figured they could simply cultivate the ground themselves, without the use of slaves. There was something honest, satisfying, about your own blisters and calluses, about lying down in your bed at night aching in body but satisfied in heart. Together they had agreed: being a farmer was much better than being a jailer.

Though the temperature was still a bit brisk, sweat rolled down Maxwell's face as his feet dug into the rich loam. Another day's work, and this field would be ready for planting. Movement in the trees to the south caught his eye, and he looked up, motioning for the others to stop. Mack bent over, placing his hands on his knees and rasped, "What's wrong, Dad?" His tattered denim shirt was soaked with sweat.

"Look," was the quiet response.

The others followed Baker's gaze. Emerging from the trees, on old State Route 60, were two horsemen. It was the first time any of them had seen a man riding a horse. For a moment the farmers were speechless. Then Neil wriggled out of his harness and unslung his assault rifle. "Better get ready," he advised. The rest of the group snapped out of their amazement and cast off their harnesses, bringing their weapons to a ready position.

The horsemen spotted the group, and kicked their animals into a canter, heading straight for them. Neil raised his M4, but the elder Baker reached over and gently pushed the muzzle down. "Wait," he cautioned. "That's Jim Trebane on the right. And I believe the young man on the left is that Jacen character. Let's see what they have to say," he directed, his curiosity getting the best of him.

Jacen and Jim rode up, and sat on their horses looking down at the weary men. The two were heavily armed, but made no attempt to go for their weapons.

"Max, Mack, Neil," Trebane acknowledged. The men nodded but made no reply. "Hello, George," he offered in a friendly tone. The silence grew uncomfortable. Jacen's mount shifted, and snorted softly.

"Afternoon, Jim. Been a long time," Max finally said. "Are you coming peacefully?"

"We're coming peacefully, Max. We've no intention of causing trouble. We were hoping to camp here tonight, and

do some trading with you, if you're of a mind to bargain.
Then we'll be movin' on, headed west."

The farmers looked at each other. Max shrugged. "Why
not? The two of you can't be that much trouble."

"No, Max, not two, twenty-one. And we've got forty-five
horses, twelve colts, and 8 large wagons. The others are
coming up behind. Where would you like us to camp?"

"Why don't you take this end of number ten?" Maxwell
Baker suggested, referring to the western threshold of the
old landing strip.

"Sounds good. How many of you are there?"

"Why do you want to know?" Baker replied suspiciously,
a hard edge to his voice.

"Relax, Max. I want to know because you're all invited to
dinner. I told you, our intentions are peaceful. We're here to
trade, and then we're moving on."

Max looked again at his companions. They nodded
assent, so he turned back to Jim and Jacen, and replied,
"There's but ten of us. It just kind of fell apart after you left,
Jim. Most of 'em have gone to the other settlement, up
northwest. We here all decided we were done with slaving,
never really did like it, so we stayed put. Tim Shanks ran off
with Mike and Sam Beaufort. Mike deserted his wife. Three
more worthless men have never drawn breath on God's
green earth. We hear an occasional report of 'em from folks
we trade with. They're off murdering and thieving
somewheres to the west. Last I heard they'd gathered a
whole gang of cutthroats. Murderin' scum, that's what they
are," he said, spitting the last words out with disgust.

Jim nodded. "Tim never was any good. His brother is a
different story; Gary's a prince." Trebane looked over at
Jacen, and asked, "All this sound okay to you, Jace?"

"Uh-huh," the young man agreed. "We'll go back and let
the others know. They're a couple of hours behind us. And
Maxwell, your people can relax. We bear no hard feelings
anymore. Our group worked through all that this past fall

and winter. Tell your ladies we'll have a dance after dinner. I expect we can talk Elijah into breaking out his fiddle."

"You want us to bring anything?"

"How 'bout you folks bring some vegetables, and fresh water? We'll provide the meat and the music."

Maxwell Baker wiped a dirty sleeve across his sweaty forehead, and grinned at Jim and Jacen. "Sounds good to me. We'll see you in a couple of hours."

Half a mile to the west, hidden on the crest of a hill, two men watched the scene through binoculars.

"I wonder what all that palaver was about," said one thoughtfully, as he watched the two horsemen disappear into the trees south of the field.

"Beats me," said the other. "But I'd sure love to get my hands on those horses. Looks like it beats walkin' hollow."

"Yep. You and me both," agreed his companion. "Wonder how they got 'em all trained up and everything. C'mon. We'd better tell Shanks. This might change our plans for tonight."

****

Dinner was a great success. Both groups were hungry for news, and they swapped many tales of the past winter, and winters long ago. After supper was cleared away, Elijah tuned up his fiddle, several others produced wooden recorders, and Maxwell Baker brought out a banjo. Gus built up the fire, and many began to dance, while others clapped to the tunes. The music had a decidedly Irish flair to it. After an hour of this, Frank Tulley walked behind Elijah while he was playing a jig, and whispered something to him. Elijah smiled and nodded.

When the jig was over, he immediately began to play a slow and mournful tune, and Frank began to sing. The Phoenix company's heads all turned as one in surprise, except for Hakim. Frank sang in a rich, clear baritone. It was the first time any of them, other than Hakim, had heard him sing.

It was an old ballad, a love song of a beautiful young woman who was waiting for her betrothed. He was off seeking his fortune, for he would not ask her to be penniless, as he was. So off he went to adventures to earn his fortune, while she waited. He never returned, and she never stopped waiting.

As the final strains of Elijah's fiddle faded, the whole group fell into a sweet, sad silence. The only sounds were the snapping and popping of the fire, and a the haunting cry of a loon in the distance. The moon began to rise over the ridge to the east. Somewhere off to the north, a pack of coyotes serenaded its appearance.

Jacen was loathe to break the spell, but he finally stirred and looked across the fire at the elder Baker. "Max, why don't you meet us in the morning, and let's do some trading. We'd like to trade for some of your canned vegetables. Tomorrow night we can all eat together again, and then come morning, we'll be on our way."

Max nodded. "What time tomorrow morning?"

"Coffee's ready at sunup. Fresh biscuits and venison steaks and gravy will be ready shortly after. You're welcome to join us."

"Don't mind if I do. I'll see you in the morning, then."

****

Hakim Abdul al Malik and Francis Tulley reined up, and studied the tracks in the mud in the morning light. They had been riding a large perimeter around the camp site, looking for any signs of unwanted company.

"What do you think?" Frank asked, after dismounting and examining the prints.

"It's a big group. Twenty-five, thirty, I'd say."

"Uh-huh. These look to be no more than twelve hours old, unless I miss my guess."

"Yep."

"Trouble?"

"Yep. An outfit this size, traveling off-road, can only mean one thing: they don't intend to be seen. These guys are hunting something, or someone. You'd better go back and warn both groups. I think I'll just follow these boys, see what they're up to." Hakim jacked a round into the chamber of his old M14, and unsnapped the flap on the shoulder holster of his Colt. He gathered his reins and stepped into the saddle. "Frank, don't gallop back. Just trot, kind of casual, like. If they have the group under surveillance, we don't want to tip our hand."

****

"I still think a night attack would be best," Mike Beaufort insisted.

"You can think whatever you want to think, but we're not going to hit 'em at night. It's too easy to start shooting our own men in the confusion. Plus, this guy, I think his name was Hakim, owns the night. He's really good. If we attack in the day it takes that advantage away from them," Tim Shanks added confidently.

Shanks then told the others the story of the raid on the slaver community last August that freed all the slaves. He related the tale of the trickery that the Arab had used to divide and conquer the settlement's forces. And finally he spoke of the last day, when Jacen had shared his vision of starting a new society in Colorado, and had invited others to join him. Shanks ridiculed Jacen's idealistic notions. "We are going to put an end to that fool's dreams today!" he boasted.

Mike Beaufort didn't say what he was thinking. Over the last several raids the distinct realization was growing that Shanks was in over his head. He was no tactical leader, and one of these days he was going to get them all killed. Going against farmers and unsuspecting families was pretty easy,

323

but now they were going to attack the curly wolf who'd freed the slaves back in August.

"Okay, here's the plan," Shanks instructed. "That old landing strip they're camped on is like a tabletop. The ground drops down from there on both the north and the south, in steep, heavily wooded gulleys. On the north side, the gulley splits like a 'Y', the two arms bounding the camp on the north and the west. We split into four groups, and we'll have them in three-way crossfire. Mike, you pick seven men. Where the draw splits, you take the south fork. I'll take nine men, and we'll go up the fork to the east. Sam, you're going to circle around with three men, and come up from the south. Just stay put, in hiding. If any of the group breaks to run away, they will run right into your hands. Kill the men, capture the women if you can. If you can't, kill them, too.

"Skinny," he said, addressing a slovenly-dressed, big-boned, heavy man," you take two men and come through the woods near where Baker is plowing. Once you hear us shooting, let 'em have it. Shoot 'em down. Don't let 'em get back to their cabins or their women.

"Does everyone understand? Okay, good. Now listen, I'll kill any man of you who hits a horse. Don't shoot the horses! Understand? We want the horses! And as many of the women as we can capture.

"Let's get moving. You've got about three hours to work into position. Then I'm gonna let the hammer drop. If anything happens, or you get separated, meet back at the falls on Raccoon Creek tonight."

****

"We've got plenty of dried corn, canned corn, potatoes, peas, green beans, squash, tomatoes, peppers, dried apples and peaches, and dried fish, plus numerous herbs. What have you got?" Maxwell eyed Jacen, Gary Shanks, and Jim

Trebane shrewdly. He considered himself to be better than most at striking a good bargain and coming out on top.

"We've got lots of skins, and plenty of dried and jerked meat," Jacen offered.

Baker rolled his eyes with disgust. "Son, *everyone* has skins and dried meat. You *die* during the winter if you don't have dried meat. And any nitwit who has meat sure as the devil better have skins. You need to do better than that, a lot better."

Jacen looked at Jim and Gary innocently, and shrugged his shoulders. "Well," he said, pretending to think long and hard, "I don't know. There's not much else we're of a mind to give up."

Baker sat sipping his coffee, waiting. Try as he might, he couldn't avoid casting an occasional glance toward the makeshift corral, where the horses were bunched. He tried to look disgusted and disinterested.

"I reckon I could do some blacksmithing. I 'spose I could set up a temporary forge for a day or two, fix your implements," Jim Trebane finally suggested. "You've probably got a whole passel of stuff needing fixed."

"That we do. Two full days of steady smith work will buy you, maybe, fifty pounds of dried apples, and twenty quart cans each of corn, snap beans, and tomatoes."

"No. Sweeten the deal," Trebane insisted.

"I'll throw in twenty quarts of canned potatoes. We got lots of those."

"Make it twenty-five quarts of each, and add a pound of dried herbs."

"Why, that's robbery, man!" exclaimed Baker, pretending to be offended.

"You're forgetting something, Maxwell," retorted Trebane, eyes twinkling.

"What might that be?"

"I used to *live* here. I *know* how much we traded for my services. I know what it's worth to you, you old curmudgeon."

"Oh, yeah," replied Max Baker, the ghost of a grin flickering around his lips despite his attempts to look grim, "forgot about that. Okay, you got a deal."

Jacen stood up, and held his hand out. "Good doing business with you, Max. Too bad we don't have anything else you want."

"Now wait a minute, Jacen, don't be so hasty. Maybe we can think of something. Sit down. Hmm . . . Say! You've got a lot of livestock!" he exclaimed, as if only now noticing, "that's a lot of mouths to feed—"

"Max, they eat *grass*," snorted Gary Shanks dryly.

"Well, you just never know how much grass you'll run across," replied Max stubbornly, wearing his best poker face. "Maybe we could do you a favor, take two or three of those animals off your hands, save you some trouble. They ought to be worth, oh, maybe ten or fifteen quarts of vegetables or so."

"What?" said the three Phoenix men in unison, genuinely shocked. Jim Trebane spoke up, spluttering, "Max, you don't have a clue! Any one of those horses is worth ten or fifteen *men*, easily!"

"Well, I don't know about th—" Baker began to say, trying to hide his interest.

"They're not for sale," Jacen said flatly, cutting him off.

It was Baker's turn to be surprised. "Not for sale? Not even one?" he blurted out, unable to hide his disappointment.

"No, because you couldn't afford it," claimed Jacen confidently. "Why, just one of those adult horses is worth five hundred cans of every vegetable you've got. That's probably more than double, or even triple, your entire stock of goods." In truth, after having discussed the matter with the former slavers that were now part of Phoenix, Jacen knew for a fact that the Pittsburgh community probably had six to seven hundred cans, each, of most of their vegetables. "Think, Max!" he continued. "One horse plus one man can easily plow half an acre of good ground in a day. How long does it take you, with *four* men, to plow half an acre? Maybe two days? Three? No, indeed. There's no way you could afford one of our horses," said Jacen, shaking his head sadly.

The men sat silently for a moment. Max chewed on his lip, thinking. It was his pride that was in the way, and he knew it. This young kid had neatly maneuvered him into showing his hand, right from the start, and he had no aces left up his sleeve. It wasn't the asking price that was the problem; it was that the kid had bested him. *That* was the problem. The worst part was that Max knew he would give them virtually anything they asked for, if only he could get one of those horses.

"Well, let's say that maybe I *could* afford your asking price. What would it be?"

Jacen looked at Baker and smiled. He'd guessed what Max was struggling with, and decided to let the older man save face. "Max, you're a shrewd trader. I want to get out of here before you talk me out of the coat on my back. Tell you what: I'll give you that big chocolate mare on this end of our rope corral, the one with the white face-patch, plus one of the two-wheeled carts, plus all the tack to hitch her to cart or plow, plus a colt and two fillies. If you play your cards right, in a few years you'll have a growing herd of your own. In return, you hold back a hundred cans of each type of vegetable, but give me all the rest, plus all your dried apples and peaches, less twenty pounds each, plus all your dried corn, less three hundred pounds, plus all your dried herbs less one pound each."

Baker scratched his chin, and drawled, "Now, suppose–"

"Nope," Jacen interrupted firmly. "That's the deal. Take it or leave it."

Baker frowned. "Do I still get the two full days of blacksmith work?"

Jacen looked at Jim Trebane, who nodded. "Yes, plus Hakim will spend those two days teaching several of your people how to care for and handle the horses."

"DEAL!" Maxwell exclaimed with a grin, slapping his palm down on the table with glee.

Jacen smiled back. It was a good bargain for both sides.

****

Frank trotted his horse past the table where the four men had just completed their deal. "Mornin' gents," he said cheerily.

"Morning yourself, Frank," Jacen called back.

"Any coffee left?"

"I think we could squeeze another cup out of that pot."

"Why don't you pour me one while I strip the saddle off my horse. Don't you guys go anywhere. I need to talk to all four of you. Be right back." Tulley trotted off to the corral and took care of his horse, while Jim Trebane got him a cup of coffee. In a few minutes, Tulley strolled up to the table and sat down.

"What's up, Frank?" asked Jim Trebane.

"Listen, when I tell you what I'm about to tell you, don't react, just smile. We're almost certainly being watched. Half an hour ago, Hakim and I ran across twenty or thirty sets of boot prints down at Raccoon Creek. We back-trailed them far enough to know that they were trying to stay out of sight, and that can only mean one thing."

"It means we're about to be attacked," Baker surmised.

"Um-hmm. Probably so. Today, tonight, tomorrow morning – we don't know. But a big group of men is trying to stay out of sight, and the tracks were heading this way, winding through the deep gulleys that surround this place. Jacen, you're in charge of the Phoenix group. How do you want to handle this?"

"Okay, everybody, for starters, let's have big smiles for the sake of those watching through binoculars. Good. Don't want to show our hand now, do we?" Jacen said calmly. He took a sip of his coffee, and then continued in a pleasant, unhurried way.

"Gary, you go warn our people quietly. Everybody, men and women both, should keep weapons and plenty of ammunition close by. Frank, make sure the horses are moved to the center of the encampment. That's probably what they're after anyway."

Maxwell Baker said, "Jacen, the only way to approach your site here is through the gulleys to the north and south. You ought to set up a daylight watch schedule that will keep an eye on both, starting immediately."

"Good idea, Max. I'll do it. Frank, I expect Hakim is already tracking them, right?"

"Yep," Frank nodded.

"In that case, heaven help 'em. Hakim is not one to be tangled with." Jacen turned back to Baker. "Max, not to open old wounds, but do you remember our assault on your settlement this past August?" Maxwell nodded, a shadow passing over his face.

"The direction of these tracks, according to what Frank just told us, is coming the same way Hakim and I did that night, right through the ditch east of your cabins. You'd better go warn your people. In fact, Jim, why don't you go with him and help them set up a defense. You two can discuss the blacksmith work that needs to be done while you're doing that. We're not going to let these people, whoever they are, pen us up. Other than good caution, we'll have a normal schedule today. Agreed?"

"Sounds good," Baker affirmed, along with the others.

As each went to their respective tasks, Tulley marveled at Jacen's savvy, calmness, and understanding. Hakim had taught him well.

****

Hakim watched from within a dense pocket of mountain laurel, as the eighteen armed men below him split into two groups. A mile back he had already observed two smaller groups breaking off and heading south. Hakim had stayed

329

with the larger force, keeping track of their movements while he remained hidden. He had tied his horse back over the hill, out of sight.

The Arab was positioned high on the northern shoulder of the gulley just north of the Phoenix encampment. The shallow gorge lay between him and the raiders he was surveilling. He observed as they carefully climbed up the opposite side and quietly took up positions in the foliage at the north rim of the flat ground on which Phoenix was encamped. They were no more than two hundred feet from his position.

"Oh, Lord Isa! Now what? I don't want to shoot these men in the back. I don't want to be the first to fire. But if they cut loose on my friends without warning, many of our people will die. I'm so tired of killing. But I won't let my friends be attacked unawares."

It was clear from the surreptitious movements that the attackers were about to open the ambush. Hakim spotted a large boulder, and moved behind it. It afforded excellent protection. He set his assault rifle down, and then stepped into the open. All of the raiders had their backs to him, and were beginning to train their weapons on the unsuspecting occupants of the campsite.

"Hello! Hello over there! I say, can any of you tell me what day it is?"

The startled group whipped around as one man, and stared at him with shock that quickly changed to rage. For the first time, Hakim got a clear look at the leader, and recognized him: it was Tim Shanks! Four or five raised their weapons and began firing, and Hakim dove behind his boulder. The ground and foliage where he had been standing was instantly shredded by the lethal fusillade that Hakim could hear whizzing past, just inches away.

"Well, Lord, I reckon that qualifies as *'hostile intent.'* Thanks for answered prayer!" He grabbed his rifle, switched the selector to full-automatic, rolled out from the opposite side of the boulder and fired from a prone position. His wild spray of lead caused the attacking group to dive for cover themselves.

All across the settlement and the encampment, the staccato burst of gunfire had the same effect: everyone dove for their weapons, and hunkered down. Several dozen easy targets immediately disappeared, and were transformed into armed and angry defenders. Hakim's quick thinking had prevented a massacre.

The three other groups of attackers interpreted the gunfire as a signal to begin the assault. The mid-morning stillness was shattered by chattering pockets of automatic weapons, spraying their lethal payloads across short, deadly spaces.

****

The initial clatter of shooting dwindled, and was replaced by short sporadic bursts, scattered across the battle site. There were no clear targets, on either side. The fight was turning into a stalemate, at least temporarily. The defenders held the high ground, but had little cover on the flat, treeless ground on which they camped. They pressed down into the turf, which was warming comfortably as the sun rose higher in the sky. The only way they could safely move was to roll from one position to another.

The attackers had the advantage of mobility: they could creep back into the safety of the gulleys and maneuver. But in order to get a good shot at targets lying flat on the ground, they had to expose themselves, raising up high enough to get an angle.

****

Jacen had mentally marked one area of the rim from which a stream of gunfire had come. He was lying on his stomach. He brought his rifle up, nestled the stock in his shoulder, and trained his weapon on that spot. He thumbed the selector to single-shot, eased his safety off, and waited. Two minutes later, his patience was rewarded. A bearded, dirty face popped up. Jacen squeezed the trigger, and the attackers' advantage was reduced by one soul.

****

Hakim saw the stalemate develop and realized that the attackers had retained the advantage. They could reposition their forces at will. The Phoenix company was in an unsustainable position. *Maybe I can even the odds*, he thought.

"FRANK, CAN YOU HEAR ME?" he shouted from behind his boulder. It drew a couple more shots, but they zinged past, harmlessly.

"LOUD AND CLEAR," Tulley bellowed back.

"I'M IN THEIR REAR. IF I KEEP 'EM BUSY, CAN YOU ADVANCE ON THE RIM?" the Arab hollered.

"I THINK SO! IT'S WORTH A TRY. JUST DON'T TELL 'EM WHAT WE'RE UP TO," Frank shouted back. That brought a grin to most faces, attacker and defender alike.

Hakim rammed a fresh magazine into his M14, and studied the situation. The boulder he was hiding behind was actually part of a limestone formation that traversed the hill, near the top. Every ten or twenty feet, enough of the formation jutted up to provide good cover. One such location some sixty feet away would allow him to creep safely over to the far side of the hill, where Hadar was tied, waiting for him.

Darting up from his hiding place, he sprinted for the next bit of cover, firing as he went, and recording in his mind the positions of all the attackers. On his next sortie, he would concentrate his fire. He waited until the fire died back down, and then sprinted to the next location. As he ran he squeezed off three shots, and another attacker fell.

Jacen, Sam Oxford, and Frank Tulley wormed closer to the rim, but immediately drew enfilading fire from the arm of the gulley to their west.

"GUS?" Jacen shouted.

"I'M ON IT, JACEN," shouted his big friend. Gus, Phil, and Elijah Moore shifted to confront the attackers on the west. "When you hear firing on our right," Gus called out, "spray the rim in front of us. That will give Jace a chance to move forward."

Two more dashes by Hakim brought Jacen and his group sixty feet closer to the rim, and also resulted in three more of the attacking force being put out of play. Hakim lay flat, and peered slowly around his cover. The opposing force was getting nervous about Jacen's group, and had turned the rim, backs to him. Hakim squeezed off two unopposed bursts, and scored one hit.

****

Tim Shanks was furious. For the second time, that meddling Arab had interfered! If Shanks lost many more men he'd have to fall back. There were just four left in his own squad, including himself.

"Culver, come here," he barked impatiently. "We've got to nail that raghead! Have you seen what he's been doing?"

The other man nodded.

"Okay, here's what *we're* going to do. Put in a fresh magazine, set to full automatic, and you point your weapon halfway between the rocks on the left of his current position. I'll point mine halfway between the rocks on the right. When you see any movement at all, no matter which side of his hiding place it is, pull the trigger, and empty your gun at the halfway spot. I'll do the same. No matter which way he runs, he'll run right into our fire. Got it?"

****

Hakim had one more gap to cross before he could safely retreat to the other side of the hill. Once over, he'd regain his horse, and figure another way to break the back of the assault.

He slapped another magazine in, counted to ten, and then sprinted for the last rock. Something knocked him down, and he tried to scramble to safety, but his arms and legs refused to cooperate. Time slowed down to a crawl. He heard a scream, and realized with a shock that it was his own. In slow motion he looked down. Blood was blossoming from a small hole in his chest, and more blood from another hole in his arm. While he watched, several more bullets ripped through him. He lay back on the matted leaves on the forest floor, no longer hearing gunfire. It was quite peaceful. A lovely young woman approached him, running gaily through a green, sunlit meadow, with two laughing little girls in tow. "Sarah, is that you? Ruthie! Naomi!" he cried out with delight.

****

In one coordinated action, Jacen, Sam, and Frank rolled off the rim into the gulley and came up firing. Tim Shanks took several shots right in the stomach, and sat down hard. His remaining three men were cut down an instant later. The north gulley was clear.

Sam Oxford walked up to Shanks and ripped the M4 right out of his motionless hands. He searched him briefly, collecting his other weapons. Shanks' eyes followed Sam's movements, but Tim said nothing. A trickle of blood was drooling out of his mouth. A brief moment later, his eyes glazed and his breathing stopped. Oxford stared at the corpse for a moment, and then said quietly, to no one in particular, "So ends the life of one of the most worthless individuals I have ever had the misfortune to know."

"Quick! Gather all the ammo you can from these buzzards. We'll follow the gulley around and take that other group from behind. Hurry!" ordered Jacen.

"Where's Hakim?" Tulley asked, as rifled through the clothes of one of the other corpses, shoving all the ammo he found into his pockets.

"He's probably pulled out to stalk the group in the gulley to the west. I'll bet we get there just in time to support him."

****

Energized by adrenaline, Jacen, Sam, and Frank raced down the gulley until they reached the point where the other draw opened to the south. Choosing the western slope, they picked their way through the new growth, holding to cover as much as possible. Sporadic firing continued to their front, and they could hear answering fire from the campsite. No sounds of combat could be heard above them to the right, where the cabins of the Pittsburgh settlement were located.

"Listen, here's the plan," Jacen whispered. "We'll spread out with maybe fifty feet between us. Find good solid cover and give me a hand signal when you're set. Our first burst will be coordinated: fire with me, when I open up. After that, just take targets of opportunity. We'll probably kill several in that first round, and it will draw their focus away from the rim. That should enable Gus and his boys to advance. Don't take any chances! It's not necessary. Pick good solid cover."

Frank listened, again impressed with the young man. *I feel like I am listening to that crazy Arab*, he thought to himself. Tulley crept through the laurel and fresh spring growth, and found a good spot behind a large tree.

A moment later, all was set. Jacen gave the signal, and the three men stepped from their cover and hosed down the opposite side of the gulley, up at the rim. Two of eight attackers dropped, screaming. The six remaining were frozen for the briefest instant, surprised that they were being assaulted from the rear. Then they scrambled for cover to protect themselves from the new direction. Thirty seconds later, another attacker dropped, drilled neatly through the skull.

Up on the rim, Gus, Phil, and Elijah heard the new firing in the gulley to their front. The suppressing fire that had been coming their way ceased. Gus took a chance and ran, crouched over, a good thirty feet before he dropped to his stomach. No opposing fire came his way. Phil and Elijah did the same. Soon they were close to the rim. They crawled forward, and then caught the remaining attackers in a devastating cross-fire.

"Clear!" shouted Jacen.

"Clear!" responded Gus. The Phoenix men stood up cautiously, and met in the bottom of the gulley.

****

Ten minutes later, the remaining attackers from the two smaller groups to the south and west melted back into the wilderness. Later that day they made their rendezvous at Raccoon Creek: neither Shanks nor Beaufort were among the survivors. Nineteen of their original twenty-five men had been killed; losses to the defenders were unknown.

For a few minutes, the six men stood arguing about what to do next. They had no heart for a second try. In the end, the remaining band of raiders dissolved and scattered, individually, to the west. Two eventually took up with other bandit groups. The other four, by default and not intention, came upon other small communities, joined, and ultimately became productive citizens.

But as they scattered each carried with him the tale of a westbound group of tough, competent people who had a vision of starting a new society in the outlands of Colorado. The tale slowly spread through the mouths of traders and wanderers, until it came up against an impassable object, the Mississippi River.

CHAPTER 33

"Where's Hakim?" Jacen asked. The group had just climbed out of the gulley, headed for the encampment. "Last I heard him, he was on the north side of the gulley above the camp."

"We'd better find him," Frank said, a note of concern creeping into his voice.

The six changed direction, and walked to the north rim. Blood-soaked corpses were scattered in various positions. "What a waste," Jacen muttered, as they picked their way down the side. When the six companions got to the bottom, they fanned out and started up the opposite side.

"Oh, no!" cried Phil. The others ran to him. There on the ground, his sightless eyes looking into the blue sky, was Hakim. His bloody body was riddled with bullets. But the expression frozen on the Arab's face was one of utter contentment.

Jacen wailed, "HELP! SOMEBODY, GO GET SOME HELP! Sam! Get some bandages! Frank, help me, help me carry him back!" He was frantic. He dropped to the ground next to Hakim, searching for a pulse.

"Jacen, Jacen," Frank said gently, reaching down and taking the young man by the shoulders.

"NO!" Jacen shouted furiously, throwing off Tulley's hands. He reached for Hakim's bloody neck again to search for a pulse. The others stood by, consumed in their own grief.

"Jacen, it's too la–"

"NO, NO, NO! It's NOT too late. It CAN'T be . . . ," Jacen's voice trailed off, his shoulders beginning to shake until finally he was overcome by body-racking sobs.

****

Frank Tulley hammered the wooden cross into the soft earth at the head of the mound. Nailed to it was a wooden placard into which were burned the words,

Hakim Abdul al Malik

Worshiper of Jesus Christ

Died May 10, 2121,

in the living hope of the Resurrection

The Phoenix community had gathered at the open grave. Tulley had read several passages from his Bible. He couldn't use Hakim's, as it was in Arabic. Frank and Gary had said a few words. Then each had thrown dirt and wildflowers on the body. Left standing at the grave when it was all over were Jacen, Mary Anders and Frank Tulley.

Hakim's death meant different things to everyone, as he had played multiple roles in all of their lives. He had been Tulley's best friend, with a shared faith and many shared experiences throughout their lives. The Arab had rescued the former slaves from their slavery. He had been instrumental in Gary and Ellen Shanks coming to faith, and learning to forgive. He had been a quiet voice of courage, wisdom, and competence for the entire community. He had been their teacher, and their storyteller.

Mary Anders had been courted by Hakim, in his own way. Her hopes of marrying the man she had grown to love died a bitter death on the side of that bloody gulley.

For Jacen, Hakim had been a father figure, a brother, a best friend, a mentor, instructor, trainer and encourager. And now he was gone.

****

The Phoenix community remained encamped at Pittsburgh. A pall hung over the group; not only was Jacen unable to break it, he was gripped by it as firmly as the others. Sensing the young man's despair, Frank Tulley temporarily took over scheduling the watch duties and chores, and assigned various ones to help the Pittsburgh settlement with plowing and planting. Both groups continued to fellowship and eat together. If there was a bright spot, it was that the attack drew the two communities close, and the old distinctions of slave versus slaver never reappeared, even for Elijah Moore. Jim and Buck Trebane carried out numerous repairs on the Pittsburgh tools and implements, and Maxwell Baker was good to his word: they brought out the canned food supplies for which they had negotiated. Elijah trained the Bakers and Agees how to care for the horses, and together they built the necessary corrals and training pens. Meanwhile, Phoenix was mourning privately, each in their own way.

A week after Hakim's death, Jacen resumed functioning as the leader of the Phoenix community. He didn't mope or become absorbed in self-pity, but it was obvious that the spark had gone out of his life, at least for the moment. He was clearly not motivated to get the group back on the move.

Meanwhile, the weather had become gloriously beautiful. The leaves, the colors of grass and forest, cloud and sky, the flowers, and the warm temperatures had a healing, restorative effect.

****

Jacen's eyes popped open. He lay for a moment, studying the star-studded, black night sky. He could tell from the constellations that it was about thirty minutes before he was to relieve the watch. Quietly he got up and dressed, shook out his boots, put them on, and then neatly rolled and tied his bedroll. Twenty feet away, Francis Tulley was going through the same routine. Gathering his coat and weapons, Jacen walked over to the low-burning fire, added a few logs, and then poured a cup for Tulley and one for himself.

Frank walked over and sat down. Despite the fact that it was late May, the night air still had a chill to it, and he warmed his hands. Jacen brought Tulley's coffee to him, and then sat across the fire. For a few minutes, neither spoke. They just sat, sipping their coffee and enjoying the quiet fellowship.

Finally Tulley stirred, and spoke in a quiet voice, "Well, boy, what are you going to do?"

That's exactly what Hakim would say, Jacen thought. *He'd say, 'Well, boy, what are you going to do? Are you going to cry forever, or are you going to get on with your dream, get on with your life?'* The memory of Hakim brought a lump to Jacen's throat and for a moment he could not respond. He cleared his throat a couple of times, and then looked up. In the dancing firelight, Tulley could see that Jacen's eyes and cheeks were glistening, but his voice was strong as he quietly replied, "I'm going to Colorado. Think I'll leave tomorrow. Want to come?"

Tulley took a long sip of his coffee. He nodded, a grin slowly forming on his face. "Don't mind if I do."

****

Breakfast was over and cleaned up. Jacen had called a meeting of the whole Phoenix group. In the distance, the Bakers and Agees could be seen with their new horse, cultivating one of their fields.

"Folks, listen up," Jacen called out. Those still standing or straggling about walked over and seated themselves in the circle. "Over the last nine or ten months, you have gathered to our community. You've heard my dream, and you've bought into it, so that it's no longer mine but ours. We've worked through an assortment of crises and catastrophes, personal problems and difficulties, together. We've drawn closer as a result. We function well together. We've even agreed on a name for ourselves: we're the *Phoenix* community.

"We've spent the last nine months preparing for a long trip west, and about a month ago we started that trip. But here, at the Pittsburgh settlement, we've suffered a great and tragic blow, a loss so grievous that I expect all of us have stopped to catch our breath and to re-evaluate our commitments and our goals.

"We can never replace our dear friend, Hakim. We can't replace his leadership, his wisdom, or his fierce ability to fight and protect. Without Hakim, not one of us would be here today contemplating a journey as free people to a distant place. And," Jacen chuckled at this, "we'd have *eaten* those horses instead of learning how to *ride* them." The memory brought knowing smiles to many faces.

"In all likelihood," Jacen continued, "others among us will be lost on this trip. Hakim used to say, *Jacen, it's a fallen world; grief comes naturally to it*. Well, you know I don't share Hakim's belief in God, but I certainly do share his belief in the fallenness of this world. I expect that here, at Pittsburgh, this is just the beginning of our sorrows.

"But I also fully expect that we'll make it all the way to Colorado, and that we'll be successful forming a new society, with Phoenix as its core, and that, in the end, it will be worth the difficulty. I believe that a new world awaits us. And I think it's time to leave this place, and find that new world."

"Tomorrow morning we're pulling out, headed west. If you've decided to stay here with the Pittsburgh community, and to go no further, well, . . . I certainly understand. But the rest of us are leaving tomorrow. All of the horses, except what we traded to Pittsburgh, all of the wagons, and all of the food for which we have traded, are going with us. I'm sorry, but that's the way it has to be. Those of us who will be traveling will need all of it.

"I hope that all of you will come with me. But if any of you have changed your mind, there are no hard feelings, and we'll part as dear friends. You'll always be welcome at my campfire. Please let me know by noon today what your decision is."

By lunch time, the entire group had made known their choice. They were all sticking together and traveling west. Very early the next morning, all the members of both communities gathered at Hakim's grave to say their goodbyes. Surprising everyone, and most of all, himself, Jacen asked Gary Shanks to offer a prayer of thanks for Hakim's part in each of their lives, and then for safety on the journey to come. By eight o'clock, the campsite was deserted and the last wagon had rolled west.

CHAPTER 34

Gus and Phil sat on their horses, and looked with disgust at the sight in front of them. The bridge over the Mississippi appeared to be intact, but the approach was gone. The embankment on which the highway had once rested was completely washed away, and had been for several decades, by the looks of things. Now the bridge simply ended, thirty feet above their heads.

"This is the first bridge we've seen all summer that spans the entire river, intact," Gus observed.

"Um-hmm. But it's not gonna do us a scrap of good. Not unless wagons and horses can fly," Phil drawled dryly.

"Yep. And if they could do that, wouldn't need a bridge anyway."

Gus reined his horse around. "Right. Reckon we'd best go tell Jacen."

The two cantered back down the trail. They were now, as were all of the Phoenix group, expert horsemen. The wagon train had encamped where the old I-74 and I-80 roadbeds intersected. Jacen had sent pairs of horsemen out to reconnoiter the major crossings in and around the Moline – Rock Island ruins. The news that came back was not good.

****

It had been a long, slow summer. They had initially followed old Interstate 70 from Pennsylvania all the way to the ruins of St. Louis. The hard roadbed was an excellent surface for traveling with wagons, and they had made good time, even during rainy periods. Upon arrival in St. Louis, their westward progress had stalled. The bridge over the Mississippi was washed out. In their wintertime discussions, Hakim had identified this as a distinct possibility. He'd advised Jacen to head north since the river narrowed the closer one came to its source. So the wagon train had turned north, but had found none of the bridges passable to this point.

Not all the news was bad, however. As they had been visited with sorrow in Pittsburgh, the Phoenix community experienced great joy with the birth of a healthy little girl, Rebecca Marie, to Gus and Katie Blackwell in late June. In early July, Buck Trebane and Misty Randall got married. Later in July, Gary and Ellen Shanks announced to the community that they were expecting their third child. Perhaps the one most delighted with that news was Elijah Moore, as he had adopted the role of grandfather to Peter and Elizabeth Shanks. Then, in August, Patty Linder and Sam Oxford tied the knot.

****

Jacen listened patiently as all three groups reported back. None of the bridges they had checked out were passable.

"Now what?" Jim Trebane growled with disgust.

"Well, let's hold the I-280 bridge in our hip pocket as a last resort. It would take some engineering, but perhaps we could rig something to lift the wagons and horses up to the bridge roadbed. But I think we should continue north. We have yet to check out the I-80 bridge north of the ruins, and

344

according to Hakim's map there are still three more bridges between here and the ruins of Dubuque," Jacen said.

"You *have* kept an eye on the calendar, haven't you, Jacen?" Gary Shanks asked doubtfully. "We'll need to build shelters before winter hits, and we've come a fair ways north already."

Jacen nodded. "I know, Gary. And you're right, of course. But we still have time. We must cross the river before winter. In fact, it's vital."

Gary looked puzzled. "Why? Other than making a few more miles before we go into winter camp, why does it matter which side of the Mississippi we are on this fall?"

"Because this river has huge floods every spring. We could be held up a month or more, waiting for it to clear up. And if we don't choose carefully where we make our winter camp, *we* could be in terrible danger from the flooding."

"How can you possibly know that? You've never even been here before."

"Hakim told me. Hakim had made the Mississippi one of the focuses of his studies, for some reason. He never told me why. But he read everything he could get his hands on regarding the river."

"Jacen's right," Tulley said. "Hakim spoke with me a great deal about the river. The flooding was one of the topics he always brought up. We need to spend the winter on the west side of this thing, and as far from it as we can get."

****

The next morning, the group headed north for the I-80 bridge. If it was out, they intended to continue north on Route 84 to the bridges at Clinton. The trail they were on—or highway, as it once was—was particularly overgrown with heavy brush and vegetation coming right up to the roadbed. That, plus the proximity to the ruins, made Jacen nervous. As his team plodded on he bent around and reached for his

M4, behind him in the wagon, although he wasn't entirely sure why.

The action saved his life. Gunfire erupted from the brush on either side of the road, and a bullet burned his side, leaving a superficial wound. It would have caught him full in the chest, a perfect lung shot, had he not been reaching for his weapon. Jacen lost control of his team, and his wagon turned over, throwing him to the ground.

It was pure chaos behind him. Three other wagons were overturned and several horses lay on their sides, still in harnesses, kicking and neighing in fear. People were screaming, and the string of spare horses was racing wildly back down the road behind them. A horse galloped past him, empty saddle, stirrups flapping madly. It was Tulley's horse, Jacen realized with a sinking feeling.

But amid the cries of the wounded and the terrified, Jacen also heard return fire beginning. Spotting muzzle flashes in the brush on the west side of the road, he emptied a magazine in the general direction, temporarily suppressing the hidden opponents in the brush. *Good thing we have plenty of ammo, because we're gonna need it*, he thought to himself, as he slapped a fresh magazine in place. He continued hosing down different places in the foliage. Things were happening so fast that the whole Phoenix group was confused, simply reacting, emptying their rifles into the brush around them, without any unified plan.

But within a minute or two, the training Hakim had conducted began paying off. Jacen heard Hakim's calm voice in his mind, '*When you are out-numbered or out-gunned, never fight from a fixed position unless it's unapproachable by the enemy. You must stay on the move.*' Move, move, we've got to move! "MOVE" he shouted, as the thought raced through his mind.

"What?" a voice called from behind his wagon. Jacen recognized it as Elijah Moore.

Jacen's mind raced, forming a plan. It was crazy, but the alternative was to be slaughtered.

"Elijah! That you?"

A long burst from an M4 ripped through the morning, and then Elijah answered, "Yeah," sounding bored. It helped steady Jacen.

"I'm coming to you. Can you give me covering fire to the west?"

"Yep. You say when."

Jacen slung his M4 across his back, and crawled on his stomach into his wagon, which was lying on its side. He rooted through the contents, and then shoved two heavy metal boxes out of the back of the wagon. He filled his pockets with extra magazines for his assault rifle, and then crawled out of the wagon. Grabbing one of the boxes, he shouted, "NOW!"

Elijah opened up to the west, and Jacen heard another M4 shooting to the east. He hoisted the box, and ran around the wreckage, hitting the ground next to Elijah. He noted with approval that it was Ginny providing covering fire to the east.

"Can you do it once more?" he asked.

"No problem, boss. Looks like you got nicked," Elijah said as he fed his hungry M4 another magazine.

"Um-hmm. FRANK – CAN YOU HEAR ME?" Jacen shouted.

"YES," came the call above the din of gunfire.

"NEED YOU OVER HERE, PRONTO! BRING BUCK AND PHIL!" Jacen looked at Elijah and Ginny and said, "Covering fire, one more time?"

"Ready when you are."

"Now!" Jacen raced back to the wagon, grabbed the other box, and raced back.

"What's that got in it, lunch?" asked Elijah, as he reloaded again. At that moment, Frank, Buck, and Phil came diving into the little cover that the group had. Frank was bleeding from the shoulder, Buck from the side.

"You guys still in action?" Jacen asked.

"We're good to go. Just got winged in unimportant places," Frank said cheerily. "What's up? OH! GRENADES! Jacen, I LOVE YOU, man!"

"What's a grenade," asked Buck, confused.

"Something you don't ever want to play with, son!" said Frank sternly. "Hakim teach you how to use those things, Jacen?"

"Yeah. I've thrown two cases of them in practice."

"Well," Frank said with surprise, "that's one case more than I have. What's on your mind?"

"We stay here, we'll be slaughtered. Once the bad guys get up their courage, they'll advance, and we'll be done for. From the sounds of it, we're pretty badly out-numbered. But I don't get the sense that they really know what they're doing.

"We need to get moving, bring the fight to them. I've got a box of M67 frag grenades here, and a box of M8 smoke grenades. Frank, you and I are the only ones who know how to safely use these things. I need you to take command here on the road. Buck, Phil, and I are going to clean out the west side of the road, starting here on the northern-most edge and working south. Once we get to work, concentrate your fire on the east side, so you don't hit us, and so they don't sneak up your backside."

Jacen was interrupted by a BOOM! BOOM! BOOM! Someone in the brush on the east side of the road began to scream, fifty yards south of Jacen's position. Frank looked at Jacen and smiled. "Sounds like Mary Anders just got her 12-gauge semi-automatic into action. She was hunting for it when I ran by."

Jacen continued, "We're going to lay a screen of smoke on both sides of the road up here, to allow me and my guys to maneuver safely. Once that smoke gets cranking, Frank, you chuck four of those M67's into the brush in a nice north-south spread. Warn our people to lay flat on the ground, and make sure you get those things at least 75 feet out. As soon as I count four bangs, these guys and I are going to charge through that smoke and kill anything still moving. Everyone got it?" The little group nodded. Jacen put two of the M67's into his pockets.

Ginny Moore's eyes were as big as saucers. "You be careful, Jacen Chester! If you get shot, I'll, I'll, well, I'll shoot you myself!" she insisted.

"Well," Frank said dryly, "sounds like you just got orders from headquarters, Jace."

Jacen smiled, "Guess I did. Let's do it."

Frank and Jacen each tossed several M8's into the brush on either side of the road. Dense white smoke began to drift through the foliage, obscuring everything. Surprised voices could be heard in the brush.

Frank shouted down the road, "GET DOWN! PHOENIX, GET DOWN! LIE DOWN NOW!" He turned to Jacen. "Ready?"

"Ready."

In quick succession, Frank hurled a spread of four M87 grenades into the smoke on the west side of the road, and then hit the ground. BOOOM! BOOOM! BOOOM! BOOOM! The grenades went off in quick succession. The voices that had been stirred up by the smoke grenades now became agonized screams. Shouts of fear came from the Phoenix company, most of whom knew nothing of Jacen's plan, nor had they ever heard of grenades.

Jacen counted four explosions, then shouted, "NOW NOW NOW!" He and his men jumped up and charged into the brush on the west side of the road.

Frank shouted to the Phoenix company, "UP! UP! DEFEND TO THE EAST! DEFEND TO THE EAST! DON'T SHOOT TO THE WEST!"

"Everyone you see, shoot in the head, even if you think they are dead," Jacen instructed as they fought quickly through the smoky brush. The smoke burned their lungs. Jacen came upon his first body, and shot the unfortunate in the head, point-blank. He noted mentally, as he moved on that it was an Anarch, with a tattoo of a scorpion on his cheek. Soon the three of them were into an area dense with stunned and dead Anarchs. Each one was shot without mercy.

"FRANK," Jacen called out.

"WHAT?"

"THEY'RE ANARCHS!"

"I WONDERED."

Jacen continued through the brush westerly another thirty yards, until he knew they had gone beyond the Anarchs' positions along the road. He then turned south, and soon they were into more Anarchs. From then on, they moved carefully, killing every Anarch they found. Meanwhile, the gunfire at the road continued steadily.

Suddenly the brush in front of Jacen, Buck, and Phil blossomed with more automatic gunfire. Jacen took a round through his left forearm, and another through the fleshy part of his shoulder. Both missed the bones. Buck was hit in the thigh, but Phil was unscathed. All three dropped to the ground and began returning fire.

"Get ready to cover me," Jacen wheezed painfully, "and for crying out loud, hit the dirt and cover your heads when I throw this thing." He carefully fished a fragmentation grenade out of his pocket and removed the safety clip. "Ready?" he asked. Both men nodded. "Covering fire NOW!" he commanded. The two hosed the area down, M4's on full-auto. Jacen got to his knees, hurled the grenade, and cried "DOWN! DOWN! DOWN! PHOENIX, DOWN!"

BOOOM!

The three hobbled to their feet, and charged into the brush. They found seven dead or dying Anarchs, and finished them off. Stumbling further through the brush to the south, they verified that the west side of the road was now clear of Anarchs.

"PHOENIX! PHOENIX, WE'RE COMING IN ON THE WEST! DON'T SHOOT!" Jacen cried. The three men ran to the last, southern-most wagon. Melissa Trebane was lying calmly on the ground behind her husband's anvil, a sawed-off shotgun in her hands pointing to the east.

"Glad you boys warned me, or I would've aerated your hides."

Jacen, Buck, and Phil continued running, crouched down, back to Frank Tulley's position.

"How's it going, Frank?"

"Ask me afterwards, Jacen, not now." His tone was somber. Somehow, Jacen didn't want to know, not until the danger had passed.

"Good enough. Are you ready to do the east side the same way we did the west?"

Frank nodded, and pulled more smoke grenades out of the box. The two men heaved them into the brush, and fresh smoke again began filling the east side of the road.

"PHOENIX, DOWN! DOWN! DOWN!" Tulley shouted. Four more fragmentation grenades went into the woods to the east.

Jacen counted off four explosions, and then jumped off with his men. As he ran he called back to Frank, "Bring some '87's and follow me, Frank!"

The Anarchs were violent, but they weren't stupid. When they heard the warning shouted out, most of the Anarchs on the east side of the road hit the dirt, too. Far fewer were killed or stunned by the grenades. Consequently, the fighting on the east side was much more intense. It took half an hour, and six more fragmentation grenades before the east side of the road was pronounced clear. By that time, a fire had started in the brush, but thankfully the prevailing breeze blew to the east, and the wagon train was not endangered by it, not yet, anyway.

****

Jacen walked wearily up the road, his M4 cradled in his arms. As he surveyed the scene, he realized what a disaster it had been. He didn't yet know the injury situation, but what he could see was bad enough. Four wagons had turned over, three horses were down with broken legs and would have to be destroyed, and their entire remuda was gone, last seen galloping south. Fire was crackling to the east of the road, close enough that he could feel the heat. Smoke everywhere. The adrenaline was still flowing fast enough that Jacen did not yet feel his own injuries, but he knew he was covered in blood.

He slowly realized that he was hearing a wailing cry, coming from the middle of the wagon train. Heedless of his injuries, he sprinted toward the sound. He found Gary Shanks holding Ellen and Peter, the three of them sobbing. Tears streaming down his face, Elijah was kneeling on the road, working with a lifeless little form, Elizabeth, lying on the road. He was sponging away the blood, straightening out her little shirt, tenderly arranging her hair. She had taken a bullet squarely in the chest. Elijah looked up, his face contorted by grief. "I'm sure she died quickly. I don't think she suffered," he rasped, caressing her head.

At that moment, Gus walked up, tears running down his face. "Angie Bartwell is dead," he told the group. "Just found her. When her wagon spilled, it threw her into the weeds. The fall broke her neck."

Jacen surveyed the scene. He knew what he had to do, though he hated doing it. But he was their leader. Their safety depended upon his leadership.

"Gus, Jim, Buck, Sam! Get these wagons righted and reloaded! Frank, take the Linder sisters. Saddle up some horses, and go find our remuda! Elijah," he said gently, "You load Elizabeth into the back of the wagon, and help Gary and Ellen and Peter."

Gus answered sharply, "JACEN! Let it go! Let us grieve! We're all hurting here!" Multiple voices murmured their agreement with Gus.

Jacen looked around the group, and said gently, "Gus, we will grieve. We will stop tonight, and set up camp for several days, and heal and grieve. But at the moment we must move, and we must move *now*. If the wind shifts, that fire will come back over the road and burn up everything we have, and us with it. If that happens, things will be even worse than they are now. We've got to go several more miles, to safety. Then we'll stop and bury our dead and heal our wounded."

Gus looked at him, his jaw working with anger and sorrow mixed together. Finally he wiped his eyes on his sleeve, then nodded, "Yes, you're right. We must move. Sorry, Jacen, I wasn't thinking."

It took the rest of the day, but Phoenix was finally gathered in a good spot four miles north of the site of the battle. The several intact wagons had to be unloaded, sent back to site, and the cargo from the broken wagons transferred, and then additional trips made for the wagons themselves. By the time of the final trip, the wind had indeed changed and Jacen's decision to move quickly was vindicated. The fire had blown back toward the road, and they were almost unable to recover the final wagon, which was Jacen's, because of the smoke and heat. In the end, however, all the goods, wagons, and carts were recovered, including their cargo. Unfortunately, about ten percent of their canned goods were a loss, as some of the glass jars broke when wagons overturned.

****

For ten days Phoenix camped in one place, grieving, burying their dead, sorting out the broken pieces, fixing the wagons, healing injuries. The loss of little Elizabeth Shanks was crushing, and it hit Elijah almost as hard as it did Gary and Ellen. Since Gary and Elijah had been reconciled, they had grown extremely close. Elijah had become the grandfather figure that the Shanks children needed, and the kids had given the old man an outlet for his affection. For several days following Elizabeth's burial, Elijah would go to the little mound and just sit in the dirt and weep.

This period was the greatest test of leadership Jacen had yet faced. Morale was lower than it had been when Hakim died. Fully three-quarters of the group had received at least superficial injuries from the gun battle with the Anarchs. There was every reason in the world to let discipline go, for just a little while.

But discipline is the key to morale. Hakim had taught that very important truth to Jacen, and Jacen had learned his lesson well. For several days, Jacen was very unpopular. He insisted on a vigorous watch duty, and on a standard schedule for the wagon train, rousing everyone before sunup, completing chores, and carrying out horseback patrols for three miles around the encampment.

Only Francis Tulley, Elijah Moore, and oddly enough, Gus Blackwell supported Jacen's decisions. It was the discipline that kept the group from slipping into the morass of despair. Gradually, the entire community began to understand, and support for Jacen's leadership was renewed.

The remuda of horses had been rounded up, most of them, anyway. They were now down to thirty-eight adult horses, down from forty-five when they left Bedford. Jim Trebane finally got all the wagons repaired, and at the end of the ten days Phoenix rolled out once more.

They found that the I-80 bridge was impassable. The group turned north, headed for the little ruin of Clinton. It was now late September, and the leaves were beginning to turn.

EPILOGUE

Jacen pulled his team to a halt. On the road ahead of him several hundred yards was a man waving his arms. Jacen reached for his M4, and jacked a shell into the chamber.

Frank Tulley trotted up on his horse, and dismounted, looping the reins around a tree branch. "What do you think, Jacen?"

"Don't know, Frank. He doesn't appear to be armed."

The west, or river side, of the road was a short-grass meadow, with no foliage in which to hide. The right side had a thicket, but it was fairly small.

Elijah walked up from the wagon behind. "Everyone's armed, Jacen. We're ready for trouble, if need be. I told Gus and Phil to watch the road behind us, in case this is a diversion of some sort."

Jacen nodded, "Thanks, Elijah. Good work. Let's go check this guy out."

The three walked toward the stranger, rifles at the ready. As they drew near, they saw that he was indeed unarmed. They stopped about twenty feet away, and studied the thicket off to the side, alert for any movement.

"Hello!" the stranger called. He looked to be around forty, with black hair peppered with streaks of gray. About six feet tall, he appeared to be powerfully built. He was wearing a fairly new looking coat, but his boots and blue jeans were worn.

"Hello," Jacen replied coolly. "Who are you, and what do you want?"

"The name is Harry Kline, my friends call me Hank. My wife and kids are with me. Come on out, Sally." A woman stepped out from behind a large tree, and four children materialized from various hiding places. They all walked warily up onto the road, and stood next to Harry. Jacen relaxed a little, doubting that the man would put his family in danger.

"What do you want?" Jacen repeated.

"We're looking for the man called the *Outlander*. We've heard that he's leading a group to Colorado, to start all over again, and build a new world. We want to be a part of that."

Jacen started to respond, but Frank Tulley interrupted him, "Looks to me like you've found him."

Jacen looked at Frank and hissed under his breath, *"What? You know Hakim is dead!"*

Tulley ignored him and called to Harry, "This fellow here is the Outlander," gesturing to Jacen, "although his friends call him Jacen. If you want to join us, he's the man you have to talk to." Turning to the surprised Jacen, Frank said under his breath, *"You've earned your spurs, Jacen."*

Elijah grinned, and said, "I reckon you're right, Frank Tulley."

Harry spoke up again, "If you'll let us join up, we've got some things we can contribute. I've got a dozen chickens, good egg-layers, a rooster, and a few cows and goats."

"Well, that settles that," muttered Elijah, smacking his lips, "they surely got my vote."

Jacen and his men lowered their weapons, and walked up to the family. "How on earth did you know where to find us?" asked Jacen.

"Simple," responded Harry with a smile, "this bridge behind us, in Clinton, is the only one left standing across the

Mississippi. I knew you had to pass this way sooner or later. So, we've been camping out, just waitin' on you."

****

One week later the Phoenix group, enlarged now with the addition of the Klines and their livestock, reached the ruin of Cedar Rapids, and set up their winter encampment. It would be a brutal winter, but all members of the group would survive. When spring finally arrived, the twenty-four souls of Phoenix would be but 800 miles from their destination. But that's another tale; maybe someday I'll tell you about it.

ABOUT THE AUTHOR

Chris Cobb's resume reads like a patchwork quilt. He's driven a forklift, worked as a technician doing board-level repair on digital circuitry, been a programmer-analyst, a data-center shift operator, taught high school science and mathematics, and been an Information Technology Director at a graduate school. Most of his career he's been a pastor.

He lives with his wife, Doris, in western Ohio, and is presently the teaching pastor at Bible Fellowship Church in Greenville, OH. They have three adult children, and a fine son-in-law and daughter-in-law, all of whom are actively engaged in the arts at some level.

Chris received Jesus Christ as his Savior in 1974, and seeks to incorporate a biblically faithful worldview into everything he does, including his writing.

Find other works by Chris Cobb at www.chcobb.com.

PLEASE HELP INDEPENDENT AUTHORS

Independent authors usually don't have someone managing their book's publicity plan or marketing. We don't have the support of an organization getting our novels in front of retailers who will carry them in their store. Other than what marketing efforts we can cobble together on our own, we have only one source of publicity that can encourage others to buy our books, and that's you, our readers.

Your word-of-mouth recommendation, your Facebook comment, your tweet, your Amazon or Goodreads review is likely the only way an unknown author will get the word out about his or her book.

Let me hasten to admit that the reader is certainly under no obligation here. If you don't like the tale, or if the editing was sloppy, the cover or packaging amateurish, then by all means don't encourage someone else to read it. The last thing the independent publishing movement needs are products that fall short of genuine quality.

Even if you think the product is the best work since Bunyan's *Pilgrim's Progress* or Tolkien's *Lord of the Rings*, you still aren't obligated. Art doesn't create a debt or obligation on the part of the viewer. You're free to enjoy it and walk away. Artists take that risk when we create our work.

But if you find a tale you like and you'd like to read more by that author, give him or her a hand by letting your friends and loved ones know where they can get a good story. Post a review, mention it on Facebook, send a few emails, tell a few friends. Once the word gets out, a good story will sell itself; but getting the word out is the challenge. Thanks for your help!

www.ingramcontent.com/pod-product-compliance
Lightning Source LLC
Chambersburg PA
CBHW070045120726
47909CB00002B/297